Volume Four

SIERRA JENSEN COLLECTION

Hold On Tight

Closer Than Ever

Take My Hand

ROBIN JONES GUNN

Multnomah Books

THE SIERRA JENSEN COLLECTION, VOLUME 4
published by Multnomah Books

© 2006 by Robin's Ink, LLC
International Standard Book Number: 978-1-59052-591-3

Cover photo by Steve Gardner, www.shootpw.com

Compilation of:
Hold On Tight
© 1998 by Robin's Ink, LLC
Closer Than Ever
© 1999 by Robin's Ink, LLC
Take My Hand

© 1999 by Robin's Ink, LLC

Poem on page 402 is from *The Complete Poems of Christina Rossetti*, Vol. 1
(Baton Rouge, Louisiana: University Press, 1979).

Unless otherwise indicated, Scripture quotations are from:
The Holy Bible, New International Version (NIV)
© 1973, 1984 by International Bible Society,
used by permission of Zondervan Publishing House
The Holy Bible, New King James Version (NKJV)
© 1984 by Thomas Nelson, Inc.
The Living Bible (TLB)
© 1971. Used by permission of Tyndale House Publishers, Inc.
All rights reserved.
The Holy Bible, King James Version (KJV)

Published in the United States by WaterBrook Multnomah, an imprint of the Crown Publishing Group, a division of Random House Inc., New York.

Multnomah and its mountain colophon are registered trademarks of Random House Inc.

Printed in the United States of America

For information:
MULTNOMAH BOOKS
12265 ORACLE BOULEVARD, SUITE 200 · COLORADO SPRINGS, CO 80921

Library of Congress Cataloging-in-Publication Data
Gunn, Robin Jones, 1955-
The Sierra Jensen Collection Volume 4 / Robin Jones Gunn.
    v. cm.
Previously published as separate works.
Contents: Hold On Tight—Closer Than Ever—Take My Hand.
    ISBN 1-59052-591-4   [1. Interpersonal relations—Fiction. 2. Conduct of life—Fiction. 3. Christian life—Fiction.] I. Title.
PZ7.G972Sie 2006
[Fic]—dc22

                                                    2006008136

14—10 9 8 7

TEEN NOVELS BY ROBIN JONES GUNN

THE SIERRA JENSEN SERIES

THE CHRISTY MILLER SERIES

Book Ten

HOLD ON
TIGHT

one

SIERRA JENSEN STEPPED INSIDE Mama Bear's Bakery. She had worked here for almost a year but never tired of the fresh fragrance of cinnamon and warm bread that greeted her as the tiny bell over the door announced her entrance. This clear spring afternoon she wasn't working. She was meeting friends.

Glancing at the empty corner table by the front window, Sierra realized she was the first one to arrive for the Monday afternoon gathering. For months she and her friends Vicki and Amy had bent their heads close together over that same table every Monday at four o'clock. They shared secrets, settled arguments, gave free advice, and teased each other mercilessly.

Mrs. Kraus, the owner of Mama Bear's, called to Sierra from behind the counter. "I just pulled out a pan of fresh rolls. Will you girls be sharing your usual large one with an extra dab of frosting?"

"I'm sure we will," Sierra said. Six other customers were seated in the bakery, and Mrs. Kraus appeared to be the only person working in the front of the shop. "Would you like me to get the tea for us?"

"No, I think I can remember what you always have. I'll get it." The cheerful, round Mrs. Kraus turned to greet an older woman who had entered the shop.

Sierra settled her slim frame into her usual chair, welcoming the stream of sunshine that spilled through the window and cascaded down her long, blond curls. She loved the feelings of promise this time of year brought, especially this spring. It was her senior year in high school, and endless possibilities stretched out for her future. That was probably why she felt impatient for Amy and Vicki to show up. She had a very promising possibility to tell them about.

Across the street a battered old Volvo pulled into a metered parking space. Sierra watched as petite Amy flipped her sunglasses onto the top of her head and fingered the ends of her short, dark hair at the base of her neck. Amy glanced right and left and then hurried across the street. Her dash had a slight zigzag pattern to it. She kept her head down and didn't watch where she was going.

That's the way Amy approaches life, Sierra thought, *zigzagging with her head down. I'll have to tell her that.*

"Personality observations" is what Vicki had first labeled these insights, when she communicated to Sierra that the way Sierra bit her lower lip was a sign of worry. Sierra accepted the observation with grateful surprise. She had never realized she bit her lower lip.

Amy, however, wasn't interested in observations lately. The openness she had demonstrated in February was gone by the beginning of March, and it didn't seem to be returning. Sierra was just glad that, even though Amy hadn't been saying much during their get-togethers, at least she kept coming. Sierra had nearly lost her friendship with Amy once, and she didn't want that to happen again.

When Amy entered, Sierra smiled and waved. The pair had certainly experienced their ups and downs in their year of friendship. In spite of their differences, they respected and deeply cared for each other, and that's what kept them close.

"Vicki's not here yet?" Amy said, slipping into a chair across from Sierra.

Sierra shook her head. "When I saw her at lunch, I told her I had something to tell you guys, so I thought she would be the first one here."

"Guess you'll have to tell me first, then," Amy said, her dark eyes glancing at Sierra's outfit. "I like that shirt. When did you get it?"

"Believe it or not, I found it stuffed in a bag Mom was taking to the Salvation Army. I think it was Tawni's. I'm actually wearing something my sister liked!"

Amy reached over and felt the sleeve of Sierra's lavender chenille top. "I like this material. It sure brings out the blue in your eyes." Amy smiled as she added, "If you get tired of it, you can always toss it in my direction."

Mrs. Kraus arrived at their table, balancing a tray with their snack. Sierra reached for the mugs of hot tea, and Amy grabbed the plate with the cinnamon roll.

"It's my turn to pay," Amy said. "I'll bring it up to the register, Mrs. Kraus."

"No hurry. Just enjoy," Mrs. Kraus said.

The bell above the door announced Vicki's arrival. She swished past Mrs. Kraus and, with a flushed face, began to talk before she even sat down. "Sorry! I was almost out of gas, and I didn't have any money, so I had to go to the bank, and the line at the drive-up was terrible and, oh, you already ordered? I wanted iced tea today. I think I'll get myself a glass of ice and turn this into iced tea. Anyone else want anything?"

Both Sierra and Amy shook their heads.

Vicki swept past the tables to the counter. Watching her, Sierra thought about the contrast between her two friends. If Amy zigzagged through life with her head down, Vicki moved through her days at full speed, with her chin to the sky and the wind in her long, silky, brown hair. That zestful optimism eventually had linked Sierra and Vicki, even though Sierra originally had interpreted Vicki's bold approach to life as conceit. Of course, when they first met, Vicki did have an overly active bent toward flirting and was far more interested in developing relationships with guys than with girls.

Amy pulled off a corner of the cinnamon roll. "Do you suppose we can start eating without Vicki? I'm starved."

"Sure. She'll be right back." Sierra pulled her peppermint tea bag out of the mug. With a glance at Vicki, she wondered how her friends would describe her approach to life. Did they see her as a zigzagger or as someone with her face to the sun? She felt she had changed a lot during the past year, and she knew that Vicki and Amy had changed, too. What would they be like a year from now? Or even six months from now, when they all would begin their freshman year of college?

The instant Vicki returned to their table, Sierra spilled her news. "Okay, are you both ready for my big announcement?"

"It can't be that huge if you didn't tell me at lunch today and made me wait until now," Vicki said, carefully pouring her steaming tea over the glass of crushed ice.

"I wanted to tell you both at the same time."

"I appreciate that," Amy said. Amy had changed schools this year after her parents' divorce. She was at a public high school now, instead of at Royal Academy, the small, private Christian school where the three originally had met.

"So?" Vicki prompted.

"Last night my brother called and told me he's going to Southern California next week. He's pretty sure he wants to attend Rancho Corona University for his master's degree, but he wanted to check out the school before he made a final decision."

"That's your big news?" Vicki asked. Her pretty face took on a teasing grin. "You definitely could have told me that at lunch."

"Wait," Sierra said, her enthusiasm unruffled. "He's going to drive down there next week, and he asked if I wanted to go with him, and my parents said yes!"

"Good for you," Vicki said. "Bring back a surfer for each of us."

"Didn't you go to California last year for Easter vacation?" Amy asked.

"Yes."

"And you also flew down there for your friends' wedding last summer." Amy turned her lower lip into a friendly pout. "How do you expect us to be happy for you again? You keep going on these adventures, and we don't go anywhere. I've never been to California—ever—in my life. I've only been to Seattle—once."

"I hope you have a good time," Vicki said cheerfully to Sierra.

Sierra broke into a wide grin. "You mean you hope *we* have a good time."

"'We' meaning you and Wes?" Vicki ventured. "Or 'we' meaning the three of us?"

"All of us!" Sierra spouted. "My brother is driving my parents' van down, and they said I could invite my friends to go. We should be able to get an excused absence from school, since it's a college scouting trip. Wes said he would let us check out as many different campuses as we want, as long as he can spend a day at Rancho Corona."

"I'm in," Vicki said without a moment's hesitation.

"What kind of colleges?" Amy asked cautiously.

"Amy!" Vicki nudged her arm. "You just said you never get to go anywhere. Accept the invitation and say thank you."

Amy hesitated a moment before saying, "It *would* be kind of fun."

"When do we leave?" Vicki asked.

"Wednesday after school," Sierra said. "I'm going to drive the van down to Corvallis, and then Wes and I will take turns driving from there. It's going to take us at least twenty hours, so we'll sleep in the van. In Los Angeles, we'll stay with a couple Wesley knows."

"Where is Rancho Corona University?" Vicki asked.

"I don't know. Someplace down there. It's about an hour's drive from where my sister lives, so we might stay with her the next night."

"This is going to be so much fun!" Vicki sipped her iced tea and glanced at Amy for a sign of enthusiasm.

"When do we come back?" Amy asked.

"Late Sunday night. It'll be a really packed couple of days, but I think it's going be great. You do want to come, don't you?"

Amy nodded, but she still didn't look overly excited. "I'll have to get off work and clear everything with my mom."

"Me, too," Vicki said. "But that shouldn't be a problem."

"Thanks for reminding me," Sierra said. "I forgot I have to ask Mrs. Kraus for the days off."

"She always lets you adjust your schedule," Vicki said. "I'm sure she'll be her sweet self and give you the time off. Now let's just pray my boss is as understanding."

Sierra laughed. "Your boss? Why wouldn't he be?"

Vicki's boss was her dad. Mr. Navarone owned a large car dealership in Portland, and Vicki worked there part-time doing clerical work.

"I know," Vicki said. "He'll let me off. My dad is going to be thrilled I'm showing serious interest in going to college. He'll probably not only send me off with his blessing but also with enough spending money to treat everyone to a trip to an amusement park down there."

Amy's expression lit up. "Could we go do that? Really? How about Universal Studios? Do you guys think we could squeeze in a trip to Universal Studios? Or at least to Hollywood?"

"I don't see why not," Sierra answered. "Wes said we could plan whatever we wanted."

The three friends bent their heads close. As the spring sunshine lit their little corner of the world, they pulled apart their cinnamon roll and began to make plans for their upcoming road trip. Sierra felt a gleeful rush of anticipation and knew the next week and a half couldn't speed by fast enough for her.

two

"AMY AND VICKI ARE BOTH COMING," Sierra said to her brother that night on the phone. "Hope you don't mind carting the three of us around."

"No," Wes said calmly. He had inherited many of their father's characteristics, including a willingness to take on challenges with a shrug of the shoulders. "I think four is a good number. We'll have room to sleep in the van, and it won't be too much to ask of my friends when we stay at their house. You told the girls we're driving straight through, didn't you?"

"Yes."

"And that we're spending a day at Rancho Corona?"

"Yes. Where is that college, anyway?"

"It's near Temecula. South of Lake Elsinore."

Those coordinates meant nothing to Sierra.

"Don't you remember my telling you about it? I'm sure they have a website, if you want to check it out before we go down. It might be a good idea to look up all the colleges you want to visit ahead of time on the Internet and contact them to see if they have any restrictions or requirements for touring their campuses."

"Good idea. Vicki, Amy, and I came up with three colleges we would like to visit, and then Rancho Corona, of course. Oh, and Wes? How do you feel about including something fun on the trip?"

"Something fun? I thought spending five days with me would be about as much fun as any girl could ask for."

"Very funny. I mean like going to Universal Studios or something."

"Fine with me. Make sure you have enough money. None of those places are cheap."

"Do you have a preference of where we go?" Sierra asked.

"Since you're asking, I'd say Magic Mountain. I'm more interested in roller coasters than movie stars. But I'll leave it up to you and your friends."

After Sierra hung up, she sat on the living room couch for a long while, thinking. She could hear her mom in the kitchen, unloading the dishwasher. From upstairs her dad was telling her two little brothers to climb into bed. Granna Mae was quietly tucked in her comfortable, large bedroom. Sierra could sit alone with her thoughts.

The first thought was about Amy and Wes. Last summer Amy had made it clear she had a huge crush on Sierra's brother. Wesley had never given Amy reason to think he was interested in her, at least from anything Sierra had ever noticed. Now Amy hadn't seen Wesley for months, since he had gone back to school in the fall at Oregon State University in Corvallis. Sierra had no way of knowing until they met up in Corvallis next week if Amy would show an interest in Wes again. The potential Amy-Wes relationship made Sierra nervous.

Then there was the choice of what fun outing they should include. Amy seemed pretty set on Universal Studios, but since Wes was their host, Sierra thought he should choose the amusement park. Vicki wouldn't care which one they went to. Neither did Sierra. Once again, it was a thing between Amy and Wes.

Sierra bit her lower lip and then realized she was doing it and stopped. *This is crazy. I'm getting in a froth over nothing. I'll call Amy and tell her Wes suggested we go to Magic Mountain. She'll understand since it was Wes's choice. But wait. If she gives in to Wes's choice, does that mean she's trying to score points with him? Should I just come right out and ask her if she's still interested in him? Maybe I should ask Vicki what she thinks I should do. No, that would be talking about Amy behind her back. If I'm going to talk to anybody, it should be Amy.*

Sierra decided she would talk to Amy. But not tonight. Instead, she would wait another day and hope the queasy feelings about Wes and Amy would go away. Why did that bother her so much anyway?

Getting up from the couch, Sierra went into the kitchen and opened the refrigerator in search of brain food.

"How's the homework coming along?" her mom asked.

"I was just going to start it," Sierra answered. She didn't turn around, but she could almost feel her mother looking at the clock, noticing it was after eight-thirty, and looking back at Sierra with mild concern that it was so late and she hadn't even started her homework. For the past two months, Sierra had burned the midnight oil over the excessive amount of homework she had. Whoever had told her it got easier at the end of her senior year had definitely gone to some school other than Royal Academy. Between work, volunteering at the Highland House, church activities, and her mound of schoolwork, Sierra barely had a social life. That was probably why she was so excited about the California getaway.

"I know," Sierra said without turning to catch her mother's gaze. "I should have started sooner. But don't worry. I actually don't have too much tonight. Besides, I had to call Wesley and talk to him about the trip. Do we have any orange juice?"

"In the freezer," her mom said. "What about Mama Bear's? Were you able to get the time off?"

"Yes," Sierra said, opening the freezer and pulling out a can of frozen orange juice. "Mrs. Kraus told me it was no problem, but I have to work this Friday after school." She reached in the cupboard for a pitcher and went to work making up the orange juice.

Mrs. Jensen closed the door of the dishwasher and wiped off the counter. "Good," she said. "I think this is going to be a helpful trip for both you and Wesley. Do you think you would like to apply to Rancho Corona? I'm wondering if we should start filling out some of the paperwork before you go down."

"Dad said to wait, since the application fee is kind of high and he's already put out the money for those other three applications last fall."

Sierra had managed to keep a 4.0 grade average since junior high, although it didn't seem like a big deal to her. The way she saw it, she simply had a mind that easily collected necessary information, spilled it back on a test a few days later, and then promptly forgot anything that didn't hold a special attraction for her. She didn't see herself as smart; she merely knew how to work the system. That was to her advantage, since she already had received two scholarship offers and had been accepted at the three colleges she had applied to last fall. At this point, it was pretty much up to her to decide which college she went to, since her parents had been in favor of all her choices.

Well, almost all. There was one they'd said no to. The University of Edinburgh.

"Was there any mail for me today?" Sierra asked.

"I don't think so. Did you check the chair in the study?"

Sierra had a favorite chair in the room that her dad used as his office. It had once been the library of this large Victorian house that Sierra's great-grandfather had built in 1915. Since last fall Sierra had been involved in a lively correspondence with Paul Mackenzie, a tenderhearted guy she had met more than a year ago at Heathrow Airport in England. Her parents had gotten into the habit of putting his letters on Sierra's favorite chair in the study. They knew that's where she would go to read them.

The emotional involvement Sierra felt with Paul through his letters had reached an all-time high for her last December. But when she realized she was far more into their correspondence than he appeared to be, she had backed off. Instead of writing him nearly every day, she began to write him about once every two weeks, which was the same pace he had been writing to her all along.

During January, Paul had written only twice—one short letter and one even shorter postcard. His words were always rich with sincerity, never flirty or demanding. Paul openly visited with her through his letters without hinting at anything strongly emotional on his side. He never signed his letters with the word "love." Yet to Sierra, the kind, earnest, from-the-heart friendship he had expressed was far closer to the best kind of love there was. She believed in many ways it was stronger than anything she or her girlfriends shared with any of the guys they liked.

That quiet hope kept Sierra writing to Paul. In February she had sent him a valentine. She made it from a collage of pictures and words she had cut from magazines and glued to a red heart. It said, "'God is love…. We love because he first loved us' (1 John 4:16, 19)." The verse seemed an appropriate way to communicate that, yes, this was a valentine; but, no, it wasn't about Sierra revealing her love for Paul or her desire for a deeper relationship with him. It was about God and His neverending love for both of them.

That's truly where Sierra had stored away her friendship with Paul. It was hidden in the shelter of God's love for those who abide in Him. However, Sierra had discovered she still felt warm emotions when she held one of Paul's letters in her hand.

Pouring herself a glass of orange juice and returning the pitcher to the fridge, Sierra slipped out of the kitchen and checked her favorite chair. No letters awaited her.

"That's okay," she whispered in the quiet room that smelled of old books. "You just take good care of him, will You, God? I know You've been working in huge ways in Paul's life lately, and I'm really thankful. I guess I just want to ask that You protect him and keep him safe at his school in Edinburgh. Help him decide what to do about school next year. I know he has to make that decision in the next few weeks, and it's been really hard for him. Thanks, Lord."

Sierra turned on the computer at her dad's desk. Before she started her homework, she wanted to check out the website for Rancho Corona, as Wesley had suggested. As she typed in the search information, Sierra thought of how she had never tried to locate information about the university Paul attended in Scotland. Last fall she had announced to her parents, without having any information, that that was where she wanted to start her freshman year of college. All she knew was that Paul went there. Her parents said no, and she never had searched out any details about enrolling.

Tonight Sierra felt a struggle. She knew she should be content with this college scouting trip Wesley was taking her on, and she should be willing to select one of the colleges at which she had already been accepted, but something inside her refused to let go of Scotland. It was as if a closet door in her heart was pushing its way open. She thought that door had been tightly locked up months ago, after she had swept away the dreams of attending the same college as Paul. But tonight the door of that forgotten closet seemed to open a sliver. The dim light that peeked from the opening beckoned to her.

Instead of typing in "Rancho Corona University," Sierra found her fingers typing "University of Edinburgh, Scotland."

three

"WHAT DO YOU MEAN, Randy said yes?" Sierra stared at Vicki in the school parking lot. The bell was about to ring, and if they didn't move, they would both be late for their first-period class.

"I called Randy last night and told him about the trip, and he said yes, he wants to come with us. He's going to ask the other guys in the band to see if they want to come, too. I told them we have free places to sleep, but they have to bring enough money for their own food."

Sierra continued to stare at Vicki. The bell rang, but she didn't move.

"Sierra, we're late! Come on. We can go through all the details at lunch." Vicki started toward the building.

"I never said anything about inviting anyone else, Vicki!" Sierra hurried after her friend. "Why did you ask him?" Sierra thought she knew the answer. For months Vicki had been interested in Randy even though he treated Vicki, Sierra, and all girls the same. Vicki must have thought a few days in a van with Randy as a captured audience might help her win his affections.

"There's plenty of room in your van. Your parents adore Randy. He and Wes get along great. What's the problem?"

"Well…it's you, Vicki."

"Me?" Vicki stopped at the front door of the school. The innocent expression on her face maddened Sierra.

"Never mind," Sierra said, holding up a hand in defeat and turning away from her friend. "I'll see you at lunch." As Sierra went through the door, she was still boiling inside.

She dashed to her class and was thankful when her teacher waved her to her seat, meaning Sierra didn't have to go to the office for a tardy slip. It was one of the rewards for being an "A" student and rarely coming to class late. Some students were late so regularly they had developed a routine of stepping to the back of the class, pausing, getting a nod from the teacher, and then going to the office for their most recent tardy slip.

But it barely mattered to Sierra that she had been waved to her seat. Her mind at that moment was anywhere but in the classroom. What was her brother going to say? Or her parents? How could she uninvite Randy after Vicki had invited him? Fortunately, Randy was a close enough buddy that she thought he would understand if she explained the situation to him. But why should she have to? It would be fun to have Randy along, too—as long as the rest of the band didn't come. Warner, the drummer, drove Sierra crazy. If he came, the whole trip would be ruined for her.

Why am I even thinking this? This is my trip. For my friends. At my invitation. I can say yes or no to whomever I want.

By lunch Sierra had prepared her line of defense. She would say her parents and brother would decide who could go and who couldn't. If they thought Randy should come along, then he could come. Neither her parents nor her brother would think Warner should come along because Sierra would tell them it wasn't a good idea. That would take the pressure off her.

When Sierra entered the cafeteria, her usual bunch of lunchtime friends were gathered around "their" table. They all looked up at her and started to talk before she sat down.

"Hey, Sierra," Tre, one of the guys in the band, said, "Vicki told us we have to pay for our food and that's all. Don't you want us to pay something for the gas, too?"

"Are you guys going to the beach?" Margo, one of the girls at the table, asked. "If you are, I'm definitely going."

"I checked at the office," Randy said. "We do get an excused absence, since the trip is to visit colleges."

"Cool. Count me in," said Margo.

Vicki still wore her innocent expression when Sierra, standing her ground, shot Vicki a perturbed look and said, "You guys have to understand something. It's not up to me. My brother is the one heading up this trip, and he and my parents will decide who can go. I didn't mean for it to become an open invitation."

"How many can fit in your van?" Warner asked.

Sierra clenched her teeth. "Eight. But that's beside the point."

Warner did a quick count. "Only four of us want to go."

Vicki held out her fingers and kept counting. "Then Sierra, Amy, Wes, and me. Eight. That's perfect."

Sierra gave Vicki her most exasperated look. "It's not up

to me. Didn't you hear what I just said? I'll have to ask my parents and brother."

"Can you let us know tomorrow?" Margo asked. "Vicki said you were planning to visit the college where my parents met. I know they would let me go to see their alma mater."

Sierra found it hard to stay irritated with Margo, who had no idea this wasn't a free-for-all. Actually, Sierra realized she wouldn't mind if Margo came along. While it hadn't occurred to Sierra to invite her, it would be nice if Margo did come. She had arrived at Royal Academy this year, fresh from the mission field. Her parents had served for years in Peru. Margo slowly had blossomed into a fun friend who was always doing little things for their group, such as bringing cookies to share or sticking notes of encouragement in their lockers. Sierra would feel bad not returning some kindness to Margo now that the opportunity was before her.

"I'll try to let you know tomorrow," Sierra promised. This was becoming complicated. How could she tell her friends that Wes had said yes to Randy, Tre, and Margo but no to Warner? Especially when everyone knew the van had enough seats. That in itself might be the deciding factor, since Wesley had said he thought four people was a good number. There would be very little sleeping if everyone had to sit up the whole way.

I guess the easiest, fairest answer would be to tell everyone, "Sorry, but you can't come." Everyone except Vicki and Amy. And maybe Randy. Oh, and Margo. Man, this is turning into a nightmare!

Sierra wanted to express her frustration to Vicki but forced herself to bite her tongue and wait so she wouldn't say anything she would regret later. Plenty of times in her life she had exploded first, then thought about what she had said later. Those times always required an apology on her part, and she wasn't interested in starting off this trip with hurt feelings all around.

By the time she had explained the situation to her parents after dinner, her dad had a strained look on his face. The skin on his forehead had turned into a bunch of ripples and tightened between his eyebrows. It looked as though a headache was starting from the outside and working its way to the inside. Sierra knew exactly how that felt.

"Well," her mom said, breathing a deep sigh, "let's think this through."

"Only you, Sierra," her dad said, shaking his head.

All Sierra's defenses rose to the surface. "Hey, I didn't mean for this to happen. Vicki shouldn't have said anything without asking me first."

"Did you tell her that?" her mom asked.

"No. I knew if I tried to say something, it wouldn't come out very nice."

"Good for you on that account," her mom said. She reached across the dining room table and gave Sierra's hand a squeeze. "We know you didn't try to complicate things, so don't think you're being blamed for anything."

"All I meant," her dad said, "was that only you would find yourself caught in such a situation. You tend to end up in these tangles. I do understand it wasn't your intention, and we can work this out. Let's give Wesley a call to see what he thinks."

They tried to call Wes until eleven that night but only got his voice mail. After leaving four messages, Mr. Jensen suggested they go to bed and call Wes in the morning before Sierra left for school.

"Just tell your friends tomorrow that you don't have an answer yet. They can wait one more day," Mrs. Jensen said diplomatically.

Right, Sierra thought. *You try showing up at school tomorrow without an answer and see how popular you are, Mom.*

Sierra went to her bedroom and closed the door. It bugged her that her room was such a mess. Usually she could go weeks without noticing the clutter, but when one area of her life was unsettled, all the unorganized parts seemed intensified. She didn't have the desire or energy to clean her room since it was so late. It actually made her miss Tawni, her neat-freak sister, who, when they shared the room, used to insist Sierra periodically plow through her stuff scattered all over the place. Ever since Tawni had moved out, Sierra, for the first time in her life, had dictated her own living conditions. Only once or twice had her room ever been completely cleaned since then, and that was when company was anticipated.

Reaching for the printed-out information she had gathered from the Internet the night before, Sierra flopped onto her bed and read again about the University of Edinburgh. She had a map of the campus and a guide to each of the buildings. It was morning now in Scotland. Was Paul on his way to class? Which building would he be in? The James Clerk Maxwell Building? Or maybe the Ogston Building. She noticed a spot marked Student Centre. It made her wonder whom he spent his lunch hours with. Was he ever tardy to class because of goofy friends who complicated his life by making plans that didn't coordinate with his?

Sierra put down the papers. It was useless to slip into a daydreaming mode about Paul. She had done that before, and it had only produced a deep, insatiable longing. She didn't want to visit that place again. In her heart of hearts, she knew she wanted her love to be focused on God, the only One who could fill her completely. She didn't want to live on that raw emotional edge where fantasy and imagination devoured reality.

With a heavy sigh, Sierra reached for her Bible on her nightstand and pulled out a note card on which she had written 2 Corinthians 10:3–5 from a different version. She had been trying to memorize the passage, but for some reason it wouldn't stay in her mind. A guest speaker for their youth group had challenged all of them to memorize these verses to learn how to control their imaginations.

She read them aloud in the lonely, cluttered room: "For though we walk in the flesh, we do not war after the flesh: (For the weapons of our warfare are not carnal, but mighty through God to the pulling down of strong holds;) Casting down imaginations, and every high thing that exalteth itself against the knowledge of God, and bringing into captivity every thought to the obedience of Christ."

"...bringing into captivity every thought to the obedience of Christ," she repeated, trying to get the last section to stay in her memory.

Pulling herself up to change into her pajamas and to brush her teeth, Sierra silently prayed. She had plenty to pray about: this mess with her friends and the road trip; her thoughts and imagination wanting to go wild over Paul; and her choice of a college. Now that she had information on Edinburgh, it was even harder not to imagine what it would be like to go there. Her motive was to be near Paul, and certainly that couldn't be an appropriate objective, could it?

Sierra had a hard time sleeping with so many thoughts rushing over her. For some reason she remembered Wesley's words from the night before when he said he preferred roller coasters. Right now, her stomach felt as though she were on one. It looked as if it was going to be an emotional ride that wasn't going to stop anytime soon.

Sierra took hold of her blankets, pulled them up to her chin, and closed her eyes tight. Sleep finally found her.

four

WHEN SIERRA STOOD before her friends at lunch the next day, she felt her heart racing. She told them she hadn't talked to Wes yet, so she didn't have a decision for them.

"I can't get off work anyway," Tre said. "You can take me off the list."

"I know someone else who wanted to go," Margo said.

"Who?" Vicki asked.

"Drake. Maybe he could take your place, Tre, if you're not going."

Sierra's heart raced even faster. Drake, the school's best athlete and biggest flirt, had been interested in Sierra last summer, and she had returned the interest. They even went out—sort of. It was never a defined dating relationship, but it certainly was a relationship that had caused Sierra confused feelings and lots of conflicts with her friends—especially Amy. Amy had been interested in Drake before he asked Sierra to go out with him.

Even though Sierra and Drake were still casual friends, they rarely spoke to each other. She could only imagine what it would be like to be in a van for days with Amy and Drake, not to mention everyone else. Her head was beginning to pound in time to her heart. She couldn't stand this much longer.

"You guys," Sierra stated with a rush of adrenaline, "you need to know this trip wasn't supposed to be an open invitation. It's turning into a huge mess. I didn't know Vicki was going to ask you all to come. If I'd known, I would have told her not to invite you." The words tumbled out before she had a chance to evaluate them.

"Are you saying you don't want any of us to go?" Margo asked.

"You never said anything about its being a closed trip," Vicki blurted out. "All you said was Wes agreed to drive you and some of your friends. I thought there was room for all our friends. Why didn't you tell me it was supposed to be just you, Amy, and me?"

"I thought you understood that."

"Obviously not," Vicki said, folding her arms.

"We don't have to go," Randy said quickly, trying to bring peace to a situation full of rising tension. "It's no big deal. We understand, Sierra. It's your trip. We all kind of took over and didn't let you invite the ones you wanted."

Now Sierra felt bad. "Randy, it wasn't that I was trying to invite only certain people…"

"But that's what you did," Warner said. "The ones you invited were Amy and Vicki."

"That was her choice," Margo said. "She can invite whomever she wants. You guys are trying to make her feel bad."

"No, we're not," Warner said.

"I can't go anyway," Tre said, shrugging his shoulders. He left the table to return his cafeteria tray.

Sierra felt as if the world had suddenly turned against her. How could her friends not understand? Why was all of this her fault?

"You guys," Margo said, clearing her throat and talking a little louder. "We should all back down like Tre did. Don't give Sierra a hard time." Margo rose and said, "Excuse me. I better tell Drake we're all uninvited."

"You're not uninvited," Sierra said, dreading how this would sound to Drake. "I still need to talk to my brother. Can you guys wait until tomorrow for a final decision? This isn't supposed to be such a huge problem."

"I guess you can blame me for that," Vicki said quietly. The sweet bloom of innocence no longer graced her face. "I didn't mean to turn this into a nightmare."

"I know. You didn't do anything wrong on purpose." Sierra glanced at Randy, hoping he would say something to help smooth everyone's ruffled feelings.

He stuffed the last bite of his sandwich into his mouth and said, "If you hear from Wes tonight, call me. I'd still like to invite myself, if that's okay with you and Wes."

Sierra wanted to say, "Yes, of course. I'm sure Wes would love to have you come." But how would that look to Warner and the others?

"I'll call you," Sierra said. She knew she would call Randy whether she heard from Wes or not. Then they could have a private conversation about all this.

True to her word, Sierra called Randy as soon as she arrived home. But she got his family's answering machine, so she tried Wes. Fortunately, Wes was there.

After explaining the situation, Sierra asked her brother what he thought she should do. There was a pause on the other end, and Sierra wondered if Wes was thinking the same thing her dad had voiced the night before: *Only you, Sierra!*

"I think this should be a fun trip for you, Sierra," Wes began. "And I also think it's an opportunity to do something nice for your friends. You should consider that."

"What do you mean?"

"Turn the situation around. What if Randy were going on a trip like this, and he invited two of the people from your group but didn't invite you. How would you feel?"

"It's not as though we're an inseparable group that does everything together," Sierra protested. "Those guys go off and do stuff without me all the time. Besides, I invited Amy, and she doesn't even attend our school anymore. I wanted it to be a girlfriend trip. It changes the whole atmosphere when guys are around."

"Uh, Sierra," Wes said slowly, "*I'm* a guy."

"I know, but..." Now Sierra didn't know what to say. Wes was right. Already the possibility existed that the atmosphere would be charged because of Amy's potential interest in Wes. Maybe Sierra's dream of what this trip was supposed to be was unrealistic.

"Look, Sierra, I don't know what to tell you. I'm open to taking more of your friends if that would be helpful to them and if that's something you would like. The point of this trip is for me to check out Rancho Corona and for you to look over some colleges. It's not about going to the beach or Hollywood or wherever else your friends want to go. Maybe, if you make the schedule really clear, some of them will change their minds. We won't have a lot of time to see the sights."

"I know," Sierra said with a sigh. "You're right. I should think of what would be good for my friends. It's just that I don't like being around Warner."

"Then don't invite Warner."

"But you just said to open the invitation to all of them."

"It's up to you, Sierra."

"You're not much help. First you tell me one thing, then you change it."

"I'm not changing anything. Listen, Sierra, this is what you should do. Make a rough schedule based on the colleges you, Vicki, and Amy want to visit. Then, if there's time, we'll fit in one fun thing, like the beach or something. Show that schedule to your friends, tell them they have to pay for their food, and then see who still wants to come. If Randy wants to come, I'd be glad for the company."

"What about Warner?"

"What about him?"

Sierra curled and uncurled her toes. She felt her jaw clenching. "Wesley, help me out here. I don't want Warner to come."

"Okay, then use me as your excuse. Tell Warner he can't come because I said so."

"But you don't even know him."

"You're right; I don't. You know him. You tell him he can't come."

Sierra let out an exasperated sigh. Obviously, no easy answer was going to turn up. "What about sleeping? Won't it be impossible to stretch out and sleep with so many people in the van?"

"We'll take turns sleeping in the front seat. It reclines. You can sleep on an airplane, can't you? You can sleep in the van."

Sierra bit her lower lip until she was afraid she might draw blood. "I'm going to hang up now, Wesley, and don't try to call me back. I can't handle any more of your wacky logic."

"Okay. Let me know what you decide." He seemed untouched by her frustration.

"I will," Sierra muttered. She hung up and headed for the basement to find her mom.

Mrs. Jensen was pulling clothes from the washing machine and stuffing them into the dryer. Sierra blurted out her problem and waited expectantly for her mother to wave a magic sheet of fabric softener to make all the static go away.

Instead, her mom leaned against the dryer and said, "So, what are you going to do?"

This was the part about entering adulthood Sierra disliked the most. Her parents let her make most of her own decisions. They said she would grow more if she learned from the consequences and rewards of her own choices. It drove Sierra crazy! Her parents seemed to find a strange parental satisfaction in putting the responsibility back on her.

"I don't know yet."

"Is Warner a difficult person to get along with?" her mom asked.

"He doesn't seem to annoy other people as much as he bugs me. He used to come up and put his arm around my shoulder. He's so tall it felt as though he was hanging on me and trying to make people think we were together or something."

"Does he still do that?"

"No. I made it clear awhile ago I didn't like it, and he finally stopped. Now he's kind of mean to me. He says cutting things and gives me these nasty looks."

Mrs. Jensen smiled.

"What?" Sierra asked.

"If you were in junior high, I'd say Warner had a pretty serious crush on you."

"Exactly! That's what makes it so annoying. We're not in junior high; we're seniors in high school! Why can't he act normal?"

"Some guys take a little longer than others to mature. You know that. Don't confuse immaturity with meanness."

"But, Mom, tell me, on a trip like this do you think I have to invite someone who is immature just to be nice to him?"

"I don't know," Mrs. Jensen said thoughtfully. "A trip like this might help him grow up."

Sierra lifted her hands in a pleading gesture to her mother. "Why is it suddenly my responsibility to make sure Warner gets a life? And why is this trip about Warner? It was supposed to be a fun, fact-finding time for Wes and me, and then I included Amy and Vicki. That was it. A nice, cozy little package. Why can't it be like that?"

"What about Randy?"

"Okay, Wes, Amy, Vicki, Randy, and me." As soon as Sierra verbalized the guest list, she realized it sounded like two couples: Wes and Amy, Vicki and Randy. Sierra would be the leftover—unless Warner came, and that would make everything worse. She hadn't even considered Margo in all the deliberations. What if Margo and Warner both came, and they ended up being a couple? Three couples with Sierra as the outsider.

"I'm getting a headache," Sierra said. "I'm going up to my room. I told Randy I'd call him."

"Could you carry this basket of laundry up to the kitchen for me?" Mrs. Jensen asked.

"Sure." Sierra bent down to pick up the wicker basket by the side handles.

"Oh, and by the way," Mrs. Jensen said, "did you see the letter that came for you? It's on the chair in the study."

five

JUST THE THOUGHT of a letter waiting for her lightened Sierra's load. She put the laundry basket on the kitchen counter and hurried to her favorite spot. Lifting the envelope and skimming the bold, black letters that spelled her name on the front, Sierra smiled. Something inside her always stirred like a breeze across a meadow when she held a letter from Paul.

Settling in her chair and carefully opening the letter, Sierra began to read:

> *Dear Sierra,*
>
> *Well, I've finally made some decisions. It's taken a long time, and I've sure gone through my share of inner torture trying to discern God's direction. I couldn't have made it without your prayer support. Thank you!*

Sierra looked up and swallowed hard. She knew all about making decisions and the inner torture one could go through. Paul's words made her realize she hadn't prayed about her own situation. It seemed ironic she was able to help Paul make some decisions with her encouragement and prayer support; yet who did she have praying for her? And why wasn't she talking over her struggles with God? Returning her thoughts and attention to Paul's letter, she read on.

> *I'm not sure if I told you how they break down the academic terms at the university. The spring term ends next week. We have a month-long break, and then what they call the summer term begins; it goes from the middle of April to the middle of June. I'll be staying for the summer term, and then it looks as though I'll be returning to the States.*

Sierra felt a rush of hope and anticipation at the thought of Paul's coming home. He had gone to school in Portland the year before, but his family lived in San Diego, where his dad was a pastor. Would Paul return to Portland, or would he go to college elsewhere? She read on.

> *As you know, it's been hard for me to work through this decision. When I came over here, I thought I'd finish out my degree at the University of Edinburgh. That had been my goal since my sopho-more year in high school. I wanted to leave home and be with my grandfather. As you know, he died before I was able to come to school here. The entrance requirements were that I had at least one year at a qualifying university in the U.S., which is how I ended up at Lewis and Clark College.*
>
> *Anyway, I came over thinking that I could help my grand-mother and that the University of Edinburgh would be everything I had dreamed of when I first visited the campus as a fifteen-year-old. The truth is, my grandmother is quite self-sufficient and has*

*made it clear it has become a bother for me to impose on her hospi-
tality every weekend. I've made a few friends at the school, but not
real close friends, since I haven't stayed around on weekends. The
classes have been great, and I believe this year has been a good experience for me in many ways, especially in getting my heart set back
on the Lord. There's a rugged loneliness about this country that
makes a heart cry out. I'm grateful that when I sought the Lord, He
heard me and came close.*

*As for my future plans, those are still formulating. When I first
asked you to pray about this with me, I was considering coming
home at the end of the spring term in March, but it was to my benefit to take the classes offered from April to June. I have a month off
before those classes begin, so I'm going to do some traveling. I'd like
to check out a sailing camp on the northwest coast of Scotland. Then
I think I'll come back down to Stranraer and take the Seacat
Hydrofoil over to Belfast.*

Again Sierra stopped reading and let her imagination
drift with Paul's words. Sierra had been to Belfast more
than a year ago. She would have to write Paul right away to
tell him to visit The Giant's Causeway on the north coast.
Sierra remembered how fascinated she had been with this
natural work of God where the lava had flowed into the sea
long ago and hardened into extremely large, steplike blocks
of rocks. It did indeed look like a cobblestone path for
giants.

*I'd appreciate your prayers for safety while I travel and for all the
decisions that still need to be made about what I'll do when I leave
here in June. I need to close for now. There's a big rugby tournament at Murrayfield Stadium this afternoon. Scotland vs. France.*

You probably know that rugby is the sport over here. This game promises to be a good one and worth the study break I'm taking to see it.

Hope everything is going well for you. Thanks again for all your prayers and encouragement. I don't think you'll ever know how much they mean to me.

With a grateful heart,

Paul

As soon as she read Paul's signature, Sierra turned back to the first page of onionskin paper and started to read every word over again. That's what she usually did when she received a letter from Paul.

She had almost finished the letter for the second time when the phone rang. Mrs. Jensen answered it and called for Sierra, telling her Randy was on the line.

Carefully folding Paul's letter and tucking it back into the envelope, Sierra reached for the phone on her dad's desk. "Hi ya," she answered cheerfully.

Randy paused a moment and then said, "You sound as if you're in a better mood than you were at lunch. Does that mean you've talked to your brother?"

Sierra's cheeks flushed. She felt as though she had been caught in a private moment of interacting with Paul. She would have experienced the same sort of embarrassment if she and Paul had been together, here in the study, sitting close and looking warmly into each other's eyes, and then the door burst open and Randy barged in.

"Yes, I've talked to Wes," Sierra began, pulling together her thoughts. "I'm not sure I have a real clear direction yet, but he did say he would like it if you came along."

"Cool," Randy said. "I'm in. I got someone to do my Saturday lawn jobs for me. By the way, my parents want to know which colleges we're going to visit, and I want to know how much money you think I should bring."

Sierra listed the colleges and then told him that he would have to cover all his meals and that they would only do something fun if there was enough time in the schedule.

"Okay," Randy said. "My parents also want me to chip in some money for the gas, so I figured I'd give Wesley fifty bucks, unless you think I should give him more."

"That sounds like a lot," Sierra said.

"My dad said it's way less than an airline ticket."

"Randy, do you think Warner and Margo would still want to go if they knew we weren't sure about making it to the beach or some other fun place? I mean, are they serious about this being a college scouting trip?"

"I don't know. I think so. Drake wanted to know if we were going to swing over to the coast. He wanted to check out Westridge in Santa Barbara."

Drake! Sierra felt the panic rising again. The last bit of euphoria she had felt over Paul's letter vanished when Randy reminded her about Drake. She had forgotten about his wanting to go. Or maybe she had pushed that thought far away when she became upset over Warner.

"The thing is, it's going to be really crowded, Randy. Who do you think should go? I mean, it's definitely you, Wes, Vicki, Amy, and me. Only three more seats are in the van, if we figure enough room for everyone's luggage. If Drake, Warner, and Margo all go, I think it's going to be too crowded for such a long trip."

"Could be. I don't know. You're going to have to call the shots."

"I wish everyone would stop telling me that!" Sierra blurted out. "Do you know how frustrating it is to suddenly be responsible for all this? This trip was supposed to be nice and easy, but now it's turned into a popularity contest or something."

Randy didn't say anything.

"I mean, how would you feel if you had to make these choices?"

"I don't know. I'd probably figure out what works best for the whole trip, and if I had to tell some people there wasn't room, I'd tell them. I don't think it would hurt your friendship with anyone. Everybody understands the situation, Sierra."

"You understand because you're definitely going. What if you were one of the ones I said no to?"

"I'd understand," Randy said without hesitation.

"Yeah, well, you're Randy. You always understand. What about the others?"

"If they're really your friends, your decision won't change that."

"I don't know, Randy. They would probably say if I was really their friend there wouldn't be any discussion. I'd want them all to come."

"Maybe."

Sierra was beginning to get the same dull headache she had felt when she talked to Wes earlier in the evening.

"Do me a favor and don't say anything about going until after lunch tomorrow, okay, Randy?"

"Okay."

"I'm going to pray about all this, and then we can settle everything tomorrow."

"Whatever," Randy said.

"Right," Sierra agreed, feeling as ambivalent as Randy's comment. "Whatever."

six

ON WEDNESDAY AFTERNOON, the day of the college scouting trip, Sierra stood in the driveway watching her father tighten the luggage rack on top of the van. Randy was in the front yard, tossing a stick for Brutus, the Jensen family dog. Amy had run into the house to use the bathroom, and Vicki stood next to Sierra.

Sierra was listening to Vicki, but her glare was fixed on Warner, who already had claimed the front passenger seat of the van and now sat there like a rock.

"I wonder if Drake dropped out at the last minute because he found out Margo wasn't going," Vicki said quietly. "I've noticed they've been hanging around together this past week or so."

"Could be," Sierra muttered. When Margo's parents found out Sierra's brother, and not her parents, was chaperoning the trip, they decided Margo couldn't go. Then at lunch today Drake had come up to Sierra and simply said he had changed his mind because he had "too much going on."

Ever since Sierra had made her big decision and

announced a week ago that Randy, Warner, Drake, and Margo were all welcome to come, she silently had hoped Drake and Warner wouldn't go—especially Warner. So when Drake dropped out at the last minute, Sierra couldn't help but wish Warner would do the same.

But no, Warner was going. There he was, planted in the front seat. Sierra kept reminding herself of all the pointers her mom had mentioned the night before about Sierra's setting boundaries with him and reinforcing them whenever necessary. Mrs. Jensen also had reminded Sierra this might be the kind of experience that would have a positive, maturing effect on Warner, and she had praised Sierra for being mature enough to include him even when it wasn't her preference.

Sierra felt anything but mature at the moment. She didn't want to be responsible for driving the family van one hundred miles down to Corvallis with Randy, Warner, Amy, and Vicki depending on her. Sierra would have felt much more comfortable if her dad stepped in and volunteered to drive them to Wesley's. But she knew her dad wouldn't; he trusted her, and her friends depended on her. She never would have expected it, but being mature and responsible on such occasions was a troublesome, nerve-wracking condition.

Putting on her best smile, Sierra thanked her dad for loading the luggage rack.

"I filled the tank and checked the oil this morning," Mr. Jensen said as he handed Sierra the keys. "Remind Wes to check the oil again before you start the return trip."

"I will."

"And call us when you get to Wesley's," Mrs. Jensen said.

"I will."

"Make sure everyone wears seat belts," Mr. Jensen said. "I took out an umbrella insurance policy so you're all covered in case anything happens. But make sure you're always driving the speed limit, obeying the traffic laws, and all wearing seat belts."

"Okay," Sierra agreed. "We will." Her parents' last-minute instructions were beginning to make her even more nervous. "I'm sure we'll be fine."

"That's what we're praying," Mrs. Jensen said. "You have a good time and call if there are any problems."

"We will." Sierra reached over to open the van door in an attempt to get going. Mrs. Jensen caught Sierra before she could climb into the van, and with a big hug, she kissed her on the cheek. Her mom's demonstration embarrassed Sierra. "'Bye," Sierra said quickly, clambering into the van.

"Good-bye," Mr. Jensen called out. Fortunately, he had not tried to give Sierra a kiss in front of her friends. She felt a twinge of shame over how her parents' loving intentions were embarrassing to her.

Amy and Vicki climbed into the bench seat behind Sierra, and Randy went to the seat behind them, carrying his bulky guitar case with him.

"Seat belts on, everyone," Mr. Jensen called out. To Sierra's relief, all of them obliged without saying anything.

"Everybody ready?" Sierra asked as she started the engine. Sierra was surprised to find she didn't like being in the driver's seat or being in charge. Since her earliest years she had been told she was a natural leader. Maybe she felt awkward leading her peers. Or maybe she felt self-conscious with her parents standing there in the driveway with their arms around each other, waving at her wistfully, as if she were going out to sea for a dangerous voyage and they might never see her again. Wherever the uncomfortable feeling came from, it began to diminish by the time they were on the freeway heading south to Corvallis.

"Anybody want some gum?" Vicki offered.

"What kind is it?" Warner asked.

"Spearmint. Do you want some?"

"No way. I only chew bubble gum," Warner said. "Which reminds me, I forgot to bring some. Pull off the freeway at the next exit, Sierra. I need to buy some gum."

"I'm not getting off for gum," Sierra said. The extra-sharp edge to her words surprised even her. It was quiet for a minute. "I told my parents we were driving straight through," she added, trying to soften her tone. "You can wait until we reach Corvallis to buy some gum, can't you?"

Warner lifted his long legs and rested his feet on the dashboard. He looked like a scrunched-up grasshopper. "Guess I don't have much choice."

"Could you put your feet down?" Sierra asked.

"Make me," Warner taunted.

"Warner, your legs are blocking my view of the side mirror."

"No, they're not."

"Warner," Sierra said, losing what tiny shreds of patience she had left, "put your legs down! This is my parents' van, and my dad doesn't like people to put their feet on the dash like that."

"Your dad's not here, is he?"

"It's still his car," Sierra said. "So I'm telling you, put your legs down!"

Warner slowly lowered his feet and turned to stare at Sierra. "Are you going to be this much fun the whole trip?"

"I don't know. Are you going to be this big of a jerk?"

The other passengers remained silent.

"I'm sorry," Sierra said. "That wasn't very kind. Let's start over, Warner, okay? All I'm saying is that my parents have put a lot of trust in me for this trip, and I want to honor them. Can you support me in this?"

"Sure," Warner said with a shrug. "You're the woman. You run the tour. I'm only along for the wild ride."

Sierra couldn't help but think Warner had no idea what a wild ride this was for her emotions. She was fully aware that what she hadn't wanted to happen was happening. Warner was coming on this trip, and she had blown up at him within the first twenty minutes. Sierra also knew that once they picked up Wesley, they would be a traveling band of six. Three guys and three girls. Matched up, that meant Vicki and Randy, Amy and Wes, and Warner and her. The thought made Sierra's stomach turn. From now until Sunday night she would have to fight her aggressive dislike for Warner.

Why is this so hard, God? she prayed. *What's my problem? I thought I'd worked through all this and decided to be kind and loving to everyone the way You want me to be. I'm sorry, but this is impossible.*

"Do you want some gum, Sierra?" Vicki rather timidly held out a stick as a peace offering.

"Sure. Thanks."

Warner pulled a skateboarding magazine out of the gym bag he had smashed into the space between his seat and the driver's. He also took out a Walkman and placed the headset into his ears. For the next forty-five minutes he kept in his own little world, tapping his fingers on the dashboard in time to the headset music.

Warner also appeared to have brought a stash of junk food in his gym bag because he kept reaching in for more snacks. First he downed a can of soda, crushed the can, and dropped it on the van's floor. Then he ate a bag of popcorn, leaving bits of kernels everywhere. The large bag of M&M's was devoured without being offered to anyone else. He tossed the empty bag onto the floor on Sierra's side of the van since his side was full. Then he went for a bag of barbecue-flavored corn nuts, which smelled up the whole van.

During Warner's pig-out session, Randy sat in the backseat quietly playing his guitar. Sierra, Amy, and Vicki tried to ignore Warner and talked about some of their expectations of the different colleges and other bits of information they each had gathered during the week. It wasn't the same level of girl chat they shared at Mama Bear's every week, since they knew two guys could listen in at any time. But Sierra was encouraged that Amy and Vicki had both gotten into the spirit of the trip.

"I have some coupons my uncle gave me for Magic Mountain," Amy said. "I don't know if they're any good, but it says they can be used at any of the Six Flags Amusement Parks."

"For what? Free admission?" Vicki asked.

"No, I think it's something like six dollars off the admission price."

"My mom gave me a AAA guidebook to Southern California. It lists all the hours and admission prices for the different amusement parks and stuff," Vicki said. "I know we're not really planning on going anywhere specific, but if we decide to, at least we have some information."

"That's great," Sierra said. "I'm sure something will work out. It'll be spontaneous, though."

"That's the best kind of fun," Vicki said.

Just outside of Salem, light rain began to fall. Sierra turned on the wiper blades and slowed down. The traffic seemed to be thickening now that it was getting close to five o'clock.

"You know what, Sierra?" Vicki leaned forward to speak, but it was impossible to have a confidential conversation with Warner planted there in the passenger seat. "I know we're supposed to go straight through to Corvallis, but I need to make a bathroom stop. I don't think I can wait. Would it be okay if we stopped?"

"Sure," Sierra said.

Warner looked up from his magazine and pulled the headset from his ears. "Oh, we're going to stop, are we? May I please get out of the car, too, Miss Tour Queen? Please, oh please?"

"Warner, why do you have to be like that?" Vicki snapped.

Warner tossed the empty bag of corn nuts at Vicki and said, "Think fast."

Sierra checked the rearview mirror for Vicki's reaction.

To her credit, Vicki remained composed. "You're acting like a jerk, Warner. Why don't you cut it out?"

"What is it with all the females in this wagon?" Warner mocked.

"Don't go there, Warner," Randy warned from the backseat. It was the first time he had said anything since they had left. Sierra was surprised at his outburst, but she appreciated her friend's support.

Sierra didn't say anything. She put on her turn signal and carefully made the lane change to exit the freeway. At the first gas station on the right, she pulled in and parked to the side, near the door to the restroom.

"I'll be right back," Vicki said.

"I'm going with you," Sierra said.

"Me, too," Amy said, sliding out the side door behind Vicki.

"It's a law of nature," Warner said, loud enough for them all to hear. "All females of the species go to the bathroom in herds." Only Warner laughed.

"Here, Randy," Sierra said, tossing him the keys. "You're on guard duty."

Sierra followed Amy and Vicki into the restroom. As soon as the door was shut behind them, the three of them started talking.

"I can't do this," Vicki said. "I didn't think he would be this bad. He's going to drive me crazy!"

"Why did you invite him, Sierra?" Amy asked.

"I didn't exactly want to," Sierra said, giving Vicki a sideways glance. Quickly realizing this was no time to start placing blame, Sierra quietly added, "It was very complicated. Trust me on this, you guys. I prayed long and hard over it, and I thought I was doing the right thing by opening up the invitation to him."

"Nice to him, maybe. But it's not nice for us to have to put up with him," Amy said.

"It's not going to work," Vicki said. "We have to figure out what we can do about this. He's going to make the whole trip miserable for everyone. I thought I was going to pass out from the smell of those corn nuts."

"No kidding," Amy said.

"We could try to set boundaries with him," Sierra offered. "That's what my mom suggested. We could tell him when and how he's irritating us and ask him to stop doing those things."

"Do you really think that will work?" Amy asked.

"Everything he's doing irritates me," Vicki said.

"I know." Sierra washed her hands and looked at her reflection in the mirror. Her hair was beginning to frizz the way it always did in the rain. Tiny ringlets had already tightened at her temples.

"All I know is that we can't go on this way for the whole trip." Vicki joined Sierra at the sink and washed her hands. She also gave herself a quick exam in the mirror. "Oh, I hate my hair," she muttered.

"Don't even get Sierra started on that subject," Amy's voice called from behind the closed stall door. "Stick to the subject of Warner. What are we going to do about him?"

Vicki and Sierra looked at each other and at the same time said, "Scream!"

seven

THE THREE FRIENDS stayed in the restroom with the door locked long enough to come up with a plan. Before they drove another inch, they were going to confront Warner. They would tell him what was bothering them and ask him to try to be considerate of everyone else on the trip. If these three friends had learned one thing, it was that the right way to handle a conflict was to go to the person you have the problem with and talk it over with him in a kind manner. They only hoped it would work with Warner.

When they finally returned to the van, Randy appeared to be having his own little "correctional conversation" with Warner in the backseat. None of the trash around Warner's seat had been removed.

As soon as Sierra opened the door on the driver's side, Warner turned to her and said, "Randy says I'm making everybody mad."

Sierra looked at Randy and then at Amy and Vicki, who were standing by the open sliding side door, waiting to get in.

Amy entered the van and looked at Warner. "I don't

know what your expectations were of this trip, but I know for the rest of us we were expecting to have a good time. When you act pushy, rude, and inconsiderate of everyone else, it's hard to feel like we're having a good time. It also makes it impossible for everyone to get along."

Warner looked stumped. "Why are you guys all against me?"

"We're not," three of them said in unison. Sierra was the only one who didn't pipe up.

"It's like I was trying to explain to you, Warner," Randy said. "When you're part of a group or on a team, everyone looks out for everyone else and tries to consider other people's feelings first. Making rude comments or being sarcastic doesn't build any kind of unity."

"I'm only kidding," Warner said. "Why can't you guys take a joke? Why is everyone so uptight?"

Sierra began to wonder if her dislike of Warner had rubbed off on the others and they were now taking her side and trying to reform Warner in three easy steps to make him more acceptable to Sierra. If she honestly were a team player, as Randy said, and if she had considered Warner's feelings, she wouldn't have thrown the first stone by snapping at him about not stopping until they reached Corvallis.

And look, she thought, *we stopped after all. So my statement was worthless.*

"You guys," Sierra said, "I don't think I've exactly been a terrific team player. I was rude to you, Warner, and I apologize."

Warner looked at each of them and shrugged his thin shoulders. "Okay. Can we get going?"

"Okay," Sierra said, reaching across the seat for the keys Randy held out to her.

Vicki opened the passenger door and started to get in the front seat.

"Whoa!" Warner said, crawling out of the backseat of the van. "That's my seat."

"Your seat?" Vicki said, picking up the empty snack bags and stuffing them into the litterbag hanging from the glove compartment. "And is this your trash, too? I say whoever picks up the trash gets to ride in the front. It's not very far to Corvallis."

"I take the front," Warner said, motioning for Vicki to move with an aggressive jerk of his thumb. "I get carsick unless I ride in the front seat."

Sierra glanced at Amy, whose dark eyes grew wide. Vicki's face took on the same look of disbelief.

"You mean you expect to ride in the front seat all the way to California and back?" Vicki said, still not moving from the seat.

"Unless you want me to barf all over everyone in the back."

Vicki quietly exited and took her seat next to Amy on the middle bench. Warner scrambled in and closed the door with a slam that Sierra knew would have prompted her dad to say, "Not so hard. You'll break it."

Instead, Sierra said, "Warner, why did you want to come on this trip?"

"What do you mean?"

"I mean, I'd like to know what your idea of a road trip is."

"This," he said. "Why?"

Vicki leaned forward. "Have you ever gone anywhere with friends before?"

"The band went up to Longview a couple of months ago."

"Longview," Amy repeated. "That's like forty miles away. You've never traveled with friends or family before?"

Warner shook his head. "No. What's the big deal? I wanted to come because everyone else was coming."

"Not everyone," Vicki said. "Tre couldn't come. Margo and Drake decided not to come. I don't understand why you wanted to."

"Do I need to spell it out?"

"Yes, if you could," Sierra said calmly. "It would help."

"Because I hang out with you guys," Warner said in a monotone.

"You're saying we're your friends?" Vicki asked. "'Cause if that's what you're saying, Warner, then you need to treat us a whole lot nicer than you have been. Friends don't treat friends the way you're treating us."

"She has a point," Randy said. "You need a little work in that area, buddy. We're all willing to hang in there with you, but come on. You have to move our way a little, too. I mean, try to be a team player here. That's all we're saying."

Warner still looked as if he just didn't get it. Sierra gave up and started the van. "Let's get back on the road. Wes is going to wonder what happened to us." Secretly, she hoped that Wes would turn out to be the ideal referee for this volatile group of team players and that he could talk some consideration into Warner.

They arrived in Corvallis without any complications, mostly because Sierra ignored Warner and then focused on finding her way to where Wes lived. They located the house he shared with several other college guys, and Sierra parked the van in the church parking lot next to the old two-story house, just as her dad had instructed her. Wes came out to greet them before they even made it up the stairs to the front door. The sight of her dear older brother had a calming effect on Sierra.

Wes physically resembled their dad, especially his eyes, which were a warm brown color, and he had the same brown, wavy hair as their dad, except that Wes had a full head of hair and no receding hairline. He was over six feet tall, which comforted Sierra, because by virtue of size alone Warner was no longer the biggest of their group.

"Why don't you go in and call Mom?" Wes suggested. "I'm not quite ready. It might be a good idea for you guys to hang out here and stretch your legs awhile."

Sierra noticed that Warner immediately returned to the van. She guessed he was retrieving his skateboard, which he had stuck under the middle seat. As she walked up the steps to the front door with Wes, she began quietly to tell her brother about the conflict with Warner on the way down.

"I've done everything I can think of," Sierra said as they entered the living room. "First, I invited him. That was nice. When he was rude, I snapped at him, but then I apologized. We all talked to him about being a team player, but he just doesn't get it. He says he has to ride in the front seat the entire trip or he'll get sick."

Wesley's eyebrows rose. Being from a large family, Wes and Sierra had learned early on to share whatever they had and to be considerate of others. That included "dibs" on the shotgun seat. Everyone took a turn.

"Do you want me to tell him I don't want him to come?" Wes asked.

"How can you tell him that? He's already here."

"We could take him back to Portland. Or we could put him on a bus back, or call his parents and tell them it's not going to work out for him to come."

Sierra sighed. "I don't know. Here I thought I was solving the problem by not excluding him, and now it's worse because I invited him. I should have said no in the beginning and let him be mad at me."

"You prayed about it, didn't you?" Wes asked.

"Yes, I sincerely did."

"Then you have to go on faith at this point. You have to believe he's here for a reason."

"Does that mean he has to stay?" Sierra asked.

"Not necessarily." Wes glanced at his watch. "Why don't you call Mom and Dad? Let them know you arrived, and I'll see if my clothes are finished in the dryer so I can pack."

"You haven't started to pack?"

"It will take me only a few minutes," Wes promised as he headed for the back of the house.

Sierra called home and chose to tell her parents only that the group had arrived safely and there had been no problems with the van. She didn't want to bring up the Warner issue. "We did make one stop, though, outside of Salem. Vicki had to go to the restroom. I guess Wes is finishing his packing, and then we're leaving. I'll call you tomorrow when I have a chance." Sierra knew her parents hadn't asked her to call regularly to check in. She also knew they would really like it if she did.

"Great," Mrs. Jensen said. "Have a wonderful time. We're praying for you."

Sierra hung up, feeling a little more optimistic. Wes was

in the driver's seat now, so to speak. He would take over and work things out. He would also be the responsible one in case anything went wrong. It was a position Sierra gladly relinquished.

She was about to head back outside when Amy came rushing in through the front door. "Sierra, come quick! It's Warner! Tell Wes to come."

"What happened?"

"Warner ran into a truck!"

eight

"WARNER WAS RIDING HIS SKATEBOARD," Amy breathlessly explained as Sierra and Wes jogged with her down the street, "and this truck came around the corner. Warner caught up with it and grabbed the back bumper. Then the truck put on its brakes at the stop sign."

"And Warner crashed into the back of the truck," Sierra concluded as they arrived at the scene of the accident. Warner was splayed out on the street. A dozen people had gathered around him.

"He thinks he broke his arm," Vicki said. "One of the guys here already called the paramedics."

Sierra noticed that Warner's right arm was twisted in a scarecrowlike position, and he was grimacing. She knew it wasn't very nice, but her first thought was to scold him by saying, "What were you thinking? Didn't you even consider it might be dangerous?"

The paramedics arrived and carted Warner off to the hospital. Sierra was thankful Wesley was there to take over the job of calling Warner's parents and explaining what had happened. Warner's mom got directions to the hospital from Wes and urged them to go ahead and leave for their trip. She said that even if Warner's arm weren't broken, he couldn't continue the trip with them. As Wes relayed it, Warner's mom said that if Warner was going to take risks like that and not act responsibly, then he couldn't enjoy the privilege of going on the trip. Apparently, the last thing Warner's mom said to Wes was, "His father and I were so hoping this trip would be a breakthrough for him. Warner has never been good at friendships or responsibility."

"I didn't want something bad to happen to him," Sierra said as the solemn group of five pulled into the hospital parking lot.

"Don't start blaming yourself," Vicki said quickly. "It was an accident, and it happened because Warner was being a daredevil and showing off. It had nothing to do with any of us."

"I know what Sierra means, though," Amy added. "I can't help but feel bad, too."

"Come on," Wes said, turning off the van's engine. "We'll buy him some balloons and tell him we hope he feels better. That's the best we can do. It's all we can do."

"Are you going to tell him his mom said he can't continue on the trip?" Sierra asked.

"Unless you want to."

"No thank you," Sierra said.

After a stop at the hospital gift shop, Wes led them into the emergency room and the area where Warner was lying in bed.

"They told me it broke in two places," Warner moaned when he saw them. "The doctor showed me the X rays. I can't believe the idiot in that truck stopped so suddenly."

"Idiot in the truck?" Vicki spouted. "Warner, you were the one who shouldn't have been holding on to the bumper! What did you think would happen?" She stood the farthest from the bed and placed her hand on her hip.

"I've done it before, and nothing ever happened."

"Here," Sierra said, tying the string from the get-well balloons to the metal railing of Warner's bed. "These are to cheer you up."

"Thanks. But don't you think they'll be too much of a distraction for you in the van?"

"Warner," Wes said, "your mom is coming. She said she didn't want you to go the rest of the way. She's taking you home."

Warner looked stunned. "Why?"

"She will have to talk that through with you," Wes said.

"Did you tell her to come get me?"

"Nope. I called her and told her what had happened, and she told me exactly what I've relayed to you." Wes looked at his watch. "She'll probably be here within the next hour and a half. We can stay here with you, if you'd like."

Warner looked depressed. For a fraction of a second, Sierra almost felt sorry for him. "No," he finally said, his head down. "You guys need to get on the road. I don't want to hold you back."

"That's really considerate of you," Randy said. "We appreciate it."

"I'm sorry this happened to you," Sierra said, giving Warner a weak but sincere smile.

"We all are," Amy added. "I hope it doesn't hurt too much."

"I'll be okay. You guys just go."

"Thanks, Warner," Wes said. "I'll get your stuff from the van and bring it back in here for you."

Warner nodded and gave a weak wave to the rest of them.

"I'll put your card right here," Sierra said, opening the envelope for him and laying the get-well card on his leg. "Take it easy, okay?"

Warner met her gaze with a more settled look than she had ever seen on his long face. It almost seemed as if he had grown up a little bit.

Sierra and the others were back in the van and twenty miles down the freeway before they started to talk about Warner. They needed that much time to process their thoughts and feelings.

"Do you think God lets bad things happen so that good things come out of it?" Vicki asked. "Like, I mean, what if this broken arm turns into a real humbling and growing experience for Warner? What if the lessons he learns from the broken arm are more valuable than the lessons he would have learned on this trip with us?"

"You mean the lessons we would have tried to cram down his throat," Sierra said. "That's my problem. I'm so quick to see where I think people are wrong and need to change, and then, just because it seems obvious to me, I think they should see it, too, and instantly desire to change."

"At least you care enough to want to see your friends improve," Randy said. "That's not a bad thing, Sierra."

"Unless she crams it down your throat, as she said," Amy added.

Sierra looked at Amy, who was now seated in the front passenger seat, next to Wes. Amy didn't turn to meet Sierra's gaze, but Sierra knew exactly what Amy was thinking. "I know, I know," Sierra said. "My track record for tact and gentleness isn't that great. You've had to endure the brunt of that, Amy. I hope I'm getting a little better at being a good friend."

"Yeah, as long as we keep all air horns away from you," Amy said.

Sierra cringed. The air horn had to be one of her silliest moves. In an effort to show Amy she was on her side, last fall Sierra had followed Amy and her old boyfriend, Nathan, as they left The Beet, a local teen nightspot. When Sierra saw Nathan grab Amy's shoulders, she had sounded an air horn behind him to give Amy a chance to run away. Only Amy had had no need of Sierra's assistance and so didn't run anywhere. Sierra still couldn't believe she had done that.

"At least you admit when you're wrong," Vicki said. "That quality in and of itself makes you a good friend. My problem is I'm so afraid people will get mad at me or decide they no longer like me that I have a hard time admitting I'm wrong."

"Not always," Sierra said.

"Maybe not in the last eight months or so, ever since summer camp when I got my life back on track with God. But before then, I never willingly would admit I was wrong. Isn't that right, Amy?"

"I'm staying out of this."

"Well, it's true," Vicki said. "But that's all in the past, and it's all been forgiven, right?"

"Right," Sierra said when no one else spoke up.

"We need to move on," Vicki said. "Move on in our friendships and move on now that Warner isn't with us. We can't spend the whole trip feeling responsible."

"Right," Sierra added again.

"It does feel different, though, doesn't it?" Vicki said. "I mean, it feels like a completely different trip than the first two hours when we had Warner and didn't have Wes."

"Are you saying you made a good trade?" Wes said with a sly grin at Vicki in the rearview mirror.

"Definitely," Amy said. "No offense, you guys, but I'm so relieved Warner isn't going any farther with us. He would have been a pain the whole time."

"I think it feels more peaceful now," Sierra said. "Is that how you guys feel? It's much calmer."

"That's because Randy is asleep back there," Wes said, glancing again in the mirror.

Randy mimicked loud snoring noises from the backseat.

"Randy is just being his usual, peacemaking self and not saying much," Vicki observed.

"Snoring like that isn't going to make a lot of peace with me at night, I can tell you that," Wes said.

"Oh, right," Sierra jumped in. "You snore much worse than that, Wes, and I have proof."

"Anyone else getting hungry?" Wes asked. "I need to buy some gas, so we might as well eat, too."

"Don't try to change the subject," Sierra teased her brother. "You might as well confess to everyone now, since we're going to be in close quarters for a long time. They'll find out sooner or later."

"Okay, okay, I snore like a chain saw. There. Now you all know."

"Gavin even recorded him this Christmas to show him how loud he snores."

"He turned up the volume on the recorder," Wes said, putting on his turn signal and moving into the slow lane.

"He did not! That's exactly how you sound," Sierra said.

"Any preferences on where we stop for dinner?"

"Anywhere. Except maybe not Burger King," Vicki said. "I had Burger King last night."

"I had McDonald's for lunch," Amy said.

"I could go for a sub sandwich," Randy said.

Wes laughed. "Opinionated bunch, aren't you? Why don't I pull off the freeway first, and then we can see what our options are."

Before Wes could exit, a red light on the control panel came on and flashed a warning. "That's strange," Wes said.

"Is something wrong?" Sierra asked.

"I'm not sure. Did this light go on while you were driving?"

"No. I've never seen it go on before."

A sudden hiss of steam began to spit from the van engine and rise up like a cloud in front of the windshield.

"Oh, boy," Wes muttered. "Everybody hold on. I may have to pull over quickly. Houston, we have a problem."

Sierra shot her brother a look that said, "How can you be trying to make jokes when we're about to blow up here on the freeway?"

Wes was able to reach the off-ramp by turning on the windshield wipers and spraying the window to keep it clear.

A distinct odor of moldy socks began to permeate the van.

"Smells like the radiator hose," Randy said.

"You can tell what's wrong with a car by its smell?" Vicki asked.

"Sometimes. When you drive a truck as old as mine, you get used to these things happening all the time." Randy leaned forward and peered through the hazed-over windshield. "Is that an auto-parts store next to the gas station?"

"Where?" Wes said, driving slowly while the traffic zoomed past him. One driver honked at them and looked angry as he sped around the van.

"Over there, next to the restaurant. On the right."

"I see it."

Before Wes could put on his turn signal, a furious screeching sounded behind them. Sierra turned around and saw a huge truck barreling toward them, recklessly fast.

nine

"HE'S GOING TO HIT US!" Amy screamed.

Sierra grabbed the side of the seat, waiting for the crash. Wes stepped on the gas and swerved the van into the parking lot of the auto-parts store just as the truck driver blew his horn and rolled past them. He missed them by only inches.

"That was way too close," Vicki said, closing her eyes and putting her hand over her face.

"What was that guy doing?" Amy said.

"I wonder if he couldn't stop," Sierra said, trying to see the truck out the side window. She watched as it sped up to catch a yellow light. Then the road curved, and the truck kept on going until she couldn't see it anymore. "Bunch of maniac drivers in this town."

"The main thing I care about this town is that it has an auto-parts store that's open," Wes said, turning off the engine and getting out of the van. The rest of them followed him.

Billows of steam rolled from under the van's closed hood. The disgusting smell of moldy socks was even stronger outside.

"You're not going to open it, are you?" Amy asked. "It looks as if it's going to explode."

"I think you're right, Randy," Wes said. "It's probably a hose. I'll give it a while to cool, and then we can check it out. Do you girls want to go eat something at Denny's?"

"Trying to get rid of us?" Amy teased. "You afraid we women might get in the way of your manly car repairing?"

"You can stay here if you want. I was trying to be nice," Wes said.

"I was only kidding." Amy gave him a punch in the arm. Sierra tried to watch the interaction between them without appearing to stare.

"I'm ready to eat," Vicki said. "I'll save us a booth at the restaurant. Anyone else want to come?"

Sierra joined her, and the two of them walked across the parking lot, leaving Amy, Wes, and Randy to deal with the car.

"Vicki, do you think Amy is showing extra interest in Wes?"

"I hadn't noticed," Vicki said. She held open the door of the restaurant for Sierra. "I don't think she's overdoing it or anything. She admires Wes. She always has. I don't think you should start to worry about anything being out of balance."

"Two?" the hostess asked, greeting them with menus in her hand.

"There will be five of us," Sierra said. "And we would like nonsmoking, please."

The waitress said, "This is all nonsmoking. All restaurants are nonsmoking in California." She led them to a large booth in the corner.

"I wish they had that rule in Oregon," Vicki said. "I can't stand it when you're trying to eat, and it tastes like ashes from the person's cigarette at the table five feet away."

Sierra was only half listening. From the corner window she had a good view of the van. The hood was up, steam was pouring out, and another guy had joined Wes, Randy, and Amy in gazing into the abyss of the van's engine area. Sierra noticed that Amy was standing rather close to Wes and looking up at him as if she were hanging on to his every word.

"You really don't think Amy is going to make an effort to capture Wes's special attention this trip? I don't know if you remember my telling you, but it got a little complicated on our backpacking trip last summer. Her interest in him put a strain on our friendship. I don't want it to get like that on this trip." Sierra was still looking out the window as she spoke, so she couldn't see Vicki's expression.

"Do you know if they serve fish here?" Vicki said, scanning her menu. "I feel like having fish sticks or something."

"Fish sticks?" Sierra shook her head. Vicki hadn't heard a word she'd said. Or she had heard and was trying to get out of responding.

The waitress took their order and left glasses of ice water for them. Sierra turned again to watch the happenings beyond the window. Wes, Amy, and the other guy had gone into the auto-parts store, leaving Randy at the van with his hands plunged into its front end. She thought how nice it was to have Randy along, since he was experienced with car problems. Before Randy had suggested the problem might be a hose, Sierra had been worried something was seriously wrong with the van and their trip would have to be canceled.

"You know," Sierra said when the waitress delivered

Vicki's salad, "I'm glad Randy came, and I'm glad you invited him."

"He's glad you included him," Vicki said, picking over the lettuce and scraping most of the creamy dressing to the side of her small plate.

"You know what else?" Sierra said. "So far I haven't noticed your acting much different toward Randy."

"What do you mean?"

"You're the same person around him on this trip that you are at school and that you are when you're around Amy and me. I mean, I know you like him, and you would love for him to pay extra attention to you, but I don't see your going out of your way to..." Sierra couldn't find the right word.

"Flirt?" Vicki filled in for her. "The way I used to?"

"I wasn't going to use that exact word," Sierra said.

"No, it's true. I've given up flirting. If Randy is going to like me, he's going to like me for who I am and how I act 24-7."

"24-7?" Sierra questioned.

"You know, twenty-four hours a day, seven days a week. And, by the way, Amy isn't exactly flirting with your brother, if that's where you're headed with all this."

"I didn't say she was."

"Trust me. I know about flirting, and I know about Amy around guys she likes and wants to impress. She is being herself right now, and I don't think she is out of balance, or whatever you called it, at all."

The waitress arrived with Sierra's hamburger and Vicki's fish dinner. They prayed together quietly. Vicki's prayer and her earlier words made Sierra feel as if she were being a nosy, spiteful sister and friend. She didn't want to be like that. With all her might, Sierra tried to remember the verse about casting down her imagination. Only a few of the words came to her, but they were enough of a wake-up call to get her mind on other things—like the desserts advertised in the clear acrylic frame in the middle of the table.

"You want to split one of these desserts?" Sierra asked Vicki, holding her burger with both hands and pointing at the picture with her little finger.

"You haven't even taken a bite of your dinner, and you're already planning dessert," Vicki said.

Sierra quickly took a bite and swallowed. "There. Now I've had a bite. Let's plan dessert."

Vicki laughed and agreed to split dessert with her.

Wes, Randy, and Amy joined them and slid into the booth before the dessert arrived.

"We're back on the road again," Wes said. "Thanks to Randy and that guy who came to help us."

Randy grinned his half grin and shrugged. "Like I said, knowledge comes from experience, and my truck provides me with plenty of experience."

Sierra gingerly reached for Randy's right hand and drew it up to the light. "And what does experience teach you about coming to the table with grimy hands?"

Wes automatically checked his own hands. The two young men sheepishly slid out of the booth and headed toward the restroom.

"You know," Amy said, "there's probably just as much bacteria on our hands, even though they're not covered with grease."

"Thank you for telling us after we've eaten," Sierra said.

"I ate with my fork," Vicki said, dipping her fork into the ice cream—covered brownie she and Sierra were sharing.

"I'm going to get one of those," Amy said, slapping the menu closed and laying it on the table.

"That's all?" Sierra asked.

"And a bowl of soup. How's that for a balanced meal?"

"Who can worry about eating healthy on a trip like this?" Vicki said. "Or when we get to college, for that matter. My cousin said that when she went to college, she gained ten pounds the first semester, and she spent more money on eating out than anything else."

Suddenly Sierra realized that once she went to college in the fall, she was going to be on her own when it came to meals, or at least meals outside the cafeteria. She didn't like the idea of gaining ten pounds her first semester. "We'll just have to all watch our diets and keep each other account-able," Sierra said. "Of course, I'm saying this as I stuff myself with this decadent dessert."

Wes and Randy returned and ordered their dinners while Sierra and Vicki finished up their dessert. The con-versation swirled around, and Sierra participated in the fun. But a cloud of apprehension hung over her. The thought of going away to college suddenly was more serious than a lark of a road trip to California. Ahead of her lay more unknowns and more responsibility than she had ever experienced.

The uneasiness heightened when they returned to the van, and Wes said, "You want to drive for a while, Sierra? I'd like to go in the back and see if I can take a nap."

Sierra felt nervous. "Okay, I'll drive. Which way?"

"South," Wes said, handing her the keys with a smile.

"I'll get you back on the freeway, then you just keep going south."

Randy climbed into the front passenger seat. "I'll be glad to drive if you get too tired."

"Thanks, Randy. Just keep me awake, okay?"

Wes directed Sierra onto the freeway and then stretched out on the backseat. The traffic was light. The friends chatted, and Sierra kept checking the control panel on the dashboard to make sure no red lights came on.

"Does anyone have any idea where we are?" Sierra asked.

"Isn't there a map around here?" Randy felt beneath the passenger seat. "Sunflower seeds," he said, holding up a bag that was circled by a thick rubber band.

"No thanks," Vicki said. "I'm trying to cut back on my natural foods this trip."

"Flashlight," Randy announced, pulling out the next item. "This may come in handy." He pulled out a map just as Sierra read the freeway sign they were speeding by. "Weed, next exit."

"Weed?" Vicki echoed with a laugh. "What kind of place is that?"

"I have no idea. Randy, check the map. Tell me I didn't take a wrong turn somewhere, and we're in the middle of Idaho."

"I don't think there is a Weed, Idaho."

"Just check the map."

Randy turned on the flashlight and searched the map. "Here it is," he announced finally. "Weed. It's definitely in California. You're doing fine, Sierra. We're in the right state."

Sierra wondered if Randy understood her anxiety and was trying to get her to laugh so she would relax. She gripped the wheel tightly, very much aware that she was once again in the driver's seat, and everyone was depending on her. Being responsible while plunging into the unknown was not something she was enjoying at all.

ten

AS THEY DROVE on into the night, Sierra felt the tension building in her shoulders. It was getting foggy, and the flash of the oncoming headlights bothered her.

"According to the map," Randy said, "we're driving right past Mount Shasta about now. Did you realize the elevation of Mount Shasta is 14,162 feet?"

"You would never know it," Vicki said, leaning forward to peer out the front windshield along with Sierra and Randy. "It's totally overcast. Do you think it's going to rain?"

"I hope not," Sierra said. "I have my heart set on sunshine all the way this trip."

"You know," Randy said, "this is like following God."

Sierra and Vicki waited for an explanation. Randy's melancholy artist's temperament would cause him to be quiet for a long spell, and then, suddenly, some wild bit of wisdom would tumble from his mouth. It was as if he was always thinking, processing, and taking in information until a silent buzzer went off inside him and—bing!—he spilled out a nugget of truth.

"Here we are in the dark," Randy finally said, "with thick clouds over us, going full speed ahead, and right out there somewhere is this huge mountain, only we can't see it."

"And you think that's like God's will?" Vicki asked.

"Yeah. Because sometimes..." Randy paused as if for dramatic effect. "...we have to keep going on faith even when we can't see what's out there."

In Sierra's state of nervousness, she felt like telling Randy he was "out there" all right, but she kept her feisty thoughts to herself.

"Remember how God says His Word is like a lamp to our feet and a light to our path?" Randy continued. "Well, that's like now, when all we can see is a few yards ahead of us by the light of the high beams. We can't see the final destination or even some of the obvious markers along the way. The only thing we can see is what is right in front of us."

"That is so profound, Randy," Vicki said.

Sierra wasn't so sure it was profound, but then she didn't have a crush on Randy the way Vicki did. She wished Amy hadn't fallen asleep and was listening to this. Sierra thought Amy was the one who needed to understand God's will.

A raspy, guttural sound broke into their conversation, and Sierra said, "What did I tell you?"

"That's your brother?" Vicki asked. "Are you sure it isn't a broken muffler or something? I've never heard anyone snore like that."

"Get used to it. You'll be hearing a lot of that these next few days."

"This is how I see it," Randy said, ignoring Wes's snoring. "God's will, I mean." He pulled a straw out of the empty soda cup in the trash and held it up in the air. "This straw represents all of time as we know it, from beginning to end. We're limited to this because we're stuck on this straw. But God..." Randy cocked his head and gave Sierra a crooked smile. "God is completely outside of time. He's not limited to just this space of time as we are."

"You think God can see everything at once, so He knows what's going to happen before it even happens?" Vicki asked.

"Yes, that's what I believe," Randy said. "He is outside of the events and sequences. He isn't limited in any way, as we are. I think that at the exact same instant God went walking in the garden with Adam and Eve, He is also with us, right this second, driving down to Southern California."

Sierra felt a tiny shiver go up her spine. It was astounding to think of God being with them right now, just as He was present with Adam and Eve. Something deep inside of her began to calm down. *God, You really are right here, aren't You? You're in control.*

Vicki said, "So you think God knew Warner was going to break his arm because He could see it happen ahead of time?"

"I think so," Randy said, tucking the straw back into the trash bag. "But I don't think God, like, sent an angel to slam on the brakes and make the accident happen. A lot of junk happens to us when we go our own way and don't even try to listen to God."

"You know what, Randy?" Vicki said. "You have to write a song about all this. Don't you think? This would make a great bunch of lyrics."

"Not a bad idea. Can you reach my guitar back there without waking up Wes?"

"I think so."

For the next two hours, Amy slept, Wes snored, Sierra drove, Randy strummed his guitar, and Vicki scribbled down every random phrase as Randy sang:

The high beam is all I have
to lead me down Your way.
Darkness hides Your wonders;
I beg for light of day.
Is Your face right there, behind that cloud?
I wanna know. I wanna see You.
Outside of time,
inside my mind,
it's You—always You.

"This is going to be an awesome song," Vicki said.

"It's a start," Randy answered and went back to strumming his guitar.

After all the anxiety Sierra had been feeling, Randy's soft strumming and coming up with song lyrics brought a calmness. The next few hours turned into the most peaceful time Sierra could remember experiencing—and the most astounding. She couldn't stop thinking about how God was right there with them.

When they needed to stop again for gas, they were close to Sacramento, and it was the dead of night. Yet Sierra didn't feel afraid.

Wes woke refreshed and thanked Sierra. He hadn't expected her to drive so far. When they hit the road again with Wesley at the wheel, Sierra was the one stretched out in what Vicki now called "the snore zone" on the backseat.

Sierra slept soundly until they stopped somewhere in a busy parking lot. She opened her eyes and felt stiff all over. Raising her head, she looked out at what appeared to be her brother's reason for stopping.

"In—N-Out Burger!" Wes announced. "Everybody out."

Sierra yawned and tried to get her eyes to unstick at the corners of her lids. "What time is it?"

"It's time for a Double-Double and a vanilla shake," Wes said.

This fast-food chain hadn't found its way to the Great Northwest, but Wes had made it known, when they first talked about going on the trip, that he planned to stop at every In—N-Out Burger they came upon. Apparently, this was the first one, which meant they had to officially be in the southern region of California, since that's the only part of the country where In-N-Out Burgers could be found.

Sierra knew by the brightness and warmth of the sun coming through the windows that they were well into the new day and that none of the clouds from the Mount Shasta area had followed them down here.

As the others scrambled from the van, eager for something to eat, Sierra fumbled for her backpack and, with another yawn, locked the van doors behind her. There was a line inside the restaurant. From the large menu over the register, it appeared that the place served only hamburgers, fries, shakes, and soft drinks.

"Do you want me to order for you?" Wes asked Sierra.

"Sure. I'm going to the restroom."

"What do you want?"

Sierra twisted her dry mouth into a grin and said, "Fish sticks."

"What?"

"Never mind. Surprise me."

Wes shook his head. Sierra didn't see Amy and Vicki in the food line, so she guessed they were already in the restroom.

"At least there's not a line for the bathroom," Sierra muttered as she pushed open the door and saw her friends standing in front of the long mirror.

"I look like roadkill," Amy said flatly. "Look at my hair!"

Vicki wasn't moaning. Instead, she had gone to work, pulling a few necessities from her backpack: a toothbrush, washcloth, hairbrush, and makeup bag. She even had a clean T-shirt, which she quickly slipped over her head after she had washed her face and the front part of her hair.

"That's not fair," Amy said, examining Vicki after her three-minute freshening-up routine produced impressive results. "You can get gorgeous with just a sink and a squirt of hair spritz. I need a hot shower and a minimum of an hour."

"You guys want to borrow anything?" Vicki asked, holding out her stuffed backpack. Her complexion looked flawless, her eyes were bright and clear, and her silky, brown hair was pulled smoothly back with a clip. She even smelled sweet.

"Leave the whole bag," Sierra said.

"Yeah, and go tell the guys we'll be out in an hour," Amy added. "I could sure use a change of clothes about now. All my stuff is tied up on the top of the van. I doubt Wesley would want to undo everything for a clean T-shirt."

"I have another one you can wear," Vicki said. "It's at the very bottom. It's white."

"Only one?" Sierra asked disappointedly. Her jeans weren't bothering her, but the light blue, short-sleeved shirt she had put on yesterday morning was a crumpled, less-than-fresh mess with dots of chocolate stains on it.

"Sorry. Only one," Vicki said. She brushed past a woman with two little girls who were entering the restroom in a hurry. "I'll tell the guys you'll be right out."

"Don't hold your breath," Amy said. She began to pull stuff from Vicki's backpack and hand it to Sierra. "This is hopeless, really. We'll never be able to pull off the same transformation trick Vicki just did."

"I'll settle for a clean face," Sierra said. "And does she have any large hair clips in there? It's hot here. I want to get my hair off my neck."

Amy and Sierra made a noble attempt at freshening up. They encouraged each other all the way, saying how much better the other now looked. Only, Amy's short, dark hair still bulged a little in the back, despite the way she doused it with warm water. And Sierra's eyes remained bloodshot— evidence that she had strained them during her stint as the midnight road warrior.

"I give up," Amy said.

She zipped shut Vicki's backpack, slung it over her shoulder, and exited with Sierra.

Wes, Randy, and Vicki waved at them from one of the tables in the far left corner of the small eating area. Before them were five cardboard tray boxes, all stuffed with burgers and fries. The drinks were in large white cups with red stripes around them.

Sierra examined one of the cups. "Are these little palm trees between the stripes? How cute!"

"How California!" Amy added, enjoying the discovery.

"Look on the inside rim on the bottom," Wes said.

All four of them lifted their cups and checked the underside, looking for a door prize.

"Hey!" Randy said, the first to find the treasure. "That's cool."

"It has John 3:16," Sierra said, looking closely at hers. "That is so cool."

"And did you see how fresh these are?" Randy asked, a handful of the thin, golden fries in his hand. "A guy is in the back shoving potatoes into a slicer and then dipping them in the fryer. You have to try these."

"We'd better hurry," Vicki said, grabbing a handful from the mound in front of them. "Before Randy eats them all."

They agreed, after they had stuffed themselves, that Wes was right about enjoying the full California experience by stopping at In-N-Out Burger. The only problem was they all groaned when they got back in the van and were sure that the seat belts wouldn't fit them anymore.

Sierra sat beside the window in the middle seat. Amy was next to her, Vicki was in the front, and Randy was happily stretched out in the snore zone. Within minutes they were back on the freeway with the windows open and the warm breezes swirling through the van.

"Mind if I try to find a good radio station?" Vicki asked.

"Wait a minute," Sierra said. "First I have a few questions for you, brother dear. Where are we? Where are we going, and how long before we get there?"

"We're south of Bakersfield. Our first stop is Valencia

Hills Bible College, and we should be there in an hour or less, depending on how quickly we get over the Grapevine."

"Now I have a question," Amy said. "Will we have a chance to take a shower between now and then?"

Wes laughed.

"I'm serious," Amy said.

Wes glanced over at Vicki, and after looking her over quickly, he said, "Why? You guys look fine. Am I starting to smell or something?"

"No," Amy said, "but I think I am."

"You're fine," Wes said. "Besides, the idea is for you to check them out. No one will be checking you out."

"Oh, thanks a lot!" Amy said.

"No, I didn't mean it that way," Wes said, glancing at Amy in the mirror. "I meant you look fine. You look good just the way you are, really."

Sierra tried to discern how Amy had taken Wes's comment. His words had brought a subtle smile to her lips.

A red light on Sierra's emotional control panel lit up as she thought, *Did my brother just flirt with Amy?*

eleven

"CAN I TRY FINDING A RADIO STATION NOW?" Vicki asked.

"Go ahead and try," Wes said. "As soon as we start to climb the Grapevine, it'll be hard to find anything. You'll have more success once we drop down into the L.A. basin."

"Is that the Grapevine?" Sierra said, noticing that the wide highway ahead led into an impressive bank of hills. It appeared even more impressive because of the long, flat, straight stretch of freeway they were traveling on. Sierra looked out the back window and thought the valley behind them was beautiful in a desolate sort of way. It seemed strange to think that all the flat farmland they had raced past was about the last undeveloped area of western Southern California. She knew that once they drove over the Grapevine into the San Fernando Valley, it would basically be one long stretch of developed civilization all the way to the Mexican border.

"Can you hand me the map?" Sierra asked. "I want to figure out where we are." Locating the red line on the map that was marked as the 5 Freeway, Sierra said, "I don't know why they call it the Grapevine. It's a pretty straight-looking road."

"Maybe the original highway had more twists and turns," Wes suggested.

"We're going to drive through the Los Padres National Forest," Sierra remarked. "Fraiser Mountain on our right is 8,026 feet high, and Sawtooth on our left is more than 5,000 feet." Then, because she realized she sounded like a tour guide, she added, "And postcards will be available at the end of our tour."

"Are we going to Santa Barbara?" Amy asked.

"No," Wes said. "That's on the other side of the mountains on the coast."

"Drake was the one who wanted to go to Santa Barbara," Vicki said.

"That's right. So, where are the colleges located that we'll see?" Amy asked.

Sierra went over the list, and she and Amy tried to find the campuses on the map.

As the van climbed the steady incline of the Grapevine, Vicki searched for an agreeable sound on the radio. All she managed to come up with was a loud song in Spanish and lots of crackling static.

"I give up. Oh, you guys, look at the hills!"

Sierra looked up from the map and was amazed at the sight. As far as they could see, wild California poppies poured over the hillside, waving to them with their bright-orange petals raised high.

"It's beautiful," Sierra said.

Randy, who had been quiet back in the snore zone,

perked up at the sight of the flowers. "Wow," he said appreciatively. "It looks as if some giant devoured a huge bag of cheese-flavored chips and then wiped his hands on the hills."

Sierra laughed. "You have such a way with words, Randy!"

"Yeah," Amy teased, "as long as those words have to do with food."

At the In-N-Out Burger, Randy had eaten half of Amy's hamburger because she couldn't finish it. He also had scarfed down everyone's leftover fries.

"We all find our inspiration in different forms." Having said that, Randy lay back down, quietly humming to himself.

He was still humming after they had toured the Valencia Hills Bible College campus. He gave Sierra the impression of an absentminded composer trying to get the melody just right for his new song.

The five of them were leaving the main part of the campus and returning to the parking lot when Sierra looked around one more time. She tried to picture herself going to school here. She decided she liked the campus. She liked the way the dorms were set up in suites with a common living room area. She liked the friendly students. Two of them even said hello to Sierra and her friends. She also liked the warm weather and wished she were wearing shorts instead of jeans.

What Amy liked the most was the student adviser who took them on tour. "Noah," Amy repeated to Sierra as they walked ahead of the others back to the van. "Isn't that a great name? Noah. It's so strong. And did you see the tattoo on his thumb?"

"That was a birthmark," Sierra said.

"It was not."

"Then it was a weird tattoo because it was a big brown splotch."

Amy shook her head. "It was a tattoo of a bear or something."

She tugged at the front passenger door of the van, forgetting it was locked and Wes had the key. As she jiggled the door, the car alarm went off. Amy shrieked and jumped back. Sierra turned to see if Wes was still behind them. All he had to do was push a button on the keypad, and even from a distance, this terrible racket would stop. But Wes was nowhere in sight. Neither was Vicki or Randy.

"Where did they go?" Amy shouted with her hands over her ears.

"I don't know. They were right behind us."

Two college guys in a red compact car slowed down in the parking lot and looked out the driver's window at Amy and Sierra. A collapsed windsurfing board and sail were strapped to the roof.

"You okay?" the driver asked.

He had short, bleached hair, a deep tan, and an engaging smile. From the look of the rippling muscle on his left arm when he stuck it out the window, he definitely knew how to use the equipment he was carrying.

Amy immediately dropped her hands away from her ears and went over to his car. "The alarm accidentally went off," she called out, leaning over to see the driver. "Wes has the keys. He should be here any minute."

Sierra was amazed at how Amy could start up a comfortable, friendly conversation with any guy anywhere.

"Wes Langerfield?" the guy asked.

"No, Wes Jensen. He doesn't go here."

"Oh," the guy shouted back. "You go here, don't you?"

"No."

Sierra watched as Amy smiled, and she wondered if her cute friend with the little bump of wayward hair on the back of her head would admit she was still in high school.

"Do you want a ride back to the main campus to find Wes?" the driver offered.

"Sure," Amy said.

"I think we'd better wait here." Sierra quickly stepped in.

The guy in the passenger seat leaned over and smiled at Sierra. He was definitely another trophy-winning, lifeguard type.

"Are you sure?" he asked.

"Yes, I—" Before Sierra could finish her sentence, the screeching alarm stopped. Sierra looked over her shoulder to see Wes jogging toward them, still pointing the alarm pad toward the van.

"That must be Wes," the driver said.

Amy smiled. She nodded.

Sierra smiled. She nodded.

They both stood there, smiling and nodding.

"We'll see you around," the driver said as he gave a wave and put his car in first gear. "Take it easy." And off they went.

"You big flirt," Sierra teased, giving Amy a swat on the arm.

"Flirt? *Moi?*" Amy's dark eyes twinkled. "You were a little taken yourself, if I'm not mistaken."

Sierra shared a giggle with her friend. "You have to

admit, they were two gorgeous examples of God's creation, weren't they?"

Amy gave Sierra a perturbed look. Sierra guessed it was because she had brought God into the conversation. "Hey," Sierra said quickly, "I'm only giving glory where glory is due."

"What happened?" Vicki said, rushing up to join them. "Did someone try to break into the van? Here? At a Bible college?"

"No," Sierra said with a wry grin. "Amy was demonstrating to me some of her techniques for meeting men on a college campus. And I do emphasize the word *men*!"

"And my techniques seemed to work quite well," Amy added, sharing another laugh with Sierra.

"I missed something," Vicki said.

"And how!" Sierra said.

"All I know," Amy said as she climbed into the front passenger seat of the van, "is that we can turn around and go home now. I know where I'm going to college in September!"

Sierra laughed again. "September? I thought you would want to start this summer. I imagine they offer windsurfing during the summer. You do have a growing interest in that sport, don't you?"

Amy laughed even harder. "I do now!"

"What is with you two?" Wes said.

He got in and closed the door. Rather than putting the keys in the ignition and driving off, he turned in his seat to face the group. Sierra slid in next to the window on the middle seat. It gave her a strange sense of comfort that Amy was talking so freely about the guys they had met in front of

Wes. Or was that a subtle way of letting Wes know some guys had ended up "checking her out"?

"We need to make a choice now," Wes said.

"There is no choice," Amy said. "I get the driver!" Again she burst out laughing, and Sierra with her.

"I think sleep deprivation is catching up with us," Vicki said. "Amy is going to lose it in about two seconds. You watch. When she starts laughing really hard, she snorts."

"I do not!" Amy protested, pulling a straight face. Her shoulders shook slightly as she tried to contain her laughter.

"Yes, you do, Amy, and you know it," Sierra agreed.

Wes gave Amy a sympathetic look. "Don't feel bad. They accuse me of snoring."

"You do snore!" Amy said. "I heard you last night sawing logs back there in the snore zone."

"We all heard you, Wes," Sierra said.

"Well, can you all hear this? We need to make a decision. Now, you guys, listen."

Amy stifled her giggles.

"I told my friends we wouldn't be at their place until late tonight because I thought we were going to spend more time here on campus. But you all said you checked out everything you needed to."

Sierra nodded and noticed the others doing the same. It wasn't a very large campus, and none of them had any interest in sitting in on one of the doctrine classes, as Noah had suggested. The catalogs they had picked up would give the specific information on classes and registration. They were all ready to move on.

Wes checked his watch. "It's five after four now. We

could do a couple of things. We could drive into Hollywood—"

"Yes!" Amy said.

"We would hit traffic all the way, and to be honest, Amy, I think you're going to be painfully disappointed with the real Hollywood once you see it. There's Grauman's Chinese Theatre with the handprints of the stars in cement, but aside from that, it's not much more than a crowded downtown strip of old buildings, junky souvenir shops, and lots of homeless people."

"When were you there?" Sierra asked.

"About a year ago when I came down with Ryan. Let me finish what I was saying. We can go on into L.A., as I said, or we can go a short way down the freeway to Magic Mountain." Wes ended his suggestion with a Cheshire cat grin, which meant the last suggestion was what he really wanted to do.

"Magic Mountain," Randy called out from the backseat.

"Amy has coupons," Vicki said.

"Sounds good to me," Sierra said.

Everyone looked at Amy.

"Am I going to be the only one who doesn't go on the roller coasters?" she asked.

"Yes!" they all answered in unison.

"Okay, fine. Let's go to Magic Mountain. I can feed my rejected soul excessive amounts of cotton candy and sit on a bench waiting for you."

"Or you can live a little and come with us," Randy said.

In a scramble of searching for coupons and checking the map for directions, Amy, Sierra, Vicki, and Randy plotted their course while Wes drove.

"You can't miss the off-ramp," Sierra said. "This guidebook says you take the Magic Mountain Parkway exit, and it's right there."

"We'll be able to see it from the freeway," Wes said.

"You know what? This is great because these coupons are only good on weekdays," Vicki said, examining Amy's contribution. "We couldn't use them if we came back on the weekend. This is going to be so much fun!"

Sierra agreed with Vicki. She had never been to Magic Mountain, and today she was definitely in the mood to go a little crazy and have some fun.

"I only wish I could have had a shower," Amy said. "It's so much hotter here than at home. Doesn't anyone else feel a little less than fresh?"

"Don't worry," Wes said. "There are rides here guaranteed to freshen you up even if you don't go on them."

"What is that supposed to mean?" Amy asked.

"I can't tell you. I'll have to show you," Wes said as he pulled into the huge parking lot. The lot wasn't completely full, which made Sierra think going late on a Thursday afternoon was a lot better than trying to go on Saturday.

"Is anyone else going to take a sweatshirt?" Sierra asked. She was warm now like Amy, but she knew it could get chilly once the sun went down.

"Not a bad idea," Wes agreed. "Once we're inside the park, I don't want to have to come all the way back out here."

Armed with money, sweatshirts, and Amy's discount coupons, the five friends headed for the park entrance, joking and laughing all the way.

twelve

"HEY THERE! How's everybody doing? Are all five of you together? How about if all of you stand right there, and I'll take your picture?" A young man wearing a park uniform held up a large camera. He and several others stood at the entrance to Six Flags Magic Mountain Amusement Park offering to capture the entrants on film.

"Sure," Vicki answered for them. She struck a pose with her arm resting on Randy's shoulder.

Sierra caught Randy's expression under the bill of his baseball cap. He looked surprised that Vicki was leaning on him. Surprised, but kind of enjoying it.

Sierra looped her arm through Wes's, and Amy did the same with his other arm. Vicki moved closer to Amy and wrapped her other arm around Amy's neck.

"Terrific," the photographer said, quickly capturing the shot while they held their chummy pose. "Here's a ticket for you. If you would like to buy a copy of your photo, you can turn this into the photo station and pick up the picture when you leave the park."

"I definitely want a copy," Vicki said.

"So do I," said Sierra.

"Me, too," Amy said.

The three girls looked at Randy.

"Whatever," he said with a shrug.

"I'll visit your picture, Sierra, whenever I need a memory," Wes said, leading them to the photo station.

His comment made Sierra realize how great he had been about this whole trip. Wes was so much older than the rest of them, yet he never treated them as if they were beneath him. If there were an award for the best big brother, Sierra would have nominated Wesley.

"Where to first?" Vicki asked after they had turned in their orders for the picture.

"Anybody else ready for the Viper?" Wes said.

"What's that?" Amy asked, sticking close to his side.

They walked past a large circular water fountain. Sierra felt a delicate mist as the late afternoon breeze caught the fountain spray and taunted her with its refreshing coolness.

"I could go for something to drink," Sierra said.

"What about the Tidal Wave?" Randy asked. "That one sounded pretty good from what the guidebook said."

"Yes," Wes said with a grin, "this might be a nice time of day to visit the Tidal Wave."

"Just point me to the gift shops and food court," Amy said. "That's where I'll be waiting for you guys."

"Oh, come on," Sierra said. "Don't be like that. You would like lots of the rides here. I'll go on them with you. And who knows? You might just feel brave enough to try one of the really fun rides."

"Don't get your hopes up," Amy said. She wasn't wear-

ing the expression of someone who was rebelliously endur-
ing this trip. She merely looked uncomfortable—as though
she would just like to have a shower and a nice, clean bed to
crawl into.

Sierra had to admit she had seen Amy's hair look better.
And the dark shadows under her eyes appeared to be more
from fatigue than smeared makeup. Amy was definitely one
of those people who did better with a bath and a blow-dryer
than she did with going creatively au naturel, like Vicki and
Sierra.

As a matter of fact, Sierra wouldn't have minded a clean
shirt before they attacked the amusement park. A hot
shower would have been nice, too, but she could wait. They
were here, and it was time to have fun.

Wes walked briskly through the stream of people, and the
rest of them followed. He was obviously a man on a mission.
They gave up trying to offer their suggestions of where to go
and trotted after their trailblazer in the green knit shirt.

"This way," Wes called to them over his shoulder as he
headed for a bridge. The sound of people screaming with
delight grew louder as they followed Wes onto the bridge.
"Hurry! This way, you guys," he called out, looking at them
and then looking at the waterway that ran under the bridge.

"Right here, Amy," Wes said, putting his hands on her
shoulders and standing behind her. She came up to about
the middle of his chest, and as he held her in place with a
pesky grin on his face, Amy turned to look up at him with a
smile of admiration—apparently for his gentle gesture of
holding her shoulders as they gazed at the elaborately decorated canal.

Sierra realized she had lost one of her earrings.

Looking around on the ground and retracing her steps, she tried to see where the dangly silver earring had landed. People were tromping all around her, and she figured retrieving the lost jewelry was probably hopeless.

Looking up at her friends, she noticed Wes giving Randy a nod. As Sierra watched, Randy followed Wes's example and stood behind Vicki with his hands on her shoulders. Vicki's grin lit up her whole face. Like Amy, Vicki turned to give Randy a sweet look of affection.

Then it happened. A speeding boat loaded with screaming people came barreling down the shoot. On cue, Randy and Wes both ducked behind Vicki and Amy while holding the girls firmly in place. The huge spray of water from the careening boat rose into the air and crashed down on them. Amy and Vicki were drenched—soaked to the skin. Amy's hair was completely flat and dripping water down her face. Randy and Wes looked well doused, too.

Vicki laughed. She laughed hard and beat Randy's chest with her fists as well as shook her wet hair on him. Sierra laughed, too, giving up on her earring and joining all her wet friends. She unfastened her remaining earring and tucked it into her pocket.

"I promised you a little freshening up, didn't I?" Wes teased Amy.

Amy didn't respond as Vicki had. Instead, Amy stood there, dripping, stunned, and looking as if she might cry. She turned her chin up toward Wes, pulled her soaked bangs from her eyes and said, "I can't believe you did that to me."

"Believe it," Wes said, still sporting his mischievous grin. "And unless you want to get it again, we'd better move off this bridge."

A chorus of screaming passengers announced the next boat was heading their way. The group scrambled off the bridge.

"You guys will be sorry," Vicki said, grabbing Amy by the wrist, "because now we're going to the restroom, and you'll have to wait for us. No telling how long it will be before we come out."

"No problem," Wes said. "You can find Randy and me in front of the funnel cake stand. You see it over there?"

Vicki nodded and ducked into the restroom with Amy.

Sierra watched as Amy and Vicki disappeared into the restroom and Wes and Randy marched off to the food cart, slapping each other on the back. She had been afraid this would happen; she was the leftover.

Dozens of happy amusement park visitors streamed past her as she stood there. Sierra felt the same way she had when she was six and became separated from her family in a crowd at a concert they had attended one night. She had been taught as a child that if she ever got lost, she should stand still and wait. She had been promised an adult would come find her. This time, no one was coming to look for her.

At the concert, she had stood alone only a few minutes before her father's concerned face appeared in the crowd and his steady hand reached out and grasped hers. It was a vivid memory. The sudden rush of terror over being lost and alone had been replaced instantly with an overpowering sense of comfort and security when her father reached out for her. At the touch of his hand, Sierra had held on tight. She never wanted to feel that kind of loneliness and fear again.

Yet, here she was, seventeen years old, doing exactly

what she wanted to do, with all the people she wanted to be with, and fear had found her. Isolation circled her. It was as if she were six years old all over again. Only this time, no one was going to reach out his hand to grasp hers. Her father was a thousand miles away.

Then a thought came to Sierra, the kind of thought that starts in the heart and warms the spirit all the way through. Her heavenly Father was not a thousand miles away. He was here with her—right beside her. He always was, and He promised He always would be.

That realization covered her with peace. Terror and all its icy companions fled. She felt as if God had invisibly slipped His nail-scarred hand into hers, and all she had to do was hold on tight.

"You are so real," she whispered into the unseen realm. "You're right here. I know You are. And You're never going to leave me, are You?" The calmness of the presence of God's Spirit in the middle of that busy crowd amazed Sierra.

She blinked and looked around, almost expecting people to stare at her, as though her hair were on fire or something. That's how changed she felt. But no one was staring. Apparently, no one else had sensed God's presence the way she had. He had done that just for her. With her heart full to the brim, Sierra headed for the restroom. She felt changed. She wasn't a little girl anymore. She didn't feel cut off from her friends or lost. She was loved, and she knew it.

Amy and Vicki were at work in front of the mirror, using all the beauty supplies Vicki had brought with her. Amy had combed her wet hair straight back and was standing in front of the heat-blasting hand dryer. Neither of them seemed to have noticed Sierra hadn't been with them all along.

The girls ended up spending less than ten minutes in the restroom. Amy's shock over the dousing wore off, and a playful attitude took its place. When they met up with the guys, there was lots of joking, teasing, and even a little funnel-cake smashing into Randy's face.

Sierra wanted to tell everyone she had just had this amazing experience in which she understood God's presence as never before. But she found it awfully hard to have a serious conversation with someone who was holding a chunk of cake at the end of a plastic fork, ready to catapult it at her face.

"More cake, anyone?" Randy asked.

"None for me," Wes said, getting up. "I think I hear the Viper calling my name."

"Oh, yes, I can hear it," Vicki said. She made her best snake face and hissed out, "Wesssss-ley. Come to me, Wesssss-ley."

"Is that a roller coaster?" Amy asked reluctantly.

"Yes," Wes said, "it's a roller coaster."

"And does it go…?" Amy made circles in the air with her finger.

"Only twice," Wes said. "It's over before you know what bit you."

Amy gave Sierra a pleading look. "Are you sure you want to go on it, Sierra?"

Sierra nodded. "Come on, Amy. You can always close your eyes."

"No way," Randy said. "You're not allowed to close your

eyes. If you close your eyes, they stop the ride, and you have to get out and walk down the emergency stairs."

"What if you close your eyes when it's upside down?"

"They still make you get out," Randy said. "There's a safety net, so, you know, you just unhook your seat belt and down you go."

"You guys are mean," Amy said.

They were walking at a faster pace now. Wes was, once again, eager to reach his goal.

"Can't you accept that some people have a death wish and some people don't?" Amy kept talking louder. "I mean, why should this be a test of my tolerance for fear? Can't you see that in this life there are rollers and nonrollers? I'm in the minority here because I'm a nonroller. So what? Isn't it time we all started honoring diversity?"

By the time Amy finished her speech, Wes had led them to the end of the line for the Viper. After ushering Sierra, Vicki, and Randy into line, he hung back with Amy.

"You guys go ahead," he said.

The line was moving quickly. Two other guys immediately got in line behind them, making it impossible for Wes to slip in with the three of them.

As the crowd pressed forward within the railings, Sierra looked over her shoulder and was surprised at what she saw. Wes was bent slightly, looking Amy in the eyes. Then he reached over and put his arm around her.

thirteen

THE LINE FOR THE VIPER moved so quickly Sierra soon couldn't see what was going on with Amy and Wes. Was he counseling her as a big brother? Had she started to cry, and was he trying to comfort her? Or was he expressing affection for her?

Why does this bother me so much? she thought. *I'm all in favor of Vicki and Randy's getting together, so what's the big deal with Wes and Amy's getting together? Is it that I think Wes is too old for Amy?*

Sierra thought Wes couldn't be interested in Amy because he had certain criteria for what he was looking for in a girlfriend, and Amy didn't match that description. His first priority was that the woman must be a strong Christian. Amy had admitted more than once that she wouldn't necessarily put herself in that category. So why was Sierra still nervous about any attention Wes gave Amy?

Vicki and Randy talked about the roller coaster as they inched toward the front of the line. They could see the loops and hear the screams of those who had gone before them. Vicki said she didn't like the way the structure made a clanging, rattling sound as the cars climbed the steep incline to the top of the first loop. Sierra nodded agreement but only half listened as she continued to process her thoughts about Wes and Amy.

By the time she reached the front of the line, Sierra figured out what was bothering her. She didn't want to share Wes with another girl. He was her big brother, and if he became attached to someone else, it would change everything.

Instead of freeing her, the realization made Sierra feel heavy. She knew she couldn't control her brother's life, and the only area she had any influence on Amy was in selecting clothes. This was something she had to let go of or it would hurt her relationships with Wes and Amy.

What's going on, God? Sierra prayed. *Two big revelations for me right in a row. First hold on, then let go... What is this?*

The uniformed ride attendant on the platform motioned for Randy to climb into an open, single seat in a roller-coaster car. Sierra and Vicki were directed to the front seats in the first car.

"Front-row seats! What did we do to deserve this?" Vicki said, grabbing Sierra's arm as she stepped into the hard plastic car. "Is it too late to change my mind?"

They sat down, and the safety bar came down over their shoulders, locking them in. It was hard to move and impossible to say anything to Randy, who was several seats behind them.

"Yes, I think it's too late to change your mind," Sierra said. As the car lurched forward with a rocking motion, her stomach did a flip-flop. "Don't worry. You're going to love this. It'll be great!" she told Vicki.

"Are you sure?" Vicki asked in a nervous, high-pitched voice.

The car made its creaky, clanking climb to the top of the rise. With their faces toward the sky, Sierra noticed how pale blue it was. To the right, an airplane left a white, dusty streak across the wide expanse of heaven. It might as well have been accompanied by the sound of fingernails on a chalkboard because that sound gave her the same sensation she was feeling in her stomach as they neared the crest of the Viper's first loop.

"You know, you might be right," Sierra yelled over to Vicki. "I think I want off now."

"Sierra," Vicki shouted, pressing her leg against Sierra's in a show of moral support, "you're supposed to be the brave one here!"

Sierra pressed Vicki's leg back. They were at the top. Before them lay nothing but air. Sierra gripped the guard bar and let out a scream as the green nemesis plunged them into the depths of its belly. The rush of air pulled their hair straight back and drew the skin on their faces away from their wide-open mouths. In a matter of seconds, they were dropped, spun through two great loops, and spit out of the control booth with a jerk. Sierra and Vicki screamed the whole way.

Dazed, dizzied, and hoarse, they stumbled out of the car and waited for Randy. Randy's only evidence of the adrenaline rush was his crooked grin.

"Ready to go again?" he asked.

"I don't think so," Vicki said, gripping her sides.

"That was great!" Sierra said, her voice loud and raspy. "Wes is going to love this one! Where do you guys think he is?"

They exited together, awkwardly bumping into each other and apologizing with their shared laughter. Wes and Amy stood a few feet from the exit.

"You're going to love it!" Sierra announced when she spotted her brother.

"I'm ready," Wes said. "Who else is game?"

"I am," Randy said.

"Not me," Vicki said with a moan. "Why did I eat all that cake?"

"I found a ride that's more my speed," Amy said. "Anyone want to go on a kiddy ride with me?"

"I'll go with you," Vicki said.

Sierra debated before deciding to go with Vicki and Amy. "Where should we meet you guys?"

Wes pointed out a spot for them to meet, and they agreed to be there in about forty minutes.

"Are you okay, Amy?" Vicki asked as they leisurely went in search of the Goldrusher, Amy's ride.

"Yes. I'm sorry if I was being a drag on everyone."

"I didn't think you were," Vicki said.

"Well, Wes was worried, I guess."

"Did you two have a good talk?" Sierra asked.

"Yes, your brother is a true hero, Sierra. You know that, don't you? Of course you do. Wes has a way of making me think without feeling like a fool. I wish I still had a crush on him."

"You don't?" Sierra asked.

"No. Why? Have I been acting like I do?"

"Not really. Maybe a little." Sierra noticed the sign above the entrance to the Goldrusher as they were about to walk past it. "Here it is, you guys. And the line is even short."

Not only was the line short, but so were most of the people in it. Everyone seemed to be less than ten years old, except for the parents who accompanied their kids.

"There's not a height or weight limit on this, is there?" Vicki asked.

"No, I don't think so. I think it's a slow roller coaster," Amy answered.

"Not that either of you two have to worry," Vicki added.

"Are you saying we look like fifth-graders?" Amy asked.

"No, I'm saying the two of you together weigh about as much as I do by myself."

"Yeah, right," Amy said.

"Not even close," Sierra echoed. "Why do you say that?"

"Because I do weigh more than either of you."

"So? You're not too heavy or anything. You're fine. You're you. You're just right whatever size you are," Amy said. "Beauty has nothing to do with size."

"I know, I know," Vicki said. "I don't want to get into that discussion."

Sierra agreed; she wanted to discuss why Amy no longer had a crush on Wes. "So tell us what Wes said that made you feel better."

"We talked about my fear of roller coasters and heights, and Wes said he understood and wouldn't pressure me any-more. He asked if I was really upset about the water, and I told him it bothered me at first, but I got over it. I guess that's how I am about a lot of things." She shrugged her shoulders. "That was all. He was being a nice big brother to me, and I enjoyed every minute of it."

They climbed into the gold-colored cart, and Sierra scolded herself for being judgmental and suspicious of

Amy. Sierra's imagination had taken off. She realized that if she had been so incorrect in her assessment of what was going on with Amy and Wes, she might be misjudging other things as well. If she was so out of balance, was it really a good idea to try to make this huge, life-changing decision about where she would go to college?

The panicked feelings returned. It didn't matter that a short while ago she had felt God beside her, holding her hand. Right now her emotional roller coaster was going through a big loop, and she felt overwhelmed with all the unknowns that lay in her future.

"Now that was a thriller," Vicki teased when they exited the tame roller-coaster ride. It was designed to resemble a mining cart traveling through a gold mine.

Sierra didn't think it would win any awards either— especially not after the Viper.

"Hey, I liked it. It was just my speed," Amy said. "So don't be mean."

They arrived at the meeting spot. Wes and Randy were already there and had planned out their next three wild rides: Batman the Ride, Superman the Escape, and Freefall. Sierra and Vicki were all set to join them, but then they remembered Amy.

"It's okay, really," Amy said. "I don't mind going with you and waiting. These rides only take a few minutes once you get to the front of the line."

"Are you sure it's okay?" Sierra asked.

Amy shot an appreciative glance at Wes. "I'm sure."

Somehow Sierra found it hard to believe Amy no longer had a crush on him. But there was no time to evaluate the situation as the five of them tromped off to experience the thrills, chills, and spills of the Batman roller-coaster ride. Besides, Sierra's evaluation tank was already full with her anxieties over her future.

As they stood in line, the elaborately decorated Bat Cave loomed before them: dark, mysterious, and promising thrills. Sierra couldn't help but equate it with her future and her decisions about college.

"What if we don't go away to college?" she suddenly said to Vicki.

"Where did that come from?" Vicki asked.

"I was thinking. What if we stay in Portland and go to a community college or even one of the universities but live at home?"

Vicki gave Sierra a look that asked if she had suddenly gone crazy. "What are you talking about? All you've been raving about for months is going away to school. You're our world-traveling role model, Sierra. You can't wimp out on us now."

Sierra gave Amy a wistful glance over her shoulder as they moved to the front of the roller-coaster line. Amy was sitting contentedly on a bench in the shade, sipping a cold soft drink. "There's something to be said for sitting this one out," Sierra said.

"What are you saying?" Vicki asked. "Sitting out your first year of college or sitting out this ride?"

Wes slipped his arm around Sierra's shoulders and gave her a squeeze. "Sounds as though you just discovered the real world, my little dreamer girl. It's about time. I hate to be the one to tell you this, but ignoring the future won't make it go away. Time to grow up, baby sis."

Sierra felt her cheeks turning red. Amy might idolize

Wes for his counseling techniques, but at this moment his words brought Sierra only humiliation. If they hadn't been in such a public place, she would have slugged him in the stomach.

fourteen

"THAT WAS BY FAR the most fun I've ever had at any amusement park anywhere," Sierra said. She settled into the front seat of the van as they drove out of the Magic Mountain parking lot. Her conflict with Wes had dissipated after they went on the Batman ride and after she decided to force her frustration and insecurities out of her mind to fully enjoy the rest of the time in the park.

"And this is by far the best souvenir I've ever gotten," Vicki added from the backseat, where she sat next to Randy. She held what looked like a toy telescope up to her eye. The telescope was also a key chain, and the photo taken of the five of them when they entered the park was at the end of the tube.

"I know," Amy agreed, holding up her key-chain souvenir. "I like this silly little thing, too. In case I haven't said this yet, Sierra and Wes, thanks so much for inviting me along. I'm having such a great time that I don't want to go home."

"We have a couple more days," Wes said. "That might be long enough for you to change your mind."

"I don't think so," Amy said. "I wish this trip was for a month. No, two months. Or all summer. That would be so cool. A whole summer on the road with your friends."

"As long as everyone who goes is friends with everyone else," Vicki said.

Sierra knew they were all thinking of what a different experience this would have been if Warner had ended up coming with them. No one said anything, though.

"I called Brad and Alissa while you guys were on that last ride. They said it would take us about an hour to get to their place," Wes said.

"What time do we have to be up in the morning?" Sierra asked.

"I'd like to leave Brad and Alissa's around eight."

Sierra groaned. "That early? Don't you want to spend more time with your friends?"

"Yeah, while we sleep in?" Amy added.

"They have a beach trip planned for tomorrow, so they're going to get an early start, too."

"The beach sounds like fun," Amy said. "By any chance are we going anywhere near the ocean?"

"We might later tomorrow," Wes said. "The main thing is that I have an appointment at Rancho Corona at eleven-thirty. After that we can do whatever we want. I need to call Tawni to see if she's still expecting us at her place tomorrow night. She lives about two miles from the beach."

"You're kidding," Amy said. "I never realized that."

"I'm beginning to like Southern California more and more," Sierra said, stretching her arms over her head. "I can't imagine what it would be like to live near the beach." She reached for the side lever and reclined her seat halfway.

"Is the college you want to go to near the beach, Wes?" Vicki asked.

"I think Rancho Corona is about twenty or thirty miles inland from the coast. It's located on top of a mesa. They say on clear days you can see the ocean, and at sunset you can often see Catalina Island."

"What's a mesa?" Amy asked.

"It's a high, flat plateau."

"Doesn't *mesa* mean 'table' in Spanish?" Sierra asked.

"I think so. That would make sense. That's what it looks like. A big, flat tabletop."

Sierra closed her eyes and tried to imagine a college campus built on a mesa with a view of the sun setting into the Pacific. The thought brought a smile to her face and romantic images of a bright, shining citadel, a brave fortress filled with God-lovers. Even though she knew nothing about this college nor had seen any pictures of it, she liked it already.

And she liked it even more the next morning at quarter to eleven, when the van turned off the freeway south of Lake Elsinore. Ahead of them stood a vast range of hills, including the mesa Wes had talked about. It was easy to spot because it was one of the highest places along the range and was perfectly flat all the way across the top. Above the plateau rose endless miles of clear sky marred only by a few lazy puffs of ragged clouds.

Sierra sat up straighter and peered through the front windshield. Wildflowers dotted the hillsides. She felt a sense of anticipation. Something about this area reminded her of Switzerland when she had visited last summer with her friend Christy. They had hiked among the cows and wildflowers in the deep green hills. Here, the terrain was a smear of warm terra-cotta and sandy-brown tones. Instead of lumbering cows with bells around their necks, as they had seen in Switzerland, Sierra imagined wild rabbits darting across the hiking trails.

"Rancho Corona University." Sierra read the sign at the side of the road. "Turn right."

Wes turned right and headed up the road that led to the top of the mesa.

"This is a wonderful place," Sierra said dreamily.

"We're not there yet," Wes muttered. He sounded tired.

They were all tired—tired and grouchy after sleeping only five and a half hours on the floor before Wes woke them that morning. Amy had been insistent about a shower before they started the new day, and they all agreed it was a good idea for them, too. Brad and Alissa's duplex had only one bathroom, so that meant a long line.

Sierra's shower provided only cold water by the time it was her turn. She complained about it, but then felt bad later. It wasn't a very grateful attitude to show their hosts, especially since Brad had whipped up fried eggs, sliced ham, and buttery muffins for all of them, even though Wes had insisted they could buy breakfast on the road. She didn't feel any of those cranky emotions now.

"Are we supposed to meet with a counselor?" Amy asked. "I mean, can we just look around and wait for you, or do we have to talk to someone?"

"I set up a tour of the campus with one of their student volunteers, like at Valencia Hills," Wes said. "You guys can do whatever you want after you take the tour. I'll need at least three or four hours here."

The wide, steep road led to the top and then curved to the left. Two tall pillars of smooth rock stood at the campus's impressive entrance. A large wooden sign arched over the entryway bearing the words, "Rancho Corona University." They followed the signs to the admissions office and parked in one of the spaces marked "Visitor."

"This doesn't look much like a college," Amy said. "It looks more like a camp or a resort or something. I love all the tile roofs. It's like a set for an old Zorro movie."

"That's the early California look. I think this land used to be a ranch," Wes said. "We'll have to ask the tour guide. Is everybody ready? I'll leave the keys with you, Sierra, in case we go in separate directions and you guys want to come back to the van for anything."

"Somebody better wake up Randy," Vicki said, pulling back her hair and leaning forward from the rear seat to get out. Randy sat with his head against the window and his baseball cap pulled down over his face.

Amy turned around and reached over to remove the baseball cap. "Wake up, Randy. We're here."

He scrunched up his face at the sudden light and uncrossed his arms. With the back of his hand, he wiped the side of his mouth. Sierra had to smile. He looked like such a kid. She missed the way Randy looked when she had first met him and his long blond hair hung straight down from a middle part. He used to tuck it behind his ears all the time. For months now he had worn it short so that at moments like this it tended to stick out and give him the appearance of Dennis the Menace.

Sierra was eager to have a look around. The grounds were beautiful. Magenta-colored bougainvillea vines climbed up the side of the admissions building and onto the red tile roof. She followed Wes into the building as the other stragglers got out of the van. The coolness of the air-conditioned building breathed a welcome. The receptionist, a college-age student, sat behind a modern, oval desk and wore a phone headset.

She looked up at them, and her face beamed with an overly eager smile, almost as if she recognized them. "Are you Wesley Jensen?" she asked.

"Yes, I scheduled an appointment for eleven-thirty."

"We've been expecting you. And you have to be Sierra," she said. Still beaming, she rose and shook their hands excitedly. "I'm so glad you both are here. Welcome to Rancho Corona!"

Sierra glanced at her brother. This welcome was a little overdone.

"There's someone who's been waiting to see you," the receptionist said. "Let me call her."

The receptionist was about to press one of the buttons on the panel before her when the front door opened and an exuberant female voice called out, "Are they here yet?"

Before Sierra could turn around, she heard a wild and vaguely familiar squeal. She felt the tackle of arms around her and a crushing hug and heard more wild laughter in her ear. The only clue she had as to who was welcoming her so enthusiastically came from a flash of red hair that had swished across her face like an oriental fan. But that one clue was all she needed.

fifteen

"KATIE!" Sierra now joined in the squeals of surprise as she pulled back to see her friend from arm's length. "Oh, I can't believe this! Katie, what are you doing here?"

The green-eyed, red-haired fireball blurted out the whole story in one long breath. "I go to school here, you goof! You never figured that out, did you? You e-mailed Christy last week and told her all about your trip down here so your brother could check out Rancho.... Hey, you must be Wes. Hi, I'm Katie. So I had my roommate here, Dawn, check out the visitors roster, and there you are. Dawn, this is Wes and Sierra. Wes and Sierra, this is Dawn. And she told me you were scheduled for today, so like the sneak I am, I didn't e-mail you to remind you that I went here because I wanted to surprise you, and I did! Is this a total God-thing or what?"

Sierra was laughing so hard at the way Katie's face turned red when she rattled on that Sierra hadn't noticed Amy, Randy, and Vicki entering the building and standing to the side, observing the event.

"Is this our campus tour guide?" Vicki asked.

Katie spun around, swishing her shoulder-length red hair as she turned. "That's me! I volunteered just for you guys. Hi, I'm Katie. Sierra probably never told you anything about me. We only went to England and Ireland together last year."

"Oh," Amy said, stepping closer for a better look. "Did you say you're Christy?"

Katie threw up her arms and gave her audience a wild-eyed look with a bob of her head. "See what I mean? I'm the *other* one: Katie. Christy is the one everyone remembers. The one everyone talks about. The one everyone…" She paused to give Sierra a squinted glare. "…sends e-mails to. And me? I'm just Katie. Everybody's friend. Nobody's Friday night date."

Now they were all laughing, even Dawn, who was supposed to be answering the phone. They quieted down enough for introductions to be made all around and for Sierra to get over some of the shock of being greeted by her friend.

"I'd better lead us out of this area before I get us all in trouble," Katie said. "So let the tour begin. This is the admin building. The business offices are down that way, and, Wes, you get to meet with Mr. Scofield in that second office on the right, but not for another twenty minutes, so you might as well enjoy the tour."

Wes seemed captivated by Katie's quick wit and simple charm. He smiled one of his best smiles and said, "Lead the way."

Katie led them out the front door and past some more office buildings into a large central area. A blue-tiled fountain stood in the center of the plaza, and wrought-iron park benches circled the area. To the left, several tall palm trees rustled their long, elegant fronds high overhead. Their tree music gave the setting a balmy, tropical feeling. Several students sat on the edge of the fountain with their bare feet dangling in the water. Others stretched out on the benches in the shade, reading, sleeping, and talking.

"This is the Fountain Plaza and my favorite spot on campus. The long, two-story building on the right is the library; next to it is the Hannan Building. That's where all the English and language classes are taught. Behind it is the science building. And over here, on our far left, is Dishner Hall, which is the music building."

"I definitely want to check that one out," Randy said.

"No problem. We can see them all if you want. But first, you need to see the Student Center."

The Student Center was located behind Dishner Hall and to the right. Katie hurried them through the two-story building, pointing out the mailboxes and Espresso Stop on the lower level before taking them upstairs to the open lounge area that led to an outdoor deck. From the deck they could view the swimming pool, track, gym, and baseball diamond.

"The ocean is out that way," Katie said, pointing to the right. "It's all smogged out today, but sometimes we can actually see it. Usually in the very early morning or at sunset."

Sierra lingered a little longer on the deck, imagining how the view would look once the pale yellow petticoats of smog were lifted from the sky's blue gown. It was a sight she wanted to see one day.

"Come on, Sierra," Katie said, motioning from the grass area below the deck where she now stood with the rest of the group. "We have a few more places to see before we send Wes back to admin."

"I'm coming." So much was hitting Sierra so quickly she wasn't sure she could take it all in. The university grounds held enough dreamy beauty by themselves. Being led around by Katie only added to the sensation that Sierra was imagining all this.

The cafeteria was the newest building on campus and was designed more like a mall food court than a typical school cafeteria.

"You should have seen the old cafeteria," Katie said as she shooed them back toward the administration building. "They said it was like an army mess hall. I never ate in it. I arrived here four days after the 'Sacred Caf' was completed, and I have nothing but stellar reports about the food."

"When did you start here?" Sierra asked.

"January. I transferred in from the community college at the beginning of the semester." Katie leaned closer to Sierra. "I've only been here three months, so don't feel bad about not knowing that. I don't think I even told you. I just wanted to give you a hard time."

Sierra looped her arm around Katie's neck and gave her a squeeze. "It's so good to see you. You'll have to tell me everything. I want to hear about everybody."

Katie flashed a sly grin at Sierra. "That can be arranged. I thought we would escort your brother to his appointment, go back to the Sacred Caf for some lunch, and talk our heads off."

"Do you guys want me to meet up with you someplace

later?" Wes asked. He stood at the door of the administration building, appearing a little hesitant to leave the rest of them.

"After we eat, I was going to take them down to the dorms," Katie said. "When your meeting is over, ask Dawn to call my room. How does that sound?"

"Good. I'll see you guys." Sierra noticed that Wes was running his fingers through the sides of his wavy brown hair and looking a little nervous, as if he were going for a job interview.

Katie ushered them all back to the cafeteria and made sure they took full advantage of the variety of food available by using their visitors' complimentary meal passes. Sierra barely paid attention to her salad, turkey sandwich, and glass of milk. Rather, she drank in and ate up every word Katie shared across the table.

According to Katie, this was an awesome school, and she planned to stay here until she graduated. Some of Katie and Christy's friends, whom Sierra had met last summer when she came to California for Doug and Tracy's wedding, also attended this school. Sierra's imagination filled with dreams of how wonderful it would be to go to college with these very special friends, especially if Wes was going to attend the graduate school here. Lost in her daydream, Sierra didn't hear Amy when she first spoke to her.

"Would that be okay with you?" Amy repeated, giving Sierra a nudge.

"What?"

"Vicki and I are going exploring. Randy went back for seconds, and you obviously are involved with your friend."

Sierra caught an edge of hurt in Amy's voice. It wasn't

that Sierra meant to snub Vicki and Amy. It was just that this was Katie. In all the world there was only one Katie. They should understand that.

"Are you interested in seeing the dorms?" Katie asked as Amy rose to leave the table.

"Maybe a little later," Amy said.

"We'll be at the pool if you come looking for us," Vicki said. "I want to see if that California sunshine can do anything about this fish-belly white skin of mine." Vicki pulled up the sleeve of her T-shirt for emphasis. She turned to Katie. "You could tell right off we were from Oregon, couldn't you?"

"No," Katie said, swatting the air with her hand. "You guys all look like naturals around here. You fit in great."

Randy returned just then with a tray heaped with another sandwich, three drinks, a mound of French fries, and a large bowl of swirled frozen yogurt.

"Where did you find the yogurt?" Vicki said, reaching over and taking off the top swirl with her finger. "This is good. You want some, Amy?"

Whether Amy wanted any or not, she followed Vicki to the self-serve machine in the far right corner.

"What about you, Randy?" Katie asked. "Do you want a tour of the dorms, or are you going with the others to the pool?"

"I'd like to see the music building," he said, chomping into his sandwich. After a few quick chews and a swallow, he added, "That is, after I finish eating."

"Of course," Katie agreed. "First things first. And with most of the guys I know around here, food comes first—especially with Doug. Did I tell you he and Tracy come up every Thursday night to lead a Bible study?"

"You're kidding!" Sierra said. "Doug and Tracy. How are they doing?"

"Great. Cutest little married couple you've ever seen. We're calling our group the God-Lovers II, after the original group that started down in San Diego a couple of years ago."

"That must have been the group Tawni went to with Jeremy," Sierra said.

"Oh, that reminds me," Katie said. "I almost forgot. I called Tawni, and she said you guys were planning to stay at her place tonight. But if you want, you can stay here. I found a couple of people who are going home for the weekend, and they volunteered their rooms for you guys. It's up to you. Tawni said to call her. If you stay here, she'll come up to visit you."

"I'd love to stay," Sierra said. "I'll see what everyone else thinks."

"Do these meal passes work for dinner, too?" Randy asked.

Katie laughed. "No, sorry. But there's a barbecued rib place in town I've heard is good. We could all go there if you wanted."

Vicki and Amy returned with their frozen yogurt and a guy. Vicki appeared pleased with the yogurt, and Amy didn't look any too disappointed with the guy.

"This is Antonio," Amy said, smiling up at the dark-eyed, good-looking escort. But Mr. Tall, Dark, and Handsome wasn't returning Amy's affectionate gaze. He was staring at Sierra.

"*Bella* Sierra," he said in his rich Italian accent. "It has been so long." With that he leaned over and brushed a kiss across both of Sierra's blushing cheeks.

Sierra caught Amy's surprised expression and felt a need to quickly explain. "How are you doing, Antonio? I haven't seen you since the wedding last summer. Did you meet my friends, Amy and Vicki? And this is Randy," Sierra added.

Randy, his mouth full, nodded amiably at Antonio.

"Antonio rescued us at the yogurt machine," Vicki said, holding up her overflowing cup of yogurt. "Look at this mess! I couldn't get it to stop coming out."

"Katie told me you were coming," Antonio said, sitting down across from Sierra and Randy. He gave Katie a wink. "Have you told them our surprise?"

Sierra immediately suspected something of a romance was brewing between Antonio and Katie. Katie had kept no secret about how she was interested in Antonio last year. They made a cute couple, in that Antonio would bait Katie by pretending his English was insufficient, and she would fall for it every time and correct his mixed-up sentences. The only thing that seemed unusual now was that, if a romantic link existed between them, neither of them acted like it.

"Thanks a lot, Antonio," Katie said. "I was trying to keep the little surprise a surprise, but now…"

"I didn't say anything," he said, holding up his hands.

"Nice try," Sierra said. "It's no good, though. One of you has to tell us now."

Antonio leaned forward. "You are seriously thinking of coming to school here in the fall, aren't you?"

"Well, I…I don't know. Until today I hadn't even considered it," Sierra said.

"I'm interested," Randy said. "If they have a decent music department. The food passes my inspection."

Sierra motioned to Randy that he had a little smear of mayonnaise on the side of his lip. He reached for a napkin and wiped it off. "Is it always this good?" he asked.

Antonio nodded. "We eat well around here."

Katie pinched her side as if measuring her fat. She was so athletic and energetic Sierra couldn't imagine any flab under her baggy white shirt. "They call it the Freshman Fifteen. That's how many pounds you gain your first year here. Even if you enter as a sophomore, like me."

"My cousin said she gained only ten her first year," Vicki said, licking her spoon and dipping it back into the cup of frozen yogurt.

"She must have gone to a state school," Katie said with a grin. "Here it's definitely a minimum of fifteen."

Sierra began to feel those tremors of terror again. She had never tried to lose weight before, since her late-blooming tomboy figure had remained pretty constant until the last six or eight months. It was disturbing to be told she would gain weight when she went to college. That meant another area of her life where she would have to be responsible and disciplined.

"You guys," Sierra said, eager to redirect the conversation, "I believe you're attempting to change the subject. Go back to that surprise Antonio mentioned. What's the big secret?"

Katie and Antonio looked at each other. Antonio raised his eyebrows as if to give Katie the go-ahead.

"It's about Christy and Todd," Katie began.

Before she could go on, Sierra clapped her hand over her mouth to keep from screaming in public.

sixteen

"NO, NO, NO!" Katie said quickly. "It's not what you think. They haven't announced their engagement. At least not yet. At least that I know of. But then, I'm always the last to know everything."

"Who are Todd and Christy?" Vicki asked.

"Don't you remember?" Amy said, the wounded tone still in her voice. "Sierra's friend Christy is the one who took her to Switzerland last summer."

"Actually, Christy's Aunt Marti took us, but, yes, Christy is the one I went to Switzerland with. Todd is her boyfriend. They've been together forever. Only she's at school in Switzerland now, and he's over here. Isn't he about ready to graduate from college?"

Katie shook her head. "Let's just say that Todd's educational path has been a winding one. He's not going to school right now. He's working two different jobs to put some money in the bank."

"He'll start his senior year in the fall," Antonio added. "And where, might you ask, would Todd have chosen to finish his college years but here, at Rancho Corona."

"And," Katie quickly added, flashing her green eyes at Antonio, "the rest of the surprise news, which somebody couldn't keep to himself, is that Christy has been accepted here, too. This September, we're all going to be back together again."

"Oh, man, you guys are going to have such great times together!" Sierra said, remembering the closeness she felt with this group of friends. Even though all of them were older than she, they had never made her feel younger or left out.

"You guys?" Katie repeated, motioning to Sierra, Randy, Vicki, and Amy. "How about all of us guys? The four of you included. Oh, and Wes, too. You have to come here now. All of you. You have no choice."

"We probably should at least look at a catalog," Vicki said, laughing at Katie's command to them. "I mean, the campus and the student body are great. None of us would argue with you there. But those aren't the areas my parents are going to ask about when I get home."

"Some information packets are waiting for you back at the admin building," Katie said. "I should have given them to you when you first arrived. Sorry about that. We could pick them up now, and then you could check out the pool or Dishner Hall or whatever."

"Let's go," Randy said, getting up and taking his empty tray with him. "Where do I put this?"

"Over here," Antonio said. "Are you the one who wants to see Dishner Hall?"

"If that's the music building, yes."

"I'll show you around," Antonio said.

Making their way out of the cafeteria, Sierra noticed Amy still appeared to have a cloud hanging over her. Was she disappointed that Antonio didn't volunteer to go to the pool with her and Vicki?

Katie led them back to the admin building, where Dawn handed each of them an information packet. They were about to go their separate ways when Wes entered the lobby. He had a calm smile on his face. Sierra knew his meeting with the financial adviser had gone well.

After introducing Antonio to Wes, Sierra asked, "What's next on your schedule? Have you eaten yet?"

"We can recommend the food here," Randy said.

"I thought I'd head over to the cafeteria," Wes said. "I have an appointment with an adviser at two-thirty. What do you think? Should we all meet back here?"

Sierra gave Wes the information about their being invited to stay on campus rather than at Tawni's if they wanted to. Wes asked the others, and everyone was eager to stay except Amy. She said it was fine, but then she added quietly, "So we're probably not going to the beach, then." She wasn't making a big deal about it, though obviously she had been hoping. And Sierra couldn't blame her. If she had never been to the beach in Southern California, Sierra knew she would be sad about the missed opportunity, too.

They quickly made their plans. Wes would call Tawni, all of them would meet back at the van at five-thirty, and Wes would drive them to this barbecued rib place Katie recommended. They would stay in the dorms that night, and the next day, Saturday, they would head home and try to visit at least one more university campus on the way. Wes was adamant that he had to be back in Corvallis by seven

Monday morning because he couldn't miss his first class. Knowing how long the drive home would be made all of them understand Wesley's concern about staying around too long on Saturday.

The group split up, and Katie directed Sierra toward the dorm.

As soon as they were out of hearing distance from the others, Sierra said, "Katie, whatever happened between you and Antonio? I thought you two were getting pretty interested in each other."

"Tonio and me?" A glimmer of remembrance came over Katie's face. "Oh, yeah. Last year. That's ancient history."

"What happened?"

"Nothing," Katie said with a laugh. "That's exactly what happened. Nothing! Antonio is a big flirt, in case you hadn't noticed. Somehow I was the last girl on the planet to realize that all the sweet talk and kisses on the cheek were his way of communicating with everyone. Well, at least with all the girls." She shook her head. "I've always been a slow learner when it comes to guys. I really believed he thought I was something special. Then one day I finally woke up, hit my head on the headboard, and the dream was over."

"That's too bad," Sierra said sympathetically. "I think the two of you made a darling couple."

"So did everyone else," Katie said. "Try not getting your hopes up about a guy when everyone is telling you that. Here we are."

Katie gestured toward a long, three-story dormitory. It was built in the same early California style as the rest of the campus. She slipped a plastic card through the security lock at the front, and the wide double doors opened automatically.

The first sight that caught Sierra's attention was the court area in the middle of the rectangular building. It appeared more like the lobby of an exotic hotel than a women's dormitory. The patio was paved with red tiles and filled with a garden of tall trees, under which sat benches around a small fountain.

"How beautiful," Sierra murmured. "This is where you live?"

"Yep. This is Sophia Hall, named after Mr. Perez's wife."

"And who is Mr. Perez?" Sierra asked, following Katie past several students, who all greeted Katie.

"Didn't I tell you that part on the tour? Oh, no! They're going to fire me as campus guide. I forgot to tell you the history of this place." Katie stopped in the middle of the courtyard, next to the fountain, and took a deep breath. "Sometime in the 1920s or 1930s—I'm not real good with dates—all this property was owned by a man named Miguel Perez. He and his wife tried to start an orange grove here on top of the mesa. It didn't work out because there was a drought or something. He gave up on trees and started to raise cattle instead."

"How did he get the cows up here?" Sierra asked.

Katie gave her a funny look. "I don't know. They had trucks back then, you know. Anyway, Mr. Perez promised the Lord that he would give half the profit from his cattle ranch back to God, and he did. For years the ranch did a fantastic business and half the profits went to Christian organizations. One of them was the Open Bible College of Los Angeles."

"I've heard of that college," Sierra said.

"I guess it was *the* Christian college of its day. Rancho Corona is actually a satellite of OBCLA because, when Mr. Perez died, he didn't have any living children, so he left everything to OBCLA."

"What a nice gift!" Sierra said. "I take it his ranch was called Rancho Corona?"

"Actually, the Perez ranch was originally called El Rancho de la Cruz y la Corona."

"The ranch of the what?" Sierra said, attempting to translate the Spanish words.

"The Ranch of the Cross and the Crown. A stained-glass window in the chapel has the ranch symbol on it. It's a cross with a gold crown resting on it. It's really pretty. I'll have to show you the chapel before you leave."

"And which room is yours?" Sierra asked, looking up at the long row of dorm rooms that lined the three floors.

"Second floor. Follow me."

Katie's room wasn't very large. There was a shared desk in the center of the room with a bookcase to the ceiling that separated the two sides. The twin beds were against opposite walls, and the closets were built in on either side of the door. Sierra was surprised at how barracklike it seemed. The suite-style rooms at Valencia Hills were much nicer.

It was easy to guess which side of the room was Katie's. Her decorations were minimal, and her bulletin board was covered with photos, many of them of people Sierra had met. She stepped closer to the wall to examine the collage and was surprised to see one of herself there. It was in front of the big wooden front doors at Carnforth Hall, where they had met in England. Next to Sierra's face was one of the large lion's head door knockers.

"I remember when you took that," Sierra said. "I still have that jacket."

"And do you still have those cowboy boots?" Katie asked, pointing to another group picture in which Sierra's legs were dangling over the edge of a stone wall, and her cowboy boots were very noticeable.

"Yep. I still have them, and I still wear them." Sierra pointed to another picture. "When was this one taken? That's you and Christy, isn't it? You look so young."

Katie leaned closer to examine the picture of the two of them wearing big T-shirts. Both of them had their hair up on top of their heads, and they were holding a large bag of M&M's. She laughed. "That was at a sleepover when we were fifteen." She looked closer. "That wasn't the party where we first became friends, I don't think. It was probably the next one we went to together."

"It's so neat that you and Christy go way back."

"What about you and Vicki and Amy?"

"We get along great now, but we didn't used to be friends at all. At least not all three of us at the same time. We've only been doing things together for a few months. That's why I think it's great you and Christy have been friends for so long."

"And it's only going to get better in the fall when she comes to school here. We've already signed up to be roommates. We'll have such a great time with you and all your friends," Katie said.

Sierra plopped down on Katie's bed. "You make it sound so easy."

"Why not?" Katie said. "I mean, why wouldn't you want to come to school here?"

"I don't know. It's so expensive."

"So? You pray about it; apply for every grant, scholarship, and loan they'll let you apply for; and then get into a work-study program, like me, and earn your spending money while you're at school."

"What's your work-study program?" Sierra asked.

"I'm an agronomy major, if you can believe it. I know it's weird. Ever since I first studied plants in high school science, I've been strangely attracted to finding out how things work within nature. They have me in a work-study course where I work in the organic garden ten hours a week. I didn't show it to you. It's terraced down the side of the hill by the pool. We sell a lot of our organic vegetables at the Saturday farmer's market in town."

"That sounds like a lot of fun."

"I like it. For my next project I want to develop my own brand of herbal tea. I should have shown you the garden. I already have all my herbs planted, and some of them are coming up nicely." Katie dropped into her beanbag chair and said, "What's your major going to be?"

"Communications, I think. I had to put something on the forms, and that's what I'm most interested in right now."

"Perfect!" Katie said. "Rancho has the best communications department around. Radio, video, journalism, anything you're interested in. And last year their debate team placed second in the national tournament. I can see you as Rancho's star debater, bringing home all the trophies."

Sierra gave her exuberant friend a skeptical smile.

Katie cocked her head and eyed Sierra suspiciously. "It's not about money or majors, is it?"

Sierra shrugged.

"Okay. I get it. What's his name, and where's he going to school?"

Sierra was surprised at Katie's perceptiveness. Letting down her guard, Sierra smiled softly. "Paul's at the University of Edinburgh now. I don't know where he'll be in the fall."

Katie looked confused for only a moment. Then, with the dawn of recognition across her face, she said, "Paul, huh? Isn't he the one who saw you walking in the rain that one time with your arms full of flowers?"

Sierra nodded. "Daffodils. He still calls me the Daffodil Queen sometimes."

"Still, huh. Are you two together?"

Sierra shook her head. "We write each other once or twice a month. That's all. You know he's Jeremy's brother, don't you?"

"Tawni's boyfriend?" Katie asked, leaning forward. "Ah, the plot thickens. This could be interesting."

"Except there's nothing to tell. I'm not even sure why I mentioned him. He said he was coming back to the States at the end of June. I was just, I don't know..."

"Dreaming a little dream?" Katie concluded for her. "Wishing a little wish? Praying a little prayer that you would end up at the same college?"

"Something like that," Sierra said, trying hard to catch her imagination before it took off like a kite.

"It could happen," Katie said with a grin. "I mean, look

at Todd and Christy. God can move mountains when He wants to."

"I know," Sierra agreed. Katie's mentioning mountains got Sierra thinking about when they had driven past Mount Shasta and how it was cloaked in thick fog. "And then again, God can also hide mountains when He wants to."

seventeen

"YOU'LL HAVE TO DIRECT ME, Katie, once we get down the hill," Wes called out in the noisy van of people.

"Turn right at the first light you come to, go about a mile, and it's on the right side. Sam's Barbecue Pit."

Katie was in the middle seat with Amy and Antonio. Vicki was in the front; and Randy, Sierra, and Tawni were in the snore zone. Tawni had driven up to spend the evening with them and had appeared especially glad to see Sierra.

"What do you think of Rancho?" Tawni asked. She had moved to Southern California to begin a modeling career last summer. It hadn't turned out to be as glamorous or wonderful as Tawni had imagined, but she was doing well and seemed to still be glad to be out on her own.

"It's great," Sierra said. "What do you think? Should I come here?"

"That's up to you," Tawni said.

"You gave up on going to school in Reno, didn't you?" Sierra asked.

Tawni nodded. Her hair was pulled up in a French twist, and when she nodded, some of the strands on the sides fell down. Her hair color had been different every time Sierra had seen her lately. This time it was a caramel blond, similar to Sierra's hair. The sisterly resemblance stopped there, though, since Tawni was adopted.

"I can't believe I hatched that scheme to go to school in Reno just so I could meet Lina," Tawni said. Tawni had found her birth mother and discovered she was a professor at the University of Nevada, Reno. Tawni had written her a letter, but when Tawni didn't hear back right away, she made plans to enroll at UNR. However, Lina Rasmussen did write back, though not right away. She initiated a meeting for the two of them last fall, and since then she and Tawni had seen each other twice and called each other every week or so.

"Did Jeremy tell you that Paul is planning to come back to the States at the end of June?" Sierra said.

"No. When did Paul tell you?"

"I got a letter last week."

"I still don't understand why you and Paul write letters instead of send e-mails to each other. Paul sends e-mails to Jeremy all the time."

Sierra smiled quietly to herself. Written letters were so much more romantic and thoughtful. It took time to take pen in hand and compose a newsy yet tender letter. And right now, that gift of time and effort was all Sierra had to give Paul. She knew that was exactly the same kind of sacrifice he was making when he wrote to her.

"What is Paul going to do when he comes back?" Tawni asked.

"He didn't say. I don't think he knows yet."

"Hmm."

"What?" Sierra asked.

"Nothing. I'm curious about what Paul's going to do. Jeremy says most of his friends are transferring here next fall."

"Tell me about it," Sierra quipped.

"Where are we going for dinner?" Tawni asked.

Before Sierra could answer, Wes pulled the van into the crowded parking lot toward which Katie directed him. The sign over the restaurant said, "Sam's BBQ Pit—Best Ribs This Side of Texas."

"This is it?" Tawni said. "Seriously?"

"Must be the place," Sierra said as the rest of the gang began to roll out of the van.

"When Wes called and said we were going out to dinner, this isn't exactly what I had in mind." Tawni extracted her long legs from the back of the van, and Sierra followed her.

"This place is hoppin'!" Katie exclaimed when the group entered the small restaurant.

She had to yell over the country music blaring from the speakers in the ceiling. Long picnic tables lined the right side of the restaurant, and the counter where customers stood to place their orders took up the left side.

"Surely there's another place to eat in this town," Tawni said.

"I've heard good things about this place," Katie hollered back. Undaunted, she led the way to the counter and began to order.

"I guess we're stuck," Tawni said. "Do you see any salads on the menu?"

The menu consisted of one thing: ribs. The only selection customers had was exactly how many ribs they wanted. There was the Cowpoke Plate for kids that came with six ribs, the Rustler Plate that came with twelve ribs, the Hired Hand Plate with eighteen ribs, and the Rancher Special that came with twenty-four ribs and free seconds.

Tawni and Amy skeptically ordered the Cowpoke Plate, but the server objected, saying they weren't under twelve years old. Katie stepped in and, with her quick tongue and friendly smile, convinced the employee to let them go for the kid's plate. According to Katie, it would be the kid's plate or nothing for these two, and if Sam wanted their business, he had better let up on the age rule.

Sierra ordered the Rustler. She paid for it and then moved through the cafeteria-style line to pick up her tray behind Vicki, who had ordered the same thing. Both of them were shocked when they saw the amount of food on the trays. The ribs alone took up the whole plate. On a side plate came the "fixin's," which included baked beans, coleslaw, corn on the cob, and a thick hunk of white bread.

"I feel like Fred Flintstone!" Sierra exclaimed as she followed Vicki to the picnic table where the others were already seated. "If we were at a drive-in restaurant with one of those window trays, the car would tip over."

"I think I'm going to tip over," Vicki said. "There's no way I can eat all this."

"Aren't we glad we brought Randy, the human disposal," Sierra said.

"Great choice of restaurant," Wes said to Katie when they were all seated. He and Randy had ordered the Rancher Special, and each of them had to carry two trays to hold it all. Wes offered to pray for the food. Their table was the farthest from the speakers, which was good because the music wasn't quite so loud at their end of the restaurant. They could actually hear each other speak.

"Don't you think it would be more appropriate if we prayed for forgiveness for being a bunch of gluttons?" Katie asked.

Wes laughed and suggested they hold hands while they prayed. Sierra noticed that Wes was sitting next to Katie.

With a round of "Amens," the group took to the ribs like ravenous beasts. All but Tawni and Amy. They both tried to use plastic knives and forks to cut the heavily sauced meat from the bone.

"Oh, come on," Katie teased. "You're not supposed to whittle those bones into figurines. Get aggressive! Stuff them in your face." To demonstrate she picked up a rib with both hands and took a big chomp out if it. The barbecue sauce dripped down her chin and onto her tray.

"You have a little something right there," Wes said, pointing to Katie's chin after her demonstration.

With her hands covered with barbecue sauce, Katie said, "Oh, really?" She reached over and made a red smear across Wes's cheek. "You have a little something on your face, too."

To Sierra's surprise, Wes cracked up. He returned the favor and painted a streak on each of Katie's cheeks. She then evened out his war paint by marking his other cheek. Vicki and Antonio laughed the hardest at Wes's and Katie's antics. Sierra laughed and joked with the others, but she felt that strange sensation in her stomach that she got when she thought Amy liked Wes. Now it was Katie instead of Amy who was getting Wes's attention.

Drawing inward, Sierra nibbled on her corn on the cob and gave herself a lecture about giving in to these immature jealousy fits over her brother. She needed to stop feeling so possessive. Sierra knew she couldn't spend the rest of her life examining the motives of every girl who appeared interested in Wes.

Picking up her glass of milk and taking a long drink, Sierra resolved to put away her childish insecurities about Wesley. She decided if she considered him more of a buddy than her adored brother during this stage of their lives, she would be less likely to feel she was selecting whom he could date. The funny thing was, Wes wasn't dating anyone and hadn't been for a long time, as far as Sierra knew. Maybe she was afraid that since he was getting older, his dating choices would be more like potential marriage choices, and she wanted somehow to be involved in that selection.

Now she realized it wasn't her choice. It wasn't her life; it was Wesley's. Her role was to love and support him. And the only way she could do that was to let go of all these assumptions and expectations.

Strangely, the mental exercise increased Sierra's appetite, and she went after her ribs with renewed gusto.

"Do you suppose they actually serve ribs like these in Texas?" Antonio asked. He was seated across from Sierra and seemed to be directing his question to Amy, who was sitting next to him on the long bench.

"I don't know. I've never been there."

"Neither have I," Antonio said, reaching for a napkin from the stack in the middle of the table. "Where I come from in Italy, you would never see such ribs."

"What part of Italy are you from?" Amy asked.

"The north. Near Lake Como. Have you heard of it?"

"My uncle is from that area. I don't remember the name of the town. He runs an Italian restaurant in Portland." Amy gave Antonio one of her best smiles and said, "I think you would like his restaurant. The food is very good."

As Sierra watched, Amy and Antonio launched into a lively conversation about Italian food. Turning her attention to Tawni, Sierra said, "What do you think?"

"What do I think about what?" Tawni asked. She had broken off a corner of her white bread and was eating it without butter.

"What do you think about this Texas food? Do you like it?"

"It's okay. I'd probably enjoy it more if I didn't know how loaded it was with fats and carbs. I have a magazine shoot next week. That means rabbit food the rest of the weekend for me."

"Don't you hate that? Having to worry about your weight and how you look every minute of every day?"

"I try not to worry about it," Tawni said. "I don't think I do as much as I used to. It's part of the career I've chosen. If I were an athlete, I'd have to work out every day to be good at my sport. As a model, I have to spend time on my appearance. But that's not all I do every minute of every day."

"I didn't mean to imply it was," Sierra said, thinking of all the warnings about gaining weight as a college freshman. "I was just thinking it would be a pain to have to watch what you ate all the time."

"It is sometimes," Tawni said, sounding less defensive.

"I guess anything in life can be a pain. We all end up choosing the level of pain we can endure to reach our goals."

"You're right," Sierra said. "That's profound." She wasn't used to having Tawni share such thoughts with her.

"You know who told me that?" Tawni said, wiping her fingers daintily and pushing away her plate.

"Jeremy?"

Tawni shook her head. "No, it was Lina. Lina told me that was why she gave me up for adoption. You know she was only fifteen when she got pregnant with me, and her boyfriend was no longer in the picture by the time she found out. Lina said she wanted what was best for me and didn't think at that point in her life she could offer me the same things adoptive parents could. She said her goal was to finish school and become a college professor, which she did."

"I imagine giving you up for adoption was the deepest level of pain for her," Sierra said. "But I'm glad she did. Otherwise you and I never would have been sisters."

A tear formed in the corner of Tawni's eye and threatened to tumble down her perfectly made-up face. "That is so sweet of you to say, Sierra." Tawni reached over and gave Sierra a hug. "I don't know if I've ever said this really clearly to you, but I'm glad we're sisters—very glad."

"I am, too." Sierra's words were whispered into her sister's ear as the two of them hugged and cried just a little.

In the background, honky-tonk music blared, and Sam's rib slabs sizzled on the grill. It was an unlikely setting for such a bonding moment. But Sierra knew it was a moment she would never forget.

eighteen

SIERRA AWOKE EARLY the next morning with a stomachache. She wasn't sure if it was from the ribs she ate at Sam's or if it was from all the junk food she had scarfed afterward when they all went back to the Student Center and hung out in the lounge, talking until almost midnight.

Getting up quietly, Sierra peeked over at Katie, who was still sound asleep. Dawn, Katie's roommate, had offered to let Sierra sleep in her bed, but it had been too soft for Sierra, making it a night of restlessness. So many thoughts, feelings, and ideas were bouncing off the walls of Sierra's mind that she decided to dress and go for a walk. She knew it would be useless to try to sleep anymore. She would much rather greet the day by trying to glimpse the elusive blue Pacific from the deck of the Student Center.

Slipping into her jeans and a sweatshirt, Sierra pulled her hair back in a clip and quietly left Katie's dorm room. No one else appeared to be awake yet. The halls and lobby were empty. And why should any reasonable college student be up? The sun had barely risen this Saturday morning.

Sierra quietly opened the double doors and exited into the new day.

Once outside she immediately felt better. Perhaps her feelings soared because of the brisk morning air or the sweet fragrance of honeysuckle that wafted in her direction from the vine covering the far side of the building. Maybe it was the night sky just beginning to fade into a rosy shade of aqua that lifted her up. Whatever it was, Sierra drew the refreshing sensation into her lungs and headed toward the Student Center with light, energetic steps. A car engine revved in the student parking lot and passed her on the road a few minutes later. The driver, a young woman, gave a little beep and waved at Sierra as if she knew her.

That was one of the many things Sierra liked about Rancho Corona. The students were friendly and open. She rounded the back of the Student Center and took the steps up to the deck two at a time. Her efforts were well rewarded. Morning had come to the top of the mesa only minutes before Sierra arrived on the deck. The faithful sun now rose steadily behind her. Before her lay the campus, spread out like a picnic on green fields all the way to the end of the mesa. After that, far in the distance, laced with morning clouds as thin as a whisper, lay the vast, blue Pacific Ocean. The immensity of the view and the vividness of the early morning colors stunned Sierra. She felt a shiver, partly from the chill of the breeze and partly from the astounding beauty of it all.

At the edge of the campus, away from the other buildings and near a grove of trees, Sierra noticed a small white building with a spired roof. She guessed it was the chapel Katie had mentioned. Tracing the horizon with her hungry eyes, Sierra ate up the scenery. It was almost too beautiful to take in—a glorious glut of wonder.

Filled but not satisfied, Sierra left the deck and scampered through the wet grass toward the chapel. She felt like laughing aloud because her spirit was so light. Pausing along the trail only for a moment, Sierra snatched up a dandelion. She closed her eyes, made a wish, and then blew all the feathery hairs from the dandelion's head and watched them dance away on the morning breeze.

Sierra knew if anyone could see her at this moment, wishing on dandelions and fairly skipping down the path, they would label her as loony and anything but college-student material. But it was unlikely anyone on this campus was up yet, and if he were, he probably had something more important to do than watch a young heart celebrate the new day.

That's how Sierra felt: forever young in her heart. All the thoughts and feelings she had wrestled with in her sleep that had weighed so heavily upon her felt light at this moment. So many things had felt so intense these past few days, and her spirit had been unsettled. But not now, not on this morning with its promise of so much life to be lived.

Skipping along, Sierra came to where the path ended, at the door of the solemn, silent chapel. She tried the door and found it unlocked. Entering with reverence, she shuffled to the front and sat down on one of the cushioned, wooden benches. At the front of the chapel was a beautifully carved altar with a large, open Bible on the top of it. Behind the altar was a stained-glass window that shone brighter and brighter as each ray of morning light poured through it, sending its pattern and colors into a dim reflection on the floor at Sierra's feet.

She stared a long time at the stained-glass window. It was just as Katie had described it. A thick brown cross slanted to the right, and around the horizontal portion of the cross hung a golden crown studded with bright jewels.

"Father," Sierra whispered into the sacred air around her, "thank You. Thank You for sending Your Son to die for me. Thank You for making a way for me to come to You through Him. Thank You for forgiving all my sins when I surrendered my life to Christ. Thank You for giving me eternal life. I know if I can trust You with all that, I should be able to trust You with all these anxious thoughts and feelings that kept me from sleeping last night."

Sierra glanced around the small chapel before continuing. God felt so close to her here, at this moment. She almost expected to see His shadow on the wall. "I guess I'm worried about the future. I don't think I ever have been worried about it before—at least not like this. Part of me wants to go away to college, particularly a college like this. Another part of me doesn't want to leave home. I don't want to have to be so responsible. I know I've had it easy. I guess I like my life at home more than I realized. I don't think I'm ready to grow up."

Sierra rubbed her hands together. It was chilly in the little chapel. "I feel as though I didn't finish a lot of things in life when I could have. Like with Tawni. Last night, when she hugged me, I felt bad that I'd wasted all those years when she was at home. Why weren't we close friends then? And then there's Amy. Did You hear her last night? Of course You did. It really bugged me when Antonio asked her when she became a Christian and she said she wasn't necessarily one of us. Why isn't her heart open to You, God? What happened?"

For another five minutes Sierra poured her heart out to the Lord. She had unsettled feelings about Warner, fears about maintaining her high GPA through this last semester, questions about how she was supposed to know which school God wanted her to go to, or if it was His plan for her to stay home. She knew all too well that she was an impetuous person. This was one time in her life when her decisions mattered a lot. She couldn't make a snap choice. Her future was at stake.

When all her doubts, fears, and worries were poured out, she stopped talking and waited, listening to the silence. The emotional exercise left her exhausted, and she stretched out on the pew. Within minutes she was asleep.

The sound of the chapel door opening and quick footsteps woke her sometime later. Sierra sat bolt upright and startled the man who had entered. He let out a funny gasping sound and then apologized for disturbing Sierra.

"No, it's okay. I was just leaving. Do you know what time it is?" Sierra squinted in the brightened chapel and stretched her kinked neck.

"Nine-thirty," the man said. He looked like one of the professors and carried a Bible and notebook under one arm.

"Thank you." Sierra straightened her sweatshirt and hurried past the man. She jogged across the campus, not sure where to go first. If the others were up, which she was sure they were, they were probably out looking for her. The best tactic, she figured, was to go back to Katie's room.

When she reached the front door of Sophia Hall, Sierra had to wait for someone with a security card to come along and open the door. She sprinted down the second-floor hall and knocked once on Katie's door before opening it. Katie wasn't there.

Sierra was about to leave when she noticed a note on the bed. It read, *Sierra, where are you, girl? If you come back here, call 240 on the phone at the end of the hall. That's Security. Tell them you're here and for them to page us. Katie.*

Hurrying to the phone, Sierra followed Katie's instructions. The person who answered and took the information said, "Where were you? Katie had us looking all over campus for the last hour."

"I'm sorry. I was in the chapel."

"Oh," was all the person on the other end said. "I'll page Katie and tell her you're waiting for her in her room."

Sierra went back to the room and quickly packed her things. She hoped her brother wouldn't be too upset with her for putting everyone in a panic. Wes had wanted to leave early this morning. Nine-thirty wasn't exactly early in his book.

Katie's dorm room door opened with a blast of people all firing questions at Sierra at once. She tried her best to explain that she had been praying and fell asleep.

Vicki seemed to be the most understanding. "We're glad you're okay," she said. "Wes said he would pull the van around in front of the dorm so we can get going. Do you have all your stuff?"

"It's right here. Is he upset?"

Vicki shrugged. "I think he's okay. He was worried. We all were. You just disappeared."

"I didn't mean to fall asleep," Sierra explained to Wes a few minutes later as she loaded her gear into the van. "I'm sorry."

"It's okay," he said. "Next time leave a note."

"Or at least a lock of hair and a trail of bread crumbs," Katie said, still appearing flustered over the whole event. "It doesn't look good on my record as a campus host when I lose visitors. We had half the campus out looking for you. I wouldn't be surprised if your name appears in a tabloid somewhere tomorrow under the headline, 'Campus Visitor Abducted by Aliens.'"

Katie's humor helped to clear the tension with Wes and the others. Then another tension surfaced. It was time to say good-bye. Katie kept making jokes, trying to make light of the situation. They all hugged her, and Antonio gave the women his trademark kiss across their cheeks.

"So, e-mail me sometime and tell me what you decide, okay, Sierra?" Katie said. "Or just e-mail Christy. She'll make sure I get the message."

"I'll e-mail you," Sierra said. "And I'll give Christy a hard time for not telling me she was planning to come here." Sierra climbed into the van behind Vicki. "'Bye, and thanks for everything."

Sierra stared at every tree and every building as they drove off campus. It was quiet in the van, and she wondered if the others were trying to memorize every detail of the campus as she was. Or were they upset at her for wandering off and producing a Goldilocks-nap story to explain her actions? Once they had driven under the entrance sign and passed the stone pillars, Sierra apologized to everyone again.

"Don't worry about it," Wes said, catching her eye in the rearview mirror. "It's no big deal. We need to make some plans from here on out, though. The rest of us talked at breakfast, and now we need your input. Do you still want to visit another campus?"

"I guess. I don't know. Do we just need to drive straight home? What does everyone else want to do?"

"Hit the beach," Vicki said with a grin. "Wes says he's checked the map, and we can visit one of the colleges on the way to the beach and then head home. What do you think?"

"I'm all for going to the beach," Sierra said.

"That's what we thought you would say," Randy said. He turned around in the front seat, and with a more serious expression, he said, "Are you going to apply to Rancho?"

Sierra felt caught off guard. "I don't know. Are you?"

Randy nodded. "Yes, I think I am. I hadn't thought much about going away to college. I thought I'd stick around Portland. But Rancho has an amazing music program. Did you know they even have a recording studio on campus? It's the best setup I've seen yet."

"What about you, Wes? How did all your meetings go?" Sierra asked.

"Great. I'm pretty sure this is where I'll end up. I never imagined you would want to come here, Sierra."

Sierra tried to evaluate Wes's tone. Would he find it annoying to have his kid sister running around campus as a freshman when he was there for graduate school? She turned to Amy and Vicki and asked what they thought about going to Rancho.

"It's a pretty big decision," Vicki said. "I liked everything I saw. My parents will go over the catalog, and I know they'll want to know what Rancho has that no other school in Oregon can offer. I'm sure I'll have to come up with a scholarship or a grant or something."

"I'd have to get a scholarship, too," Sierra said. She dreaded the thought of presenting her parents with more paperwork after they had already filled out endless forms for her. But she hadn't even known Rancho existed then.

Amy was sitting quietly in the back. Sierra reached over the seat and gave Amy's leg a friendly squeeze. "What are you thinking? Would you want to apply to Rancho Corona?"

"I don't think so," she said in a low voice.

"Why not? What didn't you like about it?"

"Nothing. It's a great school. I just don't think it's for me."

"Why not? If we all end up applying, you might as well apply, too."

"Sierra, give it up," Amy snapped. "I'm not interested, okay? Can't you leave it at that?"

"Okay," Sierra said, still looking Amy in the eye. Sierra waited a full minute before saying, "Don't you think you can at least tell me why?"

"No."

That was the last word they heard out of Amy all the way to the next campus they were to scout out.

nineteen

THE COLLEGE CAMPUS TOUR turned out to be a quick one. It was a small college nestled in the middle of an L.A. suburb. Wes drove through the campus, and Randy ran out and picked up a catalog from the admissions office. Few students were around, since it was noon on Saturday and the weather was exceptionally nice and warm. Vicki said she guessed everyone had gone to the beach, and she was glad they were headed there, too.

Sierra had been to Newport Beach several times, but she hadn't been to Huntington, which was the beach Wes drove to. He said he had been there before with his friend Ryan and that it was nice, long, and wide. As they climbed out of the van, they realized it was much warmer inland than it was on the coast. A thin layer of fog hung over the horizon, and a strong breeze whipped Sierra's long curls into her face.

"Why is it so cold?" Amy said. "I was all set to put on my bathing suit, but this is as cold as the beaches in Oregon."

"It's spring, you know. It's not summer yet," Wes said. "Look, those surfers even have on wet suits."

"It's pretty here," Vicki said cheerfully. She reached for her sweatshirt before Wes closed and locked the doors.

"Wait. I want my sweatshirt, too," Sierra said.

"Me, too," Amy said. "And I want a pair of socks."

"Socks?" Randy said. "You don't wear socks to the beach. You have to go barefoot. Once your feet get in the sand, they'll warm up."

"Oh, like you would know," Vicki said, punching Randy in the arm. "You're such a beach bum."

"Hey, I saw it in a movie. They ran along the beach in the winter and buried their feet in the sand. They were smiling and didn't look cold at all."

"In the movies?" Vicki questioned. "Haven't you ever been to the beach in California before either?"

"Nope," Randy said, stuffing his hands into his pockets. "And I'm beginning to agree with Amy. We could have gone to the coast back in Oregon and been warmer."

"Come on," Sierra said. "We have to at least walk in the sand and put our toes in the water. I can't believe how hot it was inland and how cold it is when you hit the coast."

They huddled close and marched stiffly through the cold sand.

"My feet aren't any warmer," Amy said. "Tell me, Randy, when are my feet supposed to warm up?"

"Maybe we should run," Wes said. He took off jogging before the others had a chance to consider his idea.

Sierra broke from the others and ran after her brother. Several other joggers passed them along the wet sand where Sierra and Wes jogged in unison. A few surfers sat on their boards, waiting for the ocean to churn up a decent wave. Aside from that, very few people were at the beach today.

No one sat under an umbrella eating lunch or lazed around soaking up the rays and listening to the radio. It did seem a world away from Newport Beach in the summer, which was how Sierra remembered it.

Sierra and Wes jogged without speaking. Sierra paced her rhythmic breath by Wes's. Their mom was an avid jogger, and all the Jensen kids at one time or another had learned some of her secrets. Sierra knew they had already broken their mom's cardinal rule by not warming up ahead of time.

Wes stopped and motioned to Sierra to turn around and head back. The other three were huddled close together, still walking through the sand toward Wes and Sierra. When they saw Sierra and Wes turn around, they turned, too, and headed back to the van. Sierra was beginning to enjoy the sensation of the cold, firm sand on her bare feet. The wind was to their backs now, and the gusts felt much nicer pushing them forward than when they were in their faces. Even in its chilly, overcast state, the beach exuded a sense of power. The waves roared their way to the shore the same as they did on sunny days. The seagulls still screeched and swooped, even though the trash cans held no snacks for them today. Sierra liked the constancy of the ocean in the midst of one of its many moods. It was still the beach, and it would still be the beach the next time she came to visit it.

"Sure you don't want to go for a swim now?" Wes asked, panting deeply when they all arrived back at the van.

"I'm positive!" Amy said. "Open the door, will you?"

She wore shorts, and her slender legs were covered with goose bumps. The rest of them had on jeans, which might explain why they weren't quite so miserable. But now the bottom edges of Sierra's jeans were wet and sandy. She quickly learned that could be worse than having goose bumps. At least the goose bumps could be rubbed away once everyone jumped into the car and turned on the heater. The wet, sandy jeans would take longer to dry and feel sticky for a long time.

"I liked that," Sierra said after they had driven a few miles down the road. "I'm glad we went."

"It's nothing like in the movies," Randy said.

"Is anyone else hungry?" Wes asked.

"I am," Sierra said. "I seem to have missed breakfast this morning."

Wes stopped at the first fast-food place they came to, which happened to be a Taco Bell. They ordered enough food to host a nice little Mexican fiesta in the van as they kept pushing north. Once again, Randy ate more than the rest of them. He also did the same thing he always did when he and Sierra ate at Lotsa Tacos in Portland. He teased her mercilessly about drinking milk with her tacos.

"It's perfectly normal and very delicious," Sierra said.

"Very delicious," Randy repeated in a high voice. "You sound as though you're in a milk commercial."

"I'd rather be in a milk commercial than in one of your beach movies where people sit around acting warm in the middle of winter."

"Is that rain on the windshield?" Vicki suddenly asked.

Wes started the windshield wipers. "Guess you can tell we're heading home. The Oregon rain missed us so much it's come all the way down here to keep us company."

"That also explains why the beach was so cold," Amy said.

A dull sense of sadness came over them. Their adventure was coming to an end. All that was left were miles and miles of freeway and numerous stops at nondescript gas-station restrooms.

Vicki found a radio station she liked. Amy went to sleep in the backseat, covering herself with every spare sweatshirt and jacket she could find. Randy sat next to Sierra, looking through the information packet from the various colleges.

Suddenly he let out a low whistle. "Did you see what tuition costs for a year at this one?"

Sierra looked over his shoulder at the papers. "That's about the same as what it is at Valencia Hills. Rancho is more."

"More? You're kidding!" Randy looked shocked. "Are you sure there's a way to round up enough scholarship money in time?"

"I don't know. We probably should have started this whole process a lot sooner."

"It's kind of weird," he said, "thinking about going to college. I figured I'd go to Portland State or maybe a community college the first few years."

"That's what Katie did. She and Christy both went to community college their first year. That way they could live at home and save up some money."

Randy shifted in the seat. "Sierra, do you feel old enough to leave home and start being totally responsible for yourself?"

"No," Sierra said, looking closely at Randy. "I thought I was the only one who was feeling that way."

"You? You've already had a few chances to try your wings," Randy said. "Like when you went to Europe and everything. I guess I'm more of a baby than I realized. I didn't think this decision would be here yet."

"Exactly," Sierra said, looking out the rain-streaked window at the other cars zooming past them on the freeway. "I've felt more insecure on this trip than I ever did when I went to Europe. Isn't that strange?"

"Not really. With your other trips, you knew what to expect when you got home. Your parents would be there, and all your needs would be provided for. The thing that gets me about college is the whole money thing. I mean, even if our tuition is covered, what about spending money? Antonio was telling me he works a bunch of odd jobs just to earn some cash so he can do things like eat out with us at Sam's."

"I know," Sierra agreed. "I'm more spoiled than I realized."

"You and me both. If there's anything I learned on this trip, it's that I need to tell my parents how much I appreciate them and all they do for me." Randy stuffed the papers back into the folder. "I mean, I buy my own guitar strings and keep gas in my truck. I thought that was a big responsibility. I don't know what I'm going to do when I have to start paying for my in-between-cafeteria-meals food."

Sierra smiled. "You'll need a full-time job or at least a part-time one that pays well."

"No kidding!"

"Katie said we should look into the work-study programs."

"More paperwork," Randy muttered.

They rolled along in silence. Vicki hummed along with a familiar song on the radio. Sierra fought the urge to panic over the huge decisions that lay before her.

"You know what, Randy?" Sierra lowered her voice and confided in her buddy. "I don't think I'm done being a teenager yet. I don't cherish the idea of becoming an adult. What was that song you were working on? About only having enough light from the headlights to see a little ways down the road?"

"Oh yeah. Our Mount Shasta song. I'm still working on that one."

"Well, I feel as if I'm charging down this road to adulthood, but both my headlights are on dim. It's very hard to see the road."

"Sounds as though your battery is low," Randy said. "It'll be different once you get recharged."

Sierra wondered if Randy meant she needed to get recharged physically or spiritually. Or maybe he meant emotionally. A great deal had happened in the past few days. She stared out the rain-streaked window, feeling the same unsettledness she had experienced earlier that morning when she'd prayed in the chapel. She had expected answers to all her questions to come pouring over her like light through the stained-glass window. Instead, she had fallen asleep. Maybe her battery did need recharging.

Sleep wouldn't come to her right away as they drove home through the rain. Her imagination saw to that. Far too many decisions had to be made. Should she apply to Rancho Corona? What would Wes think if she went there? Was she interested in going there only because all her friends would be there? Was that such a bad reason? What about the finances? Could she get a scholarship? And would she need a part-time job once she started school?

Sierra looked over the seat at Amy stretched out under

her pile of sweatshirts, sleeping peacefully. Sierra knew she wouldn't feel settled until she at least knew why her friend had such an adverse reaction to applying at Rancho.

Finally, her imagination floated to Paul. What about that big unknown area in her life? Talk about a road traveled with very little light to show what lies ahead!

"Play me a song," Sierra said to Randy. "Like that first night when I was driving. You have no idea how peaceful that was."

"Oh, so you want me to put you to sleep? Is that what you're saying?"

"No."

Vicki turned off the radio and gave her vote of approval, too. "I love it when you sing, Randy. Would you play something for us?"

"How about if I play stuff we all know? Then everyone can sing." He pulled the guitar out of the case and began to strum a familiar song. He must have had his earlier conversation with Sierra in mind because the song started out,

I will trust You, Lord,
in every situation,
I will place my faith in You....

Sierra sang along softly, feeling like a hypocrite. She knew only too clearly how much easier it was to sing those words than to live them.

twenty

TWO WEEKS AFTER the California road trip, the three friends met at Mama Bear's on a rainy Monday afternoon. Vicki had stopped and bought a daffodil for each of them, and the three lacy yellow trumpets sat at the end of their long stalks in a glass of water. Sierra had already paid for the warmed-up cinnamon roll and three mugs of tea. Vicki and Sierra listened closely as Amy read from the postcard in her hand. It pictured a swaying palm tree with the word "California" arched across the top in gold letters.

> *Just wanted you to know I was thinking of you, bella Amy. I have thought often of what you said about how God isn't fair, since bad things happen to good people. My only thought there is that God is God. He can do whatever He wants. Apparently, one of the things He wants is to have a relationship with us. So, with a heart of love for you, I will pray that you will know God and experience this relationship.*
>
> *Ciao,*
> *Antonio*

Amy looked at Sierra and then at Vicki, her dark eyes flashing. "Did either of you put him up to this?"

"Of course not!" Sierra said.

Amy let out a sigh and gazed into her untouched cup of tea. "You know, all of you make it hard for me to stay mad at God."

Vicki and Sierra waited for her to go on.

"You guys, all of you, keep being nice to me and caring about me. When we were at Rancho Corona, I decided I was going to hate Katie. She was your friend, Sierra, and I was sure she was going to take you away from Vicki and me. My whole life people have been taken away from me. But it was impossible to hate Katie because she acted as though she really liked all of us, not just you, Sierra. Of course, maybe it was just a show."

"It wasn't a show, Amy," Sierra said. "People really do care about you."

Amy's dark lashes blinked back the tears. "Why?"

The verses Sierra had written on Paul's valentine came to her mind, and she quoted them to Amy. "Because 'God is love... We love because he first loved us.' Love is not something that's supposed to be done on human power. It's supernatural."

"Before you start pushing me too far, Sierra, let me say this. Being with you two and Wes and Randy for five days, and being around Katie and Antonio and even Tawni, made me realize that what you guys have is very special. You really do love each other. The way you treated Warner was with a lot more kindness than I had for him."

"Did I tell you?" Vicki said, cutting into Amy's speech. "Last week Warner had to give a speech in our communications class. He talked about being a team player and looking out for the rights and feelings of others. It was a great speech. I think the jaunt to Corvallis and the broken arm did him some good."

Sierra couldn't help but wonder if traveling all the way to Southern California would have done Warner even more good. But she was glad they didn't have to find out.

"You know," Amy said. "I think I've kind of been treating God the way Warner was treating us on the trip. He acted as if he deserved everything and got irritated when he couldn't get what he wanted. It's hard for me to admit this to you both, but I think I'm pretty spoiled and immature. I've always said it was because I was the baby of the family. But I'm graduating from high school in a few weeks. How much longer can I be the baby?"

"I was feeling exactly like that when we were at Rancho," Sierra said. "I didn't want to grow up."

"Who does?" Vicki said.

"We did, a year ago," Amy said. "I couldn't wait to have my own car and move out like my sisters did. Now I feel as though I'm not ready. My life isn't at that place yet."

"Are you saying you feel ready to turn your life over to the Lord?" Sierra asked. She knew Amy had heard all about how to become a Christian during the years she had attended Royal Academy. But knowing about God and knowing Him personally were two different things. Sierra was eager for Amy to lay down her shield and weapons and stop fighting God. In Sierra's mind, this was the perfect time for Amy to finally surrender to the Lord.

"No," Amy said firmly. "What I'm saying is that I'm taking a tiny step closer. That's all. Don't rush me."

"Okay," Sierra said, calming herself down and reaching for a piece of cinnamon roll. She knew it would be better to stuff the roll, rather than her foot, into her mouth.

"What I like," Amy said after a moment of shared silence, "is that you guys don't try to explain God to me. I mean, like this card from Antonio. He's just so honest. He says what he knows, or what he believes, and that's all. I can't stand it when people try to make excuses for God or explain why He does what He does as if they're an authority. I was just thinking yesterday that if God were easy enough to understand or to explain, then I don't think He would be big enough to run this universe or solve anyone's problems."

Vicki and Sierra exchanged expressions of amazement.

"That is so profound," Vicki said.

"Well, don't get excited," Amy said, her slight grin returning. "There aren't any more deep thoughts where that came from."

Sierra sipped her tea and then ventured to share something she hadn't told her friends yet. "I wanted to tell you guys something that happened to me on the trip. I sort of had a 'moment' with God."

"A 'moment'?" Vicki questioned with a skeptical gleam in her clear green eyes. "Where? In the chapel when you were missing that one morning?"

"No, it was at Magic Mountain." Sierra realized how ironic it was that God had seemed silent to her in the sacred chapel, but He had chosen to meet her in the middle of a crowd at an amusement park. She stored that thought away as more evidence that God's way of doing things is not the way she would choose. "I don't know if I can explain what happened. I was feeling kind of lost and by myself, and then it was as if God invisibly slipped His hand into mine and told me to hold on tight."

Amy raised an eyebrow. "You're telling us God talked to you?"

"No. I mean, yes. I mean…it wasn't like a voice. It was a thought. I don't know how to explain it. Have you ever had that happen to you?"

Amy looked down and sipped her tea. Vicki shook her head.

"I'm not saying I don't believe you," Vicki said. "I just never experienced anything like that."

"Well, I know it happened. I felt changed. It really felt as though God was right there beside me." Sierra knew there was no need to apologize for her experience. As Amy had said, she couldn't explain it. She didn't want to exaggerate either.

"I had a point to this," Sierra said. "But now I can't remember what it was."

"While you think of it, let me change the subject," Vicki said. "Did you send in all your papers for Rancho Corona and all the scholarship applications?"

"Yes. Did you?"

"My mom sent them off yesterday—finally. I heard my dad telling someone on the phone last night that I was going to Rancho Corona next year, as if it already had been decided. I didn't realize they were so in favor of my going. It took them long enough to read over all the information." Vicki reached for another bite of cinnamon roll, and without looking at Amy, she said, "Have you thought anymore about applying there, Aim?"

"No," Amy said quietly. "I don't think I want to go to a Christian college. But if I did, that's the one I'd want to go to. I can see why both of you do."

Several days after they returned from their scouting trip, Sierra had finally decided to apply at Rancho. She had discussed it for long hours with her parents and even called Wes to make sure he wouldn't mind her being on the same campus. The more she prayed about it, discussed it with her parents, and accepted going away to college as the next step for her life, the more settled and at peace she felt. She realized it was time to grow up and accept the privileges as well as the responsibilities that came with the next stage of life.

Once she decided to apply, she and her parents had scrambled madly to fill out and send off all the paperwork. The finances were the biggest challenge, especially since Wes was going to Rancho and he hadn't heard back yet on any of the grants and scholarships he had applied for in their grad program. In many ways, Sierra now understood that God's will involved simply taking the next step, without knowing the final outcome, and trusting Him to lead one step at a time. Applying to Rancho had been that next step for her. She had also taken a next step with Paul.

"You both will be proud of me," Sierra said to Vicki and Amy. "I wrote to Paul last week and told him all my plans. Then, very subtly, I added, 'And how are your plans for the fall coming along?'"

"Have you heard back from him?" Amy asked.

"No, not yet."

"At least the topic is out there for you two to discuss now," Amy said, and then added, "I didn't like it last week when you said that if it was God's will for the two of you to be together, somehow Paul would mysteriously show up in your life, and it would have all been arranged without your ever talking about it."

"I agree," Vicki said. "You're the one who's always saying we have to have open communication. Even if Paul has already made totally different plans, I think it's good for him to see you're not waiting around for him. You're going forward with what you believe is God's direction for you."

Sierra smiled at her two friends. "I'm only moving ahead as far as I can see in the headlights."

"That's right," Vicki said. "You need to keep moving ahead slowly and don't try to go too fast. Keep taking it slow, and you won't get out of control."

"Or crash and burn the way I always do," Amy said.

"What would I do without all your wise advice?" Sierra said, licking the gooey white frosting from her thumb.

"Oh yeah, like we're the love experts," Vicki said. "Me and my hopeless crush on Randy. Five days with him, and he still treats me like one of the boys."

"Well, thanks to those five days, I've decided to go on a guy diet," Amy said. "I'm becoming very selective about whom I go out with. After being treated like a princess by Wes and Antonio, I realize the guys around here are junk food."

Sierra laughed. "Now, Amy, just think what a feast of great guys you would have to choose from if you came to Rancho with us."

"Oh, now *there's* a deeply spiritual reason to select a college," Amy said.

"It might not be the best reason," Vicki said, "but it's not all that bad either."

They laughed together, and Vicki said, "Can you believe

we're sitting here talking about college and graduation as though it happens every day? I started thinking about it last night, and I kind of weirded out. I felt nervous about everything. I don't know why."

"You're just now feeling that way? I felt that way the whole trip," Sierra said. "That's why I went to the chapel that morning."

"And you got over the panicky feelings?" Vicki asked.

"Eventually."

"Last night I felt the same way I did at Magic Mountain when we were climbing up to the top of the Viper," Vicki said. "It was that same sickening feeling when everything is in motion and it's too late to go back."

"I know. Growing up is nothing like I thought it would be," Sierra said.

"I can't figure out how I got to this point all of a sudden, you know?" Vicki said. "I felt like I was fifteen for about three years, and then I turned sixteen and everything started going so fast."

"Can you believe all of us are seventeen already?" Sierra said.

"I have a better one than that," Amy said solemnly. "Can you believe we're going to graduate from high school eight weeks from this Thursday?"

The gathering around the table grew silent. They spontaneously reached around the daffodils and mugs of tea and grasped each other's hands. With a wary smile, Sierra gave Amy's and Vicki's hands a squeeze.

As the raindrops roller-coasted down the front window of Mama Bear's Bakery, the three friends sat together quietly, holding on tight.

Book Eleven

CLOSER THAN EVER

one

SIERRA JENSEN DREW in a deep breath and closed her eyes. The letter she held in her hand brought news she didn't know if she dared to believe. She looked again at the thin onionskin paper and the precise, bold black letters. Yes, it was Paul's handwriting. And the words were his, too.

I've made an adjustment in my plans for the trip home from Scotland. I'm flying out of Heathrow on the 12th, which will give me a four-day layover in Portland before I go to my parents' home in San Diego. So, what do you think? Do you have room for one more person at your graduation?

I'll ring you up—or wait...How do you say it in the States? Phone you. I'll phone you. No, it's "call," isn't it? Yes, call. (I've been gone too long!) I'll call you next week after you receive this, and you can tell me what you think. I wanted to see my uncle Mac and find out how things were going at the Highland House, so I'll be staying the four days with him.

Now, Sierra, I want you to be honest with me, as I know you always are. (I'm grinning at the thought of your trying to concoct a polite fib. Nearly impossible for you, right?) When I call, I want

you to tell me truthfully if you want me at your graduation. I know
this is an important time for you and all your friends, and I don't
want to interfere with your plans.

"My plans?" Sierra laughed aloud. As she sat curled up
on the porch swing on this warm June afternoon, no one
was there to hear her. "What plans? A walk down the aisle, a
few photos with Mom and Dad. Maybe a dinner with the
family. Those are my plans. I have all the time in the world
for you, Paul."

She flipped her long, curly, blond hair off her shoulder
and squinted at the sharp reflection of the sun that bounced
off the truck pulling up in front of her house. The cab door
slammed, and Randy shuffled to the front steps and smiled
at Sierra. He held a legal-sized white envelope in his hand.

"Guess what?" he said, adjusting his baseball cap. He
grinned his crooked smile and held out the envelope. "It
came."

Sierra quickly folded up her letter from Paul. "What?"
she asked.

Randy handed her the envelope. Taking it, she noticed
that the return address was Rancho Corona University's.
Her face turned to Randy, and she expectantly raised her
eyebrows. "Well? Were you accepted?"

Randy stood with his arms folded across his chest, waiting for her to read his letter to find out if he had been
accepted to the same university she and several of their
friends were attending in the fall. Randy had been more
excited about the college than almost any of them when they
had gone down to Southern California to check it out a few
months ago. Sierra had received her acceptance letter a few

weeks ago. Vicki hadn't heard yet, and neither had Randy—until now.

Sierra hesitated. He didn't seem too excited. Did that mean he hadn't been accepted? What would she say to him? How could she hide her soaring excitement over Paul's good news if Randy's letter brought bad news? Carefully pulling out the single sheet of university letterhead, she read aloud. "Dear Randy: We are pleased to inform you that you have been accepted for enrollment at Rancho Corona."

Sierra sprang from the swing. "Yahoo! You did it! This is great, Randy!" She wrapped her arms around him. He stood with his arms still crossed. Sierra pulled back. "What?"

"There's more. Keep reading."

Scanning the letter, Sierra went on to the next paragraph. "Blahda, blahda, blahda…'and we want you to know that your scholarship application for the music department has passed the first round of advisers and now goes into its final evaluation. We should have an answer for you within the next three weeks.'"

Sierra hugged him again, and this time Randy hugged her back.

"This is so perfect! I can't believe it! Aren't you excited?" she asked.

"Of course," Randy said. His expression looked about the same as it always did, and Sierra realized she had never seen Randy particularly emotional about anything—except maybe once when his band had received a good review in a local paper after a performance at The Beet, a teen nightclub in downtown Portland.

"We have to tell Vicki," Sierra said, turning around and

snatching Paul's letter from the swing. "I'll be right back. I'll tell my mom we're going over to Vicki's."

"I think she's at work," Randy said.

"That's right. It's Tuesday. Then we'll go…" Sierra stopped midstep before entering the old Victorian house where her family lived with her Granna Mae. "I know, let's go out to dinner to celebrate! I'll tell my mom we're eating out. Why don't you come in and call some other people to meet us?"

"Where do you want to eat?" Randy asked, following Sierra into the kitchen.

"How about someplace downtown? I don't want to just go for pizza or tacos. This is a big event." Opening the door into the basement, Sierra yelled down the stairs for her mother.

"You think maybe Italian?" Randy asked with the phone in his hand.

"Perfect!" Sierra said, pointing at Randy. "And I think Amy's working tonight, so she'll be there already. Do you think we need reservations? Mom, are you down there?"

"I don't know," Randy said. "What time?"

"Make it right away so we beat the dinner rush. We probably don't need reservations. Just call Amy to tell her we're coming. Maybe her uncle will even treat you to a free dessert when he hears your good news."

Sierra hurried halfway down the stairs and called out again. "Mom?" The light over the washing machine was turned off; the basement was silent. Sierra headed back up and met her mother at the top of the stairs.

Sharon Jensen, a slim woman with an energetic spirit like Sierra's, had raised six children. She should have been used to noise, but she greeted Sierra with a scowl. "What's all the yelling for? I was upstairs with the boys."

"Randy was accepted to Rancho! Isn't that great?"

"Congratulations, Randy!" The scowl disappeared as Mrs. Jensen patted Randy on the back. He was talking to one of their friends on the phone and responded with a smile and a nod.

"And he might receive a scholarship," Sierra said. "The letter said he'll know in three weeks."

"That's great," Mrs. Jensen said. "Good for you, Randy. I imagine your parents must be proud of you."

Randy nodded his head and went back to talking on the phone.

"I received a letter, too," Sierra said, holding up her envelope with stamps from Great Britain. She slid closer to the dining room and motioned for her mom to follow, as if she were about to share a secret. "Guess what? You'll never guess. Paul said he's coming for my graduation." She waved the letter jubilantly. "And he can stay for four days!"

"With us?" Mrs. Jensen immediately asked.

"No, with his uncle Mac. You know, at the Highland House."

"Oh, yes. Of course. Well, that's wonderful news, Sierra."

"I know. Randy and I are going out to dinner to celebrate. He's calling some people, and we're going to Amy's uncle's restaurant. That's okay with you, isn't it?"

"Who's paying?"

"We all pay our own," Sierra said. "We always do." She glanced down at the pair of baggy shorts and T-shirt she had changed into after school. "I wonder if I should change?"

Mrs. Jensen looked at Randy in his jeans, T-shirt, and

baseball cap and said, "I think you'll be okay. You could always go someplace a little more casual."

Randy hung up the phone and announced, "Okay. It's all set. Tre is going to finish making the calls so we can pick up Vicki. I think she gets off at five."

"You'd better move," Mrs. Jensen said, glancing at the clock.

"Who's driving?" Sierra asked.

"You are," Randy answered. "I'm almost out of gas, and we might need to give Tre a ride home. My truck doesn't have enough room if I have you and Vicki, too."

"Remember, Sierra," Mrs. Jensen said, "you can take only three other people in your car."

"I know, Mom. Don't worry." Only once had Sierra squeezed five friends into her old four-passenger Volkswagen Rabbit. Vicki was the one who had ended up sitting in the middle of the backseat without a seat belt. They had gone just seven blocks, but Sierra had felt guilty for days and vowed she would never hedge on her parents' seat belt rules again.

Sierra led Randy to the coat tree in the front hallway, where she pulled a small canvas bag from the outside pouch of her backpack. It was only big enough to hold her driver's license, some money, and a small container of lip gloss. But that's all she needed, since her key chain latched to the outside zipper. After Sierra tucked Paul's letter into her backpack, she and Randy slipped out the front door.

Brutus, the Jensens' overly friendly, overly slobbery, overly huge dog, watched them with his paws up on the fence that kept him confined to the backyard. He gave a deep "Woof," and Randy went over to scratch his head.

"Come on," Sierra called from the car. She had the keys in the ignition and was ready to go. "Tell the old fur ball your good news, and let's go."

Randy crawled into the car's backseat and closed the door.

"What are you doing?"

He sat in the middle of the seat with his arms spread out, playfully looking down his nose at Sierra. "I feel like being 'Prince for the Day.' Drive me around. I want to see what it feels like. It's not every day a guy gets accepted to college and practically has a music scholarship handed to him."

Sierra laughed and started the car. "As you wish, Your Highness." They both laughed.

"Just make sure you put on a seat belt. You know what my mom said."

Randy scooted to the right side. "Got it on."

"I can't believe I'm acting as your chauffeur." Sierra headed across town to the dealership Vicki's dad owned, where Vicki worked part-time in the office.

They stopped at a notoriously long stoplight, and Sierra spotted a can of soda rolling around on the car's floor. "For your enjoyment, our in-flight beverage service will now begin." She scooped up the can and handed it to Randy.

"What? No ice in a little plastic cup?"

"Sorry, sir. That's what you get for riding economy."

"Aren't you supposed to say, 'As you wish'?" Randy teased.

The light turned green, and Sierra zipped through the intersection. She pulled into a gas station and parked in front of the convenience store. Hurrying inside, she grabbed a cup, filled it with ice, popped a lid on it, and plucked a straw out of a container. She also snatched up a couple of candy bars and paid for everything—all in less than a minute. Stuffing the change into her pocket, Sierra returned to the car, where she found Randy stretched out across the backseat, with his feet propped up and sticking out the opened window.

"As you wished," Sierra said, handing him the cup of ice and the three candy bars. "Enjoy the pampering, Prince for the Day, because this is the last time you'll ever get this kind of attention from me."

Randy gladly accepted the "en route snack service" and offered Sierra first pick of the candy bars. They went on their merry way as Sierra added to her earlier comment. "But you deserve the attention today, so soak it up, buddy."

"I am." For emphasis Randy took a big slurp of his now iced beverage.

When they pulled into the entrance of Navarone's Car Dealership, Randy said, "Isn't that Vicki over there, leaving the showroom?"

Vicki had a distinctive swish to her walk. Today her silky brown hair was twisted up on the back of her head in a clip, and she carried her dark blue backpack over her shoulder.

"Looks as if we arrived just in time." Sierra honked her car's horn, and it let out a pathetic "'eep! 'eep!"

Vicki turned around and saw them. She had a concerned look on her face. Sierra pulled up next to her and called out the window, "Hey, Vicki, hop in. We're going to celebrate!"

Vicki leaned into the car and looked at Randy in the backseat. "What are you doing back there?"

"Being Prince for the Day."

"I call him 'Your Highness,'" Sierra added.

"Why?" Vicki still looked concerned.

"Because," Randy said, "I am the proud recipient of an acceptance letter from a certain university and possibly of a scholarship as well. You don't have to bow—at least not this time. You want the other half of this candy bar?"

"Really?" Vicki said, not appearing at all interested in the candy. An even deeper scowl shadowed her delicate features. "You received your letter today, too? And you were accepted for sure?"

"Yep, for sure. It's official."

"Did you get your letter, Vicki?" Sierra asked.

Vicki nodded grimly.

"And?" Sierra prodded.

"My mom called and told me it came, but she wouldn't open it. She said I should be the one to read it. I'm really nervous about this, you guys. If they say no, what am I going to do?"

"They won't say no," Sierra said. "You have to go to Rancho with us. We won't take no for an answer. We'll storm their administration building or something. I'm sure it's an acceptance letter. Let's run by your house, grab the letter, and then all go out to Degrassi's for dinner. Randy already called some other guys, and they're going to meet us there."

"I don't know. I probably shouldn't go," Vicki said. "I have so much homework."

"Homework?" Sierra said. "Who gave you homework? I don't have any. All we have to do is study for finals next week, and then it's cruise time."

"It's actually some makeup work for Mr. Ellington's

class. I'm trying to pull my final grade up, and the paper is due tomorrow."

"It's only five o'clock," Randy said. "We won't stay long. You can be home by seven. Hop in, and we'll bring you back here afterward."

Vicki hesitated before opening the front passenger door. "As long as I'm home by seven. Seven-thirty at the latest."

"Not up there," Randy said. "You have to ride back here with me."

Vicki's worry wrinkles finally gave way to a smile. "Okay, scoot over, Your Majesty."

"It's 'Highness,' not 'Majesty,' if you don't mind."

"And what exactly would the difference be?" Vicki teased.

Sierra turned her car around and headed for Vicki's house a few miles away. She felt silly being the only one in the front of the car. It was one thing to have Randy goofing off and for her to play along. But now she felt ridiculous driving through town with her two friends laughing it up in the backseat.

In one way, Sierra thought it was great that Randy wanted Vicki to sit by him. Vicki had liked Randy for a long time, but he had always played it cool with her and all the other girls. Randy's treating Vicki a little special in his lighthearted mood was probably a fun encouragement for her.

At the same time, Sierra felt a foreboding sensation. What if Vicki hadn't been accepted to Rancho? Then what? How could they celebrate Randy's good news if Vicki had bad news? A worse thought struck her. How would Sierra be able to make it though her freshman year if Vicki wasn't there? They had talked about being roommates and how they were going to make sure they had several of the same classes so they could help each other with homework. Sierra would feel awful if Vicki weren't accepted. And she knew Vicki would feel even worse.

"You know," Sierra suggested, "we could just go straight to the restaurant, since people are waiting for us. Then you could read your letter when you get home, Vicki." Sierra glanced in the rearview mirror to see if her feeble suggestion met with acceptance.

There wasn't a response at first.

"Why would I want to make this torture last even longer?" Vicki said finally.

"I was just thinking you might be able to forget about it for a little while. We could eat first and then go over to your house. If you want us to, Randy and I could stay with you when you open the letter. But only if you want us there."

"I don't know," Vicki said.

"Bring the letter with you to the restaurant, and you can open it there," Randy suggested.

"And if it's a rejection?" Vicki questioned.

"Then you'll have all of us to cheer you up," Sierra said, glancing again in the rearview mirror.

"Is that the way you would have wanted to open your letter?" Vicki asked.

Randy shrugged and met Sierra's gaze in the mirror.

"No," Sierra answered for both of them. "You're right. We should just drop you at your house and let you read it alone. Then you can come over to the restaurant to meet us and tell us the good news—because it has to be good news,

Vicki. It has to. Randy and I both received good letters today. Now it's your turn."

"One problem," Vicki said. "We just left my car at work."

"Oh, yeah."

"Then you're stuck with us," Randy said. "All for one and one for—"

Vicki leaned forward and grasped the back of Sierra's seat. "What letter did you get, Sierra? You already heard about Rancho. Did you receive another scholarship?"

"No, something better."

"Oh," Vicki said, letting go of the seat. From the tone in her voice, she seemed to understand that the letter was from Paul. Sierra had received quite a few letters from Paul over the last several months, and though she didn't always confide in Vicki what the letters said, Vicki had been keeping close track of how often he wrote and what the general tone of the correspondence was.

Vicki's interest had resulted from Sierra's request that Vicki and Amy hold her accountable for her imagination, because at one time Sierra had read more into Paul's letters than he was actually saying. With her friends keeping tabs on the relationship, Sierra's feet would stay tethered to the ground.

"You'll have to tell me about your letter," Vicki said as they pulled into the driveway of her house.

"I definitely will." Sierra set the brake and turned around to flash Vicki a smile full of clues as to how wonderful Paul's news was.

But Vicki didn't seem to notice, and her scowl had

returned. "I don't want to go in there. I don't want to read the letter."

"Come on," Randy said. "We'll go with you if you want."

"I'm sure it's an acceptance." Even as Sierra said the words, she realized she didn't have a right to say them. What if Vicki wasn't accepted? Sierra had no power over Vicki's future, any more than she had power over her own. Sierra suddenly realized they were at a major crossroads in their lives, and the words in Vicki's letter could change their friendship forever. An ominous sense of foreboding came over Sierra once more, causing her to remain silent and wait for her friend to make the next move.

"Okay, okay," Vicki finally said with a huff. "Let's get this over with. I want you both to come with me."

Reaching for her door handle, Sierra thought, *And we both want you to come with us.*

two

VICKI'S FRONT DOOR was locked. She pulled a key from her backpack and said, "I forgot that my mom said she was going grocery shopping. I'll have to leave her a note to tell her where we're going."

The three friends moved through the living room and into the kitchen at the back of the house. The afternoon sun poured in on the large, round kitchen table and seemed to spotlight the letter that was propped up against a vase of yellow snapdragons.

"There it is," Sierra said, noticing the letter before Vicki did.

Vicki picked up the envelope and stared at it. "I know this is crazy. It's not that big a deal."

"Yes, it is," Randy said. "It's a very big deal. At least I think it is."

Vicki looked at Randy. "It's just that I've never waited for a letter like this before. I've never entered a contest and waited to hear if I'd won. Nothing like that."

"So open it!" Sierra blurted out. Both Randy and Vicki

snapped their attention to Sierra as if she had invaded a private moment between them. "I mean, won't you feel better at least knowing?"

Vicki looked at the letter and sighed. "I guess." With that she slid her thumbnail under the flap and carefully opened the envelope, a fourth of an inch at a time.

Sierra was running out of patience. This was almost as bad as watching her older sister, Tawni, open Christmas presents. Tawni treated wrapping paper as if it were more precious than the gift itself and needed to be preserved from tearing or crumpling.

At last the single sheet of Rancho Corona University letterhead emerged. Vicki cautiously unfolded it. Both Sierra and Randy read along with her over her shoulder.

"Oh, brother," Sierra muttered. "All that for a letter like this."

"Well, I didn't know," Vicki said with an edge of irritation in her voice.

"What do they mean?" Randy asked. "What form is that?"

"I have no idea," Vicki said.

"It's one of the forms they send in their application packet," Sierra said. "All they're saying is that it wasn't included when you sent in the rest of your stuff, and before they can process your application, they need the form. Do you know where it is? Maybe we could fill it out right now and mail it on the way to the restaurant."

"I'll check the mailer they used to send all the material. I know right where it is in my room."

A thought flashed through Sierra's mind that it was a good thing she wasn't being asked to find anything of such importance in her room. Sierra and Vicki were opposites when it came to orderliness. They had discussed that in one of their conversations about rooming together at college. Sierra had promised Vicki she could and would adjust to Vicki's standard of neatness. After all, for years Sierra had shared a bedroom with tidiness freak Tawni, and Sierra knew how to keep up with Tawni's side of the room when she wanted to—which wasn't often.

Vicki had taken offense that Sierra had compared her to Tawni and insinuated that Vicki was also a tidiness freak. Sierra had changed the subject and silently vowed never again to compare Vicki to Tawni, although their similarities were stronger than she had realized before.

"No news is good news, right?" Sierra said brightly to Randy after Vicki headed down the hallway to her bedroom. "I mean, this isn't so bad. We can go celebrate, and Vicki will be fine."

"I don't know. I think this would be worse than bad news. This only means she has to wait longer to find out. The waiting can be more torturous than a rejection." Randy skimmed the letter one more time.

"Don't you think she'll be accepted, Randy? I mean, it's not that hard to get in."

Randy took off his baseball cap, scratched a spot on the top of his head where his short, blond hair stuck straight up, and then put his cap back on. With his voice lowered, he said, "It's not exactly the same for her as it is for you and me. Vicki doesn't have the grades you have, and she doesn't have the financial need I do. It might be harder for her to get in than we know."

Sierra plucked one of the snapdragons from a stalk in

the vase on the kitchen table and pinched the sides gently, making the "dragon" open and close its mouth. "She'll make it. She has to."

"How did you do that?" Randy said, watching Sierra's tiny finger puppet.

"You've never seen a dragon snap before?"

Randy smiled his half smile as Sierra demonstrated again.

"Cool. Let me try."

"Get your own dragon," Sierra said, playfully guarding her fragile pet.

Vicki stepped back into the kitchen with a large manila mailer in her hand.

Randy asked, "Will your mother mind if we play with her flowers?"

"If you do what?" Vicki said.

"Make puppets out of her snapdragons. Do you think she would mind?"

"No. Our backyard is overrun with them."

"Really?" Randy said. "May I pick some?"

Vicki looked up from the papers in her hand. "Are you saying you want to pick some flowers?" She looked confused.

"Yeah. Is that okay?"

"Be my guest," Vicki said, pointing to the back door.

Randy left, and Vicki said, "What's with him? He's in the strangest mood today."

Sierra shrugged and used a squeaky voice to make her tiny flower puppet talk to Vicki. "Maybe he's picking flowers for you as a sign of his undying devotion."

"Oh, right. That's it. I finally wore the right perfume

today, and Randy awoke from his coma and noticed me."

Continuing in her high-pitched puppet voice, Sierra said, "Better buy a big bottle of that perfume!"

Vicki glanced at the yellow "mouth" and smiled. "I think he's had too much caffeine today. That's his problem." She went through the papers and pulled out the missing form. "Look. I think this is it. I guess we overlooked it. It has to be signed by my parents, so there's no use spending any more time on it now. I'll leave it here with the letter and let them figure it out."

"Are you bummed?" Sierra asked, returning to her normal voice.

"A little, I guess. It's better than being turned down. But it's not what I was hoping for. Should we get going to the restaurant? I'll leave a note for my mom."

Sierra wondered if Randy was right. Maybe waiting *was* more torturous than having the bad news delivered on the spot. She decided it would help if they got out the door and on to their celebration.

Randy came in the back door but not with an armful of flowers for Vicki, as Sierra had predicted. He had one snapdragon between his fingers, and he was trying to pinch it the way Sierra had. She thought it was funny that he had gone outside to pluck his very own snapdragon. Vicki was right. He was acting strange—or at least stranger than usual.

"Do we need to give Tre a ride?" Sierra asked after Vicki had finished writing the note telling her parents where she would be.

"I'll call him," Randy said, trying to use a puppet voice and maneuver his snapdragon at the same time.

Vicki motioned for Sierra to follow her into the hallway

while Randy made his phone call. Sierra thought of how she had done the same sort of thing so she could tell her mom about Paul's letter. Sierra figured Vicki wanted to hear about the letter, too.

But Paul wasn't the guy on Vicki's mind. "Do you think Randy's acting this way because he heard what you said?"

"What? About the undying devotion?"

Vicki nodded.

"How should I know? Just go with it, girl. Maybe the whole college acceptance letter has rocketed our friend into a more serious approach to his future."

"You think so?" Vicki looked over Sierra's shoulder to see if Randy was coming. She self-consciously smoothed back her long hair.

"Who knows?" Sierra said. "But I can tell you from experience that it's sobering to realize you're about to graduate and go off to college having never dated anyone, much less kissed anyone."

Vicki looked away. "Well, you already know how I feel about that. I wish I were as inexperienced as you are."

Sierra bit her lower lip and tried not to feel a little hurt at Vicki's comment. She knew Vicki meant it in a good way. Yet Sierra still felt bad that she was so inexperienced and had never been kissed. She had been asked out only once, by a guy from school named Drake. Even though she was sure at the time that she was ready for a dating relationship, the experience hadn't turned out well.

Vicki grabbed Sierra's arm and said, "What's wrong?"

"Nothing. Why?"

"Something's bothering you. You're biting your lip."

Sierra immediately ran her tongue across the pinch she

had just made on the inside of her lower lip, as if trying to destroy the evidence.

"Ready?" Randy said, joining them from the kitchen. "Tre's going with Margo, and they're leaving his house right now."

"Sure, I'm ready," Vicki said.

"Me, too," Sierra echoed. She leaned closer to Vicki and said, "Nothing's wrong. Really." With a convincing smile, Sierra led her friends to the car and drove them to Degrassi's Italian restaurant. This time Vicki sat in the front and Randy was alone in the back.

They arrived at the same time as Warner, the band's drummer, did, and the four of them entered the restaurant.

Amy stood at the hostess station. "So what's the big event?"

"Didn't Randy tell you when he called for reservations?" Sierra asked.

Amy shook her head. Her dark bangs brushed her eyelashes as she did.

"We're celebrating!" Sierra told her. "Randy has some news. Tell her, Randy."

Randy shuffled up to the wooden podium with the same enthusiasm with which he had approached Sierra when she was on the porch swing. "I'm going to Rancho Corona. And there might be a scholarship."

Amy gave Randy a wide smile, which made her dark eyes stand out. "Good for you, Randy. That must be a relief."

Randy nodded. "What about you? Have you made any final decisions?"

Amy shook her head. "I'm still not sure I want to go away to college. Or even if I want to go to college, for that matter."

"You're coming to our graduation, aren't you?" Randy said, stepping closer. Amy had transferred from Royal Academy, the small, private Christian high school that Sierra, Vicki, and Randy attended, to a local public high school whose graduation was a week before Royal Academy's.

"Yes. And you're still coming to mine, aren't you?" She looked at Warner and added, "You're welcome, too, Warner. I'm not having a party or anything, but I was hoping all of you would come to my graduation ceremony."

"We're definitely coming," Randy said.

"You know what?" Vicki added. "We really should have a party, the bunch of us."

The wheels of Sierra's imagination began to turn. She would love to have a party; she could introduce Paul to all of her friends. "Let's!" she said. "I'm sure we can have it at my house."

Just then Tre and Margo came in. They were in the process of becoming a couple lately, and they made an interesting duo. When Tre first came to Royal, he didn't appear to speak much English, although he understood everything. The group later discovered he was quiet because he was shy. Born in Cambodia, he had lived in the Portland area since seventh grade. Tre was the strong, steady backbone of the band. He was the one who always reminded Randy they should pray before practices.

Margo's parents had been missionaries in Peru, where she was born. This was her first year back in the States, and she had gravitated toward Sierra, Randy, and their group. Royal wasn't a big school, and many of the groups were so tightly formed that it was nearly impossible to break into them. Even though they had experienced some difficult moments, the group that had been labeled "Randy and Sierra's circle" had managed to remain open enough that just about anyone could hang out with them.

Lately Margo and Tre had been spending more time together. It seemed they had a lot in common because both of them had grown up in a different culture, and English was their second language. They looked cute standing next to each other. Both of them had changed into nicer clothes before coming. About a month ago, Margo had colored her short hair a deep brown with red highlights. Sierra thought it looked good, even though Vicki had tried to convince Margo to try lightening it instead.

"How many people are coming?" Amy asked, reaching for the menus and doing a quick head count.

"I think this is it," Randy said. "Did you call anyone else, Tre?"

"Drake and Cassie," Tre answered in his subdued voice. "But they're working on the float for the parade."

Every June, Portland hosted a parade to celebrate the roses that bloomed abundantly in the rainy City of Roses. Drake's dad owned a diaper delivery service that had participated in the parade every year since the early 1960s. Drake had invited the group to help work on the float, but Sierra had forgotten about the invitation. Or maybe she had wanted to ignore it. She had a decent relationship with Drake, and he really was a nice guy. It was just that he had dated every girl on the planet—or at least every girl at Royal Academy. Sierra was still a little uncomfortable with the thought that last summer she had become one of the many on his list.

"That's right," Randy said. "Maybe we should go over there afterward."

"I have homework," Vicki said a little too quickly.

Sierra decided she would ask Vicki later how she felt about Drake and Cassie being together, since Cassie and Vicki had never gotten along. Whereas Sierra was a little uncomfortable around Drake, Vicki was very uncomfortable around Cassie. It was probably a good thing neither of them had come.

"I'll put you guys in one of the big booths in the back," Amy said, leading the group through the sparsely filled restaurant.

Warner walked beside Sierra. Any attention from him, deliberate or not, made Sierra feel queasy. She was okay with his being around all the time because enough people were in their group that he usually kept his distance from Sierra. The two of them had never found a way to be more than civil to each other. He was one of those people who just got on her nerves, even though she did have to admit he seemed to be trying harder to get along with everyone.

"So you and Randy are both going to Rancho Corona," Warner said. He was much taller than Sierra, and she could almost feel his words pelting the top of her head.

"Yes," she said without looking up at him.

"Who else is going for sure?"

"Vicki," Sierra said confidently.

"I haven't heard yet," Vicki said, turning around and taking in Warner and Sierra in one sweeping glance, "so I'm not a for-sure."

They all slid into the booth, and Sierra sat next to Randy but not near long-legged Warner, who always bumped her legs whenever he sat near her at the school lunch tables. Margo sat next to Sierra, with Tre on the other side. The nice part of the arrangement, in Sierra's opinion, was that Randy was at the center of the booth, which is where he should be for the celebration.

When everyone was nearly finished with dinner, Sierra tapped her spoon against the side of her water glass. "As you all know," she began in her best dinner-hostess voice, "our very own Randy Jenkins has received an important letter today. So we are gathered to celebrate his good news and congratulate him."

Warner lifted his water glass and, in a voice too loud for the quiet restaurant, said, "To Randy!"

The others followed Warner's lead and clinked their glasses in a toast to Randy.

Sierra smiled at her buddy and said, "And now I think the guest of honor should say a few words."

Randy shrugged. "I'm going to college."

"And how do you feel about this big adventure?" Sierra used her spoon as a pretend microphone and held it in front of Randy.

He smiled his half smile and said, "It's a day my mom said she thought would never come."

The group let out a quick burst of laughter.

Sierra cheerfully added, "Yep, only a few short months, and we're outta here!"

An awkward silence fell over the group. Reality was setting in.

Tre was the one who finally spoke for them all. "That's the end of our band."

three

"YOU GUYS STILL HAVE THIS SUMMER," Margo said, leaning forward in the booth. "You have two more bookings at The Beet, and I'm sure some others will come up."

"Just when we were getting pretty good," Warner said.

Again silence came over the small group. To Sierra it felt like the time she had stayed in her seat at the end of a movie she had particularly loved. All the fast action and bright images were replaced with a long list of names on a black screen, and yet she had sat there, absorbing the soft violin music and waiting for all the names to run to the very end. Not until she saw the rectangular logo that said "Dolby Sound" did she really believe the endearing movie was over.

Their senior year wasn't over yet. And this celebration dinner wasn't over, either.

"Anyone save room for dessert?" their waiter asked, stepping up and clearing some of the empty plates.

"Yes!" Sierra answered for them. "And would you ask Amy if she would come over to our table?"

"Certainly. Would you like to see the dessert tray?"

"I already know I want the tiramisu," Sierra said. "And don't you have some kind of cherry tea?"

"Yes, cherry almond. I'll bring you a pot of hot tea. Anyone else?"

The rest of the group placed their dessert orders, and a few minutes later Amy appeared at the table.

"When do you have your break?" Sierra asked.

"I don't know if I get one tonight. I'm here for only a couple of hours."

"Could you see if you could get just a three-minute break? I was hoping you could pull up a chair and have dessert with us."

"I'll ask," Amy said. "It's really slow tonight."

The desserts arrived, and so did Amy with a chair. "I have five minutes," she said, "so everybody talk fast. What's the plan for our graduation party?"

Sierra waited for someone to say something and then remembered she had offered her house. "We haven't decided anything yet," she said. "What do you have in mind?"

Amy's dark eyes lit up. "You know what I've always wanted to do?"

None of them ventured a guess.

"I've always wanted to make a fancy dinner. My uncle said he could get us the lobsters and anything else we needed."

Sierra remembered all too well how she and Amy had planned every detail of a lobster dinner a year ago. They were going to serve the feast to Randy and to Drake. When their dating lives didn't materialize as they'd hoped, their dinner plans had dissolved.

"Sounds good to me," Randy said.

"That would be fun," Vicki agreed.

"What if I don't like lobster?" Warner said. "Can we have something else, too? Like lasagna?"

"You don't like lobster?" Amy said.

"I don't know. I've never had it. But I know I like lasagna." Warner reminded Sierra of an oversized, spoiled kid.

"You'll like lobster," Amy promised. "We'll make it with drawn butter, and you'll love it."

"So, when are we going to have the party?" Margo asked. "The same day as graduation?"

"My family has company coming for my graduation," Vicki said. "What if we did it the night before? Sort of a pre-graduation party just for us?"

"Are you guys going on the senior getaway next weekend?" Margo asked. "I heard that not many people signed up."

"I signed up," Vicki said. "But when I found out it was three hundred and fifty dollars for only two nights on the coast, I took my name off the list. I have no idea why they made it so expensive. I sure can't afford that. And with all the other graduation expenses, my parents couldn't afford it, either."

Warner gave a full report on the senior getaway plans. A group of parents had organized a weekend on the Oregon coast for the seniors, since Royal Academy didn't have a prom or senior dinner or anything like the other schools in town. The parents had reserved two floors of rooms at a hotel on the beach. They had made it clear the guys would be on one floor and the girls on another. There would be sufficient chaperons and only two students per room. Lights-out would be at midnight. The well-meaning organizers had listed more rules on their flyer than they had listed benefits. And the highlights were supposed to be the aquarium and miniature golfing—not exactly activities at the top of the seniors' list of ways to celebrate a milestone in their lives—especially not for that price.

"I think that whole senior getaway is going to crash. Nobody has the money to go," Vicki said.

"Didn't we have to sign up by last Friday?" Sierra said. "I don't know anyone who's going."

"Then we'll do our own party," Margo said. "I think a dinner is a great idea." She flashed a smile at Tre, and Sierra wondered if this was going to turn into a date event. Sierra quickly did the math. Three "natural" matched-up couples were at the table right now. The only unmatched ones were Sierra and Warner. Her skin began to feel clammy at the thought. Then she remembered Paul was coming and laughed aloud.

"What?" Amy asked.

"Nothing. Nothing. Let's plan the party. Whatever you guys want is fine with me, as long as it's after the 12th."

"I have to get back to work," Amy said. "I'll call you later tonight, Sierra, and we can plan everything, okay?"

"Great," Sierra said. Her heart was soaring at the thought of Paul's being at a fancy dinner and fun party with her friends. He would love them, and they would love him. The thought was even more fanciful because her mom was the only one who knew about Paul's coming. It was kind of sweet to have a secret with just her mom.

Never being great at keeping secrets, Sierra told Vicki

her news on their way back to the dealership. Randy had gotten a ride with Tre and Margo because they were going to check on Drake and the parade preparations. As soon as Sierra had Vicki in the car, she told her what Paul had said in his letter.

Vicki squealed and grabbed Sierra's arm in her excitement for her friend. "I can't believe you didn't tell me right away!"

"So much happened so fast."

"That is really great news, Sierra! I'm so happy for you. What else did he say?"

"I don't know. I didn't even finish reading the letter. I only read the first few paragraphs. Then Randy showed up, and his news superseded my news. Then we went to pick you up, and we were all wondering about your letter—"

"My letter," Vicki said, interrupting Sierra and suddenly sobering. "It's awful not to know if I'm going to Rancho now that Randy has been accepted. And you too. I thought about it at dinner when Tre was talking about the band breaking up. I got really depressed. We need to make our graduation party something special, as Amy was saying."

"I agree," Sierra said.

"And you know what else I realized at dinner?" Vicki said. "Our Monday afternoons at Mama Bear's are going to be over, too."

For several months now, Sierra, Amy, and Vicki had met every Monday afternoon at four o'clock at Mama Bear's Bakery for what Amy called "soul cleansing." Sierra thought Amy's term was a little too cosmic for what they talked about. To Sierra, Monday afternoons with her two friends meant an uninterrupted time of deep, honest conversation in a quiet corner with a pot of tea and a shared cinnamon roll. Amy, Vicki, and Sierra hadn't always been on peaceful terms. So when the three of them forged this unlikely friendship triangle, they all felt a common desire to do whatever it took to hold on to the fragile bonds.

When they had visited colleges in the spring, Amy had made it clear she didn't want to attend a Christian school. That was because ever since her parents had divorced last fall, she had questioned her beliefs in God and the church. Why would she want to go to a place that taught stuff she wasn't sure was right?

Sierra thought Amy's problem was that she held too much inside. Even though she called their time a "soul cleansing," she was the one who opened up the least. She listened, though—and asked questions. Vicki and Sierra had learned over the past few months that love is patient, especially when a friend is hurting and needs someone to be there, someone who genuinely loves her and isn't bent on forcing change before she is ready.

Often the Monday afternoons had been the highlight of Sierra's week—especially during the weeks she didn't receive a letter from Paul. She had two friends who would listen to her talk at length about whatever was on her mind, and Sierra had learned she could trust Vicki and Amy to keep confidences. If it was a soul cleansing for Amy, their time together was a fragrant sanctuary for Sierra.

"You know what I'll miss the most?" Vicki said as Sierra came to a stoplight. "I'll miss the way I always feel when I wake up on Monday mornings. I used to hate to get up. Then, when we started to meet, I'd hop out of bed and think about what to wear and how the day couldn't go fast enough before we could get together."

Sierra smiled. The light changed, and she pulled into the intersection and began to make a left turn, sanctioned by the green arrow overhead. The terrible sound of squealing brakes came barreling toward them, and Vicki screamed. A pickup truck swerved to miss Sierra's car and stopped dead center in the intersection. All the other cars shrieked to a halt. Miraculously, no one was hit.

It appeared the driver of the pickup had decided to run the yellow light and then had changed his mind at the last minute but couldn't stop his vehicle. Everyone sat frozen in their cars, looking at each other. The pickup backed up slowly. The guy in the car behind Sierra honked his horn. The turn signal was now yellow, so she quickly put the car in gear and motored through the mess and onto the street that led to the dealership.

"Look at me," Vicki said, holding out her hand. "I'm shaking. How can you be so calm? We could have been killed, Sierra. A few more feet and that pickup would have smashed us."

"I know," Sierra said quietly. She drove with extra caution to the dealership and pulled into the side area where Vicki's car was still parked. Then Sierra turned off the engine, and the two sobered friends sat silently for a few minutes.

"How do people make it through life if they don't know for sure they're going to heaven when they die?" Vicki asked. She turned in her seat and faced Sierra. "I mean, stuff like that happens to everyone, doesn't it? Near brushes with disaster and split seconds where only a few feet mean the difference between life and death."

Sierra nodded, still shaken inside.

"If I didn't know for sure I was saved and that the instant I die I'll be in heaven, I think an experience like we just had would completely terrify me. I'd be traumatized for life."

"I know," Sierra said. "It's moments like this that I get this sick feeling inside when I think about friends like Amy who say they're uninterested in settling their relationships with God."

Vicki and Sierra exchanged glances of painful agreement.

"Let's talk to her on Monday," Vicki said. "We can say it in a way that she'll listen to us. I know we can."

Sierra agreed.

After making sure Vicki got safely into her house, Sierra cautiously drove home. Amy called about ten minutes after Sierra was in her room. Sierra's dad brought the cordless phone to her and asked her to return it downstairs when she was finished with her conversation because the batteries were running low.

"Amy?" Sierra said.

"Hi. I asked my uncle about the lobsters, and he said he would give me a price on them tomorrow. I thought if everyone chipped in, it wouldn't be so much. For the salad and dessert, I asked him if we could buy them from the restaurant, too. Then all we would have to do is boil the lobsters and get some bread and maybe a vegetable. What do you think?"

Sierra moved some clothes and papers from the overstuffed chair by her open window and said, "Sounds great. I haven't talked to my parents yet. Why don't I call you back after I ask them? How many people do you think we'll have?"

"Around ten to twelve is what I told my uncle."

"Guess who one of those ten to twelve will be," Sierra said, smiling mischievously into the receiver.

"Wes?" Amy guessed.

"No; guess again."

"I don't know."

"It's someone you would never guess."

"Not Nathan!" Amy said in a panic. "Randy wouldn't invite him, would he? I know they've become good friends from The Beet, but Randy knows how awkward that would be for me, doesn't he?"

"Don't worry," Sierra said, assuring Amy that her old boyfriend wouldn't be on the guest list. "It's not Nathan. But it is a guy."

Amy sounded frustrated as she said, "Come on, Sierra, just tell me."

Sierra smiled and said the one name that was often on her lips in silent prayer. The name of the guy who had written to her for almost a year. The name she thought about daily but rarely spoke aloud. "Paul."

four

"PAUL?" AMY REPEATED. "He's coming to your gradua-tion?"

"Yes. I just received the letter today. He arrives on the 12th, and he'll be here for four days."

"Oh, Sierra, you must be in heaven!"

Amy's choice of words struck an all-too-recent memory, and Sierra abruptly changed topics in response to the knot she felt in her stomach. "I want to ask you something, Amy, and I don't want you to get upset."

"Okay. Sure." Amy could change her moods faster than anyone Sierra had ever known. At the moment Amy was in a good mood, which was why Sierra forged ahead.

"When I was taking Vicki home, we were nearly hit by a pickup truck. It made us both start thinking about dying and how we know we're going to heaven. And, Amy, I know we agreed not to talk about this stuff with you, but I have to tell you, it really scared me to think you might not know you're going to heaven because you say you're undecided about God."

Silence was the only response on the other end of the line.

"Amy, don't be mad. And don't hang up. I just had to say that because I really, really care. Amy, I love you, and I don't want you to go to hell."

A thunderous "Click!" sounded in Sierra's ear, followed by the lonely whine of the dial tone.

What have I done? Sierra dropped her head into her hands and reviewed her last few sentences. *Why did I say it that way? Why didn't I wait until Monday, as Vicki suggested, and let Vicki do the talking? Why, oh why do I blast out my thoughts and feelings like that?*

Before Sierra could thoroughly beat herself up, the phone rang in her lap. She grabbed it, pushed the button, and answered with, "I'm sorry. I shouldn't have said it that way."

The party on the other end didn't respond. Then it dawned on Sierra that the caller might be someone other than Amy.

"Amy?" she ventured.

"Sierra?" the male voice answered.

"Yes."

Deep laughter came to her over the receiver. She had no idea who was on the other end. "I take it you and Amy are having another go-round."

"Something like that," Sierra said cautiously, trying to place the voice and wondering why he said "go-round."

"How are things for you, other than with Amy?"

"Pretty good," she said slowly. "And with you?" She was hoping for a clue of any kind.

The phone line began to crackle, and the guy's answer

was muffled and sounded too far away for Sierra to decipher.

Oh no, the batteries are going! Sierra thought in a panic. "Can you call back?" she shouted into the phone. "If you can hear me, I'm going to hang up, and you'll need to call back because this phone is going dead."

Suddenly, his voice was clear and loud once more. "Are you there?"

"Yes, but I have to get to a different phone. The batteries are going dead on this one. Can you just call back?"

"Sure."

The phone line began to crackle again, and Sierra hung up. She headed downstairs, wondering who this caller could be. Then the realization struck her with such a "boom" that she screamed as she thudded down the last four stairs and skidded on the hardwood floor of the entryway in her stocking feet.

Mr. Jensen came running from the living room with the remote-control switch in his hand. "What is it?"

Sierra held out the dead phone. "It's Paul! He just called, and I hung up on him."

Mrs. Jensen appeared from the living room, too, and said, "He'll call back, won't he?"

The phone rang again, and Sierra pushed the button, but the phone kept ringing. Mr. Jensen took off for the phone in the den, and Sierra followed, hot on his heels. "Don't you dare!" she called out to her dad.

He grabbed the phone before Sierra could pull it from his grasp. Sierra's dad had many fine qualities, but he had one serious, incurable flaw. He harassed any guy who called for his daughters. Now that Tawni had moved out, Mr.

Jensen had doubled his teasing of Sierra's guy friends. Poor Paul! He was calling from Scotland and wouldn't understand her dad's demented hobby. Paul might be the one to hang up this time.

"Is this Paul?" Sierra heard her dad say when he answered the phone. She tried to pry the phone from his ear, but he was using both hands to hold it firmly in place.

"This is Mr. Jensen, Paul. I'd like to know exactly what your intentions are toward my daughter."

"Daddy!" Sierra gritted out through clenched teeth. "Don't do this! Can't you just take up golf like a normal father?"

Her dad's eyebrows raised in seeming approval as he listened to Paul's answer. "In that case, I'll let you talk directly to her. That is, if she still wants to talk to you."

Sierra put one hand on her hip and held out her other hand to receive the phone.

"Or, actually," Mr. Jensen went on, dragging out the agonizing seconds for Sierra, "I should say, if you still want to talk to her. She dyed her hair blue yesterday and had all her teeth pulled. But the rash on her face is beginning to clear up."

"Dad!"

He laughed at whatever Paul's comment was. "Here she is. You take care, Paul. Pleasure talking with you."

Mr. Jensen offered Sierra the phone. She put her hand over the receiver and waited for him to close the door behind him as he left.

"Hi," she said, trying to sound calm. "I'd apologize for my dad, but there's no excuse for him when he gets like that."

"I told him you looked good in blue, so the hair shouldn't be a problem."

Sierra laughed.

"It's good to hear your laugh, little Daffodil Queen," Paul said, his voice sounding clear and as close as if he were standing right beside her. Sierra closed her eyes and let his tender nickname for her melt into her heart.

"It's really good to hear your voice," Sierra echoed. She felt as if she might start to cry and pursed her lips together. Poor Paul had already paid for two phone calls and had endured an interview with her dad. The last thing he needed was to listen to her blubbering for sheer joy. "I got your letter today," she said, forcing herself to be even-keeled.

"Good. So you know I was able to make arrangements to come on the 12th. Is it okay with you if I come to your graduation?"

"Yes, of course. I'd love to have you come. My friends and I are planning a party. Maybe a dinner. It will probably be here at my house. I'm so glad you're coming."

"Now, you are being honest with me, aren't you? I'm not crashing your party or any other plans with your friends?"

"No, not at all! Having you here will be the best part of my whole graduation."

Paul hesitated.

Sierra bit her lower lip, wondering if she had said too much. Had she sounded too eager? Too forceful? From the beginning, Paul had let her know that he wanted to take their relationship nice and slow. Never once had he signed his letters with the word "Love." Never once had he written anything that indicated they were more than friends. Sierra was the one who kept running ahead, assuming and making more of the relationship than was actually there. She had tried so hard to pull back, go slowly, and be realistic. Had she ruined everything now?

"You know what?" Paul replied slowly. "Seeing you again will be the best part of my trip home."

Sierra's heart soared. This wasn't the kind of response she expected to hear from Paul. Suddenly, she felt shy, which was out of character for her. Her mind raced with all the possibilities. What was he thinking? Was he ready to move forward in their relationship?

"I have a lot of things I'm eager to talk to you about, Sierra," Paul continued. "It will be great to finally see you again and say those things face-to-face."

"Uh-huh" was the only sound that came from Sierra's lips. She chided herself and scrambled to find something more intelligent to say.

Paul went on. "Remember that café we went to last year?"

"Yes. Carla's." Sierra spilled out the words quickly. "Of course I remember."

"Good. I'm hoping you remember how to get there. I thought it would be nice to stop in for a mug of good Northwest coffee. I know this is pathetic, but I've even had dreams about mocha lattes like I used to get at a little drive-through place. I seem to remember Carla's Café had pretty good coffee, too."

"Oh," Sierra said. Another brilliant response. She couldn't help but feel her emotions plummet when he said he had been dreaming about coffee at Carla's. Sierra had dreams about the same place, only in *her* dreams she and Paul were at the same table by the window where they had sat a year ago. This time, instead of his teasing her because he had heard she had a crush on him, Paul was holding her hand and confessing his love for her.

"What did you think of the rest of my letter?" Paul asked.

"To tell you the truth—" Sierra began.

She was going to confess to not having had a chance to read the rest of his letter, but Paul interrupted her and said, "Of course you'll tell me the truth. That's what you do best. You're a proclaimer, Sierra. You proclaim the truth. That's one of the things I wanted to tell you face-to-face, but I guess I'll say it now. I know I've given you a hard time in the past about being zealous. Lately I've come to appreciate that quality in you, and I wanted to tell you."

"Thanks." All Sierra could think at the moment was how her truth speaking might have just "proclaimed" Amy out of her life for good. But all she said to Paul was, "I appreciate your encouragement."

"I'm the one who appreciates your encouragement," Paul said. "Your letters have meant so much to me this year. So have all the verses you sent me, and all the prayers I know you've prayed for me. You'll never know what a difference you've made in my life. I'm serious, Sierra. I really think God used you in a big way to turn my life around, and that's why I wrote the poem for you that I put at the end of the letter. It's the first poem I've written just for you."

He paused again. All she could say was, "Thanks, Paul." It would be too awkward to mention she hadn't read the whole letter now.

"I was going to wait and read it to you when I saw you, but I decided to go ahead and send it. Some things are easier to say on paper than in person."

"That's true," Sierra said.

"Well, I guess I'd better hang up or I won't have enough money left to buy either of us a cup of coffee by the time we get to Carla's."

Sierra quickly tried to think of what she should ask him before he hung up. "Do you need a ride from the airport?"

"No, Uncle Mac is picking me up."

"What time do you get in?"

"Around ten o'clock."

"In the morning on the 12th?" Sierra asked hopefully.

"No, ten at night."

"Well, I'm just glad you're coming. It will be so good to see you again and finally talk in person." Sierra tried hard to contain her feelings. She wanted to blurt out crazy words like, "I love you, Paul Mackenzie! I can't wait to throw my arms around you and smell that pine-tree fresh aftershave you wear."

Fortunately for both of them, she kept her wild thoughts to herself.

"I'll give you a call from the Highland House when I get in. Or maybe it'll be the morning of the 13th if I arrive too late. It's less than a week and a half away."

"I know," Sierra said in a voice that revealed her eager heart. "I'll be counting the days."

After a tiny pause, Paul said just before hanging up, "So will I, Daffodil Queen."

five

SIERRA FELT as if all the air had been sucked from the room when she heard the click on Paul's end of the line. She was still standing in the middle of the den where she had taken the phone from her dad. The whole time she and Paul had talked, Sierra hadn't moved. She hadn't even thought of sitting down. It was as if she had been suspended in time and space. Maybe if she closed her eyes tightly enough, Paul's voice would come back over the dead line of the phone she still held to her ear. But the only sound she heard was the wail of the dial tone.

As though pulling herself out of a deep dream and back to the dawn of a new day, Sierra opened her eyes slowly and forced herself to return the phone to its cradle. She wanted to remember every word, every nuance.

The poem! My poem! She hurried from the den and grabbed her backpack from the coat tree in the entryway.

"Is everything all set with Paul's trip?" Mrs. Jensen asked, stepping into the entryway.

"Yes. He'll be here the night of the 12th, after ten

o'clock." Sierra reached into the backpack and pulled out Paul's letter. "So that ruins our plans for the dinner party."

"Our plans for the dinner party?" Mrs. Jensen questioned.

"Oh. I didn't talk to you about it yet. We were all talking about having a dinner party for graduation. Amy said she could get lobsters." As soon as she mentioned Amy, Sierra remembered the way her friend had hung up on her twenty minutes ago. She needed to call Amy back. And she needed to talk over the dinner party plans with her mom. But all she wanted to do was flee to her room, where she could read Paul's letter and take into her heart the poem he had written for her alone.

"And you wanted to have the party here?" Mrs. Jensen asked.

"Yes, if that's okay. But now I don't know when to have it. We thought the day before graduation, but Paul won't be here in time, and I really want him at the party."

"It could be just as special with your friends and without Paul," Mrs. Jensen said.

An image flashed into Sierra's mind of her being paired with Warner, and she said, "No, believe me, Mom, it won't be the same. I only want to have it when Paul's here."

They stood in the hallway, discussing options, but none seemed to work.

Mr. Jensen, who could hear them talking from the living room, called out, "Why don't you have it the night of graduation? We can have the family over the night before. Then they can go home right after graduation, and you can have your friends over. Isn't the ceremony at two? That'll give you plenty of time for a fancy dinner."

"What about the other kids, Howard? Won't they have family parties on graduation day?"

"Amy doesn't," Sierra said. "Her graduation is this weekend. And Randy hasn't said anything about a lot of company. It didn't sound good for Vicki, but maybe we could work something out."

"I suppose it's worth a try," Mrs. Jensen said. "Let me know as soon as you find out for sure, and I'll make the calls to our family."

Sierra went back to the den and took the letter with her. Eventually she would get to it, but first she had some calls to make. Sierra dialed Amy's number and waited for her to pick it up, not exactly sure what to say. On the sixth ring, Amy answered.

"It's me. I'm sorry. Can we talk?"

"Why do you do this, Sierra? Things are going nice and smooth in our friendship, and then you have to say something that puts us both on edge."

"I'm not sorry for what I said, just the way I said it. I could have said it a lot better."

"Oh, really?"

"Can we talk about something else for a minute? It's the dinner party at my house. Paul doesn't get in until late on the night of the 12th. My dad suggested we have the party on Friday night, after the graduation ceremony, which is at two o'clock. What do you think?"

"I think it's amazing the way you can switch moods so fast."

"Me switch moods? You're the one who switches moods all the time, Amy."

"But I don't go around telling you you're going to hell

and then call back and say, 'By the way, can you bring the lobsters over Friday?'"

Sierra sighed. "Did it really sound like that, Amy? I'm sorry. Can we put the whole heaven and hell topic to the side until our Monday get-together? I want to talk about it more and tell you why I feel strongly about it, but I think it would be better with Vicki there, too."

"Why? So you can gang up on me?"

"No, of course not."

"You and Vicki have no idea what I believe or where I am in my relationship with God."

"Exactly," Sierra said. "And that's why I want to talk about it. I always let you talk about the things that are important to you; now I think it's only fair you let me talk about what's important to me."

Amy paused, then said, "Okay, you're right. We can talk Monday. And yes, I think next Friday would be a good night for the dinner, mostly because I already have the night off."

"Good," Sierra said. "Great, actually. I'm going to call everyone else to see if we can set it up for then."

"Okay. I'll talk to you later."

Sierra called Vicki and Randy and told them the plan. They both said they would try to convince their parents to have their family parties the night before like Sierra's family. Neither of them expected many relatives to come, so it sounded like a good possibility. Randy agreed to call the guys in the band with the same information, and Vicki said she would call Margo and a couple of other girls they were thinking of inviting.

That settled, Sierra eagerly headed for her room, where

she could read the rest of Paul's letter without being interrupted. Passing the living room, she stopped in the doorway to watch the end of a funny commercial with her parents. Then she told them the plans were working out. Mrs. Jensen said she would make the arrangements tomorrow and told Sierra to relax about everything.

"This is your graduation, honey. We want you to have a memorable time and enjoy the occasion with both your friends and your family."

On impulse, Sierra dashed over to the couch and gave her mom and dad a big hug. "You guys are the best parents in the world. Did you know that?"

Her startled parents gave each other looks of pleased surprise.

Mr. Jensen said, "Would you mind convincing Gavin of that? He's still upset that we won't let him go to the Burnside Skate Park on Saturday with his friends from school."

"He wants to go there?" Sierra said. "He's too young. Almost all the skaters there are in high school and much more experienced on skateboards than Gavin. They would run over him. Besides, the Rose Parade is this Saturday. Downtown will be jam-packed with people."

"That's right," Mrs. Jensen said. "We should go to the parade—as a family."

"I have to work," Sierra said. "And I can't take time off because Mrs. Kraus already gave me the next weekend off for graduation."

"We still might go," Mrs. Jensen said. "It could be a nice outing for Granna Mae if the weather is clear."

"I'm going to bed," Sierra said. "Thanks again for adjusting the family plans for me."

"Flexibility is a sign of good mental health," Sierra's dad said.

Sierra looked to her mom for an explanation.

"He's been reading those pamphlets the doctor gave us last week at Granna Mae's checkup."

Sierra nodded her understanding and headed upstairs with Paul's letter in hand. Sierra's grandmother had an undiagnosed condition that had grown worse over the last few years. She was sometimes as normal and clear thinking as ever, but then, without warning, she would blip into another dimension and become lost and confused. Sierra and her family had moved here a year and a half ago to be with Granna Mae in her large Victorian house and to care for her. The Jensen family adored Granna Mae and was understanding and considerate of her difficulties most of the time. But every now and then watching her became exhausting, especially for Sierra's mom, who had to do most of the overseeing.

Alone in the cluttered haven of her beloved bedroom, Sierra went directly to the overstuffed chair by the window. She pulled back the sheer curtains and pushed the chipped wooden window frame all the way up. She had to use a board to keep it open. The soothing night breezes invited themselves in, ruffling the sheers. Two birds in the huge cedar tree began a happy concert of night songs. The sky, painted a hazy periwinkle blue in the late dusk, showed off its prized jewel, a crescent-shaped ivory moon hanging above the cedar tree.

Sierra drew in a deep breath, filling her lungs with the sweet fragrance of late spring and filling her heart with a prayer of thankfulness to God for all the beauty He had placed in her life. If she was grateful to her earthly parents for their love and understanding, she was even more grateful to her heavenly Father for His lovingkindness to her.

Feeling like celebrating, Sierra lit a candle she had received as a birthday present from Vicki months ago. Since Vicki knew Sierra liked daffodils, the candle was in the shape of a bright yellow daffodil blossom. It rested on a saucer with the trumpet part of the flower facing up and the wick in the middle of the trumpet.

Sierra placed the lit daffodil candle on her dresser. Gazing at her reflection in the mirror, she fussed a little with her unruly hair. She rummaged for some lip gloss and applied it to the cracked skin on the right corner of her mouth. Then she whispered another prayer of thanks to God for protecting her and Vicki from the near-collision with the pickup.

Since the night was still young, Sierra decided to treat herself to something she had done only a few times because it took so long. She decided she would read Paul's letter and then go back and read all the letters he had ever written to her. She kept them in the large bottom drawer of her dresser in an old hatbox she had found at Christmastime in the attic. Her dad had sent her there in search of more Christmas lights, and when she had found the old silver and gray box, she had fallen in love with it. A handful of yellowed tissue paper was stuffed into the box, but the hat Granna Mae had once stored there was long gone.

Pulling open the bottom drawer, Sierra extracted the hatbox and settled herself by the window for a long visit with Paul's precious words on a glorious spring evening.

The new letter came first. She skimmed the part she had already read that afternoon about his plans to come on the 12th and then read on.

As I've been preparing to leave here, I've been surprised at how much my life and my heart have changed since I arrived on a blustery day last June. I guess I blew into Edinburgh with about the same level of cool indifference to God as the storm that came in with me. The seasons changed, and so did I. I actually feel I've lived several lifetimes in the twelve months I've been here. Several seasons, at least.

For the first time in my life, I truly know God. Is that too bold to declare? It's what I feel. He's no longer just all around me or visible in the lives of people like my dad and my grandfather. He is alive in me. My life is no longer mine to control. I'm hidden inside His eternal life, and for as long as I walk this earth, the Good Shepherd will direct me.

You know that image of Christ's being the Good Shepherd, don't you? It's in John 10. Lately that chapter has become very real to me, especially the parts, "…he calls his own sheep by name," and "I am the door of the sheep…. If anyone enters by Me, he will be saved, and will go in and out and find pasture." I've finally entered through that door, and I'm finding pasture, as the verse says.

Scotland has been an easy place to learn about sheep and pastures. I'm more aware than ever how clueless sheep can be. They follow the rest of the flock instead of following the shepherd. More than once I've seen how the failure of a lamb to follow the shepherd's directions has ended in the damage and sometimes destruction of that lamb, especially when the storms come in.

Why am I telling you all this? Because I am a sheep, and for far too long I followed the mindless bleating and frantic scurrying of the other sheep. But I have heard my Shepherd's voice, as He has called me patiently to Himself, and I have come.

God has answered all your prayers, Sierra. There is no turning back for me now. How can I ever thank you for persistently proclaiming the truth to me, even when I didn't want to hear it? How can I tell you how much your prayers have meant to me? You never gave up on me, even when I gave you no reason to keep praying. You are one of His sheep, Sierra—a very special one. Your heart is wise beyond your years. You stood by what you believed and boldly proclaimed the truth. Thank you.

Sierra stopped reading only long enough to bounce up for a tissue. Her tears were dripping on the letter, causing the black ink to smear slightly. She couldn't believe Paul was saying all these things to her. In his previous letters, he had never been this transparent.

Blowing her nose and tossing the tissue onto the floor, Sierra read on. Two more onionskin pages of Paul's bold writing remained for her to take into her heart.

six

SIERRA CONTINUED to read Paul's letter at the top of the next page.

I've done a lot of thinking and praying about what the Shepherd wants me to do when I leave here. The first thing I believe He wants me to do is apologize to some people in Portland from school last year. I also want to tell them what God has done and how He's changed me. That's part of the reason I wanted to come to Portland before going home.

I also need to have a serious talk with my parents to set a few things right there. It sure is easier to mess things up than to put them back in order. I considered writing my parents or calling them but then decided it would be best if I talked to them in person. I need to ask their forgiveness for a couple of things, too.

I know God has forgiven me for the past, but He wasn't the only one I wronged, so I need to do whatever I can to make it right with several people. Please pray for me about this. It's not going to be easy, but I know that's the next step.

I've made a serious commitment to the Lord regarding the

future, and I believe He's invited me to go into the ministry in some form or other. I don't know if it's to be a pastor, a missionary, a full-time Christian service worker like my uncle Mac, or what. All I know is that this is the next step for me, and I'm excited about moving forward. So please pray for me as you've never prayed before!

Before I close, I wanted to send you this poem. I wrote it for you, Sierra, after a hike I took in the Highlands a few weeks ago. As I opened the gate at the end of the trail and walked through the pasture, I knew it would probably be my last hike in these hills I've come to love.

You should have seen all the new spring lambs. They were so small, huddled next to the ewes. The sight reminded me of how small I felt and how eager I was to stay close to Jesus, my Good Shepherd. It had only been two days since God and I had talked everything out and I had sensed His calling me into the ministry. Perhaps someday I'll tell you how that all happened.

But what prompted this poem was a sight I'll never forget. Past the meadow, as I climbed higher, I came to a rocky area that was covered with wild heather. I don't care much for heather. It's prickly to the touch, and the colors are so pale. There, in the middle of all this heather, next to a gray rock, stood one brilliant yellow daffodil, lifting its trumpet to the heavens. I stopped, amazed at how that single daffodil could change the dreariness of an entire hillside.

That's when I thought of you, Daffodil Queen. You stand out just like that brilliant yellow flower, defying all that is common. Your words are like the bold blasting of a trumpet across a world of pale, prickly lives. And you know what? I said it the day I met you, and I'll say it again: Don't ever change, Sierra.

With affection,
Paul

Sierra had to reach for the tissues again before she could read the poem. Her eyes were blurring, her nose was dripping, and her heart was melting.

Taking a deep breath, she glanced at the flickering light of the daffodil candle on her dresser and wished with all her heart she had read Paul's letter before he had called. She would have said ever so much more to him.

And he had signed the letter, "With affection." He had never written that before.

Tossing two more used tissues onto the floor, Sierra reached over and turned on the lamp beside the chair. It had grown dark outside. The birds had subdued their concert, and the streetlight was now competing with the moonlight. Sierra had never felt like this before in her life. No one had ever said words to her as Paul just had. No one had ever made her believe she was okay just the way she was—better than okay: She was special, unique, and appreciated.

"'With affection,'" she repeated. "That is so perfect."

Sierra held the last page with the poem in her lap. She almost didn't want to read it. *What if I don't like it? What if it's really, really mushy? Am I ready to let my feelings for Paul out of the prison I've held them captive in for so long? My life is much less complicated when I don't let my emotions run wild and cause all kinds of destruction. What happens once they're let loose?*

Then she realized she was already a changed woman. Just the few affectionate lines Paul had written were enough to alter her opinion of herself. Those words were etched in her memory. She had to read the poem. She had to devour every word Paul had written, especially when those words were a poem written for her alone.

The title was simply "Daffodil."

Bold you stand beside your Rock
    Proclaiming Truth;
Eternal, unchanging,
    To a thorny crowd,
Resistant, proud
    Who mock your words.
Still you stand firm beside the Rock
    Trumpeting Truth;
You fearless, Golden Daffodil.
    One from the crowd,
Resistant, proud,
    Took your words
Into his heart
    And never
Will he be the same.
    So stand bold and firm,
Sweet Daffodil.
    Surprise the world as only you can.

Sierra reread the poem, taking in Paul's words and noting that he called her "Sweet Daffodil." A P.S. was added at the bottom of the page:

I should tell you that the morning before I took that inspirational walk I had been reading in Philippians. Read chapter 1, verses 19— 21 when you have a chance. It reminded me of you. I wrote those verses out on a card that I now carry in my wallet. I guess you could say I've taken them on as my life verses. See you soon.
    Paul

Sierra leaned back in the chair and looked out the window into the soft June night. For a long time she just sat there, staring, with Paul's letter in her lap. All his past letters went unread. In ten days she would look into Paul's blue-gray eyes and hear his deep voice. Would he take her in his arms and draw her close to his heart in a tight hug? What would he think when he saw her? She had changed a lot in the year since they had last seen each other. At least, she thought she had changed. It made her realize how young and inexperienced she had been when she first met him.

The memory brought a smile to her lips. They had met at a phone booth—not just any phone booth, but one at the Heathrow Airport in London. She was waiting to use the phone, and Paul had borrowed some change from her to complete his call.

How funny! Sierra thought. *He was calling his old girlfriend. I actually gave him money to call Jalene! Hey, I don't think he ever paid me back. I'll have to remind him when I see him…in only ten days.*

Sierra was still floating through her private dreamland the next day at school. It seemed pointless to even attend classes, since the teachers had "senioritis" even worse than the students did. In her first class they watched a video; second period was open study for the final on Thursday; and since the weather was nice, her fourth-period teacher took them outside and let everyone sit around and talk.

By the end of the day, Sierra had accomplished nothing. She had learned nothing new. She hadn't studied a pinch. But she had crafted wonderfully sweet plans for the few days she and Paul would have together. In addition to the lobster dinner and graduation ceremony, her mental list included a picnic at Multnomah Falls; a dinner cruise on the Willamette River; an afternoon browsing through books together at Powell's Bookstore downtown; a video night at home with the family, eating Mrs. Jensen's famous caramel corn; a hike up to Pittock Mansion in the West Portland Hills; and maybe a concert or play, depending on what was available downtown. If nothing there interested them, they could always tour the art museums. And of course they would go to Carla's Café at least once.

Sierra continued to spin her plans as the week went on. She made a list and checked into each activity, calling for showtimes, prices on dinner cruises, and hours when Powell's was open. The list turned into a notebook of collected information. She even picked up a few brochures at a restaurant that advertised other activities she hadn't thought of, such as the antique stores in Sellwood and a visit to Haystack Rock on the coast at Cannon Beach. This was a good time of year for windsurfing up in the Columbia Gorge. They could each rent a Jet Ski at a landing on the Vancouver side of the Columbia River. And there was also a restored steam engine train up in Battle Ground that they could ride through a park, which might be fun for their picnic day.

Her notebook soon turned into an organized, detailed travel portfolio of the Portland area. If only Sierra could have turned it in for a grade, she would have loved to accept that grade for one of her finals.

As it was, she barely received an A- on one and two Bs on the others. It was one of the first times in her high school career that she had received anything below an A on a final. When one of her teachers questioned her, Sierra

answered that the motivation wasn't there. She had worked
for so many years to have good enough grades to make it
into any college she wanted, and now she had been accepted
at Rancho Corona, had three academic scholarships, and it
was the very end of school. What she didn't tell her teacher
was that her mind couldn't hold another scholastic detail
because it was too full of important information—information such as what time the antique stores in Sellwood closed
on Saturday and what movies were playing at what times at
the Lloyd Center.

When Sierra, Vicki, and Amy met for their Monday
afternoon teatime, Sierra brought her notebook and spread
it out on the table, asking her friends' opinions about the
two different boats that offered dinner cruises on the
Willamette.

Vicki laughed. She didn't seem to be able to stop.

Sierra felt humiliated and indignant. "I don't see why
you think this is so funny."

"You tend to do things to the extreme," Vicki said, trying to pull a straight face. "When did you have time to do all
this, Sierra? You worked two afternoons last week and all
day Saturday, and we were at Amy's graduation on Friday.
Plus it was finals week!"

"I had time."

"We always find the time to do the things we love," Amy
said, coming to Sierra's defense. "I think it's great. If you
wanted to, you could sell this to a tour company or something. You could start a side business, researching and
planning private sightseeing trips for people who come here
on vacation."

Sierra appreciated Amy's attempt to support her efforts,

but she hadn't expected either reaction from her friends. "Maybe you guys don't understand," she said, closing her notebook and setting it aside. "This is Paul I'm talking about. I haven't seen him in a year. He's coming for only four days. I've never done anything with him. I don't know what he might like to do while he's here. His only hobby in Scotland was hiking. He might want to hike here, or he might be sick of hiking and just want to go to the movies. I need to be prepared for anything. I don't want to spend half of our four days sitting around trying to decide what to do."

Vicki's expression cleared to tender seriousness. "You're right. You're exactly right. I think you did the best thing you could have, considering the circumstances. It'll really help you both to make the most of the time." With a sparkle in her eyes, she added, "Just don't pull out the notebook the minute he walks in the door. It might scare him off."

"Don't worry," Sierra said. "This information is for my benefit. Paul doesn't even know I have the notebook." Until Vicki had said that, Sierra hadn't thought of her elaborate planning as something that would overwhelm Paul. Secretly, she was glad Vicki had mentioned her concern, or most likely Sierra would have pulled it out the first day and coaxed Paul to go through it with her to plan their time.

"I guess I need to relax a little about this, huh?" Sierra said, sipping her cup of peppermint tea. She didn't feel like eating any of their cinnamon roll today and motioned for Vicki and Amy to pull it closer to the two of them so they could split it. "You're right."

Vicki reached for a napkin and dabbed at a dot of frosting that stuck to her upper lip. "Right about what? What did we say?"

"It's what you both wanted to say but were kind enough not to say aloud. I need to back off. My mind and emotions are running away from me."

Vicki and Amy exchanged cautious glances.

"Don't shut down," Amy said. "Everything you're feeling and doing is fine. Just maybe do it and feel it all a little slower."

Sierra was surprised at the wise words from her friend. "Thanks, Amy," she said, giving Amy's wrist a squeeze. "You both have to remember I'm the inexperienced one when it comes to this whole dating thing. Do either of you have any advice for me?"

Now Amy was the one to laugh and Vicki was the one who turned serious.

"What?" Sierra asked, not sure why her innocent question caused such a reaction.

"Do we have any advice for you?" Amy said. "Look out, Sierra! You asked for it."

With heads bent close, Vicki and Amy started to advise Sierra as though they were helping her cram for the most important final of her senior year.

seven

IT WAS 6:10 BEFORE SIERRA came up for air from their intense powwow. She leaned back and gave a summary review to her tutors. "Okay, let me see if I've got this right. All guys are jerks, but we love them anyway. Don't ever tell them what you're really thinking because they won't understand and they'll use it against you later in an argument. Let the guy pay most of the time, and expect to be disappointed."

Vicki nodded. "That's about it."

"Oh, and if he uses the word 'love,' it's only because he wants something—so watch it," Amy said.

Sierra shook her head. "You two are pathetic."

Vicki and Amy looked shocked.

"How could you become so cynical when you're so young?"

"Reality, Sierra. You really ought to try it sometime." Amy looked serious.

"Listen, I'm sorry you both have had such terrible experiences with guys, but they're not all like that."

"How about this, Miss Innocence and Bliss?" Vicki asked, twisting her silky brown hair up and securing it to the back of her head with a clip. "We'll meet here next Monday, and you can tell us where we're wrong."

"Not next Monday," Sierra said. "Paul will still be here."

"Okay, then the following Monday. Or maybe we'll have to call an emergency meeting after he leaves to give you the opportunity to prove us wrong."

"You'll see him at my house this Friday at the dinner party. You'll see then how wrong you are."

"Speaking of the dinner party," Amy said, "how many people are coming for sure?"

They spent the next fifteen minutes discussing the guest list, menu, and preparation plans. Sierra had overlooked a few items such as drinks, bread, and when the food was going to be prepared.

Amy stepped in and gave her suggestions. Obviously, she had thought about this a lot more than Sierra had. Amy offered to bring a tray of appetizers in the morning, which Sierra could pull out after graduation. As soon as the ceremony was over, Amy would drive to the restaurant, pick up the rest of the food, and bring it to the house so it would be hot and ready to go. Vicki volunteered to collect money from everyone so Amy would have cash on Friday to pay her uncle. Sierra would take care of getting the house ready. Whatever else needed to be done, they would do together after graduation.

"At this point," Sierra said, "Warner is the only one who can't come." She forced herself not to say anything about how that didn't bother her one bit, since Warner bugged her so much. "I thought I'd ask Wesley if he wants to join us, which I know you guys wouldn't mind."

Amy seemed to light up. "That's fine with me."

Sierra wanted to say, "I knew it would be," but instead she just added, "And I don't think I told you guys, but Tawni and Jeremy might come. They're planning to drive, but Tawni still has some scheduling logistics to settle. She's supposed to do a shoot on Wednesday, which means they would have to drive straight through if they want to arrive on time Friday. If they do come, would you mind if they ate with us, too? I thought Paul might enjoy having his brother there."

"I'll need to know by tomorrow," Amy said, "so I can order enough food."

"Okay, I'll call Tawni tonight."

"I hate to be the one to break this up," Vicki said, "but I'm supposed to be home in five minutes, and this is not the week I want to get put on restriction. I've been late on my curfews twice in the last week, so I gotta fly." She stood and grabbed her backpack off the peg on the wall behind them. "I love you guys. I'll see you later." With a swish, Vicki was out the door.

"I'd better go, too," Amy said, beginning to get up.

Sierra reached for Amy's hand to stop her. "We didn't talk about God."

Amy's winsome grin inched its way across her face. "Oh, really? Maybe another time."

Sierra wasn't sure if that meant Amy was more open to talking about God or if she was feeling relieved the topic had never come up.

"I'll see you Friday morning, then," Sierra said as she

also rose from the table. "Call me if you need anything before then."

"When does Paul arrive?"

"Late Thursday night. So I don't know if I'll see him Friday morning or if he'll just show up at graduation or what."

"It's too bad you can't call him to find out."

As Sierra drove home, she thought of how she could call Paul if she wanted. Of course, it was too early in the morning in Scotland to phone right then. She would have to wait until later that night. Where could she get the number? From Uncle Mac?

When she stepped in the door, Mrs. Jensen called from the kitchen, "Sierra, is that you?"

"Yes."

"Good. Can you come in here? I have some news."

Sierra found her mom washing dishes. A paper plate with three taquitos, rice, and beans covered with clear wrapping waited for Sierra on the counter.

"The boys had softball games, so we ate early, and Dad took them. You've had several calls. Paul called."

"He did? I was just thinking of phoning him. When did he call?"

"I'm not sure. Earlier today. He said his travel plans had changed. I wrote it all down. Do you see it on the note there?"

Sierra eagerly reached for the piece of notepaper with the little birdhouse in the top left corner. On it her mom had written the information about Paul's flight. The arrival time was listed as 4:15 p.m., and Sierra said, "This is great! Before he wasn't getting in until after ten."

"Actually," Mrs. Jensen said, drying her hands and coming over to explain the note, "he doesn't arrive till Friday. I went over the schedule with him. He's sorry about missing your graduation ceremony, but he'll come right from the airport to your dinner party."

"That's okay," Sierra said. She was a little disappointed, since she had pictured him being at her graduation, but she would rather he be at the party.

"He said something about the airline changing the schedule, so he really couldn't do anything about it," Mrs. Jensen said.

"That's okay. I'm just glad he's still coming for a few days."

"Well, that's the best part. Tawni also called, and her shoot was rescheduled, so she and Jeremy are driving up from San Diego tomorrow. They'll stay with some friends of his parents in the San Francisco area and then arrive here late Wednesday night. They'll be here for the family party on Thursday, and then Paul will ride back with them next week."

"When are they going back?"

"That's what I was saying was the good part. It's open at this point. Paul might stay more than three or four days."

Sierra smiled. Her mother must have known how important this news would be. Sierra knew her mom loved going to the boys' softball games and cheering from her lawn chair, especially on warm, clear evenings like this one, but she had stayed home to give Sierra the information personally. Sierra smiled some more.

"You had another call from Vicki," Mrs. Jensen said. "She won't be able to come until later Friday because her family is going out to dinner after graduation, but they said she could come here for dessert."

"I'd better tell Amy. She's ordering all the food tomorrow. Randy might not be here for dinner, either. His parents are still trying to decide."

"Would it help if I gave them a call to let them know what the plan is?" Sierra's mom asked.

"I don't know. It couldn't hurt, I guess."

"Well, do you and Amy need anything else? I thought you would probably use the good china. We're down to twenty-one dinner plates after that fiasco at Christmas. Do you think that will be enough?"

"That should be plenty."

"Remember that Tawni will be here in two days, in case you want to plan your expedition to find her bed before then."

"Cute, Mom. Very funny. Actually, my room isn't that bad."

Mrs. Jensen raised an eyebrow. She was a trim woman with short hair and nice lips the same shape as Sierra's. Whenever Mrs. Jensen raised an eyebrow, her lips curled up. Even though the eyebrow was supposed to communicate that she meant business, the overall look was too sweet. It always made Sierra feel like laughing.

"Okay, okay. I'll take a shovel up there tonight and see what I can unearth. Right after I eat, though."

Sierra ended up putting a little extra effort into cleaning her room over the next few days. Paul might tour the house, and that gave her a whole new motivation for straightening things up.

By the time Tawni and Jeremy arrived at eight-thirty on

Wednesday night, Sierra was adding the finishing touches to the bedroom. She had picked flowers from the backyard garden and was carrying the two vases upstairs when the front door opened and Tawni's clear voice called out, "We're here! Anybody home?"

Sierra hurried to put the flowers in her room—one on the nightstand next to Tawni's bed and one on a dish on top of her dresser. The calm evening breeze breathed through the open windows, and the room swirled with the flowers' refreshing fragrance.

Dashing back down the stairs, Sierra greeted her sister with a big hug. Tawni responded with a kiss on the cheek and an extra tight squeeze.

Tawni seemed taller than Sierra remembered. Was it her shoes? She was definitely slimmer. Perhaps it was the poise and posture she had developed over the months she had been working as a professional model. Her hair was cut just above her shoulders and was as close to its normal color as Sierra had seen in a while. Tawni had colored it everything from white blond to mahogany red in the past. But today it was a soft brown, the shade of hot tea with a splash of cream stirred in. The color complemented Tawni's fair complexion.

"Are you excited?" Tawni asked.

Sierra knew her older sister most likely was referring to graduation. But when Sierra answered, "Yes, of course I am!" she had a glimmer in her eyes because she was thinking of seeing Paul.

Paul's older brother, Jeremy, stood next to Tawni and opened his arms, inviting Sierra to give him a hug, too. She did so a little awkwardly. It felt strange to hug Paul's brother when all she had been dreaming of was hugging Paul. It was like eating imitation vanilla ice milk when she had her heart set on homemade Rocky Road ice cream. Just not the same, yet oddly similar in some ways.

Sierra tried hard to remember if Paul was taller than Jeremy was. Was Paul's hair that dark? No, she remembered its being lighter. Paul's eyes weren't as deep-set as Jeremy's, and Paul's chin was less pronounced. In Sierra's opinion, she certainly had the better-looking of the two brothers. She only let herself roll that thought over for a second because it suddenly seemed quite possible that Jeremy was standing there thinking the same thing of her—that he had gotten the better-looking of the two sisters.

Mr. and Mrs. Jensen, who had been the first to greet the weary travelers, were now asking all the usual questions about how the trip was and if they wanted something to eat.

"I'm just ready for some sleep," Tawni said. "The people we stayed with last night had a brand-new puppy, and it kept me awake all night."

"You both must be exhausted," Mrs. Jensen said.

"Not me," Jeremy said. "I slept on the living room couch last night, which was upstairs, and Tawni was in the guest room, which was right next to the garage where the puppy howled. I slept great." He put his arm around Tawni and teased her. "I kept telling Tawni to take a nap in the car, but she's not one for sleeping in moving vehicles, is she?"

Tawni shook her head, as if coaxing him not to tell the rest of the story.

But Jeremy plunged forward. "Every time I stopped at a gas station, she would fall dead asleep. Then as soon as I started the car, she would wake up. As long as she was awake,

I convinced her to drive the last few hours, and I slept. So I'm wide awake, and she's about ready to drop."

"Why don't you just go up to bed?" Mr. Jensen asked. "I'll be glad to take your luggage up for you."

"I've got it," Jeremy said, using both hands to lift the heavy bag and haul it up the stairs. He hit the side of the stairwell, and Sierra saw her mom cringe. "Which room is it?" Jeremy asked.

Sierra and Tawni followed him up the stairs, and Sierra scurried ahead of him to open the bedroom door. Jeremy stood back, allowing Tawni to enter first before he let the heavy suitcase rest on the floor.

"I don't believe it," Tawni said, glancing around. "I've never seen this room look so tidy! Did you hire a maid?"

"Very funny," Sierra said.

Tawni sat on the edge of her old bed and admired the vase of blue bearded irises. "Maybe my little sister is finally growing up after all and learning to be responsible. I just never thought I'd see the day."

Something inside Sierra snapped. She and Tawni were suddenly back to their old selves, ready to fight about anything. What made it worse was that Sierra had thought they were over that stage of their lives. Now, here she was, being treated like a child in front of Jeremy.

A frightening realization came to her. It could be like this all weekend. Having Tawni there to remind Sierra that she was the lowly little sister could mean a weekend of embarrassing situations not only in front of Jeremy but also with Paul. Plus Sierra wouldn't have her private retreat all to herself for days. Tawni had invaded her room and, from all appearances, was about to invade her life.

eight

SIERRA WAS GLAD to go to school on Thursday morning. Many of her friends were ditching, since it was the last day and it seemed pointless to attend class. But Sierra wanted to get out of the house.

Tawni had gone to sleep early but woke up a little cranky when Sierra started opening drawers at 7:05. Sierra still hadn't gotten over the slump she had fallen into the night before. It all seemed so unreal. School was over. High school was over. A whole chunk of her childhood was over.

It came to an end so fast, Sierra thought as she drove to school. *I can remember my first day of school when Mom made me wear those little red shoes with the buckles. I hated those shoes! What was she thinking when she bought those for me? Or did she buy them? They were probably hand-me-downs.*

Pulling into the school parking lot, Sierra realized that, to her mother's credit, she might not have understood Sierra's preferences then, but she sure understood them now. Sierra thought her mom was great to be willing to adjust the family's graduation celebration so Sierra could spend Friday night with her friends. Vicki's parents had made a big issue of the arrangement, and Vicki said they had had a huge argument over it.

Sierra felt extra appreciative of her mom, yet at the same time a little melancholy. On her first day of school many years ago, pancakes had been served for breakfast, a love note had been tucked into her sweater pocket, and photographs had been taken before she walked down the sidewalk in a straight line behind Tawni, who was behind Wesley, who was behind Cody. Today she had made her own breakfast—a banana. No one had even said good-bye to her, and she had driven to school alone. Not that she expected her mom to take pictures. It was all just so different from the rest of her school experience.

If this was what being grown-up and independent was all about, Sierra wasn't sure she liked it. Or at least she wasn't sure she wanted to be at this point yet in her life.

Her last day of school was one party after another in each of her classes. Most of her teachers had nice speeches they gave to the students about what a wonderful year it had been. One of her teachers handed out cards with a Bible verse as a blessing for their future. It was a fun, sweet, sad, strange sort of day.

Instead of driving directly home, Sierra stopped at Eaton's Pharmacy. A little soda fountain with red vinyl stools was located inside the corner drugstore. She ordered a chocolate shake. It was served along with a silver shake canister containing the portion of the drink that wouldn't fit in the glass. The server was the same waitress who had been there the first time Sierra had visited the fountain with Granna Mae. Sierra didn't remember the woman's name but smiled and answered questions about how her family was doing, especially Granna Mae.

Sierra slurped slowly in the quiet shop and remembered when Granna Mae had brought her here a year and a half ago, after her first day at Royal Academy. Granna Mae traditionally took her children—and sometimes her grandchildren—to Eaton's for a shake on their first day of school. It didn't matter that Sierra started Royal in the middle of the year; she still qualified for a chocolate shake with Granna Mae at Eaton's.

Now Sierra felt strange sitting here alone and grown-up and responsible and not doted on by anyone. She knew she wouldn't feel this way once the family party started that night. Tomorrow would be graduation and Paul's arrival and the start of their days together. That's when she would love being grown-up and responsible and having the freedom to do what she wanted.

But for this singular moment, she was a sad, lonely graduating senior—so sad and lonely she couldn't finish her shake.

She left an exorbitant tip on the counter, feeling that someone needed to reward that woman for working in the same drugstore during Sierra's entire high school career.

Then Sierra drove home, convincing herself that the best years of her life were still to come. She wondered if part of the sadness came from her not growing up in Portland but being a transplant in the middle of her junior year. She loved her friends dearly, but she didn't feel the same about them as she did about the friends she had grown up with in the little town of Pineville in northern California. She had thought she would stay in touch with them. When Sierra moved, she had made earnest promises about going back for her friends' graduation. She knew every one of the fifty-nine students who had graduated there last weekend, and she had known most of them her whole life. But Sierra was surprised by how quickly she had moved on and forgotten all her promises about visiting. Most of her friends had moved on quickly, too. Only two or three had sent her graduation announcements, and none of them had included a note.

As far as Sierra knew, neither she nor her mom had sent her graduation announcement to any of her old friends in Pineville. It made her sad.

How can things change like that? It won't be like that when I go to college, will it? Even though Amy doesn't have any interest in going to Rancho Corona, and even if Vicki ends up not being accepted, we'll still be good friends, won't we? When I come home for vacation, the three of us will still get together at Mama Bear's. We just have to! I refuse to believe our friendship could dissolve.

By the time Sierra walked into the house, she was in a "blue funk," as Amy once described an especially depressed mood. If some category at the Academy Awards existed for graduating seniors who act happy at the family party while they are in a level-two blue funk, Sierra would have won that year. She put on the best show she could for her loving family. Her older brothers, Cody and Wes, were both there. Cody's wife, Katrina, and their son, Tyler, showered Sierra with hugs as if she had won some talent show instead of merely graduating from high school. The hugs felt funny from Katrina because she was six-and-a-half months pregnant. Sierra wasn't used to hugging pregnant women.

Twice during the evening Katrina took Sierra's hand,

pressed it to her abdomen, and said, "There. Did you feel that? Wait. She'll kick again."

Sierra didn't know how to tell her well-meaning sister-in-law that she would love her new niece to pieces once she made a grand appearance that summer. For now, though, Sierra wasn't big on bonding through tracking the baby's tiny kicks across Katrina's bubbled-out belly.

Mrs. Jensen made a huge dinner with salads and vegetable trays, and Mr. Jensen grilled chicken. A big carrot cake with cream cheese frosting was served. It had plastic decorations of a graduation cap and rolled-up diploma on top, along with the words, "Congratulations, Sierra!"

Everyone gave Sierra gifts. Cards and money were presented from relatives who hadn't come. Granna Mae was wonderfully bright and coherent throughout the evening. And Sierra noted that Jeremy fit right in with the festivities and treated Tawni like a princess.

A letter had arrived that day announcing that Sierra had been awarded another scholarship, her fourth. Everything was ideal, and she should have been as happy as she pretended to be.

Instead, she felt numb. All the celebrating seemed to be for someone else, one of the older Jensen children, like all the graduation parties had been in years past. She was just one of the many kids at the party. Only she wasn't one of the "little" ones anymore. Sierra sensed she had crossed some invisible line and was now one of the "older" Jensen kids. Gavin and Dillon were the only little ones left of the six kids, and they had a long way to go before they graduated from high school.

Not until the next morning did Sierra believe it was all

really happening. Her mom had hung Sierra's cap and gown on the back of her closet door; when Sierra woke up, they were the first things she saw. She remembered when she had tried on Tawni's cap two years ago and thought it was the silliest-looking hat in the world. She had swung her head to make the tassel do a hula. Tawni had yelled at her, and that was that.

This morning the hat hanging on the back of the closet door was hers, and she thought it looked rather important and dignified. She knew she probably would yell at Gavin if he tried to make her tassel dance a silly hula on his unscholarly head.

This was the day she had long awaited. Paul was on an airplane this very minute, and before the day was over, she would see him and…

She forced her imagination to shut down. All in good time, she coached herself, using one of Granna Mae's familiar lines.

Sierra prayed as she showered, dressed, and tried to get her hair to cooperate. After spending an extra minute with the mascara wand, she went downstairs, where she found Jeremy and Wes engaged in serious battle with a video game.

"You guys are pathetic," she teased. Neither of them had showered yet, and both had wacky hair and wore crumpled T-shirts and shorts.

"Hey, don't make fun of our male-bonding rituals," Jeremy said.

"Yeah," Wes agreed. "Do we break into your little tea parties and tell you you're pathetic?"

"No. My apologies. Bond away, big boys."

"Whoa!" Wes said, bobbing and ducking with the controller in his hand. "You shouldn't have gotten that one, Jeremy. I was in there way ahead of you. Whoa, look out!"

Jeremy laughed. "You snooza, you looza."

Sierra smiled on her way into the kitchen. Paul would fit in nicely with this clan, especially since his own big brother was already part of the gang. Mom had set out a basket of muffins, a pitcher of fresh orange juice, and a big bowl of fruit salad. Bright, golden sunshine tumbled through the open kitchen window, lighting up the counter. Sierra could hear four-year-old Tyler in the backyard with his grandpa, laughing his adorable laugh. Brutus was barking and probably slobbering all over Tyler. Someone upstairs was running a shower. A blow-dryer ran at top speed in the downstairs bathroom.

Even though Sierra was the only one in the kitchen as she poured her orange juice, she felt surrounded by love. At times like this she enjoyed being in a big family and thought that anyone who didn't come from such a clan was really missing out.

The extended family had to take three cars to fit everyone in for the ride to Sierra's school auditorium. Sierra rode with Tawni and Jeremy. Fortunately, Tawni had slept in, so she was in the best of moods. If Sierra needed to tell Tawni that she and Paul wanted to do something alone rather than with Tawni and Jeremy, it seemed more likely her sister would understand now that she was in a cheery mood.

Sierra had laid her gown across her legs with her cap balanced on her lap. She felt nervous, but she wasn't sure why. She didn't think it was graduation. After all, she wasn't valedictorian, so she didn't have to make a speech or anything. All she had to do was walk up to the podium, shake the principal's hand, take her diploma, and walk down the stage. So why did she feel queasy?

It has to be Paul, she thought. *I'm so nervous and excited about seeing him I can hardly think about anything else. But graduation is something a person should probably pay attention to!*

She tried to imagine what Paul was doing on the plane right now. Was he sleeping? Reading? Or gazing out the plane's window, just as she was gazing out the car's window? Was he feeling nervous about seeing her?

When the car pulled into the school parking lot, Sierra put aside all her thoughts of Paul, separated from her family, and scurried with her cap and gown to the school library, where all the girls were meeting before the ceremony.

Vicki was already there, wearing her gown and adjusting her cap. She gave a happy squeal and dashed over to hug Sierra when she walked in. Several other girls greeted Sierra with hugs and nervous laughter. They helped each other get their caps on right, and Margo said, "Whoever thought up this flat-head style anyhow? I don't know why someone didn't come up with something better. I mean, really, they can put men on the moon, but they can't design a decent hat for the masses to wear when they receive a diploma."

Sierra decided this would be a good time to demonstrate her talent of making her tassel do the hula. Vicki was the first one to notice and tried to imitate the subtle head motions that set the tassel swaying just right. Two more girls copied them, and then three more came over and joined the impromptu competition. Ripples of laughter rolled over the group, providing a release for their nervous energy.

"Which side is this tassel supposed to be on?" one girl asked.

"This side," Vicki said, demonstrating. "Don't you remember their telling us at practice? Then we flip it at the very end of the ceremony."

One of the history teachers entered the library and clapped her hands. "All right, ladies, this is it. Line up alphabetically in the hall. Shall we go now? Nice and orderly."

The guys were already lined up in the hall, with big gaps where they remembered girls being from the practice session. The boys looked as if they had been goofing around, too. At practice, strict warnings had been given to all the students about attempting pranks during the ceremony. The year before some girls had smuggled bottles of soap bubbles into the auditorium and had filled the air with bubbles. The harmless trick caused more trouble than it was worth, so this year the administration had come down hard about no shenanigans of any kind. Sierra wondered if the rule would be respected.

"Sierra, over here," Randy called to her. At practice, they had discovered for the first time that they were next to each other alphabetically at Royal Academy. Sierra slipped in line between her buddy and a guy she didn't know very well who was fiddling with the tie he had on underneath his gown.

"You nervous?" Randy asked. His half grin was broader than usual.

"No," Sierra said. "Are you?"

"Naw, I've been looking forward to this."

"Me, too," she agreed.

"All right, everyone, listen up." The football coach's booming voice echoed down the hall. "Let's go. Exactly as you did it in practice. This is it. Go make your mamas proud."

The auditorium's doors opened, and the music rushed out to welcome them inside. The line of students, all wearing deep blue caps and gowns, began to march down the hallway.

Just as they were to move forward, Randy reached back and took Sierra's hand. As the music played, Sierra walked down the aisle, holding hands with her best buddy, Randy.

nine

AFTER THREE SONGS and a speech from a man who had graduated from Royal Academy and now ran a chain of furniture stores in Arizona, the principal finally moved to the podium. Sierra blew air out past her protruding lower lip in an effort to cool off her perspiring forehead. The auditorium was stuffy, and the cap and gown made her feel a little claustrophobic. Fortunately, the awards and special recognitions went quickly. The last award was a new one they had added this year for the student who had best demonstrated Christian character during his or her stay at Royal.

"It'll probably go to you," Randy whispered.

"Hardly," Sierra whispered back. "You're the one who stopped the school riot last fall when you voluntarily cut your hair."

Before they could argue any more, the principal announced, "And the winner of this award will receive a four-thousand dollar scholarship, which was generously donated by Pellmer's Furniture of Arizona, to the college of his or her choice. The recipient is...Randy Jenkins."

Randy nearly rocketed out of his chair. He gave Sierra a huge grin and playful tag on the shoulder before going up to the podium to receive the envelope and to shake hands.

This is so perfect, God! Sierra thought exultantly. *You knew how much Randy needed scholarship money for Rancho. You are so awesome! Thank You, thank You!*

Randy returned to his seat, looking as if the reality of the award had just sunk in. He was more dazed than when he first had heard the announcement.

"That was a total God-thing," Sierra whispered.

"Yeah," was all Randy could say.

The calling of the graduates' names began, and row by row the students went forward. By the time Sierra stepped onto the podium, she didn't feel nervous at all. Out of the corner of her eye, she noticed the camera's flash as her mom captured the moment on film. Sierra smiled, accepted the diploma in her left hand, and remembered to cross over her right hand to shake hands with the principal. That's when her English teacher, who stood at the microphone, announced Sierra's name and her scholastic rank with resounding clarity. "Sierra Mae Jensen, magna cum laude."

A burst of applause followed, sending a little shiver up Sierra's spine. She paused right before going down the stairs and looked in the direction of the wildest clapping. Sure enough, there was her family and her mom with the camera. Sierra held up her diploma, smiled back, and gave her mother the chance to take a shot.

Her one moment in the spotlight ended when the name of the next student was called, and a burst of applause for him followed. Sierra returned to her seat next to Randy.

They gave each other clandestine pokes in the arm to show how proud they were of one another.

The ceremony ended without any shenanigans. After a prayer and a charge to the students, they were instructed to switch their tassels. They marched out much more triumphantly than they had entered. Sierra looked for her family as she passed their aisle and gave a special little wave to Tyler and then blew him a kiss.

As soon as they were in the hallway, a string of poppers and flying streamers were released. It was impossible to tell where the party favors had come from, but it didn't matter. Everyone was cheering and hugging and tossing the streamers back into the air. Caps and tassels were flying in the crowded hallway. A can of Silly String appeared, and suddenly Sierra had long, bright pink bits of Silly String in her hair. She was laughing so hard that she could hardly breathe. She watched Randy switch hats, putting on his black baseball cap with the long ponytail attached to the back. He placed his graduation cap on top of the baseball cap. Some other friends of theirs—Tyler, Jen, and Tara—came over, and Tara put a clip-on hoop earring in Randy's nose.

By the time the parents and other guests tried to exit into the hallway, it was impossible to calm the wild seniors. None of the teachers tried to stop the antics. Sierra wanted to think it was because the students had followed the rules through the whole ceremony. They deserved to go a little crazy at the end.

The only one who tried to yell above the crowd was the football coach. He kept directing them to take their party into the parking lot, which they eventually did.

Mrs. Jensen snapped lots of pictures of Sierra and her friends. Since Sierra didn't want to stop having fun with her friends to become the photographer, she was glad. She knew these were the snapshots she would keep in her photo album for the rest of her life.

Randy was the wackiest she had ever seen him. He climbed onto the top of the planter in front of the school and acted as if he were leading a cheer with his ponytail flapping in the wind.

Amy made her way through the crowd and greeted Vicki and Sierra with a big hug. "This is way wilder than my graduation was!" Amy yelled over the noise.

Sierra nodded and yelled back, "Where's my air horn when I need it?"

Amy laughed, sharing a not-so-fun memory with Sierra that involved an air horn and Sierra's overzealous good intentions.

Vicki put her thumb and first finger in her mouth and let out the shrillest whistle Sierra had ever heard. She covered her ears and turned to her usually polite friend. "Where did you learn to do that?"

"My dad. Here, like this. Try it!"

Amy, Sierra, and Vicki worked at improving their shrill whistling as Randy wound down his final cheer. Many of the parents were trying to coax the students to calm down and get their things together so they could leave and have a nice, respectable family dinner. Sierra's family kindly stood to the side and let her have her graduation moment with her buddies.

Vicki's dad motioned for Vicki to come along. She stopped her whistling, and after another hug for Sierra, she said, "I'll be over to your house as soon as I can, but don't try to hold any food for me."

Sierra nodded. It suddenly struck her that Paul could be here already. He could be at the airport or even on his way to her house. She didn't have her watch on, but she knew it was getting late. "I'm going to get things ready at the house," Sierra told Amy.

"I'll pick up the food now," Amy said. "What are you going to wear? Do you think this is too fancy? Should I stop at home to change?"

Sierra glanced at Amy's short, sleeveless black dress. It was fancy, but it looked great on her. "I don't know what I'm going to wear. Just wear that, and if you want to change, you can borrow something of mine."

Amy nodded and took off for her car. Sierra joined her family and gestured to Randy that she was leaving. She didn't know if he saw her, since her departure didn't stop his antics. Sierra shook her head. Ever since Randy had found out he was going to Rancho, he seemed to have gone through a personality transformation. It made her wonder if he was going to be one of those guys who go berserk once they move away to college and experience freedom from parental authority. She had never thought of his parents as overly strict, but maybe they were more so than she realized.

Sierra linked her arm with Granna Mae's and walked to the Jensen family van. She noticed how many of the cars in the parking lot were decorated. Most of her friends had written congratulatory notes with white shoe polish on the windows of their cars or their friends' cars. Sierra had been so absorbed in the rush of the last few weeks that she hadn't even thought of decorating her little car.

"Such a to-do," Granna Mae said. "My, my, my!"

"It's so much fun!" Sierra said. "Just think, Granna Mae, I'm a graduate!"

Granna Mae gave Sierra a foggy look as if she weren't sure who Sierra was or what she was talking about. The blank look caused Sierra to hold her grandmother's arm a little tighter and make sure she got situated in the front seat of the van. Sierra whispered to her mom, "I think this was a little much for Granna Mae."

Mrs. Jensen nodded, and they all climbed into the van.

At home, Sierra didn't see any unfamiliar cars parked in front of their house, so apparently Paul hadn't arrived yet. She wanted to hurry inside to change, but her mom was set on taking a whole roll of family photos. It took only ten minutes or so, but each minute seemed like an hour as Sierra watched every car that came down the street. None of them stopped in front of her house.

Cody, Katrina, and Tyler left after hugging everyone, and Sierra hurried up to her room. The time was exactly four-thirty. Paul was in Portland. Was he still at the baggage claim? She stopped and smiled at her reflection in the mirror. When she and Paul met a year and a half ago, they had both grabbed for the same bag on the luggage carousel.

She could hardly stand the anticipation. She pictured Uncle Mac picking Paul up and bringing him over to her house.

Sierra had no idea what to wear. She heard the doorbell ring and knew she had better hurry and decide. The dress she had worn under her robe was kind of dressy, and it was similar to Amy's. That wasn't unusual. Sierra and Amy shared the same taste in clothes. But would it seem odd for the two of them to wear the same sort of dress at a small dinner party? Sierra couldn't remember what Vicki was wearing.

The doorbell rang again, and Sierra decided she wouldn't worry about changing. She had a party to hostess and a very special guest to greet. A quick freshening-up in the bathroom was all she allowed herself before lightheartedly skipping down the stairs to see her family and friends.

A rattle of excited chatter rose from the front porch. Sierra looked through the open door and saw the back of Randy's head with the ponytail. Tawni was in the circle, as well as Jeremy, Sierra's mom, and her two little brothers. Amy stood by the steps. The group seemed focused on something on the porch.

"What is it?" Sierra asked, opening the screen door and approaching the huddle.

Tawni and Jeremy both stepped back so Sierra could see. It was the last thing she expected.

ten

"THEY'RE ALIVE," Sierra said, looking at Amy for an explanation.

"I know."

Sierra gazed at the large bucket of fidgeting red lobsters trying to climb up the slick plastic sides. "You didn't say we were going to fix live lobsters."

"I didn't know. My uncle just said 'lobster' and that he would give them to us at cost, by the pound. I thought he was going to cook them for us."

"How do you cook them?" Sierra asked.

"It's easy. You just boil them," Wesley said, coming up the steps with a second bucket. "Haven't you ever seen how they do it in the huge vats down on the coast?"

"At least you know they're fresh," Jeremy said. Tawni playfully punched him in the arm.

"How many did you get?" Sierra asked.

"Sixteen."

"Can we have two of them?" Dillon asked. "Then Gavin and I could have a race."

"Cool," Randy said. "I'm in."

"You guys!" Sierra said. "No, you may not play with our food!"

"I don't know if I can go through with this," Amy said. "I mean, I don't know if I can eat them. They were looking at me in the car on the way over."

Wes laughed. He had worked at Degrassi's restaurant last summer as a waiter and was heartless when it came to the fresh catch of the day. "You've eaten them before at the restaurant. I've seen you."

"I know, but I never actually met any of them before I ate them."

Now everyone was laughing.

"What's this one's name?" Randy teased, picking up one of the plump fellows and holding it up for Amy to see. The claws were taped closed, but Amy pulled back as if it could pinch her.

"This one is Rory," Gavin said, bravely picking up another lobster.

"Where did you get that name?" Tawni asked.

"I dunno."

Just then a car pulled into the driveway, and Sierra moved away from the group with her heart pounding. She thought how unlike any of her dreams it would be to see Paul at this moment. She had conjured up a variety of scenarios, but none of them involved greeting Paul with half a dozen people gathered around two buckets of live lobsters.

But it wasn't Paul. It was Tre and Margo. Drake pulled in behind them. Cassie was with him, as well as Jen and Tara. Drake waved to Sierra. She waved back.

"I'm just dropping these guys off," he said. "Cassie and

I are going to a party at her house, but we might come back here later."

"Okay," Sierra called back from the edge of the porch. "Have fun, and I hope you guys do come back. Hi, Cassie."

The girl in the front seat waved back at Sierra. By then the others were up the porch steps and were being introduced to their dinner.

"Can we mark them so we get the one we want? That one looks good," Tara said.

"I'm going to see if we have an extra large cooking pot in the basement," Mrs. Jensen said. "Wes, why don't you move those lobsters into the kitchen? It's hot out here on the porch. And I think they should have more water in the buckets."

Another car pulled up, and again Sierra looked expectantly at the driver. It was Warner.

I thought he said he couldn't come, she thought sullenly. She followed her mom into the house before any of her feelings about Warner showed themselves. "Did anyone listen to the answering machine since we came back?" she asked. "I was just wondering if Paul's plane was delayed or anything."

"I don't think anyone has listened yet. Your father was trying to put up the volleyball net in the backyard in case you wanted to play later."

"In dresses?" Sierra was beginning to feel as though this party were going downhill faster than a lobster could scamper out of a bucket.

"Well, later," Mrs. Jensen said, heading for the basement. "If you end up changing. It's up to you." She took off down the stairs.

Wes entered the kitchen with the first bucket of dinner.

The frightened fellows were clambering up the sides of the bucket. To Sierra, it resembled the muted sound of fingernails on a chalkboard, and suddenly she lost her appetite.

"I still have bread in the car," Amy said as she entered the kitchen with a box of Caesar salad already prepared and packed in plastic bags. "Can you get it, Sierra?"

"I was going to check..." Sierra saw desperation on Amy's face and decided checking the answering machine could wait. Besides, Sierra might go to Amy's car and find Paul pulling into the driveway. "Sure," Sierra said. "Anything else?"

"Well, I don't want to be mean or anything, but are your brothers going to be around the whole time?" Amy looked at Sierra and seemed to notice for the first time they had on similar dresses. Amy's expression grew to a deeper level of frustration.

"Oh," Sierra teased, "you want me to tell Wesley to get lost?"

"No!" Amy said quickly. Then she looked agitated. "I meant Gavin and Dillon, and you know it."

Sierra's mom came up from the basement just then with a huge silver cooking pot. "Don't worry, Amy," Mrs. Jensen said. "This is your party. I have plans for the boys just as soon as I know you have everything you need."

Amy looked a little embarrassed. "I'm sure we have everything. Thanks."

Wes entered with the second batch of lobsters as Sierra headed for the car to bring in the bread. She wished she knew how long it would take Paul to get through the airport. When she had come back from England, her plane had landed in San Francisco first, and that's where she had gone through customs. For some reason she remembered Jeremy saying that Paul's flight was from Heathrow to Seattle, and then he would take a hopper down to Portland. He might have missed the connection at Seattle if his international flight was delayed.

Sierra tried not to worry. They still had a lot to do before they could serve their dinner, so maybe it was a good thing Paul wasn't there yet. She carried the four bags of dinner rolls in her arms and joined the rest of the group in the kitchen.

Everyone was at work. Tawni wore an apron and was trying to talk Jeremy into wearing one, too, but he wasn't cooperating. Randy was filling the cooking pot with water. Wes was cleaning up a mess he had made on the floor while trying to add more water to the lobster buckets. Warner was taking Amy's orders on where to place the croutons on the salad plates, which Margo was preparing by pulling salad from the bags with tongs. Tre was unwrapping a cube of butter and putting it on a plate Amy had set out earlier when she had brought over the appetizers.

For a moment, Sierra stood and watched this organized circus. How did Amy do it? Sierra never could have gotten so many people to work together so easily.

"Bread, Aim. Where do you want it?"

"Does your mom have two or three bread baskets we could use?"

Sierra went searching for the baskets. Sierra's mom and younger brothers had disappeared, and Sierra thought it best not to involve her mom, especially when Sierra certainly could find some baskets on her own.

Tawni was the one who finally remembered where they

were. Mrs. Jensen had changed some things around in the kitchen after the oven had caught on fire last Thanksgiving. With the bread in baskets lined with Granna Mae's white linen napkins, Sierra joined Tawni in the dining room to set the table with the old family china.

"What's the final count?" Tawni asked.

"I'm not sure."

Just then the doorbell rang, and Sierra's heart stopped. She and Tawni exchanged knowing looks of anticipation, and Tawni nodded for Sierra to answer the door.

"Someone's at the door," Warner called out from the kitchen. "Want me to get it?"

"Let Sierra," Tawni yelled back.

With light steps, Sierra hurried to the door. Her heart pounded all the way up to her inner ears. She put her hand on the doorknob, paused a moment, moistened her suddenly dry lips, and cleared her throat. Pulling open the door and putting on her best smile, Sierra sang out, "Hi!"

A gangly young boy stood on the doormat with a receipt pad in his hand. His bike lay on its side in the front yard. Apparently, Sierra's disappointment showed instantly because the boy's smile turned to a half grin of conciliation.

"Collecting for the *Oregonian?*" He said it with a question mark at the end, as if he somehow knew he should apologize.

"Could you please come back tomorrow?" Sierra tried to find a smile for him and to sound pleasant. "No one is here right now who can pay you."

The boy nodded and scampered away. He mounted his bike like a fleeing outlaw and took off into the sunset. Sierra quickly scanned the street for cars. There were none. She closed the door and turned around.

All her friends burst out laughing. They had formed a haphazard pyramid in an effort to watch her reunion with Paul.

"The paper boy!" Amy exclaimed, giggling.

"Did you see the look on that poor kid's face?" Randy said with a hoot. "He couldn't get out of here fast enough."

"Very funny," Sierra said, finding it impossible to hold back her smile. She spotted the camera on the entry table and said, "Wait, you guys. Don't move." Quickly focusing, she snapped a shot of her friends, who were all crammed into the entrance to the living room, looking like one strange, aproned body with eight heads. "Let me get another one," she said before they all lost their balance. "Hold it! Smile!"

Sierra was about to take the picture when she caught sight of something out of the corner of her eye moving toward her from the kitchen. She held the camera in place and glanced at the moving object on the floor. An escapee from the dinner bucket was flailing its way toward the front door. Sierra wanted to scream but decided she would play a joke back on her friends.

"Okay, just hold it. I'm trying to focus," Sierra said, stalling for time.

"Hurry up, I'm going to fall over!"

"My leg is asleep!"

"Sierra, I have an elbow in my ear!"

"Take the picture!"

With one eye on the lobster, Sierra slowly counted under her breath, "Three, two, one!" Right on cue, the runaway lobster scurried past the human pyramid. They all noticed it at the same time and reacted wildly. That's when Sierra snapped the picture.

She burst out laughing as Wesley lunged for the crawling crustacean and the whole pyramid crumbled. Sierra took another picture. The phone rang, and she broke away from the human pileup to answer it, but her father already had. He was in the kitchen, which made her wonder if the escapee had had a little help.

"Yes," her dad said, "this is Howard Jensen."

Sierra looked around the kitchen to see what else needed to be done to prepare dinner—besides cooking the lobsters.

"Oh, yes. How are you? Oh?"

Not seeing anything else that needed to be done, Sierra went back to the entryway to put away the camera and check if the meals on wheels had been captured. The whole group was laughing hysterically as Wes pretended to wrestle with the lobster.

"I'm not eating that one," Sierra said.

"Let's mark it and make sure Wes has to eat it," Tawni suggested. She had stepped away from the group. Roughhousing was not her idea of a good time.

"Tawni, Sierra," Mr. Jensen called from the kitchen, "could you come here a moment, please?"

Tawni and Sierra exchanged glances. They both had noticed the slight catch in his voice. Tawni followed Sierra to the kitchen. Mr. Jensen had hung up the phone. He had a strange look on his face.

"What is it?" Sierra asked. "Is it Paul?"

"Tawni," Mr. Jensen said quietly, "could you ask Jeremy to come here? I'd like to talk to the three of you."

Before Tawni could turn around, Jeremy stepped into the kitchen. The rest of the group was still laughing in the entryway. The kitchen was silent except for the boiling water in the pot on the stove.

"That was your uncle Mac," Mr. Jensen said, looking at Jeremy.

Sierra felt as if icy fingers had reached down her throat and were trying to yank out her heart. Her father wouldn't look like this or sound like this unless something was wrong—seriously wrong. Sierra felt her world screeching to a halt as she waited for her father to speak.

He closed his eyes as he said, "There's been a plane crash."

eleven

"HOW? WHERE? WHEN? What do you know?" Sierra's mind raced. She shot out questions while the others remained silent.

Mr. Jensen opened his eyes. Tears glistened in them. That's when Sierra began to panic.

"Paul's plane out of Heathrow crash-landed in Seattle," her father said. "It happened at three o'clock this after-noon. Apparently, the plane made it to the runway but caught on fire. So far they haven't found any survivors."

Sierra felt her body slump slowly to the floor. Tawni and Jeremy wrapped their arms around each other and leaned against the wall.

"My parents?" Jeremy said.

"Mac is trying to reach them."

"I'm going to Seattle," Jeremy suddenly said. He reached for the phone. "I'll see if Uncle Mac wants to go with me." He punched in the numbers, and Sierra buried her face in her hands. She had no tears. Only pain. The sharpest, most unbelievable pain she had ever felt in her life, right in the middle of her chest.

The uninformed guests paraded into the kitchen, and Mr. Jensen spoke to Wesley in hushed tones. The others heard as well. Instantly, the group fell silent. Randy came over and sat on the floor next to Sierra. He didn't say anything.

Jeremy hung up the phone and said, "My uncle is going with me. We'll drive up to Seattle."

"Do you want me to go?" Tawni asked.

"Yes."

Sierra looked up.

"Unless you think you should stay here with Sierra," Jeremy added.

Tawni and Sierra exchanged glances for the third time that evening. This time both of them had red eyes.

"Go," Sierra said hoarsely. She wanted them to include her, to know that she would want to go, too. But she knew that was asking too much. She was supposed to be hosting a party at the moment. And besides, what was she to Paul?

"Hey, it's on TV," Warner said. He had left the kitchen and turned the TV in the living room to the local news channel, expecting them all to congratulate his quick thinking.

Mr. Jensen and Wes slowly moved into the living room with the others. Jeremy hesitated; then he bolted into the room with Tawni right behind him. Only Sierra and Randy remained in the kitchen. Neither of them spoke. Randy reached over and took Sierra's hand in his and held it. It struck Sierra that he had reached for her hand a few hours ago when they were entering the auditorium, ready to graduate. Her whole world had been different then.

The news was turned up loud, and they could hear the

reporter. "Flight 8079 out of Heathrow experienced failure with the landing gear when it arrived at Sea-Tac at 3:07 this afternoon. As you can see from this earlier clip, the rescue crew began evacuation immediately. However, due to the explosion that occurred when the plane's nose hit the runway, extensive damage was done in a short time. We have been informed that so far 157 fatalities and 3 survivors are confirmed. We will keep you updated as the information comes to us. Back to you, Bob."

Sierra squeezed Randy's hand. "Three survivors!" She jumped up and ran into the living room.

"Three survivors!" Jeremy repeated when he saw Sierra.

"I heard." Inwardly, Sierra began to pray with all her might, *Oh, please, God! Let Paul be one of the three. Let him be okay. Don't let him die!*

"Did they say which hospital the survivors are in?" Mr. Jensen asked.

Wes had already gone for the cordless phone. "I'll find out," he said.

Mr. Jensen took the remote control from Warner and began to check other channels. There was a report on another channel with a rerun of the crashed plane, nose to the pavement, still in flames, with rescue workers rushing into it. Sierra had only heard the description from the kitchen floor. Now, seeing the pictures, she realized it was even more horrible than she had imagined. Black smoke billowed from the sides of the plane as sirens wailed.

The doorbell rang, and Sierra rushed with Tawni and Jeremy to greet Uncle Mac. Sierra impulsively ran into his arms and hugged him tightly, as if he were the recipient of the hug she had intended for Paul.

"They said there are three survivors," Jeremy said.

"Really?" Uncle Mac came into the living room with the rest of them.

"Wesley's trying to reach the hospital," Mr. Jensen said, shaking hands with Uncle Mac.

"Did you contact my parents?" Jeremy asked.

"No, I kept getting voicemail, and I didn't want to leave a message."

"They're at Emmanuel Hospital," Wes said, hanging up. "They won't release any information over the phone, but if you go there and you're related, they will let you in."

Tawni and Jeremy exchanged tentative looks. Sierra knew they must be thinking, *And what if Paul isn't one of them?*

"I'm ready to go," Uncle Mac said. "Who else is going?"

"Tawni and me," Jeremy said. "We'd better grab an overnight bag."

"That's right," Tawni said. "Sierra, can you help me pack some things?"

The two sisters made their way up the stairs in single file. "Mom doesn't know," Sierra said, suddenly feeling dizzy. "Where is she?"

"She took the boys miniature golfing. Do you have a small bag I could borrow?"

"Sure." Sierra retrieved the bag, and neither of them spoke as Tawni transferred several neatly folded T-shirts and a pair of jeans into the bag, along with enough underwear for three days.

"You'll call as soon as you get there, won't you?"

"Yes," Tawni promised.

"I mean, even if it's the worst, you have to call me immediately and tell me."

"I will."

With no warning, the tears came coursing down Sierra's cheeks. She had so much she wanted to say as Tawni took her in her arms and held her close. "He wanted to go into ministry, Tawni. He got his life right with God." A huge sob overwhelmed Sierra. "He was coming to Portland to…" She couldn't speak. Breaking away from Tawni, Sierra went for Paul's treasured letter, which she had kept under her pillow since the day it had arrived. She held it out for Tawni to read.

Tawni read the first page and then slowly sank to her bed's edge. "Oh, Sierra," she murmured.

Tawni was on the last page, reading the poem, when a soft knock sounded on their door. Jeremy cautiously opened the door. "Uncle Mac is ready."

Tawni was awash in tears and motioned for Jeremy to come in. Now Tawni was the one who couldn't speak. She held out the letter to Jeremy.

"What's this?"

Sierra swallowed hard and forced her voice to cooperate. "It's a letter from Paul. It's okay for you to read it, if you want."

Jeremy began to read aloud and then trimmed his choking voice down to a whisper when he read the line, "I have finally entered through that gate, and I'm finding pasture, as the verse says."

He put down the letter and wiped his eyes with the back of his hand.

"Keep reading," Tawni whispered.

Jeremy finished the letter. His tear-filled eyes went to Sierra's red face. She and Jeremy looked at each other a long minute. Then, in two quick strides, Jeremy crossed the room and took Sierra in his arms. Together they cried.

"You'll never know," Jeremy finally choked out, "what your prayers did for my brother." He held her tightly and said, "Don't stop now. Not as long as we have a shred of hope. Don't stop praying."

"I won't," Sierra promised.

They pulled apart, and Tawni stood beside them, composed but still more shaken than Sierra had ever seen her.

"And I'll be praying for you guys, too, that you have a safe trip up there," Sierra offered.

Tawni tenderly kissed Sierra on the cheek and said words Sierra had never expected. "I love you, Sierra. I love you with all my heart."

"I love you, too," Sierra said, suddenly clinging to her.

"I know," Tawni whispered, stroking Sierra's hair.

Another knock came. Mr. Jensen entered, and clearing his throat, said, "Mac's ready to go."

"We're coming," Tawni said, quickly zipping up the bag. Jeremy reached for it and suggested Tawni bring a pillow and blanket, just in case she could sleep in the car this time.

Sierra followed them to Uncle Mac's car and made them promise to call as soon as they reached Seattle. It was a three-hour drive. She knew they would be three of the longest hours of her life, waiting for the phone to ring.

Sierra's dad wrapped his arm around her as they walked back to the house. She wanted to be alone, but there were all her dinner guests. She knew she could ask them to leave and they would understand, but Sierra didn't want them to go. She needed her friends now more than ever.

Amy was waiting for them at the front door. She tenderly reached for Sierra's hand and gave it a squeeze. "You okay?"

"I don't know," Sierra said.

"Why don't you sit down. Do you want to be alone for a while?"

Sierra was surprised at how well Amy knew her. It dawned on her that Vicki hadn't arrived yet, but when she did, just like when Sierra's mom came home, they would have to relay the awful announcement all over again.

"No, I don't want you to leave," Sierra said.

"Do you want something to eat?"

"I don't know."

Wes met them in the entryway and stood close to his little sister. "They may have found another survivor. The news just announced it. Do you want to come watch the report?"

"I don't know." Sierra stood in the middle of the hall-way, suddenly exhausted and directionless.

"Come with me," Wes said, putting his arm around her and leading her to the living room couch. "I think you should watch the reports. Right now they're the only infor-mation we have."

Sierra plopped down next to Randy and watched as sta-tion after station replayed the horrifying scene of the burning airplane on the runway. One station alluded to terrorist activity. Another channel had an expert explain how the recent strike of this particular airline could have led to an oversight by the maintenance staff. CNN was announcing it as the worst disaster in the Seattle airport's history.

"Amy," Wes said after a while, "why don't you and I pull

some food together? We still have to eat. You guys just kick back here, and Amy and I will take care of everything."

Eat? Sierra thought. *I couldn't possibly eat.*

Her dad sat on her right side and pulled her close. Sierra rested her head on his arm. When she did, she caught the faint scent of the soap he used. It was a green soap that gave him a woodsy, outdoor fragrance. As soon as she smelled it, she thought of Paul and his pine-tree after-shave, which she had smelled for the first time when they sat next to each other on the plane ride from San Francisco to Portland. With the memory came a crashing wave of fresh tears that Sierra unapologetically spilled all over her father's chest.

Her friends stayed and ate tender lobster with drawn butter on trays in front of the TV. Sierra didn't eat.

"I think we should pray together," Randy said after they had seen footage of the crash at least fifteen times. No new reports of survivors were forthcoming, and in a way they were all growing numb to the information, since it had been well over an hour since they had heard the shocking news.

"Sometimes," Randy said, "it helps to have a verse to pray, you know? It helps to focus on God and His promises instead of being overwhelmed with the problem. I think it could help our prayers be more directed."

"In Paul's last letter, he wrote about Jesus as the Good Shepherd," Sierra offered.

"That's in John 10," Randy said.

Sierra's dad left the couch and returned a moment later with a Bible. "But that's a whole chapter, not just one verse," he said.

"It can be a whole chapter," Randy answered.

Then Sierra remembered the reference from Philippians that Paul had listed at the end of the letter. He had said it reminded him of her boldness. Sierra had looked up the verses once, but she couldn't remember now what they said.

"He also mentioned another verse in the first chapter of Philippians, near the end. Maybe verse 27," she told her dad.

He cleared his throat and read slowly, "Whatever happens, conduct yourselves in a manner worthy of the gospel of Christ. Then, whether I come and see you or only hear about you in my absence, I will know that you stand firm in one spirit, contending as one man for the faith of the gospel."

"Wow!" Margo said. "Is that the verse Paul wrote to you? It's kind of spooky that it says 'whatever happens.'"

"Actually, that's not the verse," Sierra said. The parallels between the apostle Paul's words in the letter to his Philippian friends and what was happening to Sierra after her letter from Paul Mackenzie were just a little too intense for her.

Then she remembered one of the verses Paul had listed in his letter. She had memorized it for Bible class and recognized it when Paul said he had written it on a card and carried it in his wallet. When she first had read the verse, it hadn't meant much to her, and she didn't understand why it was so important to Paul.

Now, as she was about to quote it to her dad and her friends, it took on special significance.

"I remember the verse," she said. "Philippians 1:21. 'For to me, to live is Christ and to die is gain.'"

twelve

SIERRA'S FRIENDS had a hard time praying, but she didn't. She didn't care if her tears and overwhelming emotions soaked through her words. And she didn't care what anyone else thought of her. This was between her and God, and she was trying to make sense of this tragic news arriving on the tail of Paul's clear commitment to God.

"I know that Your ways aren't our ways, God. And I don't understand what's happening. Did You take Paul to heaven to be with You? Or is he still alive? God, I beg You to have mercy on him if he's still alive. All he wanted to do was serve You." Sierra felt exhausted. She stopped praying, and Randy stepped right in, as if holding up her arms when she was too weak to hold them up any longer.

Randy prayed for Paul's parents, Jeremy, Tawni, and Uncle Mac. He prayed for the doctors at the hospital and for all the families who had lost someone in the crash.

Mr. Jensen prayed, and then Tre. Tre's voice was calm and steady. He was so willing to accept whatever happened as being for God's best. Sierra wasn't so willing. Margo thanked God that Paul was a Christian and that therefore, if he were dead, they all would see him again in heaven.

That's when Amy left the room.

They prayed for more than half an hour. Randy's idea was a good one. It helped to focus on God's Word as they prayed. After the last "Amen," they sat still and looked at each other.

"Sierra," Margo said, "you should be ready to accept the worst because the worst is really the best. I mean, if Paul is dead, then he's with God. He's in heaven right now, and we're the ones who have to go through a lifetime of trials before we get set free the way he is."

Sierra wanted to blast her friend's easy answer and say she wasn't ready to accept Paul's death just like that. Fortunately, the doorbell rang.

"It's probably Vicki," Randy said. He rose to answer the door when Sierra didn't get up.

"Will you tell her?" Sierra asked Randy. "I don't think I can say it."

Randy nodded. They all heard him open the door. The sound of a party horn and the snap of a confetti streamer followed. Then they heard Vicki say loudly to Randy, "Look! I brought hats and party horns for everyone. You haven't had dessert yet, have you?" The party horn sounded again.

Sierra could hear Randy's muffled voice and then a gasp from Vicki. Vicki rushed into the living room and stared at Sierra as if she had to be sure this wasn't some kind of cruel joke. When Vicki saw Sierra, her face mirrored her friend's.

"No!" Vicki whispered, slumping to the floor at Sierra's feet. "I heard it on the radio on my way over, but I thought it couldn't be Paul's plane because he was coming into Portland." Slow tears began a procession down Vicki's cheeks. "Oh, Sierra, I'm so, so, so sorry."

"We don't know yet. He may be one of the survivors." Sierra tried to comfort her friend but found she didn't have as much hope as she had thought.

"Jeremy and Tawni drove up to Seattle with Uncle Mac," Randy explained. "They're going to call as soon as they get there."

Sierra felt parched and asked if anyone else wanted something to drink. No one did. She shuffled into the kitchen, which looked like a disaster area. It smelled fishy. The counter was covered with uneaten salads, baskets of bread, and a plateful of leftover lobster. For some reason she thought of the story of Jesus' feeding the crowd of more than five thousand people with the simple offering of one little boy's fish and loaves. There had been twelve baskets of food left over, enough for each of Jesus' disciples to have his own basket.

As she poured herself a glass of water, Sierra tried to make a spiritual connection between that story and Paul's crisis. She needed to see a miracle and to know that God could take something small, like just a little bit of faith, and bless it and multiply it.

Then she remembered Paul's verse: "For to me, to live is Christ and to die is gain." What if the God-thing of all this was for Paul to be in heaven, and as a result, good would come out of his death?

The possibility was too brutal. God wouldn't do that, would He? Sierra leaned against the counter, realizing that whether or not Paul was one of the dead, 157 people had died today in that crash. Those 157 people had stepped into eternity. The ones who had surrendered their lives to God by receiving His gift of salvation through Christ were now in heaven. Those who had never come to Christ were now in hell.

Sierra felt like throwing up.

God, she screamed inside her mind, *how can You be like that? You divide us up like sheep and goats—right hand, left hand. I know what Your Bible says. I know what You require from us. But why? Couldn't You make it easier?*

As soon as the thought entered her mind, Sierra realized that coming to God was the easiest thing there was. Even a child could understand God's rules for eternal life and respond. It was a matter of choice, the free will God had put in each of us.

Her head was pounding. "Why don't people just come to You? Why do they run and hide and stay mad at You?"

Sierra hadn't realized she was saying that part of her wrestling match with God aloud until she heard Amy's soft voice answer from outside the open back door. "Because we're stubborn."

Sierra opened the screen and stepped out into the cool night. Amy sat on the steps with Brutus at her feet, contentedly letting Amy scratch under his chin.

"I didn't see you there." Sierra sat down next to her and patted Brutus on top of his noble head. "It's so hard, Aim. I mean, I know what I believe, and I'm sure it's right, but it's so severe. All those people dead. What did they do to deserve that?"

"We all deserve death," Amy said. "Have you already forgotten your verses from Bible class last year?"

Then, because all Sierra could give Amy was a blank look, Amy quoted them for her. "All have sinned and fall short of the glory of God.... The wages of sin is death, but the gift of God is eternal life in Christ Jesus our Lord."

"I know, but—"

Amy finished with one last verse. "The Lord is...not willing that any should perish but that all should come to repentance."

Sierra had no response. She knew all those verses, too. She had received an A on the test, just as Amy had. But what did they mean at a time like this? Amy knew the verses, but what did they mean to her?

"I think," Amy said, as if reading her friend's thoughts, "that the problem is in the repentance part. I haven't been willing to agree with God that I was wrong about anything. When my parents split up, all I knew was that I was hurting and nothing was going to make the hurt go away."

Sierra couldn't quite follow Amy's train of thought.

"I went my own way and tried to make myself feel better. It worked for a little while when I was with Nathan. But when you're in a dark place, there's no substitute for light."

The screen door opened. "There you are," Vicki said. She came and sat behind them. "I can't believe this is happening, Sierra. Do you really think he is, you know..."

"I don't know. Margo seems to think so. She said we should be glad because we know he's in heaven and we'll see him again." Sierra choked up.

"Margo said that?" Vicki said.

"Isn't that what you believe?" Amy asked.

"Well, of course, but..." Vicki scooted closer and put

her arm around Sierra. "This isn't exactly the time to say it. At least not that way."

"I believe it," Amy said. "Whether it's a convenient time or not, I know it's true."

Sierra and Vicki both looked at Amy and waited for her to explain this sudden confession of faith.

"For a long time," Amy said, tears gathering in her eyes, "it's as though I've been in a dungeon inside myself. It's been dark and cold and more miserable than I think either of you could ever guess. And I couldn't find the key. I couldn't get myself out of the dungeon. That's why I loved our Monday afternoons at Mama Bear's. It was as if you two came to visit me. You brought me a little bread, a little water, and some light from your two steady candles. And somehow I could keep going."

Sierra slipped her arm through Amy's and held her friend's hand, steady and calm, the way Randy had held hers. Vicki put her arm around Amy.

"I think I found the key that will get me out. I need to come back to God. All along I thought He was the one who locked me in there, but now I realize I was the one who locked Him out. I can't explain it, but I want God back."

"Then just tell Him," Sierra said, gently squeezing Amy's hand.

Amy didn't cry. She bowed her head with her two friends holding her, and she spoke simple, direct words, as only Amy could. "I've been wrong, God. I shut You out. I'm sorry. I want You back. Please forgive me and take me back. Okay?"

Then, as if Vicki could answer for God, she whispered back, "Okay."

The three of them opened their eyes and looked at each other warmly.

"Thanks for not giving up on me," Amy said quietly.

Sierra hugged her.

"Did I miss something earlier?" Vicki asked. "I mean, what happened, Amy?"

"What do you mean, what happened?"

Vicki looked at Sierra. "Did you say something to her?"

Sierra shook her head.

"You want to know why I suddenly opened my heart to God after shutting Him out for so long." Amy readjusted her position and looked at her friends. "It was the news report and the possibility that Paul might actually, you know...he could be dead right now."

Sierra felt an anxious surge of emotion begin to come over her again.

"When the news said there were three known survivors, something just hit me. It reminded me of the three of us. I wanted to be one of the survivors, not one of the 157."

Before Amy could say any more, the Jensen van pulled into the driveway. Mrs. Jensen, Granna Mae, and the boys came around to the back steps. Eager to greet them, Brutus rose and barked loudly. Mrs. Jensen instructed the boys to take Brutus to his doghouse so he wouldn't jump on Granna Mae.

"Well, hello!" Mrs. Jensen said when she saw the three friends clustered on the steps in the twilight. "Taking a break from the party?"

"Mom," Sierra began and then listened to herself tell about the plane crash and Tawni and Jeremy leaving with Uncle Mac.

Granna Mae stood at the bottom of the steps and listened quietly with her purse clutched in her hand. Sierra's mom breathed a troubled "Oh, dear" and leaned against the stair railing.

Granna Mae didn't move. She calmly said, "Paul wasn't on the plane."

Everyone turned to look at her, waiting for her to speak again.

"Paul missed the plane and went back to Saigon. That's when the bombing began."

Sierra understood then that Granna Mae was having one of her flashbacks. This one was about her son Paul, who had been killed in Vietnam. Her Paul had missed his plane ride, but the thought caused a fresh hope to spring up inside Sierra.

"What if Paul wasn't on the plane that crashed?" she said, excitedly springing up. "I mean, they changed his flight once already; maybe they changed it again. Maybe he didn't get on that flight!"

"Oh, Sierra," Mrs. Jensen said, reaching for her arm. But Sierra was already sprinting up the steps. "Dad? Wesley?" They met her in the kitchen. "Can we call the airline and check the flight roster? What if Paul wasn't on that flight?"

Mrs. Jensen and the others from outside were now in the kitchen, too. Sierra could tell that her mom and dad were exchanging glances and trying to signal to each other that their fairy-tale dreamer of a daughter was about to be disappointed. But Wesley didn't hesitate. He reached for the phone and started to make calls until he found someone who would help him.

As the whole group stood in the kitchen, waiting for the answer, Wes talked to the supervisor at the airline. Wes went through the story for the fourth time. He held up a hand for everyone to be quiet. "Can you repeat that, please? No, I don't believe he could have registered under a different name. It would have been listed as Paul Mackenzie. Yes, I'll wait."

Painful, silent moments passed.

"You're sure," Wes said. "Okay. Thank you. Yes. Good night." He hung up and turned to face Sierra. "He said Paul had a reservation on the flight, but according to their computer, he never checked in."

A wild cheer of amazement and jubilation rose from the group.

"He wasn't on the plane!" Sierra practically shouted, looking around for Granna Mae. The dear, confused woman must have gone to her room. It struck Sierra with painful clarity that because Granna Mae's Paul had missed his plane, he had met with death. But perhaps Sierra's Paul had missed death because he had missed a plane.

The phone rang, and Wes silenced the chatter before answering it. "Yes, Jeremy, listen. Before you tell me anything, I have something to tell you. We called the airline, and Paul wasn't on the flight. He had a reservation, but he never received a seat assignment, and according to their computer, he never boarded the plane."

Sierra's heart was pounding. She wanted to grab the phone from Wes and tell Jeremy herself.

"Yes. I know. You did? And did you reach them? Oh, really. Okay. Well, are you coming back, then? Sure." Wes held the phone out to his dad. "Tawni wants to talk to you."

"What did you find out?" Sierra asked the minute Wes let go of the phone. "He wasn't at the hospital, right?"

Wes nodded. "He wasn't at the hospital, and he's not on the list of the confirmed fatalities. Jeremy still can't reach his parents. He called some of their friends, who said his parents had gone to their mountain cabin for the weekend. They don't have a phone there and their cell phones aren't working, so Jeremy asked the friends to drive up and tell them."

"What are they going to tell them?"

"I guess that Paul's okay."

"Is he?" Sierra asked. "I mean, he wasn't on the plane; he isn't here." Sierra looked around and wondered why she was the only one asking this question. "So where is he?"

thirteen

WES GRABBED THE PHONE from his dad before he hung up with Jeremy and said, "Jeremy, Sierra just made a good point. Where *is* Paul?"

It was quiet for a moment. Sierra bit her lower lip and tried to imagine what had happened to Paul. For all they knew, he could have taken a different flight, and he could be at the Portland airport right now, waiting for Uncle Mac to pick him up.

"Okay, call us if you hear anything," Wes said before hanging up. He then gave everyone in the room a rundown on the plan. "Jeremy is going to call his grandmother in Scotland to find out when Paul left her house. They're going to drive back here and halfway back they'll call for an update. The friends who are going to the Mackenzies' cabin have our number, and they'll call here, too."

"He's probably stuck at the airport in London," Vicki said. "I'll bet he missed his flight and is still trying to get another one. Or maybe he's already in the air and will call when he arrives in Portland—or Seattle or wherever his plane is going to land."

Just the words "Seattle," "plane," and "land" sent shivers up Sierra's spine.

"Sierra, you don't look very relieved," Vicki said. "Are you still in shock? Paul wasn't on the plane."

"I know," Sierra said.

"It's a lot to process so fast," Amy said, coming to Sierra's defense. "I'm like Sierra. I'll feel better when we know exactly where Paul is and why he missed the plane."

"It *is* a lot to process," Sierra said, pulling Amy to the side. The others had begun to help Wesley and Sierra's mom clean up the kitchen mess. "And your decision is a pretty huge event, too," Sierra said to Amy. "I don't want you to think I don't know how big a step that was for you. I'm so happy, Amy." Sierra tried but couldn't pull up a smile for her friend. "I'm deep down happy that you said what you did and that you let Vicki and me be there when you prayed. I've been praying for this for a long time."

"I know," Amy said quietly. "Thank you."

"So," Warner said, breaking into their twosome, "is it time to let the party begin? What happened to Vicki's hats and blowers?"

Sierra pulled herself out from under Warner's lumbering interference and went over to her dad. "Do you think we should go to the airport in case Paul comes in and doesn't have money to call Uncle Mac to pick him up?" A tiny smile came to her as she remembered how Paul hadn't been prepared with enough British coins for the phone when they had met at the London airport. He probably didn't have any American coins with him on this trip.

"I think he would find a way to call," Mr. Jensen said.

"We could be wandering around the airport for hours when he could still be stuck at Heathrow. It's better to wait here and keep in contact with people calling in."

Sierra nodded and meandered into the study. She shut the door behind her and took refuge in her favorite thinking chair. The study was dark, but she didn't turn on the light. Someone might realize she was there and come in. She needed to be alone, just for a few minutes.

Reviewing the available information, Sierra tried to put together the pieces. Paul could be anywhere. Then, silently moving her lips, with her eyes shut tight, Sierra prayed. For months she had prayed for Amy, and now, just like that, her prayers appeared to have been answered and Amy had come back to the Lord. For more than a year, she had prayed for Paul to turn wholeheartedly to God, and in just the last few weeks, he had. Sierra was so experienced at praying for her friends to come to Christ that she didn't know what to pray after they did.

Party sounds floated in from the kitchen. Everyone was relieved, and after all, this was supposed to be a celebration. But Sierra couldn't find a festive bone in her body at this moment. She knew she wouldn't feel like blowing any party horns until she knew where Paul was and that he was safe. Paul's image of Jesus as the Good Shepherd entered her thoughts. For the first time in her life, Sierra believed she had a tiny understanding of what it must be like for God to have lost sheep and to long for them all to come back to Him. She remembered the story of how the Good Shepherd left his flock of ninety-nine safe sheep to search for the one lost sheep. He didn't end his search until that one was found and brought back safely.

"You brought Amy back," Sierra whispered to the Good Shepherd. "And You brought Paul back. Now please bring Paul back to me. Or, well, bring him back to his family and friends and bring him back safely. I know I can't pretend that I have any right to him. He's Your sheep. And so am I. I know You will lead us and guide us in the future, whether it's separately or together."

Sierra felt a calmness that had been missing during the last few hours of panic. She thought of her frustrated prayer earlier when Randy had gathered the group together. She had said then that God's ways weren't her ways and she was having a hard time understanding those ways. Right now, it seemed she didn't need to understand. All she needed to do was trust.

Before she left the study, Sierra drew in a deep breath. She noticed her lower lip was swollen and wondered how many times she had chewed on it during the last few hours without realizing it. A smile came to her as she thought of how terrible she was going to look when she finally did see Paul. Her lip would be swollen, and her eyes would probably still be red and puffy. Her chin was likely to break out within the next twelve hours. It usually did that when she was under stress and eating a lot of sugar.

The thought of sugar piqued Sierra's interest in eating. She had skipped lunch in all the graduation excitement and then had felt no interest in food when the lobster was served in front of the TV. Right now she could eat about anything.

Sierra's mom and Amy were the only two still in the kitchen when Sierra left the study and joined them. Mrs. Jensen's hands were submerged in soapy dishwater. She turned to Sierra and with a concerned look asked, "How are you doing?"

"I'm okay," Sierra said. "I'm actually kind of hungry."

"That's a good sign. What are you hungry for?"

"I don't know. I'll find something."

Sierra's "something," under Amy's creative direction, turned out to be a lobster sandwich. She cut open one of the dinner rolls and loaded it with lobster and sliced cherry tomatoes. It was even tastier than she imagined it would be.

Sierra found out that while she was in the study, Drake and Cassie had come by, and most of Sierra's guests had left with them to go to another party. She couldn't blame them. This hadn't exactly turned into the evening of enchantment she had planned. The only people left were Amy, Vicki, Randy, and Wes. Sierra's younger brothers had gone to bed. Her parents went upstairs but said they would stay up and wait for news.

Vicki went to her car and brought back a bag filled with yearbooks. They reminisced about Royal Academy and talked about it as if all the things that had happened to them there had taken place a decade ago. Sierra certainly felt she had lived a decade in the last five hours.

The phone rang, and Wes grabbed it. "She's right here," he said and handed the phone to Sierra.

"Hi, Sierra?" It was a deep, male voice. For one second her heart rose, thinking it might be Paul. "It's Drake."

"Oh," she said. Then she quickly added, "Hi."

"Margo just told me about Paul, and I wanted to call and see how you were doing."

"Thanks," Sierra said, pulling away from the group on the living room floor.

Vicki grabbed her leg and mouthed the word, "Paul?"

Sierra shook her head. "It's Drake," she said, covering the mouthpiece.

"Are you okay?" Drake asked. "Margo said you took it pretty hard. I saw the crash on the news. I can see how it would have rocked your world."

"It did," Sierra agreed. "We still haven't heard from Paul, so we don't know where he is. Tawni and Jeremy went to Seattle. They should be back in a couple of hours. I don't know if they'll have any more news or not."

"Well, I just wanted to call you and say happy graduation, and I hope everything turns out with Paul and you."

"Thanks, Drake. I really appreciate that."

"I also wanted to say I appreciated what you wrote in my yearbook. I think you'll always hold a memorable spot in my life, too. I don't have any backpack trips planned this summer, but if I did, I'd want you along for the hike."

"That was an interesting trip, wasn't it?"

"Interesting," Drake repeated.

There was a pause before Drake said, "Well, I, um, I don't know if I'll see you much this summer, so have a good one and maybe we'll run into each other."

"I imagine we will," Sierra said, not sure why Drake would suddenly be so nice to her. He certainly appeared sincere.

"Take care, then. And I hope everything is okay with Paul."

"Thanks, Drake."

He hung up, and she returned to her circle of friends.

"What was that all about?" Amy asked.

Sierra shrugged. "Drake wanted to tell me he hoped everything turned out okay with Paul."

The phone rang again while it was still in Sierra's hand. She jumped before pushing the "On" button. "Hello?"

"Sierra, it's me," Tawni said. "Have you heard anything from Jeremy's parents?"

"Not yet."

"We finally reached his grandmother in Scotland. That was no easy task. She said Paul left last Tuesday because he was going to travel on a rail pass for a few days before he left the country."

Sierra relayed the message to Wesley and the others, who were waiting eagerly, before she answered Tawni. "That means he could be anywhere."

"Exactly. Jeremy is more concerned now, I think, than he was before. Paul would check in; this isn't like him."

"Maybe he tried to call his parents, but they were already in the mountains," Sierra suggested.

"You're right." Sierra could hear Tawni relaying the information to Jeremy and Uncle Mac. Then she said, "Jeremy, does anyone have a key to your parents' house who could listen to their answering machine?"

Jeremy's response was muffled. Sierra heard a loud page in the background.

"Where are you?" she asked.

"We're at the airport. When you guys discovered that Paul wasn't on the flight, Jeremy thought we should come here to see if Paul took another plane out of Heathrow. We've been checking with all the airlines for the past hour, but none of them has Paul listed on any of the flights."

"So he's probably still in London," Sierra surmised.

"That's what Uncle Mac thinks. He's making a few calls right now to see if he can have Paul paged at Heathrow, just in case Paul is stuck there, trying to get a flight out. Oh wait," Tawni said. The sound of muffled voices was drowned by another loud airport page, causing Sierra to hold the phone away from her ear as she explained to the others what Tawni had said.

"Sierra?"

"Yes, I'm still here."

"Uncle Mac didn't get a response to his page at Heathrow."

"What do you think that means?"

"Jeremy thinks Paul never arrived at the airport. He thinks he disappeared somewhere between his grand-mother's house and the airport. He could be anywhere."

Like a storm cloud, Tawni's words blew in and settled over Sierra's heart. With the swiftness of a lightning bolt, the intense pain Sierra had experienced earlier suddenly returned, striking her this time in the throat. She handed the phone to Wes and lowered herself into a chair.

For the first time ever, a jagged thought pierced her. *I might never see Paul Mackenzie on this earth again.*

fourteen

SIERRA DIDN'T LIKE the thoughts that hovered over her throughout the long night. She tried to make them go away. She tried to reason them through. Nothing seemed to help. All she knew was that Paul Mackenzie probably wasn't dead. He was missing. For some reason, that was much more terrifying to wrestle with.

Randy went home around two in the morning. Amy and Vicki stayed. The three girls put out sleeping bags on the living room floor and changed into shorts and T-shirts. They waited all night for the phone to ring.

At a little past four in the morning, the phone finally rang. Sierra jumped to answer it, but the cordless wouldn't respond to her push of the button. The battery had gone out again.

"Somebody get the phone!" she yelled, scrambling for the phone in the kitchen. She grabbed it on the fifth ring. All she heard was a click and some static. The answering machine was set to pick up calls on the fifth ring, so Sierra ran into the study to grab the phone connected to the answering machine.

"Hello?" She could hear her father's recorded message playing over the line. "Wait just a second," she said.

The voice on the other line sounded like a recording also. Sierra listened hard to decipher what it was saying.

"Hello?" Wesley's voice came over the upstairs extension.

"Hang up, Wesley. The phones are all messed up."

"What?"

More static.

"Hang up!" Unfortunately, whoever was on the other end must have thought the command was for him, and he hung up.

"Sierra?" Wesley said.

Frustrated, she hung up the phone and went back into the kitchen to hang up that extension. Wes came bounding down the stairs, along with Sierra's dad.

"Who was it?"

"Our phones are messed up!" Sierra stated, pushing her hair out of her face. "If it rings again, only one person should answer it. I really think it could have been Paul."

Vicki and Amy appeared from the living room; Amy was holding the dead cordless phone.

"Are you sure?" Mr. Jensen asked Sierra.

Sierra felt like crying. "I'm not sure of anything. I tried to get it before the answering machine picked it up and then..." Before Sierra could finish, a clear thought broke through her deep blue funk. "The answering machine!"

She turned and headed back to the study. The confused troop followed her.

"Did anyone ever listen to the messages?" Sierra bent over the machine and pushed the rewind button.

They heard a beep, and then an electronic-sounding voice said, "This is the overseas operator. Will you accept a collect call from…" There was a click and then in his own voice they heard Paul say, "Paul Mackenzie." A pause followed as the electronic overseas operator tried to discern if the answer to its question was "yes" or "no." Of course all the answering machine gave was silence as the tape rolled, so the mechanical operator hung up.

"No," Sierra cried. "Why did it do that? Where is he? When did he call?"

The next message beeped, and the group fell silent again to listen. It was the same mechanical operator, only this time, instead of Paul's saying his name, he listed some numbers. Again, when there was no answer, the "operator" hung up.

"He's trying to leave you a message," Amy said. "Those numbers! Play it back, and write down the numbers. You can call them and see if he's there."

It seemed a little strange to Sierra's dad, but Sierra agreed with Amy. If Paul realized he couldn't get the phone to take a message, he had to use whatever means he could to communicate with them. Sierra wondered if Paul had tried to reach his parents as well but only got their machine. Uncle Mac had been at the airport waiting for Paul, so it was possible Paul hadn't been able to reach him yesterday afternoon, either.

Sierra replayed the message while Wes wrote down the numbers. They tried phoning them only to hear a recording that said their call couldn't go through as dialed.

"It's probably a London number," Sierra said. "Don't we have to dial another number first to get international access? I know there's a code for each country in Europe."

"I'll call the operator," Wes said.

"It'll be a machine," Vicki predicted.

But it was an actual person, and Wes set to work, trying to solve the mystery. The operator tried seven different possibilities, but none of those seven codes with the numbers Paul left was the right combination. They tried one more, and Wesley looked up excitedly.

"I have a connection. It's ringing." He held up his hand, motioning for silence. "Yes, hello," he said into the receiver. "What did you say this was? Danbury House? Yes, well, I'm not sure I have the correct number. Pardon me? Yes, I am calling from the U.S. I'm trying to contact Paul Mackenzie. By any chance is he there?"

Sierra held her breath and bit her lower lip.

"Yes, I understand. Could you check your roster, though, and see if his name appears? Oh, I see. Yes."

"What?" Sierra begged to know, tugging on Wesley's arm.

"So he left this morning, and you don't expect him to return," Wesley repeated. "Do you know if he was planning to go to the airport? Did he say anything about flying back home today?"

It was silent far too long.

"Yes. I understand. Thank you. Good-bye."

"What?" Sierra asked before Wes had even hung up the phone.

"The Danbury House is some sort of homeless shelter in London. Paul checked in last night and left this morning. She said he had to go to the free clinic to get some stitches."

"Stitches?" they all repeated.

Before they could get any more information from Wes, Tawni and Jeremy arrived, looking exhausted.

"Paul's in London," Sierra announced. "He tried to call here. Is Uncle Mac in the car?"

"He dropped us off. What did you find out?"

Wes relayed the story and added the details the others were waiting for. "Apparently, Paul arrived last night with some cuts on his face. They cleaned him up, gave him some food and a bed, and sent him to a clinic this morning. The woman I talked to remembered Paul. She talked about him as if he were a common street bum."

Sierra began to put together the pieces. "He must have been mugged," she surmised. "The robber beat him up and took everything, which is why Paul couldn't take the plane home yesterday. And they took his money, so that's why he's calling collect."

The others looked at her as if she had an overly active imagination.

"It fits," Jeremy was the first to say. "If his passport was taken, that would explain why he didn't leave England yet."

"Where would he go to get a new passport?" Tawni asked.

"The American Embassy," Sierra said. She had traveled to Europe twice and had learned enough to know what to do in an emergency. "Let's call there and leave a message for him."

Jeremy called this time. Mr. Jensen retreated to the kitchen to start a pot of coffee, nice and dark, the way he liked it. Sierra and the others waited. Tawni flopped onto the living room couch and told them to wake her as soon as there was some news.

Twenty minutes later, Jeremy met with success. He reached the embassy and found out that Paul had been there earlier and had registered all the necessary forms. The agent at the embassy wouldn't give out any further information, such as whether or not the passport had been stolen. They still didn't know where he was, but at least he was okay.

Sierra felt as if she could begin to breathe again, and she drew in generous lungsful of air. The smell of her dad's strong coffee filled her nostrils, and she decided to try half a cup, mixed with lots of cream and sugar. Paul had dreamed of drinking good coffee again, and now that they knew he was okay, Sierra felt she could start the celebration before he arrived.

At five o'clock the phone rang. Sierra answered, and it was Uncle Mac saying he had just received a collect call from Paul, and he was all right. Sierra quickly told him everything they had figured out, and Mac said, "Good detective work, Sherlock! You pretty much figured it out. He got off a bus in London in the wrong district. He had stayed the night at a youth hostel and was trying to take the bus to the airport to catch his flight. When he realized he was on the wrong bus, he got off, hoping to catch the next one. It was a bad area, and no cabs were around for him to hail. He said he waited at the bus stop for more than an hour, but no bus came. He asked someone for directions and took off walking, which was probably his second mistake. The directions led him down an alley, and that's where the hoodlums got him. It was as if they were lying in wait for him, he said."

"Did they hurt him?" Sierra asked.

"Yes. They knocked him down and took everything: his backpack, wallet, money, passport. I think he said he had four stitches put in his chin this morning at a clinic."

"This is so awful!" Sierra said.

The others were gathering around Sierra, waiting for an update. She motioned that she would tell them everything in just a minute.

"I was able to wire him some money," Uncle Mac said. "At least he can find something to eat and buy some shoes. They took his shoes, and he's been walking around London barefoot."

Sierra couldn't imagine what Paul had been through. But at least he was safe. And he would be home soon.

"How long will it take him to get his passport?" Sierra asked.

"He didn't say. He's going to try to reach his parents today and figure out his ticket home. I told him his folks were at the cabin but to keep trying them because they were heading home. If he doesn't contact them by tonight his time, I told him to call me back and I'd work out the ticket with him."

"Did he sound okay?" Sierra asked. "I mean, was he feeling all right?"

"You'll be able to tell me in a little while," Uncle Mac said. "I told him to call you and Jeremy at your house and to charge it to my account. I'd better get off the line because he was going to wait twenty minutes and then give you a call."

Sierra hung up and gave the group the update. Everyone responded at once.

"He could have been killed."

"I'm so glad he's okay."

"Barefoot? Through London? No thank you."

"When is he going to call?"

"Any minute," Sierra said, checking the clock on the microwave. She sipped her overly sweetened, cooled coffee and decided it wasn't worth the effort.

The first streaks of morning had broken into the kitchen, bringing a sense of comfort and hope to the weary bunch. Mr. Jensen decided to make a batch of scrambled eggs. Jeremy helped him with the toast, and Amy unloaded the dishwasher so Wesley would have glasses for the orange juice he was making. Sierra sat and watched, waiting for the phone to ring. She realized no one had told Tawni the good news, so Sierra slipped into the living room and woke her sister.

"Paul's okay. He's in London. He was robbed."

Tawni raised up on her elbow and squinted. "He was robbed?"

"Yes, but he's all right. He's trying to get another passport and a ticket home."

"That's awful!"

"No, it's good," Sierra said. "He's alive. He's coming home."

"I'm so glad," Tawni said, lying back down. "Do you mind if I go back to sleep?"

"Not at all. Do you want to go upstairs to bed?"

"No. I just want to…" Tawni's voice trailed off, and she was back asleep.

Sierra returned to the kitchen, trying not to appear too frustrated that the phone hadn't rung yet. Mr. Jensen was beginning to dish up the eggs, so she grabbed a paper plate and let him pile it on. The conversation swirled around the weary bunch. No one but Sierra seemed nervous that the phone hadn't rung. She could barely stand the suspense. There was so much she wanted to ask Paul.

At 7:10 the phone finally rang. Vicki and Amy had gone home. Wes had fallen asleep in a chair in the living room. Jeremy had crashed on the living room floor. Sierra and her dad were the only two still awake. Mr. Jensen had gone outside to work in the yard while it was cool, and Sierra was cleaning the kitchen. It was a good outlet for her nervous energy. She had even mopped the floor, since it was sticky where the buckets of lobsters had rested the night before.

She answered the phone, breathless from the mopping.

"Good morning," the male voice said. "I apologize for calling so early. This is Pastor Mackenzie. Is my son Jeremy there?"

"Yes, I'll get him." Sierra felt like the maid, standing there with the mop in her hand and her hair twisted up and held on top of her head with a clip. She had waited so patiently for Paul to call, but here it was his dad instead, and he had no idea who Sierra was or why she was important to his son.

Sierra woke Jeremy and said, "Your dad is on the phone. You'd better take it in the kitchen or the study because the cordless isn't working right."

Jeremy shook himself awake and stretched his long arms over his head as he went into the kitchen. "Dad?" he said, taking the phone. "Yeah. I'm fine. What have you heard?"

Sierra remained inconspicuous in the background while Jeremy and his dad compared notes on Paul's situation. She gathered from a few of the comments Jeremy made that Paul had obtained a ticket and could use it as soon as his new passport was issued. Jeremy hung up and turned to see if Sierra was still in the kitchen.

She looked up sheepishly, as if she had been caught eavesdropping. Jeremy walked over to where she stood wiping off the counter for the ninth time. He looked so compassionate and understanding that she knew something was wrong.

"What?" she said. "What is it? Is Paul okay?"

Jeremy nodded. "He's okay. But his ticket is a direct flight to San Diego. He won't be able to come through Portland."

"Oh," Sierra said, trying to appear brave. "That's understandable."

"I'm sorry," Jeremy said, putting a brotherly hand on her shoulder. "I know how much you were looking forward to seeing him."

fifteen

JEREMY'S COMMENT stayed with Sierra for the next three days as she floated in a deep blue funk, waiting for the phone to ring and for the voice on the other end to be Paul's. But he didn't call.

Sierra had time on her hands, since school was out and she had taken off these days from work. She had intended to fill the time with an unending list of adventures with Paul. Instead, she spent most of the days in her room alone, thinking of how Jeremy had tried to comfort her when he said, "I know how much you were looking forward to seeing him."

Did he mean that I was looking forward to being with Paul more than Paul was looking forward to being with me? she thought. *Jeremy read the letter. He saw how much Paul cares.*

Every now and then, Sierra could cheer herself up with the thought that Paul had several complications in his life at the moment and that he would call her when he arrived home. She was being unfair to expect a phone call when the poor guy was traipsing barefoot through London with four stitches in his chin. He had places to go, things to buy, tickets to book.

Still, she wondered how hard it would be to find a phone, use his uncle's charge number, and call her. Two minutes—that's all she needed. A two-minute call that said, "I'm fine. I'm sorry I didn't get to see you. I'll come up to Portland as soon as I can." Two minutes—that's all it would take. And then her life could go on again.

Tawni and Jeremy had left Sunday morning. Tawni's roommate had called and said a photo shoot was scheduled for Tawni on Tuesday morning that her agent had forgotten to tell her about. They left in a hurry, both tired and not looking forward to the two-day drive home. Sierra felt sorry for her sister, since she knew she had a hard time sleeping in the car. Tawni would probably end up splitting the driving with Jeremy when she had planned on the brothers' doing all the driving.

Wesley had gone back to Corvallis, where he was taking a summer-school course and working at a grocery store. Sierra missed her brother and sister more than she thought she would. In that one emotion-packed weekend, Sierra, Tawni, and Wesley had become closer than ever. Part of it might have been due to Sierra's graduating. Now she officially was a member of the older Jensen children group instead of the oldest member of the younger Jensen children group. In addition, the three of them had stood beside Jeremy as he had faced the possibility of losing his brother, and that had made them process all their feelings for each other.

Randy came by twice to try to convince Sierra that she should do something with the rest of the gang. She just didn't feel like it, and Randy seemed to understand.

Vicki and Amy seemed to understand her depression, too. Vicki had called at four on Monday afternoon to suggest that Sierra meet with Vicki and Amy at Mama Bear's. Sierra told Vicki she just didn't feel like it yet.

"Are you still waiting for him to call?" Vicki asked.

Sierra didn't answer. She felt childish waiting around for the phone to ring when she should be out having a great time now that she had graduated.

"Have you heard if he's arrived in San Diego yet? I mean, did he get home safely?"

"I haven't heard. I don't think Tawni is home yet. I'll call her tomorrow."

"Well, do you want to do something on Wednesday?" Vicki asked. "I don't have to work until noon that day. We could meet for breakfast or something."

"Sure," Sierra agreed.

Now it was Wednesday, and she was on her way to meet Vicki and Amy for breakfast. She still had received no news of Paul. Tawni hadn't returned her calls; Sierra guessed Tawni was out on a shoot. For all Sierra knew, Paul could still be in London, waiting for a new passport.

In some ways, she had moved past the emotional churning of the weekend and had grown in the process. She had slept long hours and had thought deep and hard about life and death, love and pain. She had written a lot in her diary, read a lot in her Bible, and talked a lot with her dad.

When she arrived at Mama Bear's Bakery, Vicki and Amy were waiting for her at their favorite window table. Just seeing her friends' smiling faces as she walked up to the bakery made Sierra's spirits feel lighter. She realized nothing was better in this life than friends who were there for her when she needed them.

Mrs. Kraus called to Sierra from behind the counter before she had a chance to join Vicki and Amy. "Could you come here a minute?"

Sierra joined Mrs. Kraus at the register. No customers were waiting for cinnamon rolls at the moment. "I was going to call you, so I'm glad you stopped by. Jody gave her notice yesterday."

"Oh, that's too bad. I'm going to miss her."

"Yes," Mrs. Kraus said, "we'll all miss Jody. But lots of hours are now up for grabs, and I wanted to tell you, since you had been asking about more hours this summer."

"That's perfect. Yes, I'll take whatever you can give me. But you remember, don't you, that I'll be here only until the second week of August?"

"Yes. And I'll miss you, too. But until then I'll give you most of Jody's hours, and you can earn some spending money for your college days."

"Thank you so much."

"My pleasure." Mrs. Kraus smiled. "Peppermint tea this morning?"

Sierra nodded and went over to join her friends. "Did you guys already order?"

"We're each having our own cinnamon roll today," Amy said. "Mrs. Kraus said a fresh batch would be out in five minutes, so we're waiting."

"Guess what?" Vicki's smile was wide.

"I don't know," Sierra said. "But I have a 'guess what' for you, too. Mrs. Kraus is giving me more hours. Now that is a huge God-thing."

"And this is a huge God-thing, too," Vicki said, still smiling. She pulled a legal-sized envelope from her purse.

Before Sierra saw the return address, she knew. "You were accepted at Rancho!" She threw her arms around Vicki in a hug. "I knew it! I knew it!"

Vicki laughed. "How did you know?"

"Because they can't break us up. We need each other too much." As soon as Sierra said it, she realized she had excluded Amy from the "we." "I mean…"

"It's okay," Amy said. "I guess I have a God-thing for both of you."

Vicki and Sierra waited. Amy had never referred to anything in her life as a God-thing before.

"Yesterday I sent in my application for Rancho. I guess I felt the same way you do, Sierra. They can't break us up. Besides, I've forgotten all the reasons I didn't want to go to a Christian college."

Sierra and Vicki were out of their chairs, hugging Amy and both talking at once. Mrs. Kraus showed up with the cinnamon rolls and tea, and they settled back in the chairs.

"You know what?" Amy spoke softly. "I feel as if I've changed so much in the past…what, how many days has it been since I prayed with you guys? Five days? Six now? I feel…I don't know—put back together or something."

"That is so great, Amy," Sierra said. "I feel as if I've been on a soul search, too, these past few days. I don't know if I feel put back together yet, but I'm getting there."

"You'll probably feel better once you hear from Paul and know that he's safe," Vicki said.

Sierra agreed and put the first bite of warm cinnamon roll into her mouth. The gooey frosting clung to her lower lip, and she wiped it with her napkin. Then Sierra looked out the window and noticed her mom coming toward Mama Bear's with something in her hand.

As her mom entered the bakery, Sierra immediately said, "Is everything okay?"

Mrs. Jensen smiled. "A courier just delivered this. It's from Paul, and I'll be honest, I couldn't wait for you to get home to open it."

They all laughed. Sierra took the second-day international mail envelope from her mom and coyly said, "What makes you think I'm going to open it in front of you guys?"

They all protested at once. Sierra said, "Okay, okay. Just let me read it first in private, okay?" She pulled out a single sheet of stationery from a hotel called The Edwina Courtyard and skimmed it quickly. The letter directed her to something else in the envelope, which she pulled out. It was small, thin, and wrapped in a single piece of tissue.

"What is it?" Amy asked.

"What did the letter say?" Vicki asked.

Sierra ignored them just long enough to pull back the tissue. She extracted a long chain with a silver emblem hanging from it.

"A daffodil," Mrs. Jensen said, reaching over to finger the dainty necklace. "It's beautiful, Sierra."

"Put it on," Amy urged.

Sierra slipped it over her head and adjusted the daffodil so that the finely detailed lines were showing. She grinned at her mom and then at Amy and Vicki. "Do you want to hear the letter?"

"Oh, no, that's okay," Vicki teased.

"I want to hear it," Mrs. Jensen said, moving in closer.

Dear Daffodil Queen,

What a weekend! I honestly hope yours was better than mine. However, after I heard about the crash in Seattle, I realized my experience wasn't so bad. Do you think sometimes God allows uncomfortable things to happen so that other, worse things won't happen? I've learned so much these past few days. I am convinced that, when we are God's own, we are indestructible until He is finished with us. Bad things happen to us, true. The storms come. But none of His sheep are ever out of His care.

I've enclosed your graduation gift. I had it made in the village where my grandmother lives. It's a daffodil, as you can see. It represents your bold spirit, Sierra—the way you brightly proclaim the truth. I had the chain made extra long so you could wear it next to your heart.

Now, I have to tell you, I intended to buy a proper box and wrap it before I gave it to you. However, since I didn't have a box, I wore the necklace while I was in London. It's about the only thing that wasn't taken from me. Perhaps they didn't notice it inside my shirt, next to my heart.

"Oh," Vicki said with a sigh, "this is the most romantic letter in the world, Sierra. Can you believe the necklace wasn't stolen?"

The women exchanged looks of amazement.

"There's a little more," Sierra said, continuing to read.

Since I won't be coming to Portland, I wanted to get this necklace to you as quickly and safely as possible, so I'm sending it from London as I wait for my passport to clear. There's been a hitch over my visa, since I was on a student visa this past year in Scotland.

When I finally arrive at my parents' house, I'll call you. Until
then, may the peace of our Good Shepherd be upon you.
With hope and affection,
Paul

Sierra looked up. Her mom, Vicki, and Amy were gazing at her with soft, mushy-hearted expressions.

"I think I'm going to cry," Mrs. Jensen said.

Sierra felt embarrassed. She had never shared one of
Paul's letters with her mother before. She wondered if Paul
would mind that she had read his carefully crafted words in
a public place to these women. Too late now. Looking
down, Sierra gently rubbed her thumb over the silver daffodil. "It's beautiful, isn't it?"

Vicki leaned closer and admired the gift. "Forget everything Amy and I tried to teach you about guys. Whatever we
learned from our past boyfriends is worthless. Whatever
you're doing with Paul is working perfectly."

"I'm not 'doing' anything," Sierra said. "Except praying.
You know that. I've prayed for him since the day I met him."

Amy grinned. "I predict an improvement in Vicki's
prayer life this summer!"

Vicki laughed. "If Randy mails me a guitar pick he once
used to pick his teeth, we'll know that Sierra's formula
works."

They all laughed.

"You girls are teasing, aren't you?" Mrs. Jensen said.
"You do know there are no formulas when it comes to love.
Praying for a guy doesn't guarantee he will suddenly become
interested in you."

"Oh, Mom, we're only kidding," Sierra said, folding Paul's letter and tucking it back in the mailer.

"Just checking," Mrs. Jensen said with a grin. "I guess I should get going."

"No, stay," Amy pleaded.

"Yes, please stay," Vicki agreed.

Sierra hopped up. "I'll be right back with your very own cinnamon roll and a milk."

"Nonfat, please," her mom said.

"Okay! Nonfat milk with a five-thousand-calorie cinnamon roll. That's going to make a big difference!" Sierra laughed all the way to the counter. As she walked, she could feel her new silver necklace tap lightly against her T-shirt. She fingered it again, feeling as bright, bold, and steady as the daffodil Paul had encountered on his hike.

It suddenly didn't matter that the weekend's events had nearly crushed her. Paul was right. Storms do come. But after the storm comes a gentle calm like Sierra was feeling in her heart right then. In that calm, Sierra knew she and her Good Shepherd were closer than ever.

Book Twelve

TAKE MY HAND

one

SIERRA JENSEN BENT DOWN and lifted the dust ruffle, taking one last look under her bed. Not even a dust bunny greeted her. The space was clean and cleared out, just like the rest of her bedroom.

Sierra sat up and for a brief moment admired the rare view. The warm breezes of the late August afternoon pushed their way past the sheer curtains, compelling them to hop out of the way. Then, racing around the room, past the antique dresser with the oval mirror, the overstuffed chair, and the two twin beds made up with ivory chenille bedspreads, the breezes found nothing out of place to disrupt and flew out the door and down the hallway of the old Victorian house.

Sierra's bedroom had never been so orderly—except maybe when her family moved to Portland the middle of her junior year of high school. She had been in England the week they moved, and when she first had stepped into this room, it looked this tidy. But that tidiness was due to her older sister, Tawni, who had been the one to put everything in its place.

Now Sierra was all packed and leaving for college. Tawni had moved out a year ago and last week had announced her engagement to Jeremy. It seemed only a blink of time since their family had moved here, and a sudden sadness swept over Sierra as another rush of late summer breezes muscled their way through the screen on the second-story window and rushed around her room.

"Is that everything?" Sierra's mom asked, stepping in from the hallway. She must have read the wistful look on Sierra's face because, with a knowing smile, Mrs. Jensen came over and sat down next to her daughter on the edge of the bed.

"Where did it go?" Sierra asked quietly.

"Did you lose something?" her mom asked.

Sierra sighed. "My childhood. It was here a minute ago."

Mrs. Jensen laughed softly and slipped her arm around Sierra's shoulders. "I know, honey. Believe me, I know."

"What if I want it back?"

"Sorry. It's on to the next step."

"But what if I really mess up?" Sierra said. "What if I turn out to be really bad at being responsible?"

Mrs. Jensen laughed again.

"What if I'm not cut out for college life?"

"What would you rather do?"

"I don't know. Travel, maybe. Go live in Europe for a while. Sail the seven seas. Hike Mount Fuji."

"You can do all those things as long as..." Mrs. Jensen paused.

"As long as I go to college first, right?"

"No, I was going to say, as long as you ask your Father."

"Ask Dad?" Sierra said, giving her mother a questioning look.

Mrs. Jensen pointed upward. "No, your heavenly Father. You have no idea yet what amazing adventures lie ahead of you in adulthood. God, on the other hand, has your future all planned out. So get used to asking Him. Always. About everything. He'll lead you, Sierra."

Quietly, Sierra added, "He'll lead me like the Good Shepherd that He is." She felt a warmth come over her at the memory of Paul's words from a letter he had written to her months ago. It was the last letter he had written before he left Scotland, and he had talked about God as the Good Shepherd who cares for and protects His sheep. Thinking about that made the future seem less terrifying. How could it be frightening when God had already been there?

Sierra jumped up from the bed as her startled mother looked at her.

"Oh no! What time is it? I'm supposed to meet Amy and Vicki at Mama Bear's. I almost forgot, and I'm probably already late," Sierra said.

"Oh." Mrs. Jensen rose and glanced around the room. "You have everything ready, I see. Did Wes pack those last two boxes into the trailer?"

"He took them down. I don't know if they fit." Sierra felt a little funny about the melancholy moment she had just had with her mom. After all, Sierra's older brother Wes was going to the same university she was attending in Southern California: Rancho Corona. Wes had graduated from Oregon State University. Now he was going on for his master's at Rancho Corona. And Tawni lived less than an hour's drive from the college. Sierra wasn't sure why she had suddenly felt so sad about leaving. It wasn't as if she were leaving all her family and friends.

Actually, she was going to be with most of her closest friends when she went to college. Vicki and Randy were flying to Southern California the next weekend and had brought over a lot of their belongings the night before so Sierra's dad and Wes could pack them in the rented trailer that was hooked up to the Jensen family van.

Tomorrow, Friday, in the morning, Sierra, Mr. Jensen, Wes, and Sierra's two youngest brothers, Gavin and Dillon, would leave for the two-day road trip. Mrs. Jensen would fly down on Saturday with Granna Mae, with whom the family lived. They would all gather in San Diego for Tawni's big engagement party.

"I have to run," Sierra told her mom, dashing down the stairs. "I'll be back soon. If Paul phones, tell him to call back after eight. Is it okay if I take your car?"

Mrs. Jensen stood at the top of the stairs. When Sierra turned to look to her for an answer, she thought her mom was the one who looked wistful now. Their mother-daughter moment had been cut short.

"Sure. Have a good time. The keys are on the hook in the kitchen."

At moments like this Sierra most admired her mom. Sometimes Sierra wondered if her mom had been blessed with an extra-sensitive memory so that she remembered what it was like to be seventeen and to have friends who were almost more important than family, and feelings that were almost overwhelming. Certainly she knew what Sierra was feeling now because she let Sierra go rather than try to extend their time together.

The screen door slammed behind Sierra as she went out the back door. Her dad and Wes were still reconfiguring the jigsaw puzzle of boxes that needed to be loaded into the trailer.

"Lots of junk, huh?" Sierra said.

"It's not junk," Wesley corrected her. "You'll find these few worldly possessions are your favorite treasures once you get to school."

Mr. Jensen took a swig from the soft drink can he held. The late afternoon sun hit the top of his head just right, highlighting the perspiration beaded up where his hairline was receding. "It's all this band equipment that Randy wants to send with us that's not exactly fitting into the trailer."

"He said it was okay if you couldn't fit it in, didn't he?" Sierra said. Randy and some of his friends had started a band that had pretty much fallen apart by midsummer. Sierra knew that Randy was bringing along all the band equipment only because he owned it, not because he necessarily needed it. "I mean, if you can't fit it in, you can't." Sierra rolled up the sleeves of her long, white cotton shirt. It was actually one of her dad's old shirts, which she had put on over her shorts and tank top when she was packing stuff that morning. All the windows had been open, and the air had been cool then. Somehow, having her dad's shirtsleeves around her as she packed and cleaned had been comforting, and so Sierra had left it on.

"Oh, we'll get it in somehow," Mr. Jensen said. "You might be sitting on a few duffel bags in the van for the next two days, but we'll get it all in."

"I'm going to Mama Bear's," Sierra said, pulling her long, curly blond hair up in a clip she had just discovered in her shirt's pocket. She had stuck it there a few hours ago and then, forgetting where she had put it, had wasted twenty minutes going through her packed luggage trying to find it when her room started to heat up.

"Hey, buy some cinnamon rolls for tomorrow's breakfast," Mr. Jensen said. He reached into his pocket to pull out a money clip.

"I've got it," Sierra said, patting the small wallet pouch she had tucked in her back pocket. "My treat."

Mr. Jensen smiled one of his crinkles-around-the-corners-of-the-eyes smiles. He didn't have to say any words. That look told Sierra he was proud of her and he loved her.

She turned away quickly before the sensation of her father's loving glance could work its way to the center of her tender heart. She opened the door of her mom's new white sedan and slid across the seat. It was actually a used car but new to Mrs. Jensen. Just three days ago they had traded in the old Volkswagen Rabbit that Sierra had shared with her mom for the past year. Several months ago, her parents had given the car to Sierra, but that meant she was responsible for her own insurance payments and for all the gas she used.

It wasn't hard for her to decide not to take the car with her to college. She had worked out a good deal with her parents when they said they would buy it back from her. Sierra now had enough spending money to make it through at least the first semester, so she wouldn't have to find a job right away.

Wesley had done the same thing, selling his finicky sports car and pocketing the profit. Several friends who were going to Rancho had assured Sierra and Wes that those with cars would help those without get around. Their friends also told them that the public transportation in that area was much more convenient than in most parts of Southern California.

As Sierra drove the short city blocks to the bakery where she had worked the past year and a half, she felt another wave of memories. This older part of town had become so familiar. She remembered so many amazing and frustrating things that had happened here, such as the time they thought Granna Mae had wandered away from home in one of her forgetful states and they had combed the area looking for her. Or the time Sierra had marched down the street to the mailbox, where she mailed her first brazen letter to Paul, telling him exactly what she thought of him.

That memory brought an irrepressible smile. She and Paul had come so far in their relationship since their earlier communication, when he had teasingly called her the "Daffodil Queen." Then the term had insulted her. Now it warmed her. Daffodil Queen was Paul's nickname for her, and when he called her that over the phone during one of their conversations, she always melted inside.

Still smiling, Sierra cautiously parallel-parked her mom's car along the busy street in the Hawthorne District, a few blocks from Mama Bear's. This was about the same spot where Paul had driven by her as she walked one rainy day, carrying an armful of daffodils home for Granna Mae, who was recovering from surgery. Now, as Sierra stepped from the car and made sure she had locked all the doors, she thought of how right here, on this sidewalk, the Daffodil Queen legend had begun.

She stood still for a moment, feeling the intense summer sun beat down on her shoulders. Cars roared past, shoppers bobbed in and out of the unique shops, a guy wearing dark blue knee pads jogged by with a very young golden retriever on a short leash. But Sierra stood still, eager to remember every sight and sound. Tomorrow she would leave all this and start the next chapter in her life.

Reaching instinctively, as she had countless times, for the long silver chain around her neck, Sierra felt the shape of the silver daffodil that hung at the end of the necklace. It had been Paul's graduation present to her in June and her only link to him all summer. The sporadic phone calls and few letters didn't carry the same meaning as this necklace did. This was a gift from his heart, a daffodil he had had made for her by a jeweler in Scotland. Whenever Sierra held it like this, it was as if she were holding Paul's hand. In two short days, she would exchange the cool silver touch of the daffodil for the warm grasp of Paul's hand, because in two days she would see him face-to-face for the first time in more than a year.

two

SIERRA BIT HER LOWER LIP and forced herself to move toward the bakery, where her friends were certainly waiting for her by now. Vicki, Amy, and she had met there once a week for months. They would bend their heads close, open their hearts wide, and lower their voices to levels at which only true friends dare listen in. This last meeting was going to be awful.

The bell above the door of Mama Bear's Bakery chimed merrily, as if today were any other day. Sierra had heard that bell at least a million times, she estimated. Today was the first time the sound brought tears to her eyes.

Blinking quickly and forcing herself to look at the familiar table by the window, Sierra saw Amy and Vicki in the thick of conversation and unaware that Sierra had entered. She took advantage of the moment and went to the counter, where her dear-hearted boss, Mrs. Kraus, was ringing up an order.

Sierra stood in line behind a dark-haired woman with a toddler balanced on her hip. Bending her first two fingers in a friendly wave at the boy, Sierra smiled at him. He turned away, burying his face in his mommy's shoulder, but only for a minute before shyly emerging and examining Sierra with serious gray eyes. The toddler then turned his head to the side and gave Sierra an adorable smile that she couldn't help but return.

What a little doll! Sierra thought. *If I were responsible for raising him and if he ever gave me one of those grins when I was about to say no, I'm afraid I couldn't deny him anything.*

She waved again and offered her most engaging smile. The boy kept smiling at her.

Just then the woman carrying him turned to see what had captured the child's attention, and when she turned, Sierra recognized her immediately.

"Jalene," she said without thinking.

Jalene looked closely at Sierra, raising one thin, dark eyebrow in an obvious sign of nonrecognition.

"Jalene," Sierra said again, having a hard time formulating her thoughts. "Hi."

"I'm sorry," Jalene said coolly. "Have we met before?" She had fine, dark facial features, and her hair wasn't as short and jet-black as it used to be. Sierra remembered the catlike smile that had curved up Jalene's lips when Sierra first had seen her almost two years ago. But Jalene's lips weren't smiling now.

"No, we haven't met. I'm Sierra. Sierra Jensen."

Jalene still looked confused. The toddler on her hip had lost his smile now, too.

Sierra let out a nervous laugh and wished she had kept her mouth shut for once. Now she needed to explain. "I'm Paul's...I mean, I know Paul. Paul Mackenzie."

Jalene's eyes widened, but her smile still didn't come.

"He, um, I mean I...well, we met in England, and actually we were on the same plane when he was coming back from his grandfather's funeral. I saw you at the airport when you picked him up. That's how I know who you are. Paul told me. Your name, I mean. Paul told me you were picking him up."

A faint recognition came across Jalene's face.

Sierra laughed again nervously. "As a matter of fact, I loaned Paul the money to call you from London. He didn't have enough change, and I was waiting to use the phone, and...well, that's kind of how we met."

Jalene shifted the toddler to her other hip. "And Paul and you are together now?"

Sierra had no idea how to answer that. She and Paul hadn't defined their relationship. How could she summarize it for Jalene? Her pause and probably her involuntary facial expression must have told Jalene more than her careful explanation. "Well, my sister is engaged to Paul's brother, and so that's kind of the connection."

"Oh."

Panic washed over Sierra faster than she could compose herself. She wanted to run into the bathroom and hide her face from this scrutinizing former girlfriend of Paul's. She didn't trust her tongue not to slip and say something ridiculous, like how she had ended up at Paul's old college accidentally one day and how she had seen Jalene at the gas station and then again in the parking lot and had watched her secretly and that's really why Sierra recognized her.

It felt bizarre to be face-to-face with this woman. This was the girlfriend Sierra had prayed Paul would break up with. And when they did break up, Paul had told Sierra his mother thought Sierra was an angel for praying so diligently. Sierra literally bit her tongue so she wouldn't slip up and blurt out to Jalene that Sierra's earnest prayers had quite possibly contributed to Paul and Jalene's breakup.

"Well," Jalene said after an awkward pause had paralyzed both of them long enough. "Nice meeting you. Tell Paul I said hello when you see him."

Sierra nodded and tried to smile naturally. "Okay" was the only word she let slip out of her mouth.

Jalene adjusted the little boy on her hip and lifted the white bag of warm cinnamon rolls from where Mrs. Kraus had placed them on the counter before going into the back. Two more customers had entered the shop, and now Sierra was at the front of the line. Sierra started to turn away from Jalene but felt the woman's dark eyes holding her longer than necessary in their examination.

The cat smile never came to Jalene's lips. But the little boy in her arms made up for her coolness by granting Sierra one more heart-melting grin from his tilted head. Sierra waved good-bye to him, and Jalene turned and walked out of the bakery without looking back.

"Ready for some tea, dear?" Mrs. Kraus asked when Sierra finally turned to greet her. "The girls have already picked up their tea and roll."

"Yes. I'd like to have some peppermint tea, if you have any more. I know we were out last Monday."

"I just received my tea shipments yesterday," Mrs. Kraus said. "And this is my treat. Vicki told me it was the last time for you three. I'd like to treat all of you."

"That's so sweet of you. Thanks. I also want a dozen

cinnamon rolls before I go home, and those I want to pay for. It's for breakfast tomorrow before we hit the road."

"You let me know when you're ready to leave, and I'll have them packed up for you." Mrs. Kraus stepped away from the register to fill a little ceramic teapot with boiling water. Sierra looked down at the familiar counter with the tip jar next to the register. The jar had sat on the counter ever since Sierra had worked at Mama Bear's and had a handwritten sign taped to it. The sign read, "If you fear change, leave it here." And the jar was always filled with change.

Sierra pulled a five-dollar bill from her pouch and tucked it into the change jar. Yes, it was symbolic of how she feared this change in her life, but it was also the least she could do for dear Mrs. Kraus, who had done so much for her. The world had never seen a more kind-hearted boss, and Sierra knew she would probably never again have such an enjoyable job with such a flexible schedule.

Smiling her thanks when Mrs. Kraus handed her the teapot and cup with the peppermint tea bag, Sierra realized her tongue was sore. Probably from biting it too long while she was trying not to slip up around Jalene. Sierra walked over to the window table, swishing her tongue from side to side and then sticking it out to make sure it wasn't swollen.

"Oh, well, that's real attractive," Vicki said, watching Sierra approach them.

Sierra made a goofy face, and Vicki and Amy both smiled.

Smiling is a good way to start this time together, Sierra thought. *I don't know if I'm up for how things will most likely end.*

"Who were you talking to at the counter?" Amy asked.

She was the analytical one of the trio, and Sierra wondered for a moment how much she wanted to say. Amy's steady dark eyes locked in on Sierra's blue-gray ones and seemed to pull Sierra's free spirit down to the table, where all secrets were shared openly.

Sierra took her time, sitting down and dunking her tea bag in the pot. She could feel Vicki staring at her, too, waiting for an explanation. Whereas Amy attracted attention because of her short, wavy dark hair and dramatic Italian looks, Vicki was even more attractive. She was, in fact, stunning. Her long, straight brown hair hung like silk from a center part, and her light green eyes were set like precious stones in her perfectly balanced face. Both of these friends had intimidated Sierra more than once with their piercing looks, and she knew if she glanced up from her teapot, they would both do it to her again.

So she didn't look up. She poured the tea into her cup and answered while gazing at her reflection in the steaming tea. "That was Jalene, Paul's old girlfriend."

"Really?" Vicki said.

"Why does stuff like that always happen to you?" Amy said. "I mean, what are the chances of your seeing her today, of all days, when you're about to see Paul?"

"I don't know," Sierra said, looking up. Her dad had often teased her when crazy things happened by muttering, "Only you, Sierra. Only you." It seemed now that Amy was about to join him in his muttering.

"Nothing ever happens just because it happens," Vicki philosophized. "We've said that before, here at this very table. God-things are all around us. Every day. We just don't always know at the time why they're happening."

"Do you suppose," Amy said quietly, leaning forward, "that God wanted you to see her and know that she was married and had a baby and everything so that you could tell Paul, and he would definitely be over her?"

"I think he is over her. Long over. He's never said anything about her," Sierra said.

"Why would he?" Vicki asked.

"Did she ask about him?" Amy probed.

"No, not really. She just told me to say hi to him when I saw him."

"So she knows you and Paul are together," Amy said.

"No, not really. I mean, I didn't say we were."

"Why not?" Amy asked.

Sierra looked at Amy and then at Vicki. All she could do was shrug. "Because I don't know if we are together. Not really. I mean, nothing has been defined."

"Well, it'll sure be defined by Saturday when you see him," Amy said. "And I hope you know it's killing me that I'm not going to be there to hear all about it."

The same sadness that had been blowing over Sierra all afternoon rushed over her once more. Sierra and Vicki were going to be roommates at Rancho Corona University, but Amy wasn't going to college with them. She had applied at the beginning of the summer but couldn't attend because of finances. Her parents were recently divorced, and she hadn't applied for financial aid soon enough. The three friends had been excited when Amy had decided to apply to Rancho, so when she was turned down, they were devastated. They had formulated a plan for Amy to take classes at the community college and work as many hours as she could at her uncle's restaurant. By next semester they figured she would be able to attend Rancho.

"Just promise you'll call me or e-mail as soon as you can and tell me all about it," Amy said. Sierra could tell Amy was trying to be brave about everything.

"I'll still be here next week," Vicki said. "At least the first part of the week. So when Sierra calls you, then you call me and tell me everything. Okay?"

Amy nodded courageously. Vicki shot a glance at Sierra. Sierra couldn't help it; tears were pooling at the corners of her eyes. All it took was the infallible law of gravity to pull them down her cheeks. For the next fifteen minutes, the three friends cried together.

three

SIERRA DECIDED it actually felt good to be on the road the next day. The steady bump-bumping of the tires as the van and trailer sped down the freeway meant she was done saying good-bye for a while. She was on her way to see Paul. The sadness could leave her now. She could concentrate on all the wonderful things ahead of her.

But instead of concentrating on anything, all she wanted to do was sleep. She had been up nearly all night, even though she hadn't planned on it. After the meeting time at Mama Bear's, Amy, Vicki, and Sierra had decided to go to Randy's house. Some other guys were over there when the girls arrived, and they all sat around looking at Randy's yearbook, reminiscing about the good times they had had together at Royal Academy and complaining about how all they had done that summer was work. Sierra agreed that if she had it to do over again, she would have taken a little more time off from work instead of volunteering for everyone else's vacation hours. She would have done something fun, like backpacking with the youth group the way she had the summer before.

The unofficial end-of-the-summer party stretched into the night, and Sierra had called her parents to get permission to stay later than her curfew. Her mom had said that Paul hadn't called, so Sierra felt no need to rush home. Once again, Mrs. Jensen seemed to understand how important this last good-bye was for Sierra.

By the time she left Randy's house, Sierra had hugged and cried and said good-bye one too many times. All she wanted to do was go home and crash. But when she got home, she found a note on her pillow from her dad saying they would be leaving early. They pulled out of the driveway at four in the morning, which meant Sierra had managed to squeeze in only a few hours of sleep.

Now that they were well on their way, she tried to catch up on those missing hours of rest. The van's motion cooperated with her goal, but her two little brothers didn't. Gavin and Dillon slept only the first hour or so, waking up when Mr. Jensen stopped for a restroom break in Eugene. Now the seven- and nine-year-old boys were wide awake and making sure everyone else was, too.

Sierra had made a little nest for herself on the backseat of the van with the extra duffel bags. What she wished she had were tiny duffel bags to stuff in her ears to block out her brothers' noise. She and Wesley had made this same trek earlier that spring, when they drove down with Amy, Randy, and Vicki to check out Rancho Corona. What a different experience that had been!

More than ever, Sierra was looking forward to being on her own, away from her siblings and in the company of her friends. She didn't know if she should feel guilty for such thoughts or if it was a natural part of growing up and leaving home.

Drifting into a restless sleep, Sierra tried to refresh her thrashed emotions. She knew for certain she needed them to be intact when she arrived in San Diego the next day.

For a good part of the trip, Sierra did rest. Not deeply or comfortably, but she kept to herself and pretended to be asleep a lot more than she really was. Many times she turned down pleas from Gavin and Dillon to play a game with them. When Wes tried to convince her to trade places with him when he wasn't driving, she reluctantly gave in. Instead of providing interesting conversation for her dad, she simply stuffed her pillow between herself and the door and tried to get comfortable enough around the shoulder-strap seat belt so she could sleep.

What Sierra was really doing, while appearing to be sleeping, was daydreaming about seeing Paul. By the second afternoon of the trip, she had pretty much decided to run into Paul's arms and hug him, regardless of who was around. That was, she decided, the true expression of her feelings for him, and she shouldn't hold back. She played the possible angles over and over in her mind. What would she wear? What would Paul be doing when she saw him? Who would be watching them?

Only a few times did the caution alarms go off in Sierra's psyche. She had gotten carried away with emotional daydreams almost a year ago when she had read more into Paul's letters than was actually there. But this was different. He had given her a necklace. He had a nickname for her. He said he was looking forward to seeing her. Surely she hadn't exaggerated any of the feelings between them this time. She felt certain running into his arms and hugging him wouldn't be an overdone response.

Then, while they were stuck in traffic somewhere south of Los Angeles, the van's air conditioner quit. The thick, smoggy, late-summer heat bulldozed into the van as soon as they rolled down the windows. Within three minutes in the sluggish traffic, they were all hot and grouchy.

Mr. Jensen pulled off the freeway and drove into a gas station. They spent a miserable forty minutes there only to find out the problem couldn't be fixed. At least not there and not then.

"We have to get on our way," Mr. Jensen said. "We'll just have to endure life without air-conditioning and pretend we're pioneers."

"Pioneers?" Sierra questioned. She knew she wasn't trying very hard to be cooperative or cheerful in the midst of this annoyance. If she had been with her friends, she would have been Little Miss Mary Sunshine telling everyone else to cheer up. The truth about herself bothered her—and made her even grumpier.

Crawling into the extreme heat of her backseat nest, Sierra insisted they keep the side vented windows open even though the left one rattled terribly. "It's just too hot to close it," she said. "You guys have to leave it open, or I'll suffocate back here."

She tried to sleep. It was impossible. She sat up and tried to position herself so the most breeze came her way. That proved futile. So much traffic was on the freeway that the van wasn't going much faster than twenty-five miles per hour, which was hardly enough to whip up a respectable breeze.

All Sierra wanted to do was reach their destination. She drank the last bottle of water from their ice chest and half an hour later begged Gavin to give her some ice.

Sierra leaned over the seat, waiting for her brother to pull a handful of ice from the chest and give it to her so she could rub it over her neck and cool herself down. Gavin scrounged in the small ice chest between the front two seats and said, "Hey, you can have this!" In a jerking motion, Gavin shot up, snapped his arm around, and attempted to offer Sierra the last can of root beer he had found at the bottom of the ice chest. But Sierra had moved forward while Gavin scrounged in the ice, and her face was in his line of fire. Before she could see it coming, Gavin's fist and the cold can of root beer crashed into her face, hitting her under her left eye, right on the cheekbone.

Sierra let out such a shriek Mr. Jensen slammed on the brakes. Wes quickly assessed the situation and began to give direction, telling his dad to keep driving, telling Sierra to stop screaming, and telling Gavin to put his seat belt back on.

"I didn't mean it! I didn't mean it!" Gavin kept shouting.

"I know," Sierra shouted back. She didn't mean to shout, but in the midst of a painful black eye in the making, she found it nearly impossible to respond with anything lower than a yell.

"She knows it was an accident, Gavin," Wesley said calmly. "Don't worry. You didn't do anything wrong. You were trying to be nice and give her the last soda. It's okay."

Despite Wesley's calming words, Gavin was crying as if he were the one who had just gotten clobbered. Sierra was crying, too, more from frustration than pain. She knew by the way her face was throbbing that she was going to have a doozy of a black eye.

Wonderful. Just wonderful, she thought as her eyes smarted with tears. *The perfect way to show up on Paul's doorstep. I can't believe this happened to me! Go ahead, Dad, say it. "Only you, Sierra. Something like this would only happen to you."*

Her dad wasn't saying anything. He was trying to change lanes without much success, and Sierra could see his aggravated expression in the rearview mirror. Wesley was directing him from instructions he had on a piece of paper. She knew the best thing to do was to sit back and not create any more trauma for the group.

Taking a deep breath, Sierra picked up the cold can of root beer that had fallen onto the seat. She pressed it to her cheek, hoping the cold would at least keep the swelling down. A minute later she realized with irony that she was cooling off. The can was extremely cold, almost too cold to hold directly against her skin. That, plus the receding burst of adrenaline, cooled her off.

"Gavin," Sierra said calmly.

He turned around and cautiously looked at her with moist eyes. For a moment he reminded her of the charming little boy Jalene had been holding at the bakery. All Sierra's frustration dissolved.

"Gavin, please don't feel bad. I know you didn't mean to do it. Wesley was right. You were being nice to me. It was an accident. So don't feel bad about it anymore, okay?"

Gavin nodded and said, "Okay."

Dillon, who had been watching the fiasco with the fascination of an onlooker at an accident, said, "Can we see it?"

Sierra pulled away the can. She could feel her eye's lower lid swelling despite the cold compress. Several years ago, Sierra had accidentally knocked out a janitor at an airport with only a can of orange juice in her hand. She now knew how the stunned janitor felt when she had moved closer to him for an examination of his bruise.

Dillon made a gruesome face. "There's blood," he announced.

Sierra touched the thin portion of skin at the corner of her eye, and indeed there was blood. Only a drop, and it felt as if the tiny tear had already closed up. Definitely not a cause for panic or for stitches. "It's okay," Sierra said, returning the cold can to her throbbing eye.

"It's on your shirt, too," Dillon announced.

Sierra looked down, and sure enough, the white T-shirt she had saved for today so she would look fresh when she saw Paul and hugged him had a splattering of red drips down the left side. It looked as if a dizzy bird had dipped its feet in red paint and tried to walk down her shirt.

Sierra calmly assessed the situation. Or at least she *tried* to calmly assess the situation. They were a couple of hours away from San Diego by her calculations. That would give the swelling around her eye time to go down. Certainly they would need gas or someone would need to go to the bathroom before they arrived in San Diego. Then she could persuade her dad to open the back of the trailer, and somehow she would find her bag and a clean shirt. The duffel bag under her feet held only dirty clothes from the last two days.

With another rush of sadness, Sierra realized she couldn't simply take her bloody shirt home and ask her mother to remove the stain. From now on, Sierra was responsible for all her laundry. The realization sobered her and for some reason made her eye hurt more.

Then, to her surprise, her dad pulled off the freeway. She hoped it would be the gas stop she was counting on, but she didn't want to bug him about opening the jam-packed trailer until they actually stopped. The problem was he didn't stop. He followed Wesley's directions, weaving through a residential area until they came to a large house with a blue tile roof and a long driveway. That's when Mr. Jensen stopped the car.

"We're here!" he announced, smiling at Sierra in the rearview mirror.

four

"HOW CAN WE BE HERE?" Sierra squawked, removing the can from her eye and staring at her father. "This isn't San Diego. Paul's family doesn't live in a big, fancy house overlooking the beach."

Mr. Jensen turned around to view Sierra's eye. He winced slightly, and she began to wonder just how bad her injury was. "This is Lindy's parents' home," he explained.

All three of Sierra's brothers were already out of the car and headed for the front door.

"Lindy?" Sierra echoed, placing the can back on her eye.

"Lindy Mackenzie. Paul and Jeremy's mom. Didn't you hear the plans for this weekend?"

Sierra shook her head.

"Lindy's parents offered to have the engagement party here and let all of us stay with them because they have more room than the Mackenzies do. That way we don't have to rent a hotel room."

"How long will we be here?" Sierra asked, feeling lost and out of the loop for all the weekend plans.

"Tawni and Jeremy are at the airport right about now picking up Mom and Granna Mae. We'll stay here tonight and tomorrow night. Tonight is dinner with the two families, and tomorrow is a reception at the Mackenzies' church in San Diego. On Monday I'll take you and Wes to Rancho and get you all set up. Don't you remember our discussing any of this?"

Sierra shook her head again.

"Let me see your eye." Mr. Jensen leaned closer and made a sympathetic sound with his tongue behind his teeth. "Let's get you in the house and see if we can find a better compress. You're going to have a nasty shiner."

"Great," Sierra muttered. She peeled her sweaty legs off the seat and the mound of duffel bags and crawled out of the van. At least it was cooler outside, with a nice ocean breeze blowing. And it felt good to stretch. But she felt fear, embarrassment, and excitement over seeing Paul. She glanced at the house's front door, which was now shut. Her brothers apparently had disappeared inside. Did that mean Paul knew she was here and was waiting for her to go all the way to the front door before he greeted her? What would be so hard about his coming halfway or even all the way out to the car? How could she run into his arms and hug him if he wouldn't even come out of the house? But then again, how graceful would it be to run into his arms with a can of root beer held fast to her face, hiding her hideous eye? Maybe it was better that he hadn't come out to the car. Maybe it would be darker inside. The bloodstains might not look so bad inside the house.

Sierra and her father walked up to the front door and rang the doorbell. Sierra kept her head down. She noticed the large clay pot by the front door full of bright yellow flowers with little blue flowers brimming over the edges and trickling down the sides.

The door opened, and a large woman with short, stylish white hair and large, light blue-rimmed glasses welcomed them in. She was older than Sierra's mom and younger than Granna Mae, based on Sierra's one-second evaluation. The woman wore a gold charm bracelet that clinked pleasantly as she waved Sierra and her dad into the narrow entryway.

"Please, please, come on in. The boys wanted to go right out to the back to see the view. I haven't met you yet, Sierra. I'm Jeremy's grandmother. Please call me Catherine." The gracious woman smiled, revealing unusually white teeth. They weren't perfectly straight, but they were so white they were pretty when she smiled. She was young for a grandmother. Sierra could never imagine her grandmother inviting anyone to call her "Mae."

"How was the trip, Howard?" Catherine asked, motioning with her charm-braceleted hand for them to come into the sunken living room, which was two steps down from the entryway.

Sierra followed her dad. Two things bothered her. First, she was walking around with a can of root beer pressed against her face and Catherine hadn't even blinked. And second, where was Paul?

"Please sit down. May I bring you something to drink, or…" For the first time Catherine seemed to notice Sierra wasn't sipping from the can of soda in her hand.

Sierra slowly pulled down her hand to reveal her wound.

"Oh, gracious!" Catherine said. "You come into the kitchen with me, and we'll get a proper bag of ice on that. Goodness gracious! What happened?"

Fortunately, Mr. Jensen followed Sierra into the kitchen and explained the situation. He also took over the preparation of the compress by suggesting they use a small bag of frozen peas wrapped in a dish towel. It felt much better than the can of root beer.

"So, where's everyone else?" Sierra asked, trying to sound casual and trying to look natural with a bag of frozen peas covering the left side of her face.

"My husband is out back with the boys. Tawni and Jeremy went to the airport to pick up your mom and grandmother, and I expect Paul to arrive with his parents shortly after six. He had to work today, so if they don't hit much traffic, we should be ready for dinner by six-thirty." Catherine gave Sierra a compassionate smile. "I could show you to the guest room where Tawni and you will be staying, if you would like to rest a bit or maybe freshen up." She said it so nicely that Sierra decided she really liked Paul's grandmother. After hearing about his grandmother on his father's side, who lived in Scotland and rationed the heat when Paul had stayed with her on the weekends, Sierra found it hard to picture this elegant yet friendly and gracious woman as his other grandmother.

Sierra accepted the invitation to go to the guest room. As soon as Catherine closed the door, Sierra made a beeline to the adjacent bathroom, where she examined her eye. It was a lulu, no doubt about it. She was going to have to brace herself for all the "Rocky" jokes because there was no hiding this one.

Tawni's things were already unpacked in the room. Sierra wondered if her sister would mind if she borrowed a clean shirt. Certainly Tawni would understand when she saw the damage. She knew how deeply Sierra cared for Paul. Tawni would want to do everything she could to aid Sierra in a successful reunion, wouldn't she?

Sierra's judgment instructed her not to touch any of her sister's things. Noticing the alarm clock on the dresser, Sierra saw it was only three-thirty. Paul wouldn't be there for two hours. Maybe the best thing would be to stretch out on that inviting bed and let the ice pack work on the swelling. When Tawni arrived, Sierra would ask about a shirt or persuade Tawni to have their dad open the trailer for the luggage. Things were looking up. Maybe Sierra's reunion with Paul wouldn't be a disaster after all.

Stretching out on the queen-size bed, Sierra felt as if she could fall asleep then and there, it was so comfortable. Not a single lumpy duffel bag touched her anywhere. Within a few minutes, she did fall into a luxuriously deep sleep.

Tawni woke her some time later by gently shaking Sierra's shoulder and asking in a louder than normal voice the silliest question in the world, "Are you asleep?"

"I was," Sierra mumbled, forcing her eyes to open and trying to figure out where she was. Her left eye wouldn't open all the way. That's when she remembered.

"Did you lose this?" Tawni asked, holding up the defrosted bag of peas, which had fallen onto the floor.

"Ouch," Sierra said, sitting up.

"I guess," Tawni said, leaning closer for a more thorough examination of the swollen eye. "Why do these things always happen to you, Sierra?"

"Don't start with me, Tawni. I'm in a bad mood."

Tawni reared back and put her hand on her hip. She was a beautiful woman, even when she was putting on a mock show of being offended. Her year of working as a professional model had given her natural loveliness and grace added polish. She had tried out a variety of looks over the past year, including a wild array of hair colors. Today she looked more like her childhood self: Her hair was a soft strawberry blond color, and she wore little makeup. She was still gorgeous, and once again Sierra felt the familiar stab of pain at being the little sister in the shadow of the perfect Tawni. The black eye only added to the tomboy memories from childhood. She felt more like a fifth-grader than a high school graduate who was moving into her dorm room next week.

"You don't have to leave it like that, you know," Tawni said, her voice soft but still carrying an edge to it. "Take a shower, and I'll put some makeup on it for you. I also have a few techniques to help with the swelling."

"I don't have any clean clothes."

"You can wear whatever you want of mine," Tawni offered.

Sierra hesitated only a moment before complying with her sister's directions. "Are Mom and Granna Mae here?" she asked.

"Yes. Granna Mae is taking a nap. Paul and his parents should be here in less than an hour, so you had better hurry."

Prompted by her sister's reality check, Sierra picked up the pace. Just before she closed the bathroom door, she turned and gave her sister a grateful smile, which also made her eye hurt. "Hey, Tawni, thanks. And congratulations on your engagement and everything."

Tawni's smile broadcast that she was a woman in love and nothing could ruin her mood, not even her kid sister with a black eye.

five

SIERRA HURRIEDLY SHOWERED. She was beginning to feel anxious about seeing Paul. Tawni was nice to offer to give Sierra a speedy makeover for the event.

Stepping back into the bedroom with the towel around her, Sierra spotted her mom sitting on the edge of the bed.

"Hi!" Sierra said, her mood definitely improving. "How was your trip down?"

Mrs. Jensen looked closely at Sierra. "Obviously a lot less eventful than yours. Gavin told me what happened. I'm so sorry, honey. He said you told him not to feel bad about it. I appreciate your saying that to him."

"It was an accident," Sierra said, adjusting her towel and wishing she had a robe to put on. It was much cooler in the bedroom than the bathroom, and she was getting goose bumps on her arms.

"I'm going to work a wonder on her," Tawni said, swishing past Sierra and carrying a large makeup case into the bathroom. "Let's decide what you're going to wear first because that might determine the hues I select."

"The hues?" Sierra questioned, giving her mom a silly grin. "Is that model talk for color?"

"Of course," Tawni said, making her way back into the bedroom with quick yet fluid motions. She reached into the closet and pulled out a short summer dress on a hanger and gave it a snap in the air to chase away any wrinkles. "What about this one?"

"For me?" Sierra skeptically scanned the short, thin, straight dress. It was an earthy bronze color with embroidery in matching thread around the scoop neck. This was definitely a departure from the usual long, gauze skirts Sierra picked up at the vintage thrift stores in Portland. Tawni's selection had a Southwest, hot-summer-in-Arizona look about it and was nothing Sierra would ever have been drawn to in a store window.

"It might be a little short on Sierra," Mrs. Jensen said.

Suddenly, Sierra didn't think it was so short. Tawni was taller than Sierra, and if Tawni could wear this dress, why couldn't Sierra? Besides, they were in Southern California now, and it was definitely hot. The dress would make her look much older, and since Paul was two years older than Sierra and had, in the past, alluded to her need to grow up, this dress might just be the right item to wear. With a little help from Tawni and her wardrobe, Sierra decided she could grow up in the next half hour.

"I like it," Sierra said decidedly. "I'll put it on."

"Oh, no," Tawni said, pulling back the dress. "First the makeup. Here, you can wear this robe, if you want. Start drying your hair, but be sure to leave my diffuser on the dryer. I don't want you to blow all the curl out."

Sierra gave her mom another comical expression and

then said, "Right, like that would ever happen. The curse of the curls is with me for life, dear Tawni. As if you had never noticed."

"Don't worry," Tawni said, with another vivacious grin. "I have plans for all those curls."

"Well," Mrs. Jensen said, rising from the bed. "I'm not sure I should stick around for this. It's hard on this old heart of mine to watch both of you turn into such lovely women before my eyes."

"You're just not used to seeing us get along so well," Sierra said. "It's the new, improved Tawni-and-Sierra relationship."

Mrs. Jensen stood another moment admiring her daughters before leaving the room. Her parting words were "I love you both."

"Here," Tawni said, handing Sierra a bottle of hair spritz. "Spray this on before you start drying. It'll protect your hair from the heat. And hurry."

"I'm hurrying, I'm hurrying." Sierra slipped into the bathroom, put on the robe, squirted the fine mist all over her hair, and went to work drying it. Tawni came in and began doing Sierra's makeup. Sierra gave up trying to dry her hair, since Tawni kept complaining that the air was blowing on her face.

Sitting as still as she could, Sierra allowed her sister to work her miracle. Tawni worked quickly and expertly, giving Sierra compliments along the way.

"You have the perfect shape of lips, you know. I wish mine were like that on top. I have to draw in the heart shape. And your skin is really clear. Have you been using anything special?"

"No."

"I always get blemishes right here on my chin. It doesn't look like you do."

"I get them behind my ears."

"At least you can hide those." Tawni stepped back and admired her work around Sierra's swollen eye. "Take a look."

Tawni moved away from the mirror, and Sierra was startled by her reflection. She looked stunning. The blackness had disappeared, and even the swelling had seemed to go down after Tawni applied a clear cream under her eye. The amount of makeup was more than Sierra had ever worn. Her blue-gray eyes were emphasized dramatically, and her lips were colored and looked ready for kissing.

"I look…" Sierra couldn't find the word.

"You look gorgeous," Tawni said. "Here, blot your lips. I know it's more than you would normally wear, but to get it all to blend with the color under your eyes, I had to go heavier. I think you look stunning, and Paul will be stunned when he sees you."

"You sure?"

Tawni nodded and checked her watch. "Oh no! We're running out of time. Let me get your hair up, and then you can dress. I have a pair of sandals that match the dress perfectly. You have shaved your legs recently, haven't you?"

Sierra quickly ran her fingers up her right leg. "They're not too bad."

"Honestly, Sierra. I shave my legs every time I take a shower. I've never understood how you could stand to have prickly legs."

"They're not prickly."

Tawni quickly ran her finger up Sierra's leg, taking her own test. "They're prickly. But that's the least of your concerns right now. First the hair, then the dress."

Eight minutes later, Sierra stood before the bathroom mirror trying to decide what she thought of her reflection. Tawni had arranged Sierra's wild blond curls on the top of her head by scooping them all up in a hair tie then letting the curls bubble out the top. With a dozen bobby pins, Tawni had twisted the larger curls and pinned them to the side of Sierra's head. She had a magazine in front of her the whole time with a picture of this style and told Sierra that when she first saw the picture she wanted to try fixing Sierra's hair that way.

Sierra had to admit the effect was dramatic, which meant the fancy hair went with the heavy makeup and the short dress. It all went together. And it wasn't too much, really. Tawni dressed like this all the time. It just didn't feel familiar, and that made it a little scary.

For a moment Sierra considered telling Tawni she couldn't go through with it. She couldn't meet Paul's parents for the first time looking like a junior Tawni model. And she couldn't meet Paul looking so different from when he had seen her last, more than a year ago. Could she? But then she thought of how this was Tawni's weekend, this was Tawni's party, and Tawni had had so much fun fixing Sierra up like this. It would certainly put her sister in a bad mood if Sierra rejected the makeover. She felt stuck.

With one more glance in the mirror, Sierra convinced herself she looked good. And she did look good. Stunning, actually. No one would disagree with that. Maybe stunning was a good thing for one night. One special night.

"Do you think they're here yet?" Sierra asked.

"No. I asked Jeremy to knock on the door when they arrived."

"Do you have your ring yet?" Sierra looked at her sister's hand and realized she should have asked this question an hour ago.

"No." Tawni held up her unadorned left hand. "Jeremy is going to give it to me tonight, I think. We picked it out, but it had to be sized."

Just then a knock sounded at the bedroom door. Tawni and Sierra spontaneously reached for each other and squeezed each other's arms. They had good reason to be a little excited and nervous. Those Mackenzie boys were the kind who took a girl's breath away.

"Yes?" Tawni called out.

"It's me." Jeremy's voice sounded through the closed door. "Just wanted to let you know my parents are here."

"Thanks. We'll be right out." Tawni checked her hair in the mirror and touched up her lipstick. The summer dress she wore was a pale tangerine and looked much more sophisticated than the "Arizona summer" outfit Sierra had wiggled into. Tawni's sandals had much lower heels than the ones Sierra had borrowed from her sister, so for one of the first times in their lives, the two sisters stood nearly eye level with each other.

"You look ravishing, as always," Sierra said.

Tawni flashed her a smile. "So do you. Come on. Let's face the cameras."

Sierra assumed that was some kind of model talk. She should have joined in the spirit of the comment when Tawni put her arm through Sierra's and led her from the guest room. She should have felt ravishing and confident. Instead of her tomboy cutoff jeans, her unruly hair flying every which way, and of course, the hideous black eye, she was dressed like a model and was a fitting counterpart for her sister. She should have been smiling for the cameras.

Yet all she could think as they exited the room was, *I'm about to make one of the worst mistakes of my life!*

six

JEREMY'S COMMENT when the two sisters entered the living room should have been reason enough for Sierra to take flight back to the guest room and conduct a little makeover of her own. Actually, it wasn't his comment so much as his expression. He said, "Sierra, is that you?" And he said it not as though he was impressed, but more as if he was amused. The tone was condescending, like an older brother discovering a younger sibling who has helped herself to Mommy's perfume and makeup.

"Doesn't she look terrific?" Tawni asked, going to Jeremy's side, slipping her hand into his, and standing back to admire her handiwork.

Sierra nervously fingered the silver daffodil necklace. Tawni had tried to convince Sierra that it didn't go with the outfit and she should tuck it under her dress, but Sierra wanted to wear it proudly so Paul would see how much she treasured his gift.

"Ah, yes," Jeremy said after a pause. "Terrific. I hardly knew it was you, Sierra."

Mr. Jensen walked in then with Wesley and Mrs. Jensen. They all had a stilted nod for her after hiding the surprised looks on their faces.

"You did a good job of covering up the shiner," Sierra's dad said graciously.

"What do you think of her hair? I got the style out of one of my bridal magazines. I wanted to try it out. It might be kind of cute for all the bridesmaids to wear their hair that way, don't you think?"

Sierra swallowed, waiting for all the Lookie Lous of her family to finish staring. She definitely wasn't cut out to be Tawni's guinea pig. In that moment Sierra decided she couldn't go through with this.

"You know what? I have a headache from my hair being coiled on top of my head like this. No offense, Tawni, but I'm going to take it down."

"Oh. Are you sure the headache is from your hair? Maybe it's from your eye. You could try some aspirin first, couldn't you?" Tawni looked heartbroken, but Sierra felt certain, as she heard voices approaching up the front walkway, that some things in life were more important than Tawni's feelings. A good impression with Paul and his family headed the top of Sierra's list at the moment.

"I'll take some," Sierra said, quickly turning to dash for the guest room, which was situated on the other side of the entryway. She was too late. Just as her sandaled foot hit the tiled entry, the front door opened, and a rush of voices overwhelmed her. Sierra tried to duck out of the way, but a large, friendly woman with brunette hair took her wrist and said, "Sierra? Are you Sierra?"

Sierra timidly nodded and could feel her pinned curls

bob on top of her head. She didn't dare look behind the woman in case Paul was standing there.

"Sierra dear, you don't know how long I've waited to give you this!" And with that, the woman, who smelled of honeysuckle, wrapped her arms around Sierra and gave her about the biggest hug she had ever received. When the woman pulled away, she looked Sierra in the face and said, "I'm Lindy. Lindy Mackenzie. Paul's mom. And you're the little angel who prayed my boy back to us." She scooped up Sierra's hands in hers and held them tightly. "You'll never know how much I cherish you, sweet Sierra." Tears were in her eyes. "And I understand we even share the same birthday—November 14th."

Suddenly, Sierra knew her outward appearance didn't matter to this woman. Lindy Mackenzie saw straight to the inside of people and embraced them heart to heart. Sierra felt at ease, and not ridiculous, in her fancy hairdo and tight dress. Paul's mother had showered her with the happy scent of honeysuckle, and Sierra knew somehow she could face whatever the rest of this weekend might hold.

Mrs. Mackenzie gave Sierra's hands another good squeeze, and with a twinkle in her eye, she said, "I'd like you to meet my first husband, Robert."

"First husband?" Sierra questioned as she reached out her hand to shake with Pastor Mackenzie. He was a calm, gentle man who had lots of dark, wavy hair like Paul and wore small, wire-rim glasses.

"Lindy likes to call me that to see people's reactions," Pastor Mackenzie said with a wink at Sierra. "I also happen to be her only husband."

Sierra got the joke, as silly as it was, and nodded her understanding to Pastor Mackenzie.

Mrs. Mackenzie jumped in with another story. "An older woman from the congregation of our last church lived in a retirement community, and you'll never guess what she did. This is a true story. She went up to one of the gentlemen who lived there and said, 'You look just like my third husband.' And the gentleman said, 'Third husband? How many have you had?' And she said to him, 'Only two...so far.' And would you believe, they were married the next month? Robert performed the ceremony."

Lindy Mackenzie filled the room with her cheerful chuckle, and Sierra decided she had never met a woman like her. Sierra adored her.

Mr. Jensen stepped into the entryway and said, "That's some pickup line. How are you, Robert? Good to see you again, Lindy."

Sierra glanced over Pastor Mackenzie's shoulder to see if Paul was standing on the front door step next to the clay pot with the tiny blue flowers spilling over the sides. She saw only Dillon bending down to pet a large calico cat, and she could hear Gavin calling to him from around the side of the house. Unconsciously biting her lower lip, Sierra wondered if she should venture outside in hopes of finding Paul so the two of them could share a private reunion. Of course, either of her little brothers might bombard her with a bunch of immature comments about her appearance, and that was the last thing she needed in front of Paul—especially since Mrs. Mackenzie had managed to lift her spirits in such a way that Sierra's attention was off herself.

Pastor Mackenzie closed the front door behind him and headed for the living room.

"Is Paul still coming?" Sierra asked in a voice that sounded much too squeaky.

"He's here already," Pastor Mackenzie said. "He drove up himself after work so he could have his car here. It was in the driveway when we arrived. He must be out back."

Now Sierra felt nervous all over again. She had to figure out a way to casually wander through this chattering crowd in the entryway and living room and figure out how to get to the backyard. Slipping around the giddy relatives, Sierra tried the hallway that contained her guest room. She passed a bathroom, two closed doors, and then entered a large kitchen and dining area with huge windows that faced the ocean. The view was spectacular. A wide patio stretched out behind the house and was met by a carpet of deep grass. To the left, on the grass, was a small white gazebo, and next to it was a trail that appeared to lead down to the beach.

Sierra leaned up against the counter by the sink, hoping to be hidden just a little as she scanned the backyard for Paul. Dillon was running with a croquet mallet in his hand and yelling for Gavin to come back and finish the game with him. She saw no sign of Paul. But the view captivated Sierra, and she watched the white, soaring seagulls as they circled in the pale blue sky.

As she stared out the window, someone quietly entered the kitchen behind her and said, "Excuse me. Do you know what time my grandmother is planning to have dinner?"

Sierra couldn't move. She knew that deep male voice. She would know it anywhere. Ever since the first time that voice spoke to her at the phone booth in London and said,

"Excuse me, but do you have any coins? I'm desperate!" she had known that voice. But now she couldn't respond.

"Oh, ah," Paul said to the back of Sierra's head. *"¿Qué tiempo esta noche es la comida?"*

Sierra nearly burst out laughing. Paul apparently thought she was a maid his grandmother had hired to help with all the company. Slowly turning to him, with a straight face, she answered in her equally broken Spanish, *"Yo no sé, señor."*

Paul gave her the strangest look.

Sierra tried hard not to crack up. He kept staring at her until the corners of her mouth finally pulled themselves up in a huge grin, and she said, *"Hola,* Paul."

"Sierra?" It was barely a whisper. Then again he said, "Sierra!" as if he finally did recognize her through the makeup and hair and imperfect Spanish accent. Now it was his turn to start laughing.

Sierra's big plans for their romantic reunion turned into the kind of story Mrs. Mackenzie might tell at a church social. There Paul and Sierra stood, four feet from each other in the middle of the kitchen, both laughing their hearts out, but neither of them moving toward the other. Theirs was a nervous, relieved, caught-in-the-act kind of laugh. It helped Sierra to realize Paul must be feeling all the same crazy things she was feeling.

The first wave of laughter subsided, and Sierra caught her breath. She inched closer to him, moving awkwardly in the high-heeled sandals across the slick kitchen floor. Paul didn't move, though. He stayed still, staring at her with a strange look on his face, as if he couldn't quite figure out if she really was Sierra or if this was some kind of bizarre joke.

"It's really me," Sierra heard herself say, shrugging her shoulders and feeling her heart beating all the way up into her throat.

Paul was wearing a white cotton shirt with the sleeves rolled up, khaki shorts, and a pair of sandals with dark straps. His brown, wavy hair was cut short and combed back on the sides. A few rebellious strands curved at his right temple, and across his broad forehead were hints of thin worry lines. His stormy, blue-gray eyes met hers and stayed locked on her for an unblinking moment.

"Hi," he finally said.

Unsure of what to do or say, Sierra swallowed her disappointment over this not being the fairy-tale reunion she had planned. She found her shaky voice and whispered back, "Hi."

seven

"OH, GOOD!" Lindy Mackenzie declared, making a grand entrance into the kitchen. "There you two are. So you've found each other. Isn't this wonderful? I've been looking forward to this get-together more than I can tell you." She stepped over to Sierra's side and gave her a quick, around-the-shoulder hug. "How about something to drink for you two? I see a pitcher of lemonade there on the table. Would either of you like some?"

Sierra couldn't answer. She didn't want lemonade. She wanted Paul's arm around her instead of his mother's. And she wanted him to stop staring at her and to smile. Really smile. Smile the unspoken message that he had been looking forward to this get-together more than his mom had and that he was happy to see Sierra.

Before either of them could answer, the group from the living room had made its way into the kitchen, and with the crowd came noise and confusion. Sierra was instructed by her mother to wake up Granna Mae from her nap. Lindy announced that they weren't eating at the house, as Paul had supposed. They were going out to dinner and planned to leave in five minutes.

Sierra turned away from her mom, preparing to head back to the hallway, which meant she had to walk past Paul. Maybe he would duck out with her, and they could have their hug in the hallway. But when she turned, Paul had disappeared.

She strode to the hallway, hoping he was already there waiting for her, but the hall was empty. Sierra tapped on the first closed door and called out for Granna Mae. When Sierra heard no answer, she opened the door and tapped again lightly. Granna Mae was asleep on top of a blue and white floral bedspread with a thin blanket over her legs. Her soft, white hair billowed between her head and the pillow, making it look as if she were sleeping on a cloud. Her wrinkled face wore a blissful expression.

Leaning over, Sierra touched her grandmother's shoulder and whispered, "Granna Mae, time to wake up."

Granna Mae's eyelids fluttered open. The instant she looked at Sierra, Sierra knew her sometimes-confused grandmother didn't recognize her. A cloudy look was in Granna Mae's eyes, and her blissful expression had turned into irritation. "What?" the old woman said impatiently.

"Granna Mae, we're at Tawni's engagement party, and we're all going to go out to eat for dinner now. Are you ready to wake up so you can come with us?"

"What?"

Sierra repeated the information more slowly and then gently coaxed her grandmother to get up. "That's good," Sierra said as Granna Mae swung her legs over the side of the bed. "You'll feel better once you've had some dinner."

"I'm not sick," Granna Mae snapped.

"I know you're not sick. It's just that it's dinnertime, and we're all going to a restaurant now." Sierra realized she looked different to Granna Mae, since she had never dressed up like this before; the transformation could have been confusing even to someone who didn't have memory lapses. Sierra's appearance certainly hadn't impressed Paul.

Sierra held out her hand. After scrutinizing her for another moment, Granna Mae hesitantly took her hand and allowed Sierra to lead her out of the bedroom.

Mrs. Jensen met them in the hallway and gave Sierra a raised-eyebrow look that Sierra knew meant, "How's she doing? Is she coherent?"

Sierra shook her head and lowered her eyes, letting her mother know that this was not one of Granna Mae's clearer moments. When Granna Mae was thinking clearly, she would call Sierra by her childhood nickname, "Lovey." For some reason, Sierra was the family member Granna Mae recognized most often in her fuzzy spells, which was why Mrs. Jensen had sent Sierra in to wake up her grandmother.

"We're going in Jeremy's car," Mrs. Jensen said to Granna Mae. "We're all going out to a Mexican restaurant for dinner."

Granna Mae looked at Sierra and then at her mother. "I don't know anyone named Jeremy. Where's Paul?"

Mrs. Jensen and Sierra snapped a glance of surprise at each other. Sierra was the first to respond. "Paul is here. He'll be glad to see you, too."

Sierra had no way of knowing if Granna Mae truly meant Paul Mackenzie or if she was referring to her son

Paul, who had been killed in Vietnam. Granna Mae had met Paul Mackenzie when she was in the hospital more than a year ago. Paul had paid her an unannounced visit and brought her a daffodil, which Granna Mae declared was her favorite flower. Earlier Paul had seen Sierra parading down the street with her armful of daffodils for Granna Mae in the hospital, and he had dubbed her "Daffodil Queen" shortly after that in a letter.

They stepped into the crowded entryway, and Sierra could tell all the loud voices were frightening Granna Mae. She looked at the group as if she didn't know anyone, not even her own son Howard, who was Sierra's dad. Granna Mae clutched Sierra's hand tighter, and together they maneuvered through the group and out the front door. As soon as they were outside, Granna Mae seemed to start breathing again, and she loosened her grip on Sierra's hand. Sierra was amazed at how soft her grandmother's hand felt even though the skin was sagging around her bony fingers and wrist.

"Mom said you're going to ride in Jeremy's car," Sierra said slowly, leading Granna Mae to the driveway, where all the cars were packed in, bumper to bumper. "You and Mom will ride to the restaurant with Jeremy and Tawni."

"And you," Granna Mae said, quickly tightening up on Sierra's hand.

Sierra didn't know how to tell her grandmother that Sierra's secret plan was to go in Paul's car—just she and Paul, alone at last so they could talk. She hadn't spotted Paul since he had disappeared from the kitchen, but she had thought through the seating arrangements in the car, as well as when they arrived at the restaurant. Her plan was to put herself next to Paul the whole time—not next to Granna Mae.

"Well, Mom will be with you," Sierra said. The others were following Sierra and Granna Mae out to the driveway, and Sierra expected to turn around and see Paul any second.

Granna Mae held tightly to Sierra's hand and looked confused.

"My mom," Sierra explained slowly. "My mom, Sharon Jensen, will be with you in the car."

"Sharon?"

"Yes. You know, she married your son Howard."

"Oh." Then after a pause, Granna Mae said, "Is this their wedding party?"

"No. It's Tawni's engagement party. Tawni and Jeremy. We're going out to eat with Jeremy's family and our family."

Granna Mae looked up at the crowd that was now gathered in the driveway. Sierra knew they were all watching her with her grandmother and waiting to take a cue from her as to what to do next.

"Would you like to ride in the backseat?" Sierra asked.

Suddenly, Granna Mae let go of Sierra's hand and held both her arms out to the group of relatives. "Paul dear," she said cheerfully. "Oh, Paul, how wonderful to see you."

Sierra looked at the surprised group and watched as Paul moved around from the rear flank next to his father and came toward Granna Mae with his arms open to her. Paul was reaching with open arms for her grandmother, when all along Sierra had planned for him to run to *her* with open arms. He hugged Granna Mae gently, and as Sierra watched from less than a foot away, Paul tenderly pressed his lips against Granna Mae's soft cheek and gave her a kiss.

Granna Mae gave no indication if she knew he was Paul Mackenzie or if she thought he was her son. Sierra admired Paul all the more when he spoke to Granna Mae. He knew she might be confused about who he was, but that didn't matter to him. He treated her with dignity and tenderness. "Would you like to ride to the restaurant with me?" Paul asked Granna Mae, bending down so he could look her in the eyes.

"Oh, yes. I'd love to go with you and Becky."

Paul shot a questioning look at Sierra. She gestured that she had no idea who Becky was.

Sierra's mom stepped forward. "That's a great idea, Granna Mae. Why don't we all go in Paul's car?" Mrs. Jensen took Sierra by the elbow and urged her into the backseat of the dark blue sedan while Paul helped Granna Mae into the front seat. Mrs. Jensen leaned over and whispered to Sierra, "Becky was Paul's fiancée. They got engaged the week before he left for Vietnam. You've probably met her. She married Mrs. Kraus's brother."

Sierra shook her head. She didn't remember any relatives of Mrs. Kraus's named Becky ever coming into the bakery. It was all too strange—too connected. It reminded Sierra, as she had noted in the past, that everyone is so connected it's a good idea not to alienate or offend others. Right now Paul was doing an exceptionally good job of honoring Granna Mae and helping Sierra and her mom make this a comfortable situation for both families. Sierra's heightened opinion of Paul almost made up for their reunion being awkward. Almost, but not quite.

As they drove through the beach town's narrow streets,

Sierra considered what maneuvers might be necessary for her to sit next to Paul at the restaurant. If she could make those arrangements, she felt certain she and Paul could relate on a more comfortable level. All the letters they had exchanged for the past year and the phone conversations in which they had laughed together late at night had led Sierra to believe they were very close—boyfriend-and-girlfriend close, even though they had never used those terms nor had they ever defined their relationship. The only part that had been missing over this year had been the physical contact. Sierra felt certain that if they could just break that barrier, their relationship would move forward.

By the time they pulled into the parking lot of the large Mexican restaurant, Sierra had dreamed up a lovely plan. She would sit next to Paul, nice and close, and without anyone else knowing it, they would hold hands under the table. Her plan was to be close enough and her hand accessible enough that Paul would know instinctively to take it. That way he would be making the first move—sort of. She also had a backup plan. If he didn't take her hand, she would slip her fingers over his, and then he could decide what position their holding hands should take, and they could adjust.

It seemed perfect. Of course, being inexperienced at these things, Sierra was a little unsure of how it would all actually happen. The most important thing to her was that it would be natural. The memory of it would be wonderfully sweet and would help erase the memory of their silly encounter in the kitchen.

But none of her careful planning included Granna Mae's unpredictable actions and her selective memory.

eight

BEFORE SIERRA had stepped three feet away from Paul's car, Granna Mae reached for Sierra's hand and held it tightly. Her grandmother smiled happily and appeared coherent. Then she reached out her hand to Paul, inviting him to take her other hand. While Mrs. Jensen waited for the others to arrive, Granna Mae, Paul, and Sierra walked hand in hand through the parking lot and into the restaurant.

Sierra tried to steal a glance at Paul to see how he was reacting to this. He was studying his sandals as he walked and seemed unaware of Sierra's glances.

They entered the restaurant, and Granna Mae proudly announced to the hostess and several people waiting to be seated, "They're getting married!" She held up her arms so that Sierra and Paul's hands were raised as if in triumph.

"Congratulations," the hostess said.

"We're, um…" Paul hesitated. He glanced at Granna Mae and then flashed a quick look at Sierra. "We're here for the Mackenzie party. I believe we have the back room reserved."

"Oh, yes. For the engagement party. Congratulations again."

Paul nodded his thanks, playing along for Granna Mae's sake. Sierra noticed his neck had turned red. His face was turned away from her, but Granna Mae still had a lock grip on both their hands.

Sierra wanted to burst out laughing again. She knew if she did, it would take the tension out of this crazy situation and help Paul relax. But an outburst of Sierra's wild, pent-up laughter would probably upset her grandmother. Opting for Granna Mae's stability, Sierra swallowed her nervous laughter and prayed that Granna Mae wouldn't make another announcement to the Jensen and Mackenzie families, which had now entered the restaurant.

As hard as she tried, Sierra couldn't get Granna Mae to let go of her hand. The way they were headed, Granna Mae would be sitting between her and Paul the entire dinner. Sierra panicked at the thought.

Like a bad plot in a TV sitcom, Sierra's worst predictions came true. Granna Mae did sit between Paul and her. The speaker above Sierra's head played loud mariachi music throughout the whole meal. Everyone else was so busy chatting that no one noticed that Granna Mae kept holding Sierra's hand under the table, as if she were insecure and couldn't bring herself to let go.

Sierra tried to remind herself that this party was for Tawni. It was her engagement, her time to shine. And she did so—beautifully. Every now and then Tawni and Jeremy exchanged tender looks. Twice he kissed her on the cheek, and once she burst out laughing at something he said. Her laugh was wonderfully melodic, the kind Sierra had heard only a few times from her sister. Sierra knew Tawni was happy—deliriously happy—and that was supposed to matter the most.

However, Sierra was experiencing a desperate, sinking feeling—a deep sadness because none of her dreams were coming true. She had waited so long to see Paul, to be with him. And now nothing was going the way she had hoped.

Why isn't Paul trying to talk to me? she thought as she picked at her meal. *He could have found a way to sit next to me if he had wanted to. Maybe he doesn't want to. Maybe the feelings I have for him don't match any he has for me. Maybe this is all a huge mistake, a big joke, and I'm the punch line.*

Sierra's head hurt. She knew it was partly due to the impractical hairstyle. With all her heart she wished she could go back to the house, change out of her tight dress that was becoming uncomfortable to sit in, wash the sticky makeup off her face, and release her curls from their fashion prison. Then she would find her way down the trail by the gazebo, dig her bare feet into the sand, and let the gentle Pacific waves tickle her toes.

The evening dragged on as each of the fathers stood to say something wonderful about their children. Tomorrow afternoon a big engagement reception would be held at the church in San Diego where Paul and Jeremy's dad was the pastor. Tonight was just for family, and so the speeches were personal.

Both fathers pledged their wholehearted support to Jeremy as he took this next step into manhood. Sierra's dad invited Jeremy to come to him at any time if he needed anything, and then he charged Jeremy to take his responsibilities to Tawni seriously as he now made public his pledge to marry her. Pastor Mackenzie then stood and read a verse from Ephesians about Christians being Christ's bride and how Christ gave Himself for her. Jeremy's father talked about the Hebrew tradition in which the bridegroom would declare publicly his love for and commitment to his bride and then go to prepare a place for them to live.

"This is a beautiful picture of what Christ has done for us," Pastor Mackenzie said, his deep voice booming over the piped-in mariachi music. "Christ came to earth to declare His undying love for us. He even called us His bride. Then He returned to His Father's house to prepare a place for us. One day soon He'll come back for us and take us to be with Him forever. Until that day, Christ has left the Holy Spirit with us as evidence of His commitment to those who believe in Him. The Holy Spirit is God's engagement ring around our lives, His promise that we will one day be united with Him."

Sierra felt a rush of goose bumps stream up her arms. She had never seen the parallel before. Being a Christian meant she was, in a sense, spiritually engaged to the Lord. He loved her and wanted her to be with Him forever. The truth burrowed itself in her heart.

Pastor Mackenzie sat down, and Jeremy stood. He looked a little nervous but determined. In his hand he held a small black box. Turning to face a radiant Tawni, he said, "I now want to make a promise to you, Tawni. This ring is a symbol of my commitment to you and evidence to others of my love for you. In giving it to you, I'm asking that you will save yourself for me alone and that one day soon you'll marry me and spend the rest of your life with me."

Tears clouded Sierra's eyes. She saw the twins of her

own tears running down her sister's cheeks as Tawni stood and gracefully held out her hand to Jeremy. "I accept this ring with all my heart, Jeremy. And yes, I promise to marry you."

Sierra could hear sniffs all around the table as the women and some of the men tried to keep back their tears. Sierra noticed that, miraculously, the annoying music had stopped, and the room was silent as the family watched Jeremy take the ring from the box and slip it on Tawni's finger. The newly committed couple tenderly, comfortably, kissed each other.

Enthusiastic applause burst from around the long table, and as if on cue, the music cranked up again, with trumpets blaring right above Sierra's head. She clapped and wished her oldest brother, Cody, could have been there. He and his wife, Katrina, recently had had a baby girl, and she had been sick with an ear infection, which made it unwise to travel since she was so young. If Cody and Katrina had been there, then it would have really felt as if the whole Jensen family were entering into this engagement with Tawni. A Mackenzie family member was missing, too. Paul and Jeremy also had an older brother who wasn't able to join them, although Sierra never heard exactly why.

Tawni sat down and admired the sparkling diamond ring on her finger. Her smile was electric, and Sierra was sure she had never seen her sister happier.

Wiping away her tears with a napkin, Sierra noticed she left a streak of foundation on the white cloth. She had wanted to look past Granna Mae over at Paul to see how he was reacting to all this, but the realization that her tears had probably made a mess of Tawni's makeup job prompted

Sierra to quietly excuse herself and make an exit for the restroom.

One glance in the mirror and Sierra knew she couldn't take the hairdo or the heavy makeup another minute. It wasn't that she looked bad or overdone by the standards of most magazines. Tawni had done an expert job, and the mascara must have been smudge-proof because no evidence showed of its smearing. Sierra just didn't look like herself. And that bothered her.

She was about to start pulling out the bobby pins when the door to the restroom opened and her mom stepped in.

"Are you all right?" she asked Sierra.

"Yes. I thought I'd smeared this makeup all over my face when I started to cry. Wasn't that beautiful—what the dads said and when Jeremy gave her the ring?"

Mrs. Jensen nodded and smiled. "It was wonderful. I wanted to make sure you were okay, though."

Sierra nodded. "I'm tired of being Tawni's beauty makeover project. I want to wash my face and take down my hair."

"You had better wait," Mrs. Jensen said. "Everyone is ready to leave now. Catherine has dessert for us back at the house, and I think Granna Mae is about as confused as she's ever been."

"I know," Sierra said. "She thought Paul and I were announcing our engagement! She told the hostess and everyone in the waiting area that we were getting married."

"Oh dear," Mrs. Jensen said, biting her lower lip. Sierra never noticed it before, but her mother did that often. That had to be where Sierra picked up the habit. "I've noticed you and Paul haven't exactly said a lot to each other. Is everything okay between you?"

Before Sierra could answer, Paul's mom entered the bathroom and said, "There you two are. We're ready to go. Paul and Jeremy have already left, so you can both come with me."

"What about Granna Mae?" Mrs. Jensen asked.

"She went with Paul. I don't think she was willing to let go of his arm for anything. It's kind of sweet the way she has taken to him."

Sierra followed her mom and Paul's mom to the parking lot and sat in the car's backseat. As soon as they reached the house, Sierra rushed to the guest room. She wriggled herself out of Tawni's bronze dress and slipped into her cutoff jeans. It felt wonderful to breathe again. Rummaging through Tawni's neatly organized clothes, Sierra found a sweatshirt and carried it into the bathroom.

She released her captive curls, scrubbed her face, and removed all the eye makeup. The face that returned her gaze a moment later was a much happier, less sophisticated, much cleaner face. The only problem was the shiner. It hadn't magically gone away while the makeup covered it.

Sierra considered trying to dab a little of Tawni's concealer back on the blackened area, but she wasn't sure it would work without all the other layers Tawni had applied. She pulled the sweatshirt over her head and shook out her tangled tresses before running a hair pick through them.

"This is the real me," Sierra declared to her reflection, as if she were preparing for what she would say to Paul when he saw the downsized version of her hair and face. "Take me for what I am or walk away now, buddy, because this is reality."

As soon as she said it, Sierra had a terrible thought. What if Paul did decide to walk away? What if all this reality was a little too much for him? And could she blame him? The guy had just spent a quiet year in the Scottish Highlands, and here he was, with her wacky Granna Mae clinging to him and making false public announcements, and his brother and her sister entering into a sacred agreement. What if Paul did get a good look at the reality that was and would always be "Sierra Jensen"? What if she walked into that living room and this guy, who had captured her heart through his words written in bold, black letters on a hundred sheets of onionskin paper, decided to walk away?

Time seemed to freeze.

"There's only one way to find out," Sierra finally told her reflection. "It's now or never."

nine

WHEN SIERRA ENTERED the living room, wearing her own familiar sandals, her well-worn jeans shorts, and Tawni's sweatshirt, she found the room empty. All the voices seemed to be coming from the backyard.

Walking through the kitchen and out the back door, she found the group gathered around the patio table and sitting on the chaise lounges and cushioned patio chairs. Lindy Mackenzie was busy helping Gavin and Dillon scoop ice cream for themselves from the cartons set on the table. It appeared that dessert was a make-it-yourself ice cream sundae bar.

Sierra looked around for Paul. He wasn't there. Her heart started flip-flopping again. What if he had left? What if he already had done a reality check, and, having fulfilled his duty as a good son and brother by attending the engagement dinner, he had taken off?

Before she could sink into a bog of despair, Paul's deep voice sounded from behind her. "This was the only one in the freezer in the garage." He placed a carton of vanilla ice cream on the table. "Do you want me to go to the store for some more chocolate ice cream?"

"No, this is fine. Just fine," his mom said. "I think we have plenty." When Lindy looked up at Paul, she noticed Sierra standing at the table with her back to him. Sierra hadn't quite gotten up the nerve to turn around and face him. The look on Mrs. Mackenzie's face showed that she was surprised by Sierra's transformation. Sierra saw a trace of a wince, too, which was probably directed at the black eye. Then Mrs. Mackenzie smiled just as she had when she first had hugged Sierra and said, "Did you get yourself a sundae yet, Sierra?"

"Not yet." She was thankful Mrs. Mackenzie hadn't made a big to-do about how different Sierra looked. She could almost feel Paul staring at the back of her head, willing her to turn around, but she kept her chin tucked and bit her lip.

"Me neither," Paul said. He stretched his arm past Sierra on her left side, reaching for a bowl. She felt his arm brush her shoulder. He picked up two bowls and held one out for Sierra. "Here you go," he said.

Sierra drew in a deep breath and slowly turned to face him. She hoped her sincere, fresh, clean smile would make up for the shock when he saw her like this, only inches away.

Paul didn't even flinch. He stared the way she remembered him staring at her on the plane when they first met. His hand went gently to the black circle under her eye, and he touched her cheek just to the side of the bruise, the way a child might touch a floating soap bubble in fascination.

"It was an accident," Sierra explained before Paul could ask. "In the car on the way here. A can of root beer."

Paul nodded slowly, sympathetically. He seemed to be taking in her face and hair as if for the first time.

Sierra continued to whisper her explanations to Paul as if no one else were around. "Tawni wanted to fix me up for the dinner. I guess she thought the other hairstyle went with the makeup she used to cover my black eye."

Paul nodded again, this time with a smile on his lips. He took Sierra by the elbow and whispered one word in her ear: "Come."

It was all she could do not to drop the ceramic ice cream bowl on the patio. She managed to place it on the table, and although Paul had let go of her elbow, she felt he had an invisible hold on her as he led her past all the chattering guests and across the grass toward the gazebo. Without saying anything, Paul led the way to the trail and down the wooden steps to the beach. The farther away from their families they walked, the louder the pounding surf grew.

The sun was hidden behind a bank of thick clouds that seemed to ride the edge of the horizon like a great battleship. In only a few minutes the sun would surrender behind that hulk of a ship, and this day would be over. But Sierra felt sure that, for Paul and her, this day was just about to begin.

When she reached the last step, Sierra slipped off her sandals, just as Paul had done, and followed his lead. She tucked the sandals under the step for safekeeping until their walk brought them back this way.

Paul shuffled through the sand with Sierra beside him. She loved the way the brown sugar grains felt between her toes, cool and soothing like millions of tiny massage balls on the bottom of her feet.

They strolled and watched the glow of the sun diminish. Side by side, step matching step, neither of them spoke. A salty breeze whipped Sierra's hair into her face. A sandpiper scurried after the receding waves, pecking the bubbles in the sand, hoping to find its dinner.

No words seemed to come to either Sierra or Paul. With so much to say, Sierra didn't know where to begin. She felt peaceful and yet wired at the same time. Finally, she couldn't stand it. "Wait!" she said. "Stand right there. Don't move."

Paul stopped and stood with his bare feet sinking into the wet sand. Sierra walked a few feet away and turned to face Paul. The wind was now in her face, and it blew her curls away from her eyes. Paul stood still as a wave came up and covered his feet, burying them deeper in the sand.

In the cool evening light, Sierra could see his peaceful expression. He looked happy enough without adding anything to this moment. Sierra was the one who needed something else.

"Okay," she said, hoping this wasn't going to look strange to Paul. "This is how I wanted it to be when we first saw each other." She smiled and held out her arms, delightfully crying out, "Paul! It's you! It's really you!"

Paul caught on to her game, and holding out his arms, he declared, "Sierra! After all these long months, we're finally together!"

The scene was silly and more melodramatic than any Sierra had rehearsed in her imagination, but the essence was still there. They could now run into each other's arms.

One problem, though. The surf had buried Paul's feet in the sand, and Sierra was the only one running. She hit

Paul's chest with a thud and bashed the underside of her sore eye.

"Ouch!" she yelped, pulling away and doing a little circle-of-agony dance.

"Are you okay?" Paul released his feet and stepped to her side, gently touching her shoulder.

"I hit my eye on your chest. What have you been doing? Working out or something? It felt like a rock." For emphasis, she playfully swung at Paul's chest and hit something hard again.

"Careful," he said, pulling out a cassette tape in a plastic holder from his pocket. "This was supposed to be a present for you. I forgot I put it in that pocket." He held out the tape. "It's some Scottish music. Remember? I told you I'd buy you a tape."

"Oh, yeah. Thanks. I think." She still held her left hand over her sore eye. "Actually, why don't you keep it for me? I don't think it would fit in any of my pockets."

"Sure." Paul took the cassette back and tucked it into his shirt pocket with a pat. "Just remember it's there, and don't go crashing into it again."

Sierra slowly lowered her hand and tried her best to smile without making the muscles under her eye move upward. "Ouch," she said again. "It hurts too much to smile."

"You don't have to smile," Paul said. He was looking at her warmly, and she could tell he was content just to be with her.

After the endless hours of staring at the picture Paul had sent her, Sierra had thought she had his face memorized. But now she knew she didn't. The soft summer evening light, the way his hair was cut shorter than in the photo, and the gentle expression were all different from the image she had memorized of Paul Mackenzie. This was real. He was real. And he was here, only a few inches away from her.

"Take my hand," Sierra heard herself say. It was exactly what she had been thinking, but she hadn't planned to say it aloud.

"Yes, ma'am," Paul said with a laugh, responding playfully to her command. He reached for her hand, and she met his halfway and grasped it securely. Paul stopped laughing.

Wow! He felt that, too, Sierra thought with a thrill. *I know he did.*

Sierra's left arm had turned warm, as if low-wattage electricity had shot through it. She and her buddy Randy had held hands before, but she never had felt like this inside when they did.

"Let's walk," Paul suggested, still holding her hand firmly in his.

They walked silently for many minutes along the shoreline before loosening the grip they each had on the other. Sierra felt as if she had waited too many months for this experience to let go now. But their hands were getting sweaty, and Sierra felt a tiny muscle cramp in her thumb. The loosening of their grasp was a good thing. It relaxed their hands and arms and seemed to relax them as well.

"I wrote you a poem," Paul said, breaking their long silence.

"You did?"

"I wrote it last week when I was thinking about what it would be like when we finally saw each other again."

Sierra could feel her heart beating faster. She wondered if Paul had been looking forward to seeing her as much as she had been looking forward to seeing him. He must have if he wrote her a poem.

"Let's see if I can remember it." Paul led Sierra to where a cliff met the sand and a hollow had been dug out of the ancient rock by the high tide. He let go of her hand, and she settled herself into the cleft of the rock, out of the wind, where it was quieter and warmer and she could hear Paul's rich voice.

He looked into Sierra's eyes and began his poem:

"I asked you once
     If you could fly;
You promised me
     You had no wings.
Why did you lie?
     How else
Could you have come
     Across the sea
To my dark tower,
     Bringing bread and light
To me?
     I learned to know
The sound
     Of stirring air,
Of candlelight,
     And whispered prayer.
Can you tell me truly
     You weren't there
Far across the sea?
     Now distance

> *Is a walking space*
>> *In full light I see your face.*
> *But tell me,*
>> *Now*
> *Where do you hide your wings?"*

"Wow," was the only word that came to Sierra's lips. "Say it again," she urged him.

Paul repeated it and added for her interpretation, "I was thinking of how all we've had for so long were words between us. Words we wrote in letters and words we sent to heaven as we prayed for each other." Paul reached over and took Sierra's hand from where it rested in her lap. He laced his thick fingers in hers and said, "Or mostly your prayers for me, and then my returned prayers for you more recently."

Sierra affectionately gave Paul's hand a squeeze and added her interpretation to his poem. "And those words flew back and forth across the ocean and into the heavens for a year. Now we're close enough—what did you call it?—distance…"

"Distance is a walking space."

"Yes. A walking space and…"

Paul finished for her. "In full light I see your face."

Sierra felt herself blushing. A smile crept up her face, making her tender left eye hurt. "And let me guess," she said, pointing to her black eye. "This isn't exactly the face you expected to see."

"Actually," Paul said, tilting his head and looking at her closely enough to count every blessed freckle on her nose, "this is much more what I expected to see than what you surprised me with in the kitchen."

Sierra laughed. "Ow! That hurts." She tried to make her face go straight.

"Come here," Paul said tenderly. He let go of her hand and slid across the sand so that he was sitting next to her in the partial windbreak of their private little cove. He put his arm around her shoulder and invited her to rest her unbruised cheek against his shoulder.

Sierra felt herself relax as she snuggled up next to Paul. He smelled good. Not like the fresh evergreen scent of pine trees at Christmas when she had first met him. Now he smelled like pure soap and fresh laundered sheets that have hung on the line. His arm felt warm across her shoulders. His chin rested against the side of her head.

Together they sat close in the sand and watched the waves roll in and out. Neither of them said a word.

ten

SIERRA LAY IN BED a long time that night, finding it impossible to fall asleep. Tawni, beside her in the guest bed, was already sleeping when Sierra had tiptoed in well after midnight. Sierra had undressed for bed quietly and then lay there wishing her sister would wake up so Sierra could share the details of the evening with her. Especially because it had ended so confusingly.

Sierra coughed to see if that would disturb Tawni. It didn't. Then Sierra was glad it hadn't. She changed her mind about talking to Tawni. These details were hers alone; maybe she didn't want to share them with anyone. At least not until she had made some sense of them herself. She knew Amy and Vicki would never forgive her if she didn't provide them with an update before the weekend was over. She had a lot of fast figuring out to do.

Sierra turned over onto her back and stared at the tiny flecks of silver that glistened in the paint of the textured ceiling. The night-light in the bathroom gave the silver flecks their glow, but they were nothing compared with the glow of the stars Sierra and Paul had watched. The moon, wearing a half-grin, had looked down on them. And Sierra had worn a half-grin all evening, too. It hurt her face too much to smile, but it hurt her joyful heart too much not to smile.

For a wonderfully long time, Sierra and Paul had sat silently snuggling in their little cave. Then they rose and walked along the beach, hand in hand again. This time they didn't clasp hands so tightly. A settled peace had come over them, and they held hands playfully. First, with their fingers intertwined. Then, sometime later, when the conversation turned to Granna Mae and Sierra's appreciation for Paul's being so understanding, they linked only their first two fingers together and let their arms swing.

Sierra saw a shell and bent to pick it up. Paul teasingly pushed her toward the oncoming surf. She kept her balance and pulled herself up by his grasp. Then, using a self-defense technique Wesley had taught her a long time ago, Sierra hooked her foot around Paul's ankle and, with a quick jerk, toppled him to the sand.

He was so startled that he sat for a moment, his ego obviously flattened that Sierra had managed to bring him down so quickly. Sierra took off running in the sand, laughing into the night wind. Paul was a much faster runner and overtook her in only a few yards. He grabbed her by the shoulders and pushed her toward the water, playfully threatening to "feed her to the fish." Their laughter echoed off the rocks that formed the end of the bay. The sand ended there, and the only way to reach the sand on the other side of the cliffs was to wade through the rocky tide pools that jutted out between the two beaches. So Paul and

Sierra turned around and headed back to the center of the bay, the wind in their faces.

"I love being here with you," Sierra called out over the wind. Then she impulsively put her arm around Paul's waist and welcomed his arm around her waist.

Paul stopped walking and took Sierra in his arms, wrapping her in a tight hug. She felt warmed all over. It lasted only a minute, and then Paul let go. He didn't hold her hand or put his arm around her again but took off at a sprint across the sand.

Sierra laughed and started to run after him. And she had thought she was the impulsive, moody one. It appeared that, in melancholy Paul, she had met her match.

They arrived breathless back at the stairs, grabbed their sandals, and climbed up to the yard, out of the rush of the wind. Sierra brushed back her tangled hair with her free hand and said, "Paul, wait. Stop." She stood alone on the grass. "Look up. Isn't it beautiful?"

Paul didn't return to the grass to join her but looked up from where he stood on the patio. "Spectacular," he said quietly.

"What if we just stayed out here all night and watched the stars together?" Sierra said, smiling at Paul.

Paul gave her a strange look and said, "We need to go in."

"Wait, I wanted to ask you something," Sierra said, joining him on the patio.

"What is it?"

"Well, can we sit down?"

Paul moved the lounge chair back a foot or so from the chair where Sierra landed. He slowly sat down and folded his hands, waiting for Sierra to speak.

She couldn't understand why all the closeness and snuggling was suddenly over. "I just wondered if you've figured out your schedule for the fall."

The last time she and Paul had talked about it, he had planned to keep working at the construction site where he had been employed all summer, make good money, and take one or two evening classes at the community college. That way he would have enough saved up by the second semester to attend Rancho Corona. Paul's plan was similar to Amy's, only Paul would be less than an hour's drive away from Rancho, and he and Sierra could see each other every weekend.

"I'm registered for sociology on Monday nights," Paul said. "And I'm the first one on the waiting list for a statistics class on Tuesday and Thursday nights. I can take it at another school on Wednesday nights, but it costs twice as much."

"Good. I'm glad your weekends will still be free," Sierra said, leaning back and looking up at the stars.

As she lay in the guest bed now, looking up at the silver flecks in the ceiling, she remembered Paul's answer had made her feel even more distanced from him.

"We'll see," was all he said. Then he stood up and announced, "I'm going in."

Sierra rose and followed him across the patio. For the last several hours she had been imagining what it would be like when they said good night. Sierra thought for sure Paul would kiss her before the night was over. She was certainly ready to kiss him.

But he didn't kiss her. Instead, he briskly led her around to the side door that let them into the house through the garage.

Once inside, he quickly drank a glass of water, as if he were dehydrated. Sierra filled a glass for herself and awkwardly waited around. She thought Paul would at least hug her or somehow say good night in a romantic way. But he didn't. He seemed to be pulling away. As soon as he put the glass in the sink, he turned to Sierra and, with a quick nod, whispered, "Sleep well." Then he turned and left through the dining room while she stood alone in the kitchen.

As Sierra reviewed the details of their time together, she couldn't think of one thing she had said that would have made him pull away. Maybe he realized how late it was, and he was concerned about getting her in trouble with her parents. If she had been at home, her parents would never have agreed to let her stay out that late.

Sierra knew that was about to change. She was going to be the one to set her own curfew now, and if she and Paul wanted to stay out and walk on the beach until the sun came up, that would be their decision. The thought was very satisfying.

She strained to read the luminous green numbers of the alarm clock on the dresser—2:27. Tomorrow would be another full day. She had to try to sleep. The worship service at Paul's church would come early in the morning, and after that was the reception for Tawni and Jeremy in the church fellowship hall. During it all, Paul and Sierra would be together.

As it turned out, Paul and Sierra were indeed "together" all day Sunday, but no one observing the two would have guessed they were acquainted, let alone friends who were close enough to walk along the beach holding hands. Paul managed to keep his distance from her all day.

They sat next to each other during the church service, but Paul literally put the hymnbook between them. Sierra went from being mystified to being angry. By the time the grand reception was over and the two families were ready to wearily go their separate ways for the evening, Sierra had a long string of angry words all lined up for Paul.

"You ready to go?" her dad asked, tagging Sierra's arm in the church parking lot. "The boys are on their way to the van."

Sierra was waiting to see what Paul was going to do. He was still inside the church, probably taking down the last of the tables in the fellowship hall. All during the reception Paul had been running around, fixing things, unlocking cupboards with his dad's keys, and answering questions for the women who handled the refreshments. He barely had stopped the whole time and hadn't spoken to Sierra at all.

Then a thought washed over her. Maybe she wasn't being fair. Paul was more or less "on duty," since he was trying to make things go smoothly for his brother, and he was the pastor's son who knew where everything was.

"Sierra," her dad said when she didn't move, "are you coming with us?"

Softened by her revelation, Sierra wanted to talk to Paul. Even if she couldn't talk to him, maybe she could help put away tables so she could at least be with him. "I think I'll go with Paul, Dad," Sierra announced. "You guys go ahead."

"Are you sure Paul is planning to drive all the way up to his grandparents' tonight? I thought he had to be at work early tomorrow, so he was going to stay at his parents' house."

Sierra hadn't counted on that. "I'd better go ask him," she said. "Do you mind?" She turned and met her dad's gaze.

She must have given him a look of overeagerness about to turn into panic because he spoke to her softly. "Honey, if Paul were planning to take you back to his grandparents' house, I think he would have mentioned it by now."

Sierra felt like bursting into tears but refused to do so. "It will only take me two minutes to go ask him," she said.

Her dad nodded sympathetically. "Two minutes."

Sierra charged back into the church gym and immediately spotted Paul with a long broom in his hand, sweeping the floor. He looked up when she came in and gave her enough of a smile that she felt she could march across the floor and speak her mind.

The incident reminded her of when she worked at the Highland House her junior year. It was a halfway house that Paul's uncle ran in Portland. Sierra had helped out at the Highland House when Paul worked there as well. They didn't have much of a relationship then, and they didn't speak to each other much, but Sierra remembered feeling as if Paul were watching her. It had intimidated her.

Today she refused to be intimidated—especially by a guy who had written his heart to her for months and had only twenty-four hours earlier held her so tenderly on the beach and quoted poetry he had written for her alone.

Whatever the reason was for Paul's aloofness, Sierra was going to find out. She wasn't going to Rancho Corona tomorrow morning without things being settled between them.

eleven

"ARE YOU GOING BACK to your grandparents' house?" Sierra asked while still a few feet away from Paul.

"No, I hadn't planned on it."

"Oh," Sierra said, not sure if she should be mad or understanding, since he did have to start work early tomorrow.

Paul leaned on the broom handle, and Sierra took a deep breath. Before she could let her words come out, Paul said, "Sierra, we need to talk."

"Funny," she said, "that's exactly what I was going to tell you."

"I want to be honest with you," Paul said, glancing around as if to make sure no one could hear him. "I'm not exactly ready to have this talk with you because I haven't decided what I want to say yet."

"Well, when do you think you'll be ready? Because as it stands, my dad's waiting for me, and tomorrow morning I go to Rancho. You work all week, so what does that give us? Next weekend maybe? Do you think you can figure out what you want to say to me by next weekend?"

Paul looked surprised by Sierra's words. Or maybe it wasn't the words but the angry, sarcastic tone she used to say them.

"I'm sorry," Sierra said. "It's just that I'm so upset with you right now I don't know what to say. Last night I thought everything was wonderful and close, and I was completely open with you, Paul. And you were close and wonderful and open with me, too." Sierra fought hard to keep back the tears. "Suddenly, you act as if I have the plague. You won't talk to me, you won't touch me or look me in the eye—"

"I'm looking you in the eye now," Paul said with his clear, blue-gray eyes fixed on her.

Sierra looked into his eyes and didn't look away. With her voice much softer and lower, she said, "What is the problem, Paul? What happened?"

Paul pressed his lips together, still looking into Sierra's eyes. "We got going too fast. I was afraid."

"Afraid of what?"

"Afraid of things between us getting out of control."

Sierra didn't understand. They had held hands and sat close and snuggled. He had recited his poem to her. They had laughed and gazed at stars together. How was any of that "out of control"?

"I've been there before, Sierra. Please trust me when I say I didn't want that to happen to us."

"You didn't want *what* to happen to us?"

"You know," Paul said, scanning her face, as if looking for assurance that she understood the deeper meaning of his words. "Physically," Paul finally said. "I didn't want things to get out of control between us physically."

Sierra was still in the dark. "How could they have gotten

out of control?" She lowered her voice to almost a whisper. "You didn't even kiss me."

"I know," Paul said, looking relieved. "And you'll never know how glad I am that I didn't."

If Paul had slapped her across the jaw, it would have hurt less than his words and the deeper meaning she read in his facial expression. Flinching, Sierra pulled back. "I see." She looked away.

"Do you really?" Paul tilted his head and gave Sierra a charming, innocent look.

Just then Mr. Jensen called from across the empty gym floor, "Sierra, we need to get going. I have the boys waiting in the van. We need to go now."

Sierra wouldn't allow herself the luxury of one more view of Paul's blue-gray eyes or his broad forehead and wavy brown hair, even though her heart was telling her it would be her last look. She kept her eyes down as she turned away from him. "Good-bye, Paul," she managed to say as she hurried to join her father at the other side of the gym.

"Call me!" Paul hollered as she left the gym. "Call me when you get your new number at Rancho."

"Everything okay?" Mr. Jensen asked, slipping his arm around Sierra as they walked quickly to the waiting family members in the hot van.

"Sure," Sierra said flatly. Inwardly, she was building a mighty dam of determination to hold back all her feelings for the rest of her life. She had been naive to give her heart so quickly to Paul. He flat out didn't want her. He didn't like her the way she liked him. She had made a fool of herself, and he had played along with it, writing poems that he knew she would like to hear, holding her hand because he knew she wanted him to. It had all been a big lie. All his words in all those letters. All the dreams she had stored up. It was all a big nothing. A long, elaborate joke played out on inexperienced Sierra. And the punch line was, "You'll never know how glad I am I didn't kiss you."

There. Now it was over. Ha-ha. So this was why people wrote songs about love and cheating hearts and broken dreams. It was all real now—too painfully real. All Sierra could think of was the time Amy said to her, "I promise I'll be there for you when Paul breaks your heart."

Sierra, of course, had assured Amy that would never happen because Sierra knew what she was doing. Now here she was, finding enough hidden strength from somewhere deep inside that she could walk silently beside her father across the church parking lot and act as if a sinkhole of despair hadn't just opened up and swallowed her whole.

Somehow Sierra managed to keep up the act the rest of that night and into the next day when her father drove her to Rancho. Twice Wesley asked her if something was bothering her, but Sierra said she was nervous about moving into the dorms and going away to college and everything. She didn't know if he believed her or not.

Mr. Jensen moved Sierra's belongings into her room, but before they had finished he said, "Don't forget to call Paul. He said he wanted you to call as soon as you got your new number."

Sierra only vaguely remembered Paul's calling out those words at the church gym. The person she wanted to call was Vicki. Sierra wanted to try to persuade Vicki to come down as soon as she could. Classes didn't start for more than a week, and Sierra didn't want to be alone in their dorm room. Without a car or a roommate, Sierra suddenly realized she was facing a lonely week. In her original plans, this time was going to be filled with Paul during every one of his spare moments.

Walking her dad down to the men's dorm, where Wes was unloading Randy's band equipment, Sierra thanked her father for all he had done to get her to college and to set up her room. To her surprise, he slipped his strong hand over Sierra's and held it as they walked. "You're going to be just fine, Sierra Mae. Your mother and I are the ones who are going to have trouble making the adjustments. It's probably a good thing she flew back with Granna Mae this morning. If she had come here and tried to say good-bye to both you and Wesley on the heels of Tawni's engagement, well, I think it would have been hard to convince her we should stay in Portland. She would have wanted to move down here—especially after she saw this campus. It's exactly as Wes and you described it."

They were walking past the plaza fountain at the center of the campus, still holding hands. Sierra didn't mind that several other early-bird students who sat at the benches surrounding the fountain were watching. She guessed that any one of the three girls sitting there would love to have a dad like Sierra's.

Suddenly, one of the girls on the bench called her name. Sierra stopped, and both she and her dad turned. The long-legged girl who rose from the bench and eagerly came toward them had a bright, welcoming smile. Her long, nutmeg brown hair was pulled back in a braid, and she wore sunglasses, which kept Sierra from recognizing her. The girl wore shorts and a short-sleeved T-shirt, and when she raised her arm to wave at Sierra, the sun glistened off a gold ID bracelet on her right wrist.

"Christy!" Screaming, Sierra ran to hug her dear friend. "I can't believe you're here! How are you? When did you get back from Switzerland?"

Christy hugged Sierra a second time and took off her sunglasses, revealing her distinctive blue-green eyes. They sparkled when they saw Sierra. "It's so good to see you," Christy said, taking a closer look at Sierra's left eye.

"I had a run-in with a can of root beer," Sierra explained. "It's actually lots better than it was a couple of days ago."

Christy smiled. "Katie is going to want to hear the whole story. Did she ever tell you about the time on the houseboat when Doug gave her a black eye?"

"No, but I'm sure with very little prompting she'll tell me the whole story. Oh, Christy, this is my dad."

"I'm pleased to meet you, Mr. Jensen," Christy said, offering her hand to him.

"It's a pleasure meeting you," Mr. Jensen said, shaking Christy's hand. Sierra felt so grown-up. Her friends in high school never shook hands with her parents. Christy seemed even more grown-up. Sierra hadn't seen her friend for more than a year, ever since the two of them had gone to Switzerland with Christy's aunt so Christy could check out the school she ended up going to for the past year.

"Is Todd here?" Sierra asked.

"You just missed him. He and my parents picked me up at the airport a few days ago, and then he stayed with us and helped me move in earlier today. He'll be back." Christy smiled when she said it. "He's going to work the rest of this week and then move into the dorm on Friday."

Sierra felt a bittersweetness come over her. If things weren't going to work out between Paul and her, at least she could be happy for Christy that she and Todd were together. Sierra would have to ask Christy exactly how many years she and Todd had been together. Five? Or was it six? Either one was amazing, especially since Sierra couldn't manage to maintain a dating relationship for even five to six hours.

"Katie should be here this afternoon," Christy added.

"You know," Mr. Jensen said, "I can find my way from here, Sierra."

"You sure?" Sierra asked.

"Yes, I'm sure. Let me give you a hug, and I'll be on my way."

Sierra hugged him tightly and whispered in his ear, "Good-bye, Daddy. I love you. Thanks again for everything."

"I love you, too," he whispered back.

As Sierra pulled away, she could see that her dad was "overly" smiling, and the lines by his eyes were crinkling the way they did when he was trying not to cry.

"You okay?" Sierra asked quietly.

He nodded and kissed her soundly on the cheek. Then he turned and headed for the men's dorms.

"I just said good-bye to my dad," Sierra said solemnly as she turned her attention back to Christy. "I didn't think it would be like that."

"Do you want to go with him?" Christy asked.

"No."

"You sure?"

Sierra watched her dad's familiar gait another minute as

he turned down a path behind the library. Then he was gone.

"So many good-byes," Sierra said as a sense of loss came over her.

Christy gave Sierra's arm a squeeze. "And many hellos, too."

Sierra smiled at her understanding friend. "If all the good-byes don't kill me, I'll probably start to enjoy some of these hellos."

"I know what you mean," Christy said. "Come on. I brought you something from Switzerland. It's in my room, and it just might cheer you up."

"You brought me something?"

"Yep. And I know you're going to like it." Christy flipped her sunglasses back on and led Sierra toward the upperclassmen dorm. Sierra couldn't imagine what Christy had brought her, but she did know she was going to like being around Christy and Katie and all their friends. For the first time, the thought crossed her mind that maybe Paul truly was a "good-bye," and some guy at Rancho Corona was going to be her newest "hello."

twelve

CHRISTY'S DORM ROOM was completely set up on the left side. The right side had only an unmade bed, an empty closet, an empty desk, and vacant bookshelves. Christy was already at home here, and Katie would have to catch up when she arrived.

"Wow, you settled in fast," Sierra said, examining some of the pictures on the wall. Next to the window was a framed poster of a tropical waterfall with a quaint bridge across the top of it. At the bottom of the frame was what looked like a piece of fabric that had been cut from a T-shirt. It read, *I Survived the Hana Road.*

Next to the desk was another framed poster. This was a more familiar scene to Sierra: a mountain trail in the Alps, complete with cows wearing bells around their necks, snow-capped peaks, and a colorful carpet of blue, yellow, and white wildflowers.

"This looks like where we had our picnic with Alex," Sierra said.

"I know," Christy responded. "That's why I bought it. I

went back to that same spot several times this past year. And each time I thought about you and Alex and his verses about loving each other fervently."

Sierra smiled at the memory. *See?* she told herself. *Other guys in the world have been interested in you. Paul isn't the only one.*

"Did I tell you I saw Alex last month? He was visiting his uncle at the school, and guess what? He's engaged!"

Cross Alex off my list of potential interests, Sierra thought dismally. "That's great," she said generously. "He deserves someone wonderful. Did I tell you my sister and Jeremy just got engaged? We had a big family party this weekend."

"I take it you finally saw Paul," Christy said, reaching for a tiny white box on the shelf above her desk. Sierra noticed it was next to a beat-up metal Folgers coffee can, which Christy had placed on a white lace doily. Sierra made a mental note to ask Christy why in the world she had a funky old can in a place of honor.

"Yes, I finally saw Paul. And it was both wonderful and horrible, and if I start to talk about it, I'll cry."

"Well, here," Christy said, holding out the tiny white box. "See if this brings back any sweet memories. It got a little squished in my suitcase. Sorry."

Sierra opened the tiny box and found three exquisitely decorated pieces of chocolate candy. "Truffles! From that bakery we went to with your aunt, right? I can't believe you remembered."

"I was going to try to bring home one of their pastries, but the truffles fit in my suitcase better. Remember when we sat on that bench in the sunshine and had our first bites of amazing Swiss chocolate?"

"Oh, do I! And your aunt told us we couldn't chew

them but had to savor the moment and let the chocolate dissolve in our mouths." Sierra broke off a corner of one of the squished truffles and offered the box to Christy so she could take a piece. Before popping it into her mouth, Sierra added, "And remember how mad your aunt was because we knocked over the card rack at that shop across the street? I still have one of the mangled cards she had to buy. I think I brought it with me. I should put it up on my wall."

Christy laughed and pointed to the large bulletin board next to her closet. "Look—there's mine." Sure enough, in the top right corner was a card with a crease right down the middle of an illustration of a wildflower bouquet.

Sierra laughed and held her piece of chocolate up in the air. Christy did the same. "On the count of three," Sierra said. "One, two, three!"

The two friends lowered the precious chocolate into their mouths and slowly let it melt, echoing a duet of "mmm's" and "ahhh's."

Christy plopped onto her bed and moved a stuffed Winnie the Pooh from on top of her pillow. "I'm sure going to miss that bakery," she said.

Sierra made herself comfy on the foot of Christy's bed. She noticed how soft the comforter was. It was a faded yellow patchwork design, and Sierra guessed it probably held sentimental appeal for Christy because it didn't match anything else in the room. Looking up at the dresser, Sierra noticed a vase filled with white carnations. She assumed they were a welcome-home bouquet from Todd.

"What else are you going to miss about Switzerland?" Sierra asked.

Christy gazed out the window before answering. "I'm not sure I even know yet. It was my life for a year, and now all of a sudden I'm here. I don't think it's all hit me."

"Didn't you miss Todd fiercely?"

"Yes and no. I needed to grow up some and settle some things in my heart before I could move on in my relationship with Todd. And he needed to do some growing up, too. He kept changing schools and majors. He had a bunch of jobs but never anything consistent—and he never had any money. He needed time to make some decisions, too."

"Katie told me a while ago that Todd's been working like a crazy man. She thought he was trying to save enough so you guys could get married."

Christy's calm, gentle face took on a determined look. "Todd needs to graduate first. That's his goal in coming to Rancho this year. He's decided he wants to be a youth pastor."

"I can see him doing that. He's a great teacher and a natural leader. I would have loved for him to be my youth pastor when I was in junior high," Sierra said. "Sounds like a good choice."

Christy nodded. "It does. He'll be a great youth pastor. It just took him a while to come to that conclusion. For so many years he wanted to be a missionary in some tropical jungle, live in a tree house, and eat coconuts."

Sierra laughed. "You're kidding."

"No. That's exactly what he wanted to do. You can ask him."

"What changed his mind?"

"God."

"Oh," Sierra said.

"And it wasn't an easy task, from my point of view." Christy adjusted her pillow behind her and smiled. "Todd wanted to be a Bible translator, but he doesn't have a natural ear for languages. He tried taking some linguistics classes but had to drop them because he just couldn't get it. Then he signed up with a missions organization, thinking they would send him to Papua New Guinea, and they sent him to Spain instead."

"That's where you saw him when you and I first met on the missions trip at Carnforth Hall."

"Exactly," Christy said. "It's been a long journey for Todd to figure out what God wants him to do, and I think it was easier for Todd to go through that process while I was far away."

"Now what?" Sierra asked.

Christy shrugged. She didn't look distressed, just hopeful and dreamy. "We just 'keep on keeping on,' as the director of the orphanage in Basel used to say. It was so wonderful being together these last few days when Todd was at my parents' house and helped me move in here. Now we're going to see each other every day. I don't want to start making any predictions, though. We need to take each day as it comes."

Sierra reached for the white candy box on the desk, and after taking another truffle, she offered the last bite to Christy. Since Christy had been so open about her relationship with Todd, Sierra felt compelled to tell Christy about her wonderful-horrible weekend with Paul.

As soon as the piece of chocolate melted, Sierra drew in a deep breath and said, "I'm really glad everything is working out between Todd and you. I guess I should tell you that all my dreams about Paul crashed and burned yesterday."

"Do you want to tell me about it?" Christy asked. "I mean, I'd really like to hear, but only if you want to tell me."

Christy was two years older than Sierra, which made her the same age as Tawni. But Sierra had never thought of Christy in the same way she thought of her sister. Christy was more of an equal, a close friend, yet more experienced and therefore a wise counselor.

"He basically acted as though I was his girlfriend on Saturday and then ignored me on Sunday and said he didn't want to ever see me again."

Christy looked surprised. "He told you that?"

"Well…" Sierra tried to make her emotions pull back so she could relay the information accurately. "Not exactly. That's what it felt like. You see, on Saturday night we walked on the beach, and he held me and quoted a poem he had written just for me. I'm telling you, Christy, I was sure this was 'it,' you know? This had to be what it felt like to be in love, and nothing could ever break us up. I was so…so…"

"Vulnerable?" Christy filled in for her.

"Okay. Yes, vulnerable. And happy. I was so sure of my feelings."

"And you gave him your heart," Christy suggested.

Sierra nodded.

"And he took your heart in his hand, and with a friendly smile but a critical eye, he scanned it, then set it down and said, 'It is still unripe, better wait awhile.'"

"Where did you get those words?"

"From a Christina Rossetti poem. I have it copied in my diary. I went through the same thing with Todd a long time ago. But I still remember how much it hurt. I'm sorry you're going through this, Sierra. It doesn't necessarily mean everything is over between the two of you, though."

"I don't know," Sierra said, kicking off her sandals and sitting on the bed with her legs tucked under her. "Paul said I would never know how glad he was that he didn't kiss me. That feels pretty terminal to me."

"Why did he say that?"

"He said things were going too fast, and he didn't want things between us to get out of control physically because he had been there before."

"Did he mean he had been in a physical relationship?"

"I guess. But how could things be going too fast and becoming too involved for us? All we did was hold hands. He didn't even kiss me!" Sierra was picking up steam as she released her emotions. "How can hugging and holding hands be too involved? I think he was saying all that as an excuse to cover up what he really meant. He doesn't care for me the way I care for him. He doesn't want to be around me."

"Sierra, holding hands and hugging are the first steps, you know. It can be hard to pull back once you're familiar with each other that way. Paul obviously knows where his guidelines and standards are in a relationship. Are you sure that's not what he was trying to communicate? That he had a line he didn't want to cross physically in your relationship?"

Sierra refused to accept such a simple explanation. "But why would he say he was so glad he didn't kiss me?"

"Obviously, kissing is the next step, and he wasn't ready to go there."

"I was," Sierra said. "It was such a romantic evening. It would have been the perfect place and time for my first kiss."

"But, Sierra, think about it. You guys went from nothing to step one, holding hands, and on to step two, hugging, in just a few hours. It sounds to me as if Paul wanted to pull back and take things more slowly. I think that was really kind of him."

In Sierra's mind, she saw Paul sitting like a rock on the second step of a long, winding staircase. His arms were folded across his chest as if to say stubbornly, "This is as far as I'm going, Sierra. Take it or leave it." Her heart began to melt. Why hadn't she seen that before? If he didn't care for her so much, he wouldn't have stopped on the second step. How could she have misinterpreted everything so badly?

"You know what, Christy? You're right. I had it all backward." Sierra remembered how Paul had looked, standing in the church gym, leaning on the broom, his head tilted with that charmingly shy expression on his face. He had looked so innocent. Just like the toddler with the gray eyes that Jalene had held on her hip at Mama Bear's.

"I admire Paul for treating you that way," Christy said. "Especially since he's apparently been further up the steps in other relationships."

Suddenly, the image of Paul planted like a rock on the second step disappeared, and a new, disturbing image took its place. Paul was on an escalator, running up the steps. Another girl was running up the steps with him. That other girl was Jalene.

thirteen

"OH, CHRISTY, I think I'm going to be sick." Sierra slid off the bed and curled herself up in a ball on the floor, hugging her legs to her chest.

"What is it? What's wrong? Was it the chocolate?"

"No, no, no!" Sierra moaned.

Christy sat on the floor beside her and gently touched her arm. "Sierra, what is it?"

Sierra lifted her head and faced Christy, trying to make the escalator image in her imagination go away. "I should have seen this before. Why didn't I guess? I am so naive!"

Christy reached for a tissue and handed it to Sierra even though she didn't have any visible tears.

"No wonder Paul said he wasn't ready to talk. He said he didn't know what he wanted to say to me. He knew I didn't know, and that's why he said he didn't want things to get out of control. He said he had been there before. He asked me to trust him when he said he didn't want that to happen to us."

"Paul didn't want *what* to happen?"

Sierra looked away from her concerned friend and spoke the words she didn't want to hear herself say. "Paul's last girlfriend got pregnant. They obviously went to the top of the stairs. I've seen her baby—Paul's baby. He has gray eyes and tilts his head just like..." Sierra couldn't finish. The tears she had been holding back came gushing out. She buried her face in her raised knees and let the tears flow.

"Oh, Christy," Sierra said at last, "how could I have been so blind?" She sniffed and choked out the words. "Paul wasn't walking with the Lord when he dated Jalene. No wonder he left for a year and ran away to Scotland. When he was planning to come to Portland for my graduation, he said he had a few people he needed to set things right with. He must have meant Jalene and their son. He wanted to see their son!"

Another wave of frantic tears washed over Sierra, and she exhausted herself with the emotional outburst. The worst part was that the excessive crying made her left eye ache around the bruise, and she was sure it was beginning to swell again.

Christy sat quietly beside Sierra and let her cry. Several times Christy handed Sierra tissues, and twice she stroked Sierra's wild, curly mane in a gesture of understanding.

When the last of Sierra's tears had been released, she looked up and tried to breathe deeply. She had just regained control of her emotions when they heard a key being inserted into the door's lock. A second later the door flew open, and boisterous, red-haired Katie burst inside.

"Home sweet...Sierra? What's wrong?" Katie dropped the box in her arms and flew to Sierra's side. "What happened to your eye? Are you okay? Christy, what's going on?"

Christy quietly stood and pulled Katie along with her. "Come on. I'll help you unload your stuff and carry it in." Then, turning to Sierra, Christy asked, "Do you want me to tell Katie or would you rather tell her later?"

Sierra pointed at Christy. "You tell her. I don't think I can."

Katie and Christy left, closing the door behind them.

"Oh, Father God," Sierra mumbled in the still room, "I never expected anything like this. Why didn't You warn me? Why didn't You make me pull back a long time ago? I put so much hope and trust in Paul. I never expected…"

The phone on the desk rang. Sierra jumped. It rang again, and she thought she should answer it. Clearing her throat and reaching for the receiver, Sierra said, "Hello?"

"Hi, I'm not sure I have the right room," the male voice said on the other end. "Is this Katie?"

"No, but she'll be right back." The voice sounded so familiar that Sierra had to venture a guess. "Is this Wes?"

"Sierra?"

"Yeah. What are you doing calling Katie?"

"I was trying to find you, since you didn't answer the phone in your room. I remembered you knew Katie from when we visited in the spring, and I guessed you might be there."

"Well, I am here," Sierra said, reaching for another tissue. She tried to blow her nose quietly.

"Dad left a little while ago," Wes said. "I wondered if you wanted to meet me at the student coffee shop for some lunch."

"I'm not very hungry," Sierra said.

Wes paused and then said, "Are you okay?"

Sierra wasn't sure if she should be open with her brother or not. She decided she should say something but not too much. "I just figured some things out, and they hit me kind of hard."

"You mean about being on your own now?"

"No."

"Is it anything you want to talk about?"

Sierra sighed deeply. "I've been talking to Christy. She's Katie's roommate. She's the one I went to Switzerland with."

"Well, I won't interrupt then. But if you feel like calling, I'm at extension 3232."

"That's an easy number to remember."

"Call me later if you want. I'm going to get something to eat."

Sierra hung up and looked around the room. She felt dizzy. Or maybe she *was* hungry, and lunch with Wes would have done her some good. Before she could reconsider meeting him at the coffee shop, Christy and Katie reappeared, both carrying large boxes, which they promptly lowered to the floor.

"You guys need some help?" Sierra said, scooping up her crumpled tissues and looking for a wastebasket.

"If you want my opinion," Katie said, her green eyes flashing above her rosy cheeks, "I say, 'Big whoop.'"

"Big whoop?"

"I told her everything," Christy said.

"Yeah, big whoop. Whatever happened with Paul and his old girlfriend is in the past. He wasn't a Christian then, was he? Or, if he was, he was totally backsliding from what I remember your saying about him. So whatever happened in the past is the past. God forgave all that stuff when Paul came back to Him. If God isn't holding it against Paul, then none of us should hold it against him, either."

"You haven't even met Paul," Sierra said.

"But he's a brother in Christ, right? So the Bible says I'm to forgive others as Christ has forgiven me. You can't hold this against him, Sierra. That would be so unfair."

"But Katie, a few other lives are involved in this."

"Remember what Jesus said when He was hanging on the cross for us? He said, 'Father, forgive them. They don't know what they're doing.' Every day people make mistakes. They don't have any idea what they're doing. If they ask God to forgive them, then we're supposed to forgive them as well. Don't you remember that verse on the wall at Carnforth Hall: 'Love will cover a multitude of sins'?"

"Actually, it says, 'Love...bears all things, believes all things, hopes all things, endures all things. Love never fails,'" Christy said.

"Well, both of those love quotes are from the Bible," Katie said, wiping the perspiration that had beaded up on her forehead. "My point is, Sierra, what does it matter? Does Paul's past have anything to do with your future?"

"I don't know." Sierra felt as if all the wind had been knocked out of her. "I don't know much of anything at this moment."

"Maybe we should all eat something," Christy suggested. "It's after two o'clock, and I don't know about you, but breakfast was a long time ago for me."

"Let's finish unloading my car," Katie said. "Then we can all drive into town for some food. I want to stop at a drugstore, too. I don't have any shampoo."

The three of them worked quickly, hauling several heavy boxes out of the heat into the air-conditioned comfort of the room. Sierra had never seen Katie's car before, and she thought the bright yellow vehicle was perfect for Katie. It was a cross between a Jeep and a dune buggy. Katie called it "Baby Hummer."

Sierra, Christy, and Katie all climbed into Baby Hummer after they had stacked the boxes on Katie's side of the room and drove down the hill into the town of Temecula. They all agreed on the first fast-food place they came to and ate in the car on the way to the drugstore. Sierra bought some toothpaste, a box of snack bars, and a bottle of apple juice. After Katie collected a small basketful of necessities, she and Sierra went searching for Christy.

They found her in the laundry soap aisle looking dazed. "Look at all these boxes of soap," Christy muttered. "How do you know what to buy? In Switzerland I had only three brands to choose from. There are so many choices here. Liquid or powder? Do I need fabric softener? What is this color-safe bleach? And do I need a stain remover?"

"She's losing it," Katie confided to Sierra. "I knew it would catch up with her real soon. She's been back only a few days, you know."

"Jet lag?" Sierra questioned.

Katie shook her head and took Christy by the arm, leading her to the checkout stand. "Cultural reentry," she said. "It's really bad on missionaries who have been in remote areas for a long time. They forget what a land of abundance America is."

"There are just so many choices," Christy said again.

"We learned about this last semester in my intercultural

studies class," Katie informed Sierra. Turning to Christy, she said, "You'll freak out if you stay in this store much longer, Christy. Let's go back to the dorm and unpack my stuff. We can buy you some laundry soap tomorrow."

Back at the dorm, Christy seemed to have lost all her energy. She blamed that on the jet lag and afternoon heat.

"You guys, I'm going to bed," Christy said, crawling under her covers with her clothes still on.

"Will it bother you if I unpack?" Katie asked.

Christy didn't answer. She appeared to already be asleep.

"I'll stay and help if you want me to," Sierra said in a low voice.

"That would be great. Are you already moved in?"

"Not really. My side of the room looks just like this, all boxes. Vicki doesn't arrive until the end of the week. To be honest, I'd rather stay here than go back to my room right now."

"Then stay all night," Katie suggested. "In one of these boxes, I have an air mattress. If you don't mind sleeping on the floor, it's all yours."

They set to work, talking about school, parents, their summer jobs, and their expectations for the coming school year. Several times they started to laugh and then remembered Christy was trying to sleep, so they lowered their voices and tried to be quiet. It didn't seem to matter, though. Christy was in a deep sleep.

Sierra appreciated that Katie didn't bring up anything about Paul. It gave Sierra a chance to even out her emotions.

Since Katie didn't have a lot of treasures to hang on the

wall, it didn't take long to set up her side of the room. Sierra was beginning to understand why Wes had said a few boxes of belongings turned into valuable treasures when that's all a person had of home and the past. It made Sierra eager to unpack her boxes—but not tonight. Tonight she would cheer herself with the warmth of Katie's energetic personality. Sierra would have tomorrow to make her own little nest cozy.

She slept well on the air mattress and borrowed a clean T-shirt from Katie the next morning before the three of them went to the coffee shop in search of breakfast.

"When does the cafeteria start to serve meals?" Sierra asked.

"Thursday dinner is the first meal," Katie said.

"I'm going to go broke before then," Sierra said as she paid for her bagel and orange juice.

"I know," Christy said with a yawn. "I just can't seem to wake up, you guys."

"There's no reason you can't go back to bed," Katie said. "Nothing is going on today."

"I thought we were going to help Sierra set up her room."

"There's not that much to do," Sierra said. "You should sleep while you can. This seems like the quiet before the storm."

Just as Sierra said it, her brother entered the side door of the coffee shop. He noticed her right away and marched over to their table. He didn't look happy.

fourteen

"WHERE HAVE YOU BEEN, SIERRA?" Wes looked more angry than worried.

"I've been with these guys. Katie, you know my brother Wes. Wes, this is Christy."

Christy held out her hand to shake with Wes. He shook quickly and then looked back at Sierra. "Didn't you go back to your room last night?"

"No. I stayed on the floor in Katie and Christy's room."

Wes looked flustered. "Then will you do me a favor and give Mom a call and then call Paul?" He handed Sierra a slip of paper with a phone number on it. "He's called me four times since I got here yesterday, trying to track you down. You were supposed to call him and give him your number."

"I, um…" Sierra stalled, feeling embarrassed that her brother was chewing her out in front of her friends. She felt as if she were back in junior high and not at all like an independent college woman. "I'm not sure I'm ready to talk to Paul," she said. "Can you tell him that for me, if he calls you again?"

Now Wes was the one who looked embarrassed, as if she had reduced him to a junior high messenger between two friends who weren't speaking to each other. "And why can't you tell him that?"

"I..." Sierra couldn't answer.

Just then some of Katie's friends walked up and visited with her for a few minutes. It gave Wes a chance to cool down. He pulled up a chair and sat on it backward, leaning his arms on the backrest at the end of the table next to Sierra. Then he reached over and took half of Sierra's bagel and chomped into it.

"Hey, I paid for that!" Sierra said. "And I'm on a very tight budget. Go buy your own bagel."

"Okay, okay. I'll buy you a bagel." Wes took another bite and rose to order some food. "Anyone else want anything?"

"See if they have any of those little packets of peanut butter," Katie said. "Smooth, not crunchy."

As soon as Katie's friends left, and while Wes was still waiting for his bagel, Katie leaned toward Sierra and said, "Are you going to tell Wes about Paul?"

"I don't know. It's starting to bug me that Wes is checking up on me."

"I think you should tell him," Katie said. "Otherwise he's going to be caught in the middle—Paul will keep calling Wes and you'll keep saying you don't want to talk to him. It's not really fair to Wes, if you're asking him to relay those messages for you."

"Do you agree?" Sierra asked Christy. For a blink of a moment, Sierra felt as if she were back at Mama Bear's with her head bent close around the table with her two friends. Only these two friends weren't college freshmen, like

Sierra, Amy, and Vicki. Katie and Christy were both going to be juniors. They had much more experience to draw on when it came to complications with guys.

Christy said, "You know, I've been thinking. I know we should speak the truth in love, and the truth would help Wes in this situation. But we shouldn't spread rumors about other people."

"You think I'm making that up about Paul?" Sierra felt her defenses rise. "Is that what it seems like to you? That I'm gossiping and making up a rumor about Paul and Jalene having a baby?"

Christy and Katie both looked over the top of Sierra's head as if signaling her that Wes was returning. She instantly went silent and waited to see if he had overheard her. She suspected her voice had grown a little loud at the end.

Wes sat down. He flipped half of his bagel onto Sierra's paper plate and tossed the peanut butter to Katie. Turning to look at Sierra, he raised his eyebrows as if inviting her to explain what he had just heard.

"Okay," Sierra said with a huff. "I saw Paul's old girl-friend at Mama Bear's the day before we came down here. She had a little toddler with her. After some of the things Paul said this weekend, I just figured out the little boy was his—his and Jalene's. Paul doesn't know that I know yet, and I'm not sure I'm ready to talk to him about everything. He said on Sunday that he wasn't ready to have that conversation with me, and I'm not ready to have it with him, either. Not yet."

Wesley looked skeptical. "Are you sure?"

"Yes, I'm sure. That's why I asked if you could tell him I wasn't ready."

"No, I mean, are you sure Paul and Jalene had a baby? That's pretty intense, Sierra."

"Tell me about it."

"But he wasn't walking with the Lord then," Katie said, slipping into the conversation. "I think if God's forgiven him, then Sierra should forgive him, and they should just go on from there. We should never torture our brothers and sisters in Christ by holding past failures before them."

"You're right," Wes said. Then, turning to Sierra, he added, "And you know what? This is going to get way out of hand unless you have a private conversation with Paul. The sooner the better."

Sierra didn't agree with Wes. He didn't understand how high her hopes had been for her relationship with Paul. Wes would only give her a lecture about why he thought girls should stay "emotional virgins" if she tried to tell him how deeply this revelation about Paul hurt her.

"I think I'd better go," Sierra said, feeling that she would be better off dismissing herself before she said something she would regret. She collected her carton of orange juice and bagel and slid out of the booth.

"I'll walk back to the dorms with you," Christy said.

"Well, I'm staying," Katie said. "I told the guys who were just here that I'd eat with them when they came back. They went to get some money."

Wes gave Sierra a fatherly look, which irritated her. As she and Christy were leaving, he said, "I'll trust you to talk to Paul soon."

"Why did he have to say that?" Sierra muttered as they exited. "And why did I ever think going to the same university as my brother was a good idea?"

Christy didn't answer. They walked across campus in the brightness of the late morning sunshine, and Christy asked Sierra if she wanted to stop at the fountain. At first she didn't want to, but then Christy coaxed her to stop for just a minute. No one else was around, and in the warmth of the day, the coolness of the water was appealing.

Christy slipped off her sandals and stepped into the fountain. Sierra took the last swig of her orange juice and then followed Christy's example. When her feet first touched the smooth blue tiles, the cool water felt shocking. But then she settled in next to Christy on the edge of the fountain wall, and the two of them silently splashed their feet. The sensation seemed to revive both of them.

"I was thinking," Christy said, "did Paul actually say the little boy you saw was his son?"

"No. He doesn't know I saw him."

"Did Paul ever say anything about Jalene's getting pregnant?"

"No. Not exactly. He just said he had been there before and he didn't want us to end up there."

"Well, Sierra, what if the baby you saw wasn't Paul's? I mean, what if it was some other guy's? Or what if Jalene was never pregnant, but she was baby-sitting the day you saw her? Did you think about that? I mean, what if this is all a misunderstanding?" Christy pulled her long brown hair back and twisted it up on top of her head.

Sierra dismissed Christy's suggestions. "Then why would Paul have pulled back from me the way he did, and why would he have said all the things he did about not wanting to lose control physically?"

Christy let her hair go, and it cascaded down her back,

untwisting itself as it fell. "I don't know Paul at all, so I don't have any guesses as to why he did or said anything. But I know from talks Todd and I have had that a lot of times it's different for a guy than it is for a girl. Do you know what I mean?"

Sierra shaded her eyes from the sun and tried to look directly at Christy. The sun was shining off the water, causing an extra-bright glare on their faces.

"Like the other night when Todd and I were at my parents' house. It was about ten o'clock, and everyone else had gone to bed. Todd and I were talking out on the front porch. We were sitting on the top step under this trellis my dad built. A jasmine vine has grown over the trellis, and in the summer, especially at night, it's the most fragrant canopy you can imagine. Todd had his arms around me, and my back was against the side of his chest. You know, like this." Christy demonstrated by leaning against Sierra and resting her head on Sierra's shoulder.

Sierra laughed. "I've got the picture."

"Well, that's just cozy, right? Balmy night, fragrant jasmine, Todd and me back together again after a very long year. And we're talking about cars. Should he sell ol' Gus."

"No, never!" Sierra said.

"Well, that's what we were discussing," Christy continued. "And I was sitting there thinking how cozy and comfortable it was to hear his voice so close to my ear and to be planning together—even though it was just a little thing like cars. We were together, and I was so happy."

"Sounds perfect," Sierra said.

"Right. Because we're women. But you won't believe what happened. Todd leans over and snuggles his nose into my hair above my ear and kisses me right there." Christy points to a spot on her head above her left ear.

Sierra smiled, drawn into the romance of Christy's story.

"And then Todd says to me, 'I can't do this anymore.' Then we got up and went inside. I went to my room, and he went to David's and slept in the sleeping bag on David's floor."

"Why did he do that? Weren't you mad?" Sierra said. "He ruined the beautiful moment you two were having."

Christy smiled. "No, he preserved a beautiful moment rather than creating a moment of regret."

"I don't get it. You were just snuggling."

"I know," Christy said. "But what's cozy snuggling for me can be something much stronger for Todd. I have to understand and honor that, even though I don't feel the same way. It's taken me a long time to figure out that he and I are wired differently. He's a microwave, and I'm a Crock-Pot."

Sierra laughed.

"Todd always says this is the season for us to save, not spend."

"What does that mean?" Sierra pulled her feet from the cool water and felt them tingle as they dried in the sun. Having her feet washed and cooled had brought a refreshing sensation to her whole body. For some reason she thought of how Jesus had washed the disciples' feet as an act of love for His closest friends. She wondered if Christy's trying to understand Todd's feelings was also a loving act for her closest friend.

"During these years while we're dating, we're holding

back physically from each other," Christy said. "Even when we want to express ourselves, we're saving those expressions instead of spending them. I think of it as putting coins in a piggy bank. The only way that bank can be opened is to break it and let everything come pouring out at once."

Sierra could picture Christy and Todd sitting together under the jasmine trellis with imaginary handfuls of coins. They spent a penny or two each as they cuddled, but then, because they stopped, they were able to save their more valuable coins in their "piggy banks."

Christy pulled her feet from the water, too, and swung around to shake them out in the warm sunshine before slipping them back into her sandals. She stood and said playfully, "I can tell you, Miss Sierra, that by the time my wedding night gets here, whoever I marry is going to get one very full piggy bank, if you know what I mean!"

fifteen

SIERRA BURST OUT LAUGHING at Christy's comment. She was refreshingly transparent and honest. It made Sierra glad all over again that they would be together this school year.

"Well, maybe I should go buy myself a piggy bank," Sierra teased. She leaned back and scooped up a handful of water, which she splashed all over Christy.

Christy gave a muffled squeal and laughed with her hands up in defense. "Hey, I don't need a cold shower! I told you I have my hormones under control."

They laughed together and headed off to Sierra's dorm room. Overhead a clump of tall palm trees swayed in the breeze, making a swishing sound that Sierra loved. It wasn't quite the same as the wind in the birch trees outside her bedroom window at the house where she grew up, but it was similar enough to make her feel happy and at home at Rancho Corona.

When they reached the dorm, Sierra and Christy went to work opening Sierra's boxes and settling her into her room.

"Do you think it's dumb to have matching bedspreads?" Sierra asked as she smoothed the deep green comforter on her bed. "Vicki's mom insisted we buy matching bed-spreads. We even have matching throw pillows. I noticed Katie and you don't have anything that matches."

"Katie and I didn't have time to think about that," Christy said. "These comforters will look great together. You were smart to pick a solid color because in these small rooms a print might get old real fast."

"Wait until you see what Vicki is bringing. She has a huge beanbag chair, a stereo and speakers, and a little nightstand. It's going to be so crowded in here."

"It will all fit somehow," Christy said.

They worked together another hour before Christy curled up on Sierra's bed and helped herself to a catnap. Sierra took the opportunity to go down the hall to the pay phone so she could call her mom without waking Christy. She reached the answering machine and left a message that she was doing fine, setting up her room, and enjoying her friends.

After she hung up, she looked at the paper in her hand that listed Paul's home phone number. For the first time she realized she couldn't just decide never to see Paul again. Her sister was marrying his brother. Numerous occasions in the next year would bring them together. Whatever she decided to do with this relationship would affect both families as well. It reminded her of the thought she had had on the way to the Mexican restaurant, that nothing happens to us alone. Her life was connected with those of others, which was why it wasn't a good idea to alienate anyone.

Still not ready to have a heart-to-heart talk with Paul,

Sierra used her phone card to call Vicki. Vicki wasn't home either, so Sierra left a quick message and then dialed Amy's number, only to get Amy's voice mail. At least Sierra had tried. She would try again this evening when everyone was home from work. Sierra realized she had just used up precious minutes on her phone card, and she had only been given three cards. After the cards, she would have to pay for all her calls. That was a sobering thought. *That's it. I'm buying myself a cell phone before this semester is over. I can't believe I've gotten this far in my life without one!*

Christy was still asleep when Sierra went back to the room, so she collected her towel and a change of clothes and acquainted herself with the shower room located halfway down the hall. The shower was industrial-sized and seemed to magnify every sound she made. Sierra thought it was funny and started to sing, enjoying the wacky echo the shower made. But soon she realized playing in the shower was a way to avoid thinking things through while under the influence of warm, pelting shower drops. Maybe that was okay for right now.

Refreshed and clean all over, she returned to her room just as the phone on her desk rang. Christy stirred, but Sierra reached it before Christy could.

"Hi ya. It's Katie. Is Christy with you?"

"Yes. She's taking a little snooze."

"Well, tell her someone came looking for her. I'll send him over to your dorm."

Christy sat up and asked sleepily, "Who is it?"

"It's Katie," Sierra replied. "There's someone here to see you."

"Who?"

"Hey, Katie," Sierra said into the receiver, "Christy wants to know who you're sending over."

"Ask her if tall, blond, and surfer-dude mean anything to her."

Sierra smiled. "It's Todd. He's on his way over here."

"He is?" Christy sat all the way up and opened her eyes wide. "What's he doing here? I thought he wasn't coming until the end of the week."

"Hey, Katie, Christy wants to know why he's here."

"Why is he here?" Katie repeated. "Oh brother! Tell her if she doesn't want him, she can send him back over here, and he can take *me* out to dinner."

Sierra turned to Christy, "Katie said—"

"I could hear her," Christy said. "Tell her never in a million years, and I mean that in a nice way."

Sierra had been holding the phone out and now put it back to her ear. "Did you get that?"

"Yeah, well, just tell her that next time he comes offering food and she's not around, I won't be so diligent about tracking her down. And I mean that in a nice way, too."

Christy borrowed Sierra's brush and started to untangle her long hair.

Sierra laughed and hung up. She began to relay Katie's line to Christy when the phone rang again. It was a student who'd picked up the phone in the dorm lobby.

"Is this Sierra Jensen?

"Yes."

"You have a visitor, Sierra," the voice said. "He wants to know if you can come meet him in the lobby."

Sierra guessed who her visitor was right away. "Thanks. Tell him I'll be right there." Sierra hung up and said, "My brother is here. No doubt he's checking up on me again. You know, I thought it was going to be great having my big brother here so I could have someone to go to with all my problems, but if the rest of this year is anything like these first few days, the guy is going to drive me crazy!"

"Wes and you can get something to eat with Todd and me. Come on. Grab your key and let's go."

"My hair is still soaking!" Sierra said.

"It'll dry in two minutes outside," Christy said. "At least you smell good, which is a lot more than I can say for myself."

They hurried down the long hall and took the elevator to the main lobby area, where residents met their guests. The central lobby of Sierra's dorm, Sophia Hall, was as gorgeous as a tropical hotel lobby, with a court area in the center of the rectangular building. The large patio was paved with Tecate tiles, and the area was filled with trees and bushes, like a jungle. A number of benches were placed throughout, and a small fountain was located in the center.

Sierra looked around for Wes but didn't see him. Todd didn't appear to be anywhere visible, either.

"Knowing Todd, he's probably climbing one of the palm trees," Christy said, venturing into the arboretum area. Sierra followed her and noticed a guy walking around the backside of one of the trees as if he were examining it or trying to hide.

"What do you think?" Christy asked. "Is that one yours or mine?" All they could see was a bit of a gray T-shirt.

"Yours," Sierra guessed.

Then the guy rounded the tree, and they saw his face.

"Oh!" Christy whispered in surprise. "It's neither of ours."

"No," Sierra said slowly. "It's mine."

Christy reached for Sierra's arm. "Paul?" she whispered.

Instead of answering, Sierra found herself moving forward at the same pace Paul was moving toward her. He looked serious and had on his dirty work clothes, so Sierra guessed he had driven there right after a long, hot day of construction work.

"Hi," he said.

"Hi," Sierra answered.

Even sweaty and dirty he looked great. Sierra found it hard to slow down her heart enough for her to come up with some words. Paul looked past Sierra at Christy, and Sierra quickly introduced them, explaining that Christy was the friend Sierra had met in England and then later went with to Switzerland.

Paul nodded and said, "I've just come back from a year in Scotland."

"That's what Sierra told me."

Sierra could see Todd sneaking up behind Christy as she spoke. He had on a pale blue T-shirt that made his silver-blue eyes shout with mischief, but the finger to his lips told Sierra not to announce his approach. Paul played along as well, and before Christy knew what was happening, Todd stepped behind her and scooped her up in his arms.

She let out a startled squeal, which was overpowered by Todd announcing, "Me Tarzan, you... Hey, you not Jane!"

He put Christy down, and she looked at him with astonishment. "Todd, whatever got into you?"

"I've always wanted to do that," he said, returning to his easygoing manner. "Hey, Sierra. How's it going?"

Sierra introduced Paul, and the four of them stood there rather awkwardly.

"Do you want to get some dinner, Christy?" Todd asked.

"Sure," Christy said. She turned to Sierra and Paul. "Would you guys like to join us?"

Paul and Sierra exchanged uncomfortable glances.

"I guess," Sierra finally said. She didn't know what to do.

"Actually," Paul said, "I'd like to talk with you, Sierra."

"Why don't you guys go ahead," Sierra said. "I'll see you later."

"Okay, later," Todd said. He gave Paul a chin-up nod and said, "See you around, Paul."

Paul nodded back, and Todd and Christy left, hand in hand. Sierra thought Todd had never seemed happier. And why not? He had Christy back and the "distance between them was a walking space." Sierra had hoped she and Paul would be that happy together, but all her feelings were so tied up in knots she didn't know if she could ever untangle them.

"I saw a bench back there," Paul said, motioning to where Sierra had first seen him behind the tree. "I was looking for a little more private place to talk." He walked into the center of the garden lobby and motioned for Sierra to follow him to a bench in the far right corner.

Sierra's mind raced with all the different directions this conversation might go. She could tell him that she had seen Jalene and their son and that he didn't have to hide that part of his life anymore. But then what would she say? That it didn't matter? That the two of them could go on and that she would be content to sit next to him on the "second step" and not go any further physically?

Right now Sierra wasn't sure she even wanted to be with Paul, let alone take any steps with him. It suddenly seemed ironic that after years of gaining a reputation around her friends as the "queen of confrontation," the last thing she wanted to do was have a heart-to-heart talk with Paul.

sixteen

"THIS IS A BEAUTIFUL PLACE," Paul said as he sat on the bench and motioned for Sierra to sit next to him.

Sierra nodded her agreement.

"I can see why you said in your letters you liked this school so much. I'm even more interested in coming here now that I've seen the campus. It's very different from the University of Edinburgh." Paul was looking at her, but she was having a hard time looking at him.

"Sierra," Paul said, trying to get her full attention, "can you tell me what's going on?"

Sierra bit her lower lip.

"I don't understand why you didn't call me." Paul's voice was low and calm. "I know it wasn't the best timing on Sunday in the gym to try to talk about physical guidelines for our relationship, but I wanted you to know why I was spooked Saturday night. We were just getting too close too fast."

"I understand," Sierra said softly, looking down.

"Then why didn't you call me?"

"I wasn't ready to talk to you."

Paul balanced his arm on the back of the bench and rested his unshaven cheek on his knuckles. "Why?"

Sierra knew this was the perfect opening to tell him that she knew about Jalene and the baby, but she couldn't do it. She couldn't say the words. Not used to being tongue-tied, she fingered the silver daffodil around her neck and wondered where all her boldness had gone.

"Listen," Paul said, reaching for one of her still-wet curls and gently brushing it off her shoulder. "Neither of us has told each other much about our past relationships."

Sierra turned to look at him, ready for his confession.

"And I just want to say that I realize you may have been more involved with guys in the past, so you're expecting more from me at this point. But I've set some pretty rigid standards for myself. Maybe we should have talked about that before we saw each other."

Sierra was startled. "You think I've been more involved with guys in the past?"

Paul's eyes showered her with understanding. "Hey, you don't have to tell me about any of that. I'm not your judge. I'm just saying you obviously were comfortable with a lot of physical expression the other night, but that's not the direction I'd like our relationship to go. That's why I thought we should pull back."

Sierra stared at Paul in disbelief. All she could do was repeat his statement. "You thought I was comfortable with a lot of physical expression?"

Paul nodded. "That might be what you're used to in relationships with other guys, but I want us to take it more slowly. That's what I've wanted from the beginning, which is why I suggested we write letters instead of e-mail. I'm not judging you for your past; I'm just saying this is how I'd like it to be for us."

Sierra sprang from the bench and said in angry disbelief, "You're not judging me?"

Paul stood, too, caught off guard by her reaction.

Before Sierra could blurt out that she was as pure and innocent as a lamb and that Paul was the only guy with whom she had ever expressed the kinds of physical affection she gave him the other night, two girls walked in their direction, talking loudly. Paul and Sierra stood frozen, staring at each other, waiting for the girls to pass.

Sierra's startled anger overtook any sense of reason, and she blurted out, "You're a fine one to be going around overlooking my past! What about your past?"

Paul looked stunned. "What about my past?" His voice was rising to meet the intensity of Sierra's.

"Jalene and you."

"What about Jalene and me?"

"Oh, come on, Paul. You kept it from me all this time. But then I saw her last week, and I figured it out."

"Figured what out?"

"I saw him, Paul. I saw him with Jalene, and I figured out why you wanted to go to Portland last June."

"I wanted to go to Portland to see you," Paul said loudly.

"And a few other people so you could make things right with them. Isn't that what you said?"

Paul still looked frustrated and confused. "What are you getting at, Sierra? This is making no sense."

"Oh, it's not?"

"No," Paul said, lowering his voice. "It's not. Can you just tell me what you're trying to say?"

"Okay, I'll tell you. It's Jalene," Sierra said, looking at him like an eager lawyer making her closing statements to the jury. "Jalene and the *baby*." She gave extra emphasis to the last word, raising her eyebrows in a knowing expression. "And since you didn't tell me and I had to figure it out myself, well, to be honest with you, I haven't quite decided where my trust level is in this relationship at the moment. I thought you—"

"You thought what?" Paul cut her off, his arms folded across his chest.

"I thought—"

"You thought the kid you saw with Jalene was mine?" Paul's face was turning red.

Sierra folded her arms, too, and stood her ground. "I'm not saying I'm judging your past in any way. But it sure would have been nice if I'd heard it from you first."

"Listen, Sierra," he stated, "you didn't hear it from me first because there was nothing for you to hear. I don't know whose baby Jalene had when you saw her, and I don't know what she told you, but there's no way it's mine. Absolutely no way! It's not possible."

"It's not?"

"No! And I can't believe you assumed it could be, Sierra! How could you have jumped to such conclusions?"

Instead of meekly apologizing at the revelation, Sierra let her nervous fury fly. "And what is it you assumed about me? Just a few minutes ago you said you thought I was comfortable with a lot of physical expression because that must be what I was used to. Well, guess again, Paul! There haven't been any other guys—ever. Not even one."

His expression softened. "What about Randy?"

"Randy is my buddy."

"What about that guy you told me you met in Switzerland?"

"Alex?" Sierra laughed. "He hugged me good-bye at the airport by pressing his cheek against mine. How's that for physical intimacy?"

"And there hasn't been anyone else?"

"Well, let's see, there was Drake. He put his arm around me once when we were walking the dog together. Oh, and he held my hand when he prayed with me one time in the car."

Paul rubbed his neck as if he were trying to relax his thick muscles.

"Paul," Sierra railed, still fired up, "you are looking at one of the world's oldest pair of virgin lips! They've been on my face for almost eighteen years and have only been used to kiss the cheeks of grandmothers, the feet of infants, and Brutus."

"Brutus?"

"Our dog."

"Oh," was all Paul said. Sierra's ravings seemed to have calmed him down a bit. "I misunderstood," he said. "The way you were coming on to me Saturday night, I assumed you were much more experienced."

Something inside of Sierra went *Twang!* "The way I was coming on to you!" she yelled. "I can't believe you're saying that! You were the one who took me down to the beach and held me in that little cave and quoted me your poetry. Are you telling me that's not coming on to me?"

"Is that what you thought I was doing?"

"I thought you were treating me the way you would treat your girlfriend."

"And what were you doing?" Paul asked.

"I was treating you the way I'd treat my boyfriend. My first boyfriend in my whole life, I might add, not that that matters at this point."

Paul rubbed his neck again. "Is that what we are? Are you saying we're now boyfriend and girlfriend? Are we a couple, Sierra?" Paul looked at her, his jaw clenched, his blue-gray eyes clouding over, waiting for her answer.

seventeen

SIERRA CROSSED HER ARMS around her middle, trying to keep her upset stomach from grumbling loud enough for Paul to hear. "I don't know," she answered with her chin held up defiantly. "You tell me. What are we?"

"I don't know," Paul said, folding his arms across his chest. "And maybe I don't want to feel pressured to figure it out right now."

"Who's pressuring you?" Sierra said. "Certainly not me."

"That's right," Paul said, slapping his forehead with the palm of his hand as an exaggerated gesture. "You're not pressuring me. As a matter of fact, you're not even calling me when I ask you. So I have to wonder what's wrong and rush up here from work so I can find out. And here you are, dreaming up some promiscuous past life for me!"

Sierra had a half an impulse to apologize and admit she had been wrong to jump to conclusions. But she couldn't let herself. It still bothered her that he had jumped to conclusions about her as well. "Oh yeah? Well, what about the promiscuous past life you dreamed up about me? Or doesn't that count?"

Before Paul could answer, Katie appeared. "Hi, kids!" she called across the courtyard. "Did Todd and Christy leave already to go eat? Hey, you must be Paul." Katie gave him a friendly punch on the shoulder. "I was wondering when I'd get to meet you. Sierra has told me all about you."

"Really?" Paul said, looking at Sierra and then back at Katie. "And did she tell you about a certain baby boy in Portland who is supposedly my son?"

Katie looked at Paul. Her clear green eyes showed sincere compassion. She nodded and said, "And you know what I told Sierra? I told her, 'Big whoop.' What's past is past. As long as everything is settled between God and you, then it's time to move on, right?"

Paul hesitated only a moment before saying, "Right. Time to move on." He shot a pain-filled expression at Sierra and said calmly, "You know what? I don't think I can do this." He brushed passed her and headed straight for the door.

Sierra felt her heart pounding in her throat. Everything inside her told her to run after him, but she couldn't move a muscle.

"Was it something I said?" Katie asked. "If it was, I'm sorry."

"No, it was me. I messed up, Katie. I messed up bad! Paul and Jalene never had a baby. I jumped to all the wrong conclusions. I should never have said anything to you or Christy."

"Then go tell him that," Katie said, motioning in the direction Paul had gone.

"I can't. It's too messed up. And I'm still mad at him. He assumed I had a very active past, too. He thinks I'm pressuring him to be my boyfriend or something." Sierra sank onto the bench, her arms still folded tightly across her stomach. "I think I'm going to be sick."

"Hey, don't get sick here," Katie said, pulling Sierra up by the arm. "You should go back to your room. I'll go talk to Paul."

"No, Katie, don't."

"Hey, it's the least I can do after what happened. You go back to your room, and I'll call you, okay? I need to apologize to Paul." Katie was already moving away from Sierra as she said the last sentence. "I have to run if I'm going to catch him." With that, she sprinted toward the front doors.

Sierra called out to Katie one more time before giving up and heading to her room. With each step, she remembered vividly Paul's assumptions of her, and her hurt and frustration fanned the fire that had not yet died down inside.

Stomping down the hall, Sierra entered her room and slammed the door behind her—something she was never allowed to do at home. That particular habit had been curbed when she was a small child and she would throw what her mother called "dramatic displays of independence."

Sierra certainly was in the mood to throw one of those "dramatic displays" right now, and no one was there to stop her. Or discipline her. Or listen to her. Or comfort her. She was all alone.

Sierra picked up one of her throw pillows and threw it at the wall. That didn't do any good, so she began pacing back and forth, trying to make sense of everything, picking out each feeling and trying to identify it.

First, she knew she felt remorse over her assumption that Paul and Jalene had had a child. Her imagination had gotten way out of control on that one. Why hadn't she listened to Wes or Christy when they tried to get her to look at other possible explanations? Why did she always get carried away with her zealous, impulsive assumptions? She didn't blame Paul for being mad at her. He had every right to be furious. If he never spoke to her again, she wouldn't blame him.

But then, her other feeling was anger at Paul because he had made assumptions about her, too. And that wasn't fair. Those assumptions hurt her more than she would have expected.

And why did Paul have to walk away from the problem? Why couldn't he have stayed so they could fight it out? Sierra almost always preferred a good fight to silence.

But then she recalled Paul's red face and arms folded across his chest. That image made her smile against her will. *So the man's got fire in his spirit*, she thought.

She had never seen that side of him. Some things don't come up in written words, even after dozens of letters. The maddening thing was, Paul's ability to communicate so clearly what he was thinking and feeling only made Sierra adore him more than ever. She knew she could never love or respect a guy who couldn't match her zeal. And she certainly didn't want to end up with a guy who would let her bulldoze him with fiery words. That revelation acted as cool water, quenching the fire within her.

Sierra lifted the silver daffodil from the end of the chain around her neck and pressed the cool metal to her lips. *Oh Paul, I'm sorry. Please come back. I want to apologize. Father God,*

can't You make him come back? I can't let the sun go down on my anger. I
need to make things right with Paul.

In the silence, Sierra thought, waited, and prayed. When Katie didn't call, Sierra decided to ease her loneliness by eating a granola bar and drinking some apple juice. It proved an unsatisfying solution.

Just as she was about to start in on a second granola bar, she heard a knock on her door. It was Katie, and she was shaking her head.

"I couldn't find him. He must have parked out front and taken off immediately. I'm sorry, Sierra. I've been thinking about all this, and I really feel bad. I never should have jumped to those conclusions about Paul without all the facts."

"I know," Sierra said. "But it's my fault, not yours. It was my assumption, not yours."

Katie flopped onto Vicki's empty bed and lay on her back, staring at the ceiling. "Have you prayed about everything yet?"

"Yes."

"And what do you think you should do?"

"I don't know. I want to talk to him."

"We could take Baby Hummer and go down to Paul's house in San Diego, or you could borrow Baby Hummer and go by yourself." Katie turned on her side and faced Sierra, who was sitting tensely on the edge of her bed.

"I don't know where his house is. Maybe I could call Tawni and ask her for directions."

"Do you have the address?" Katie asked. "We could look it up on the Internet."

"What if he calls here?" Sierra said. "What if he drives

halfway home and calms down the way I have? What if he comes back here or calls? Oh, I wish I had a cell phone!"

"I could go find someone who has their laptop already online, and you could wait here," Katie suggested.

"You would do that for me?" Sierra asked.

"Are you kidding? As the last honorary member of the P.O. Club, I find it my duty to serve former members whenever the opportunity arises."

It took Sierra a moment to remember what Katie was referring to. When she did, she smiled. "Oh, right, our little 'Pals Only Club' we dreamed up in England. You and I vowed to be only pals with guys so we wouldn't have to experience all the emotional trauma our friends were going through with their boyfriends." Sierra felt a little sad as she said, "Looks as though I might be back in the club after I talk to Paul. That is, if he still wants to even be friends with me."

"He will," Katie said confidently. "When I saw him standing there next to you, I immediately knew who he was, and honestly, my first thought was that you two look like you belong together."

"Why do you say that?"

"You just do. Some couples match. You know, like Doug and Tracy, and Christy and Todd. Paul and you go together."

Sierra let out a sigh. "Yeah, well, we'll see."

eighteen

A FEW MINUTES after Katie left the room, the phone rang. For half a second, Sierra considered not answering it. *That'll show him,* she thought defiantly. *He thinks I'm waiting for him to call.* But Sierra had never been good at playing hard to get, so she lunged for the receiver on the second ring.

"Good, you're there," the male voice said on the other end.

Sierra sighed. "I'm not interested in getting something to eat, if that's what you're going to ask, Wesley."

"No, I'm not offering food. I want to ask a favor."

"Well, what is it? This is kind of a bad time."

"I want to know if you would go to the chapel in about ten minutes."

"Why?"

There was a pause. "This is really important, Sierra. I have rarely asked you to do anything for me. I'm asking that, just this once, you do something for me without all the details up front. All you have to do is say yes or no. Can you go to the prayer chapel in about ten minutes?"

Sierra drew in a deep breath. "Oh, all right." She figured that by the time she had completed this silly secret mission of Wesley's and returned to her room, Katie would be back with the map. If Paul did call while she was gone, he would leave a message for her, and she could call him back and talk to him with a much calmer spirit. "I'll be there in ten minutes, Wesley."

"That's great. Thanks, Sierra."

She hung up the phone and gave herself a quick look in the mirror. Her hair had dried during her "heated" discussion with Paul. Her black eye had toned down some, and none of her previous fiery or queasy feelings now showed in her skin tone. She scribbled a quick note to Katie, grabbed her room key, and left the note on her door.

As Sierra hiked across campus, she figured out Wes wanted to meet with her to instruct her not to jump to conclusions about Paul. The prayer chapel was probably the most private place on campus. If her brother was going to lecture her, it might as well be in private. Well, she had news for him. She had already figured out she shouldn't jump to conclusions. What she hadn't quite figured out was how to make peace with Paul. She hoped Wes would be in an extra-understanding mood when she told him everything, and he would be able to give her some advice.

Sierra thought it was ironic that now she wanted her brother's advice. It made her realize how much her opinions had been swinging back and forth the past few days. If this was all part of getting used to being on her own and charting her way through her relationship with Paul, then Sierra hoped she could find some calm middle ground soon.

Rancho Corona's campus covered nearly twenty acres on the top of a mesa. The prayer chapel was on the southwest corner of the mesa, and the walk there, in the cool of the evening, refreshed Sierra. She thought of how the Bible talked about the Lord God walking with Adam and Eve in the Garden of Eden in the cool of the evening. It made her wonder what that must have been like, to walk and talk with God. Then it struck her that the same God who went walking with the first woman was still here, invisibly walking beside her, down this trail past the large meadow.

Sierra impulsively began to talk with God aloud. "I guess Paul and I aren't the first man and woman to have a conflict, are we?" she said. "Not that it's a good thing, but it's not unusual, is it?"

Only the evening breeze answered her with soothing strokes across her cheeks. Suddenly Sierra realized that her most important relationship was with God. He would never leave her. He would never make incorrect assumptions about her because He already knew everything. He would never give up on His relationship with her because He had promised in His Word that His love for her was forever.

Picking up her pace, Sierra felt eager to reach the prayer chapel. She wanted to have time to kneel and pray in that quiet, holy place before Wes arrived. She wanted to reaffirm her commitment to Christ and ceremoniously surrender her relationship with Paul. An urgency seemed to envelop her, and when she turned onto the path that led to the chapel, the wind seemed to push her forward into the chapel's sanctuary.

Opening the door cautiously and peering inside, Sierra was glad to see no one was there. She tiptoed up to the altar at the front of the chapel and got down on her knees, folding her hands to pray. Above the altar was a stained glass window that bore the emblem of the ranch that had occupied this mesa years ago. It was a gold crown with a cross coming out of the center of it at a slant. She bowed her head and noticed how the evening sunlight spilled through the golden glass that formed the crown and settled in a shining circle around Sierra's heart.

She closed her eyes and prayed in a whisper, "Lord God, thank You so much for bringing me here to Rancho. I want to honor You with my life. I want what You want for the relationships in my life, especially with Paul. God, forgive me for messing things up, and please give us a fresh start. I don't know how to do this boyfriend-girlfriend thing. Will You teach me? I want to trust You in every way with every area of my life. I love You, Jesus."

With her whispered "Amen," Sierra heard the chapel's door open, and she wondered if she should jump up before Wes saw her kneeling at the altar. But it didn't matter to her. She had just shared a meaningful moment with the same Lord God who had walked with Eve in the garden. Sierra had no reason to run and hide the way Eve had when she disobeyed. Sierra had been forgiven. She knew it. She could face God and Wes without shame.

Sierra didn't turn to look at her brother. Instead, she listened as his footsteps approached. She wanted to linger one more moment, gazing at the light coming through the stained glass window and reveling in the fresh, clean feeling that had come over her.

She felt her brother's hand on her shoulder and impulsively pressed her cheek against it. Then with a quick kiss on his knuckle, she said, "I know what you're going to say."

"Oh, do you?" the voice behind her answered. But it wasn't Wesley's voice.

Sierra froze.

Paul knelt beside her. She slowly turned her head to look at him, all her defenses down. "I'm sorry," she said, the instant her eyes met his.

"I'm sorry, too. I'm not sure what happened," Paul said. "But instead of leaving, I decided to talk to your brother, and I'm glad I did."

Sierra noticed Paul had on a clean shirt. It was one of Wesley's new, short-sleeved, blue cotton shirts. Paul smelled fresh, too. He obviously had calmed down—maybe in a cold shower—and was ready to talk the way Sierra was.

"You know what I think?" Paul said.

Sierra waited for him to go on.

"I think we got off track. I'd like to get back on track."

"I would, too," Sierra said. "Only now I understand I had way too many expectations and assumptions."

"I did, too," Paul said. "Can we start again and take it nice and slow?"

Sierra nodded.

"I need to apologize for not communicating more clearly before we went for our walk on the beach. I realize I was being very familiar with you physically. That's why I was trying to say I didn't want our relationship to go in that direction. It could become an expectation that every time we see each other we have to hold hands or whatever just to keep the relationship at the same level. Does that make sense?"

"Yes," Sierra said, adjusting her position so now she was

sitting on the floor in front of the altar.

"I've written out these verses I found in First Thessalonians." Paul settled in on the floor across from her. They both were speaking in hushed tones and using tender expressions, a vast difference from their earlier confrontation. He pulled a folded piece of paper from his back pocket and said, "This is what I want for our relationship."

He read the first eight verses of chapter four quickly, and Sierra asked him to go back and read part of it again.

"For God wants you to be holy and pure, and to keep clear of all sexual sin so that each of you will marry in holiness and honor." Paul looked at Sierra and said, "I don't know whose wife you're going to be someday, but I don't want to dishonor that guy, whoever he is, or you, by taking anything that is meant for him alone."

Sierra felt her heart melting into a little puddle.

"So I don't want to take advantage of you by becoming too physically involved."

"You know what, Paul? I don't want to take advantage of you either. And I don't want to steal anything that belongs to your future wife. But I have to tell you something: I really pay attention to your words. What you say to me or write to me is how I gauge our relationship. So if you write incredible poems just for me, I'm thinking our relationship is deepening. Your poems may be saying more to me than you mean for them to."

"I didn't realize that."

"I know you've been careful with your words to me in your letters, but I have to tell you, your words capture my heart."

Paul nodded his understanding. "I guess that's similar

to how it was for me when we were on the beach and you were so free with your physical expressions. I think I took it to mean more than it was."

Sierra shrugged. "I'm a rookie at this. Now I know not to be so expressive."

"And I'll watch my words."

Paul reached out and, touching the silver daffodil around Sierra's neck, said, "But don't go too far the other way and clam up, Sierra. I've always admired your zealous spirit. I like the way you openly and honestly express yourself."

"But it wouldn't hurt if I tried to control that zeal a little more, right?"

Paul tilted his head. "Maybe. And I need to control my poetic spirit, right?"

"Maybe," Sierra said, smiling at him. "So, where do we go from here?"

"I think I know," Paul said, letting go of the necklace and holding out his hand, inviting her to take it. Sierra slipped her hand into his, and Paul held it lightly. He looked at the blue and amber hues of the stained glass windows that were sprinkled across their hands. "We just keep going from here, helping each other learn how to live controlled lives of sanctification and honor."

"And lives that are a little more balanced," Sierra said, thinking of how much she had been swinging emotionally back and forth the last few days.

"Balanced," Paul repeated. "And since the next chapter in First Thessalonians says to greet one another with a holy kiss, here's my answer to that balance." Paul lifted her hand to his lips. With hushed words, he said, "This is from my heart to yours. A holy kiss for the Daffodil Queen." Paul tenderly kissed the top of Sierra's hand as only a romantic poet would.

She smiled, repressing the impulse to throw her arms around his neck and return his kiss on his lips. To her surprise, Sierra found she could sit there, without having to act on the impulse. She remembered Christy's story about the piggy bank, and Sierra secretly decided that she had just saved a very huge kiss for her future husband in her invisible piggy bank.

"You interested in getting some dinner?" Paul asked.

"Sure," Sierra said, feeling settled and at peace about where their relationship was and where it was headed.

Paul stood and offered her his hand to pull her up. She rose, and together they left the quiet chapel. The air around them seemed charged with a holy presence. Sierra imagined that Adam and Eve must have experienced the same somber stillness when the Lord God walked with them in the cool of the evening.

"He's here, you know," Sierra said to Paul.

"I know," Paul said.

They paused just long enough to watch the bright orange September sun dip into the horizon. Then, circled by the golden light of God's presence and His promise, Paul and Sierra walked side by side along the trail that led toward the campus and on toward their future.

Happenstance... or God's Great Plan?

She's the bold, free-spirited type. She's cute, she's fun, and she's following God. She's Sierra Jensen, Christy Miller's good friend, ready for her junior year of high school! All twelve books in the popular Sierra Jensen series come together in four volumes to reveal the ups and downs of Sierra's incredible God-led journey!

Volume One: In *Only You, Sierra*, she's nervous to be the "new girl" after her family moves to Portland and wonders if meeting Paul in London was only by chance. Just when everything important seems to elude her, all it takes is one weekend *In Your Dreams* to prove otherwise. But even a vacation doesn't keep her troubles away in *Don't You Wish*.
Available Now!

Volume Two: Paul's voice lives in her memory, but now it's loud, clear, and right behind her in *Close Your Eyes*. With summer fast approaching, it is *Without a Doubt* bound to be Sierra's best yet. In *With This Ring*, she can't help but ponder the meaning of first kisses and lifetime commitments.
Available Now!

Volume Three: An exciting trip to Europe challenges Sierra to *Open Your Heart* to loving others without expectations. At the start of her senior year, only *Time Will Tell* the truth about Sierra's friendships. And in *Now Picture This*, she wonders if her relationship with Paul is as picture perfect as she thinks!
Available Now!

Volume Four: In this final volume, Sierra Jensen's only just beginning the roller coaster of adventures leading up to college. Join her in this exciting, challenging time of faith and fun!
Available Now!

www.ChristyMillerAndFriends.com

ROBIN JONES GUNN

As You Wish

ROBIN JONES GUNN

Until Tomorrow

ROBIN JONES GUNN

I Promise

Don't Miss the Next Chapter in Christy Miller's Unforgettable Life!

Follow Christy and Todd through the struggles, lessons, and changes that life in college will bring. Concentrating on her studies, Christy spends a year abroad in Europe and returns to campus at Rancho Corona University. Will Todd be waiting for her? CHRISTY AND TODD: THE COLLEGE YEARS follows Christy into her next chapter as she makes decisions about life and love.

CHRISTY AND TODD: THE COLLEGE YEARS by Robin Jones Gunn

Until Tomorrow • As You Wish • I Promise

SISTERCHICK® Adventures by
ROBIN JONES GUNN

SISTERCHICKS ON THE LOOSE!

Zany antics abound when best friends Sharon and Penny take off on a midlife adventure to Finland, returning home with a new view of God and a new zest for life.

SISTERCHICKS DO THE HULA!

It'll take more than an unexpected stowaway to keep two middle-aged sisterchicks from reliving their college years with a little Waikiki wackiness—and learning to hula for the first time.

SISTERCHICKS IN SOMBREROS!

Two Canadian sisters embark on a journey to claim their inheritance—beachfront property in Mexico—not expecting so many bizarre, wacky problems! But there's nothing a little coconut cake can't cure...

AVAILABLE NOW!

www.sisterchicks.com

More SISTERCHICK® Adventures
by
ROBIN JONES GUNN

SISTERCHICKS DOWN UNDER!

Kathleen meets Jill at the Chocolate Fish café in New Zealand, and they instantly forge a friendship. Together they fall head over heels into a deeper sense of God's love.

SISTERCHICKS SAY OOH LA LA!

Painting toenails and making promises under the canopy of a princess bed seals a friendship for life! Fifty years of ups and downs find Lisa and Amy still Best Friends Forever…and off on an unforgettable Paris rendezvous!

SISTERCHICKS IN GONDOLAS

At a fifteenth-century palace in Venice, best friends/sisters-in-law Jenna and Sue welcome the gondola-paced Italian lifestyle! And over boiling pots of pasta, they dare each other to dream again.

AVAILABLE NOW!

www.sisterchicks.com

About the Author

Robin Jones Gunn grew up in Orange County, California, where both her parents were teachers. She has one older sister and one younger brother. The three Jones kids graduated from Santa Ana High School and spent their summers on the beach with a bunch of "God-Lover" friends. Robin didn't meet her "Todd" until after she had gone to Biola University for two years and spent a summer traveling around Europe.

As her passion for ministering to teenagers grew, Robin assisted more with the youth group at her church. It was on a bike ride for middle schoolers that Robin met Ross. After they married, they spent the next two decades working together in youth ministry. God blessed them with a son and then a daughter.

When her children were young, Robin would rise at 3 a.m. when the house was quiet, make a pot of tea, and write pages and pages about Christy and Todd. She then read those pages to the girls in the youth group, and they gave her advice on what needed to be changed. The writing process took two years and ten rejections before her first novel, *Summer Promise*, was accepted for publication. Since its release in 1988, *Summer Promise* along with the rest of the Christy Miller and Sierra Jensen series have sold over 2.5 million copies and can be found in a dozen translations all over the world.

For the past twelve years, Robin has lived near Portland,

Oregon, which has given her lots of insight into what Sierra's life might be like in the Great Northwest. Now that her children are grown and Robin's husband has a new career as a counselor, she continues to travel and tell stories about best friends and God-Lovers. Her popular Glenbrooke series tracks the love stories of some of Christy Miller's friends.

Robin's bestselling Sisterchick novels hatched a whole trend of lighthearted books about friendship and midlife adventures. Who knows what stories she'll write next?

You are warmly invited to visit Robin's websites at: www.robingunn.com, www.christymillerandfriends.com, and www.sisterchicks.com.

THE GLENBROOKE SERIES

by Robin Jones Gunn

COME TO GLENBROOKE...

A QUIET PLACE WHERE SOULS ARE REFRESHED

Imagine a circle of friends who enter into each other's lives during that poignant season when love comes their way. Imagine the sweetness of having those friends to depend on as the journey into marriage and motherhood begins.

Meet the women of Glenbrooke: Jessica, Teri, Lauren, Alissa, Shelly, Meredith, Leah, and Genevieve. When their lives intersect in this small town, the door to friendship is opened and hearts come in to stay.

Perfectly crafted, heartwarming, and rich in truth, Robin's Glenbrooke novels have delighted half a million readers with their insights and charm. All souls looking to be refreshed are warmly invited to come to Glenbrooke.

SECRETS
Glenbrooke Series #1
Beginning her new life in a small Oregon town, high school English teacher Jessica Morgan tries desperately to hide the details of her past.

978-1-59052-240-0

WHISPERS
Glenbrooke Series #2
Teri went to Maui hoping to start a relationship with one special man. But romance becomes much more complicated when she finds herself pursued by three.

978-1-59052-192-2

ECHOES
Glenbrooke Series #3
Lauren Phillips "connects" on the Internet with a man known only as "K.C." Is she willing to risk everything...including another broken heart?

978-1-59052-193-9

SUNSETS
Glenbrooke Series #4
Alissa loves her new job as a Pasadena travel agent. Will an abrupt meeting with a stranger in an espresso shop leave her feeling that all men are like the one she's been hurt by recently?

978-1-59052-238-7

CLOUDS
Glenbrooke Series #5
After Shelly Graham and her old boyfriend cross paths in Germany, both must face the truth about their feelings.

978-1-59052-230-1

WATERFALLS
Glenbrooke Series #6
Meri thinks she's finally met the man of her dreams...until she finds out he's movie star Jacob Wilde, promptly puts her foot in her mouth, and ruins everything.

978-1-59052-231-8

WOODLANDS
Glenbrooke Series #7
Leah Hudson has the gift of giving, but questions her own motives, and God's purposes, when she meets a man she prays will love her just for herself.

978-1-59052-237-0

WILDFLOWERS
Glenbrooke Series #8
Genevieve Ahrens has invested lots of time and money in renovating the Wildflowers Café. Now her heart needs the same attention.

978-1-579052-239-4

Excerpt from *Sunsets*

"COFFEE," ALISSA MUTTERED, pushing herself away from her cluttered desk, "a tall café mocha, and I need it now. You want anything, Cheri?"

"No, thanks," her coworker said without looking up from her computer. "Are you getting this same strange reading on the Mazatlan cruise package?"

"Yes," Alissa said after checking the computer screen over Cheri's shoulder. "I got that reading when I tried to access the Alaska cruise package for the Andersens. But I'm not ready to try again until after I've had some coffee."

Cheri looked over the top of her glasses. "We open in five minutes."

"I know. I'll be back in four. Don't sell any cruise packages until then."

The line at Starbucks was shorter than usual. Alissa examined the pastries in the case. They had Cheri's favorite lemon bars this morning and lots of other incredible-looking goodies.

She started her familiar mental workout. *Croissant. I want a croissant. But I shouldn't. Too much fat. I'll have a muffin. A low-fat blueberry. Or a bagel. I can have a bagel. A bagel with fat-free cream cheese.*

"What can I start for you?" the young woman behind the counter asked.

Alissa hesitated.

The customer behind her spoke up. "Cappuccino and a croissant."

"Excuse me." Alissa turned to the casually dressed man behind her. "I was next, and if you don't mind, I'm in a hurry."

He wore his long brown hair with a crooked part down the middle. A soft cocoa stubble curved across his broad jaw, and his gaze struck her with intense clarity. Green eyes. Green like the grass after it rains.

"So what took you so long?" he said with a teasing smile.

Alissa raised her eyebrows and decided this must be his idea of a joke. Since she had moved to Pasadena seven months ago, she had met plenty of men who acted as if the world were their footstool, and therefore they could put up their feet whenever they wanted. Southern California was full of that sort.

Turning to the woman behind the counter, Alissa said calmly, "I'll have a tall café mocha, a lemon bar, and a cinnamon roll. Thanks."

There was no point looking over her shoulder as she left Starbucks. The man with the intriguing green eyes wouldn't be watching her. Men used to watch her walk away. She could feel their gazes. Men used to offer to let her go first.

But that was thirty-two pounds ago. It had been far too long since a man had given her a second glance. Not that she blamed any of them. Much had changed in the life of Alissa Benson.

Wistfully, she remembered what it was like to be seventeen, sauntering through the sand at Newport Beach while everyone watched. That had been many summers ago, back when the ends of her long blond hair had danced in the wind like the mane of a wild horse.

Today, a linen blazer covered her rounded hips, and her shoulder-length, wavy blond hair was caught up in a twist, clipped flat against the back of her head. She rarely wore her blue-tinted contact lenses anymore. Makeup was something she bothered with only on special occasions, of which there hadn't been many lately.

Alissa's live-in companion was a cat named Chloe, and her favorite weekend pastime was reading. At twenty-six she was living the life of a sixty-year-old. And she was safe.

As Alissa opened the door to the travel agency, Cheri motioned to her. "She's right here. I'll put you on hold, Mr. Brannigan."

"Line two," Cheri said to Alissa. "And your landlord is on line one."

"Oh, terrific." Alissa handed the pastry bag to Cheri. "I picked up a little something for you."

A smile spread across Cheri's face. "Did you bring me a lemon bar? You are a honey!"

"Don't touch my cinnamon roll!" Alissa playfully responded as she slid behind her desk and reached for the phone. "Good morning, Mr. Brannigan. Did your wife tell you I was able to reserve two nights for you at the Heathman?"

With a few clicks on the computer keyboard, she tried to pull up the active file of the Brannigans as he said,

"We've decided to stay three nights. Can you add one more night for us?"

The computer screen froze. Alissa tapped on the keys. "Certainly, Mr. Brannigan. May I call you back to confirm that?"

"I'll wait for your call," he said.

Alissa knew he would. The Brannigans had to be the most active retired couple she knew. In good health and possessing excessive spending money, they traveled constantly. And with Alissa's efficiency and excessive good manners, she was their only travel agent.

"Okay. Thank you, Mr. Brannigan. Good-bye."

"Cheri?" Alissa said. "Did we go off-line?"

"I've called the repairman. I don't know what the problem is. I guess all we can do is take messages. Don't forget your landlord."

With a push of a button and a deep breath, Alissa picked up line one. "Clawson Travel Agency. This is Alissa."

"Ms. Benson," the landlord said with forced friendliness. "You have not responded to the notice we sent you last month. I have left messages on your machine at home, but you have not returned the calls. I found it necessary to call you at work to ask for a reply."

Alissa turned away from Cheri and the client who had just entered the shop and was seated in front of Cheri's desk. "I'm going to need more time to decide."

"I'm afraid there isn't any more time. I must know today by five o'clock."

Alissa heard the click as he hung up, but she kept the phone to her ear as if the answer she needed would come sometime after the dial tone. Her condo complex had been sold a month ago. The new owner required all renters to sign a new lease that included an increase of $150 a month and a minimum commitment of two years. Alissa had never lived anywhere for more than two years. It was a nice condo but not her dream home. During the past month she had found nothing else in her price range. Yet the two-year commitment scared her. She had already been in Pasadena and at the same travel agency for seven months. That in itself was almost a record.

She heard a slight rustling sound and realized a customer was now seated in front of her desk. "Okay. We'll work on that and get back to you then," she said into the dumb receiver she still held to her ear. "Good-bye."

Turning to hang up and greet her customer, Alissa forced a smile back on her face. "Yes, how can I—" She stopped. It was the guy from Starbucks. "How can I help you?"

He took a slow sip from his Starbucks cappuccino and looked at her with his grass green eyes. "You're having trouble with your computers this morning?"

It crossed Alissa's mind that perhaps this guy had followed her here and somehow overheard Alissa and Cheri say they had computer problems. For a brief flash, Alissa felt flattered that this man had apparently sought her out.

"What can I do for you?" he asked.

Alissa was glad to see Cheri come over to offer her support. "Alissa? This is Brad Phillips. I thought you two had already met. Brad works down the street at The Computer Wiz." Cheri kept her voice professional. "I called him this morning."

"Oh," Alissa said, feeling foolish for allowing herself to

think this man had come looking for her. She rose from her work station and offered Brad her seat. "All yours."

Then, reaching for her coffee and cinnamon roll, which Cheri had put on a paper plate for her, Alissa took the customer seat on the other side of the desk. She might just as well make some phone calls.

"All righty then." Brad punched the keys at top speed. The screen miraculously unfroze. "We have lift off."